PACK REFUGE

PACK REFUGE
THE SPLINTERED BOND

MERRI BRIGHT

Editing by Aubergine Editing

Cover by Get Covers

For Kristin
You gave me chocolate, birch.
Now you'll never get rid of me.

CONTENTS

AUTHOR'S NOTE AND CONTENT ADVISORIES

T hank you so much for reading Pack Refuge. This book contains on-page, graphic violence/death, profanity, intimate activities involving more than one partner, physical assault, mention of past sexual assault, and mentions of past domestic abuse. This is a medium-dark, slow-burn reverse harem romance, with scenes that may be disturbing to some readers. Please be kind to yourself when choosing to read.

I

THE NORTHERN HUNT BEGINS
FLOR

Ontario, the Northern packlands

In my imagination, the Northern shifters lived in a city, or at least close to one. The Hilliers had seemed so cultured, more refined than anyone I'd met before. But the Lodge was nestled in a wilderness, the great house situated in the center of a green, rolling valley around three miles wide. The valley was closed in on three sides by a dense evergreen forest, and the horizon dominated by a snow-dusted mountain. On the fourth side was a vast lake that reflected the trees, the mountain, and the endless sky.

It looked like heaven.

But it turned out to be hell.

I'D MET SNAKES BEFORE. Whip snakes, rat snakes, cottonmouths, and diamondback rattlers, even. But I'd never met one that wore high-heeled shoes and a cocktail dress at ten in the morning.

Seconds before, the Heir to the Northern pack had run up the wide marble steps, holding my hand, and when this particular snake had opened the door, he'd pulled me into a hug, kissed the top of my head, and handed me off to her with a hurried explanation. "Vanessa? I have to go help Mom. Dad just stopped breathing again. Please show Flor the house and give her a room." He dropped a second kiss on my hand, shocking the hell out of me before he took off. "I'll see you at dinner, if not before, Dream Girl."

Now Vanessa's curious gaze raked me from top to bottom, while she murmured something about needing to tell someone named Clara about me. "Dream Girl? Sounds like my cousin has plans for you."

"I honestly hope not," I said truthfully. "All I want is a hot meal and a bed." I felt like I could fall asleep where I stood.

"Well, let's get you sorted out, then. You look like you've been..." She grimaced.

"Like I've been chewed up and spit out? I feel that way, too." I forced a smile when she laughed.

Even without a mirror, I knew I looked like hammered shit. I'd just spent the past two days on a road trip from Alabama, and the seven days before that hiding in sewers and fighting for my life.

And the nineteen years before that being starved, or beaten. Or starved *and* beaten. My life growing up in the Southern pack had been rough, but Glen had promised me this fancy-as-fuck pack would be better.

"Well, this day is full of surprises. Aren't you just a sliver of a thing," Vanessa mused as she closed the door behind us. "With an almost... boyish figure."

"That's me, skinny as shi... uh, as all get out," I agreed.

Her green eyes flashed. "And you're here all alone?"

"Looks that way." I had no idea where Brand, the Alpha Heir from Mountain—who'd been stuck to my side since we left my old pack—had gone. The Enforcer chauffeur who'd brought us here in the black SUV had mentioned something about protocol and heightened security, and drove him to the back of the estate after they'd dropped Glen and me off at the front.

I tried not to stare at Vanessa, but it was impossible. She was gorgeous, like a model or something. Her silver dress had black accents and a plunging neckline, and ended above her knees, showing off her trim, but still curvy body. She had on diamond earrings and black high heels, the red soles perfectly matching her fresh lipstick.

I followed her through a short hall to a far more ostentatious entry room. The ceiling was fifty feet high, with a massive crystal chandelier and what had to be expensive art on all the walls, huge canvases depicting wolves running over mountains and crossing streams. Even the floors were some kind of mosaic with the phases of the moon in what might have been gold, and a word I'd never seen before: Boreal.

She caught me moving my lips as I read it, and remarked, "That was the name of our pack when it was founded two hundred and fifty years ago."

I nodded and peered around the nearly-empty space. There was one table by the door, holding a fancy ceramic urn, but no other furniture, just walls of alternating wood and some sort of glittery stone, so every footstep and scuff echoed. Everything looked old but expensive. Not like Southern, where everything was old and about to fall into piles of rust and rat shit.

"Who are your parents again?" Vanessa asked. I swallowed and shrugged, not wanting to lie. I wasn't about to admit that my mother was dead, and my father was on the run from the Council after he'd lost an Alpha challenge and fled like a coward.

Vanessa sure as heck didn't need to know he was the former Alpha of Southern. I was pretty sure no one alive knew that but me, and I wanted to keep it that way.

When I didn't answer, she pivoted and led me into a long hall. I followed close behind, even if she really did make me think of a snake. Especially the way her hips moved back and forth. How did she stay up on those stilts while she was swaying her butt like a moon-drunk wolf after a pack ru— "*Ow!*"

While I was watching her hips, she'd turned and caught my arm with her long, manicured nails, digging them into my skin. Had she shifted her nails? I glanced down, but they were human-shaped, just filed to points and painted a vivid purple.

"Flor. That's really your name? Like the thing people walk on?"

"Close enough," I snapped back. "You're really Margarette's niece?" It didn't seem plausible; this woman was the opposite of the one who'd invited me to Northern.

Margarette Hillier was the badass, tough-but-kind Alpha Mate of this pack. She'd vowed to take care of me, but her mate was on the brink of death, so I understood her not showing me around. I'd heard whispers of silver poisoning on the trip here, and he'd stopped breathing more than once.

I twisted my arm, pulling out of Vanessa's grip and putting some distance between us as she escorted me down a long hallway that was all plush carpet, dark wood, and tiny oil paintings of forests dressed in autumn leaves, each with their own miniature light.

"Yes, my mother Linn was one of the only other female Enforcers. She died fighting the Russian invaders twenty-two years ago." She muttered, "And I've been stuck here ever since."

I didn't know what that was about, but I offered a sympathetic smile. She must have been young when it happened, since she only looked like she was in her late twenties now. "I'm sorry about your mom. I lost mine a few years back. Maybe we can train together, get to know each other."

She stifled a laugh. "Train together? You've been trained to fight?"

"Ah, kind of. Not officially. Not like, lessons. Margarette said I could take those here. But Brand's planning to help me work on some new techniques. We're supposed to start tomorrow."

Her red lips made a small circle. "Brand. The Alpha Heir of Mountain. He's offered to train with you?" Her voice rose in an alarming way, and I stepped back. "He's never offered to train with me."

"Yeah, well... maybe we can all train together." That sounded about as fun as handwashing feral cats, but I didn't know what else to say.

Her eyes slid back and over me as she reached for a brass doorknob, hesitating. Considering something.

My skin prickled everywhere she looked, and I turned my head, wondering where everyone else had gone. I could smell food somewhere, and had heard distant voices when the car stopped, so I knew there must be others close. But we were alone for now.

I didn't like it. Something about this woman's assessment reminded me of the worst males back home. Trevor, or Grant. The ones who'd tortured and hunted me for years. Like she was waiting for the moment I had my back turned to pounce.

As she stared at me, she played with the ends of her long, shiny hair. My own newly short haircut was already growing out over my ears, though Margarette had mentioned it would grow even faster once I could shift regularly. I wasn't sure when that would start, though. I didn't feel much different than I had before my one shift at Southern.

I tucked a stray piece of hair behind one ear, brushing the metal circle that dangled at the top of my ear, the one I'd worn since I was a child, like every unranked shifter at Southern.

Suddenly, Vanessa gasped, and I braced myself. But for some reason, she was beaming now, her smile a real one, even if it had a strange coldness to it. She pointed at the metal tag. "That's an intriguing piece of jewelry you have, Flor. I've never seen one in person, but I've heard about it. Does it mean what I think it does?"

"That I'm unranked? Yeah, it does." I rubbed at my tag, not sure why she would care. Glen had acted like everybody was treated the same in his pack no matter how they were ranked, going on and on about integrity and honor. He'd urged me to take the tag off now that I was going to be at Northern. He'd even offered to cut it off in the car the day before. I almost wished I'd taken him up on the offer, caught under the judgmental gaze of this woman.

But it was that judgment that had me hesitating.

For some reason, now that I'd escaped my past, my tag felt less like a mark of shame, and more like a battle scar. I'd take it off soon enough, but the tag reminded me of what I'd survived.

And it was an easy way of finding out who was an elitist bitch.

I dropped my hand from my ear, deciding to play dumb. "Do y'all have ear tags for the unranked here?"

"Of course not," she scoffed. "But we do have sections of the house the unranked are not allowed in, if you're not on the staff." I could practically smell the condescension coming off her as she motioned for me to follow her.

I trailed behind her down yet another hallway, noting the number of narrow doors with latches instead of doorknobs. The wood wasn't polished here, and the brass was dull. This hall stank of chemicals, like bleach and floor polish, and I noted a few buckets and mops inside one open door. A janitorial closet?

Vanessa took a key from her pocket and unlocked a door, opening it to reveal a room with two cots, though neither one had sheets or pillows. "This is where you'll stay until Aunt Margarette tells me what to do with you. Don't leave the servants' hall without an escort or a summons. I'm assuming Glen might call you into his room at night. Just be aware that no one can see you go in or out." She winked. "Who he fucks isn't anyone's business, but we don't want his reputation to take a hit, right?"

"I'm not fucking him," I began, but she was already on her way out. "Hey! What about food?" But the door was shut before the last word was spoken. "So, they have bitches at Northern, too. Fun times," I murmured as I began looking around. The room was every bit as bare and plain as the one I'd lived in for years in the shifter dorms at Southern. The bathroom had to be down the hall, since there was no toilet here. It was a good thing we'd stopped on the drive a few hours ago. I only wished I'd grabbed some snacks.

Del's voice echoed in my mind. *In every new setting, if you're lucky, you'll have a moment to assess your surroundings. Use this time wisely. Where can you hide? What weapons can you find? Water, food, shelter—you need these. But you also need safety, and a way out.*

I hadn't needed those lessons for a while. But I wouldn't insult his memory by forgetting them now.

Got it, Del. I moved around the room, taking it all in. There was a wooden chest of drawers with sturdy handles that could be unscrewed, but nothing had sharp edges. Inside one drawer was a stack of maid's uniforms: starched white tops, gray trousers, a gray skirt, sturdy wool socks, and the ugliest granny panties I'd ever seen. No belt, which was a shame. No bra, but I didn't need one. There also weren't any shoes, so I was glad I had some on.

I glanced down. The t-shirt and loose pants I'd worn for three days—some of the only clothes I'd been able to scrounge up after all the battles at Southern—were filthy now. The Enforcers in the SUV hadn't said anything about my increasingly rank smell, although their expressions had said enough. I'd tried to wash them in the sink when we'd spent a few hours in a motel, but the small bar of soap hadn't done much good.

Fuck. I took a moment to change into the gray trousers and one of the white tops, wishing I'd been given a room with a shower.

On one wall, there was a window. It was painted shut, but I had my steak knife. I'd stolen it at the dinner with the Council only a few days before, and used it to decapitate the Head Enforcer who'd been trying to kill the Hilliers. The blade was as strong as ever, though, and I used it to loosen the paint and make sure I could open the window. Beyond was the woods.

My way out. Even better.

I scanned the room once more. Beside the bed sat a brass lamp, nice and heavy, with a cord long enough to strangle someone. The only other decent weapon was my knife.

I picked a flake of paint off the serrated blade and sheathed it in a leather knife holder one of the Northern Enforcers had given me on the way. I had no idea why he'd offered it to me, but at one of the rest stops, he'd brought it out of the small store. Brand had growled at him, but after I showed him the scrapes beside my spine from the serrated edge, he'd settled.

A sudden knocking at the door had me on my feet, one hand on the handle of my knife. There was no way to lock the door from the inside, I noted as I cracked it open, finding a confused-looking woman there.

"I heard Miss Vanessa say we had a new unranked shifter."

"Yeah, that's probably me," I said, meeting her eyes.

She dropped her gaze immediately and mumbled, "Not sure I believe that. But here you are."

"What's wrong?"

She opened her mouth to answer, when someone shouted down the hall, "They're coming up!"

"You need to go," the girl said nervously. "I'm kitchen staff, so I have a place to hide, but... are you assigned yet?" I shook my head. "Shit. Listen, some of the ranked males are on their way here. It's not safe for you to be caught alone."

Somewhere in the distance, a door slammed open. A chorus of male laughter rang out, drawing closer.

"Sorry, I've gotta go," the girl squeaked, and ran on

silent feet down the hall and through a doorway, away from the voices.

Ranked males. Hiding.

Suddenly, I was back at Southern again, afraid and alone. But this time, I had no idea where the hiding places were. I hadn't spent years making bolt-holes and stringing ropes and wires in treetops and along rooflines to escape from a pack of running wolves.

I didn't know how to get to safety, or who might help me.

A door opened at one end of the hall, and a deep voice called, "Hey, you! I heard there's some fresh meat. Is that you?"

I didn't answer him, but started for the door at the other end of the hall. Then that door opened as well.

A burly shifter with no shirt on and a lustful gleam in his eyes rested his hands at the top of the doorframe, closing off my exit. "You the new piece of fur Vanessa said wanted some company?" He licked his lips, his eyes resting on the tag in my ear. "I've never seen you around before. I would've had you already, shown you what you should aim for." He took one hand down and adjusted his dick. "Come here, unranked girl."

It wasn't a request. It was an order, and the males at both ends of the hallway were stalking toward me.

Fuck a mangy duck. I had to get out of here. I ran back into my room, slamming the door behind me. In a second, I was halfway out the window. But that was all the time it took.

"She's running!" one of them yelled.

"Get her!" shouted another.

The Hunt was on again.

2

SAY THE WORD
BRAND

I stood at the edge of the water, listening to the click of stone on stone as tiny waves lapped around my feet, wondering what in the hell I was doing here. And where my little mate had gone.

Not that she knew that she was my mate.

Glen's parents had been rushed away the moment we arrived, and I'd been taken to the training ground to report to the Sergeant at Arms and register my weapons—a ridiculous protocol for visiting Alphas and Heirs, in my opinion. The most dangerous weapons I had were my claws and teeth. But my sword had to be approved, and at least I'd been able to secure the Council's permission to come to Northern at all.

Of course, once I'd reported, the younger male shifters had insisted on watching me wrestle Sergeant, until he'd dismissed them all. I'd gone looking for my little flower then, but no one had seen her.

I could have asked Vanessa, but I made a point of staying as far from the annoying young woman as possible. The last time I'd spent the night here, she'd grasped my dick underneath the dinner table. I'd warned Glen that if she did it again, I'd tear her hand off.

I sighed and drew in a deep breath, tasting the slightest hint of jasmine and cinnamon on the back of my tongue. "Flor?" I murmured.

The rocks behind me shifted. As if I'd conjured her, I turned to see Flor standing there, her steak knife held tight in one hand. Her hair was disheveled, her eyes wild, and her clothing...

Wait. Those weren't her clothes. If I wasn't mistaken, she had on one of the maids' outfits.

"Flor? What happened?"

"Is the invitation to Mountain still open?" was all she said. Her shoulders were tight, her whole body trembling like a plucked string. I glanced at the woods, where she had to have run from. Was someone chasing her?

My wolf rose to the surface, instantly enraged. Whoever it was, we would kill them for her and present her with their heads as trophies.

She likes heads, my wolf encouraged.

I tried to regain the upper hand over my wolf side. I took a deep breath, scenting the air, but caught no sign of anyone else. Only the scent of Flor's anxiety.

"Brand?"

"Yes," I replied, my emotions still turbulent, though I kept my face and voice steady. "I'll take you to my pack-lands now. I can have a car here at any moment. Or we can shift and run there." It would take days, weeks. We would be together the entire time, in our fur. I would keep her safe as she learned how to live as a wolf.

My wolf approved of this idea.

She shook her head, but the tension began to unspool from her. "I haven't shifted since..."

The battle. Maybe some of her worry was from that? Had she been trying to shift in the woods, and been unable to? I remembered years ago how frustrating it had been to try and shift on command, when the moon wasn't full.

"Don't worry about that. The shifting will happen when it happens. We'll take the car."

She grinned suddenly, and it was like the sun had come out from behind a dark cloud. "I can leave at any time, can't I? And you'll take me. Promise me."

"I promise. Say the word, and we're gone."

Her smile grew even wider, and she tucked a stray piece of red hair behind her ear. "I trust you."

I nodded in reply, unable to speak. If I opened my mouth, I would tell her how consumed I was by her. How beautiful she was. How I wanted to honor her indomitable spirit, worship her body with mine, and claim her for the rest of our lives.

But I needed to go slow. Most women were frightened of me, of my size and strength. I couldn't bear the thought of this one, my wildflower, fearing me.

"Okay," was all she said, sinking down to the stones to sit cross-legged. I sat beside her, waiting. We stayed silent for a long moment, looking out at the water together.

"My lake is smaller," I murmured at last, knowing I sounded like an idiot.

"Does size really matter?" she replied after a moment.

I blinked, wondering what to say.

Finally, she burst into laughter, though her face was as pink as I thought mine must be. "I mean, when it comes to lakes?"

When I had myself under control, I agreed. "Size doesn't matter. Not for lakes. Not for many things, not for..."

I took in her small, upturned nose, her slender neck, her narrow shoulders. She was so much smaller than me, almost two feet shorter, and at least a hundred and fifty pounds lighter. The thought that I might hurt her inadvertently if she ever chose to give herself to me, was a terrifying possibility.

Not that I would change her if I could. If I had the chance, I would show her how gentle I could be. I would treasure her, touch her so softly she would think it was a breeze, kiss her lightly, over and over, worship her like the moon-blessed goddess she was, and taste her for hours...

"Brand?" Her forehead wrinkled, as she waited for me to go on.

I cleared my throat. "Take you, for instance. You're one of the smallest shifters I've ever seen. But you had the Northern Enforcers so impressed with you on our journey here, they couldn't speak."

The memory had my jaw clenching. The eyes of the two Senior Enforcers in our shared SUV had landed on her so often, and with such longing, my wolf had all but torn his way out of my skin to savage them. All that had saved them was her utter disregard for them both.

"Wait, what?" She laughed again. "*That's* why they were so quiet? That can't be true."

"But it is. I heard them say it. They saw what you did in the fight against Trevor. They saw what you did to the one who attacked Margarette and Bradley." I paused, my teeth grinding at the memory. "One of them even wrote a poem about you. Another drew some sort of sketch, with charcoal. A picture of you."

"Really? Can I see it?"

I coughed. "It was not a good likeness." Not after I punched the asshole who'd drawn it in the face, and the paper had been splattered with his blood. He'd deserved it. He'd made some wild guesses as to what my mate looked like without clothing. I felt no regret in taking the drawing from him, and taking the price for his disrespect out on his face.

"Poems and sketches? How mortifying. You're kidding, right?"

She seemed disgusted, and I found myself smiling. "No. These Northerners are very artistic. The winter nights are long. They've had to develop their odd little hobbies."

I could tell she was stunned. "I see. Um, do you have an odd little hobby?" I spluttered and evaded the question, until she begged, "Come on, tell me what you do when you're not hunting or watching the lake. Or doing whatever Alpha Heirs do."

Finally, I sighed. "I make sculptures."

She sat up, her side so close to me, I could feel her warmth. "With stone? Or clay?"

I folded my arms over my chest to keep from drawing her onto my lap. "You'll have to be patient. I'll show you when you visit my packlands."

"Big sculptures, carved out of tree trunks with chainsaws?" she teased. "Enormous, bear-sized saws to fit your hands?"

My heart sank. "I know I'm too big. I suppose you think I'm... slow." I turned my head away slightly, trying not to let her see how her teasing had cut me. "I'm not like Glen, or Finn. Not civilized. Most females don't talk to me." No, most of them only came near if they wanted something. Status, or influence with my father. Bragging rights that they'd been with an Alpha Heir.

"Oh, Brand. Those girls miss out." I wasn't looking, so I didn't see her reach out, but felt her small, warm hand on my arm as she pulled it gently toward her. "I don't think you're slow. I watched you fight. You're big, but you're fast, and powerful. And you make smart decisions in battle."

My heart was pounding so hard, I felt dizzy. Her touch was addictive, even this hesitant, soft one. "You truly think so?"

"I do." Her hand moved over mine like my fingers were fragile, in feather-soft, careful strokes that gave me goosebumps and made me long for more. Like I was the delicate one.

She pulled her hand free before I could return the caress. I shifted so she wouldn't notice the erection now tenting my sweatpants, the uniform I wore whenever I was training at Northern. I needed to change the subject.

"Flor, when you came out here—" Her stomach suddenly growled so loudly, it sounded like a wild animal. She laughed, but I stood, enraged. "You haven't eaten?"

I was going to kill Glen.

"No, and I'm starved. Do you think you could get me something from the kitchen?"

"We have a formal dinner in a few hours, but I'll take you to get something now. If Margarette knew you hadn't been fed, she'd be horrified."

"Would she be?" I thought I heard Flor mutter as she stood.

A howling started up in the forest, the sound of a pack of young males chasing a deer, most likely.

She shivered. "Let's go inside, Bearman."

I forgot what I was going to ask her. I forgot everything including my own name as she linked her arm in mine and pressed her cheek against me, as if I was bringing her comfort.

As if I was her safety in an uncertain world.

"We can leave whenever I want?" she asked quietly, her eyes on the trees, in the direction of the howling.

"All you need to do is say the word." I leaned into her touch.

"Which word?"

"Lake," I replied, as we walked toward the house. I didn't want her to have to say it, but some part of me hoped she would whisper it in my ear someday soon. Then I would carry her away, and show her the second most beautiful sight I'd ever seen. Just being around her calmed my wolf. I hadn't felt peace like this in so long.

"Formal dinner, huh? Guess I might need to change. Would be nice if I had clothes. Unless they want me to serve dinner—in which case, I'm fine as is."

My peace suddenly fled. "What do you mean? Wait... that *is* a maid's uniform, isn't it?"

"Yeah," she replied with a pained smile, and sketched out what had happened since she'd been left in Vanessa's hands. "Guess I thought the unranked here had it better than at Southern. Don't be shocked if I end up yelling 'lake' like some sort of lunatic over the first course tonight."

Feeling my claws emerge from the ends of my fingers, I dropped my hand from her arm. Fur prickled across my back and sprouted along my neck, my snout elongating and my teeth growing sharper. In seconds, I was in a half-shifted form, my clothes ripping at the seams.

I knew I was ruining any chance I would ever have with Flor, but the rage that rushed through me at hearing what had happened was forcing my wolf to emerge. It was all I could do not to change fully, hunt down Vanessa, and kill her, presenting her corpse to my mate.

"Brand?" Her voice was filled with an emotion I

couldn't recognize, and I rested my shifted, hairy arms on my knees, fighting for control.

"Leave," I demanded. "Leave me, Flor." My words were garbled, but I knew she heard them.

Because instead of running away, she wrapped her tiny arms around my hideous form and whispered, "Not on your life, Bearman."

3

MISCHIEF AND MURDEROUS INTENT

FLOR

B rand was magnificent, and terrifying, and watching him react in such a protective way to what he called an "unforgivable insult" by Vanessa went a long way to making my fears about how I would handle being at Northern vanish.

Of course, I'd only shared the part about her putting me in the servants' quarters, the crappy living conditions there, and how the maid had seemed to be worried about me.

As I hugged his waist, I decided not to tell him about the Hunt I'd just escaped, at least not yet. If he realized those guys had been chasing me, I had a feeling he'd run off without a word and kill them all. And I didn't want him to leave my side.

"Don't be embarrassed," I said, as he ducked his head.

"Aren't you disgusted?" he asked, his words hard to understand since his snout was still diminishing.

"By your form?" I discreetly ran my hand over the fur on his arm. I was not at all disgusted. I was fascinated. I pulled away, gazing up at his half-shifted face. He was fierce and

21

terrifying, and I didn't want to think about how turned on I was getting, seeing him like this.

Though he could probably smell my desire. I refused to think about that.

His chocolate brown eyes were still the same, and his size, but his wolf's fur was a brown so deep it was almost black, like his hair. He took a breath and closed his eyes, forcing his wolf to subside.

"By my lack of control." He laughed weakly as he finished changing, the fur receding, though he was still covered with more dark hair than many men. I wanted to bury my fingers in it.

Afraid I might do just that, I let go of his arm. "Looked pretty in control to me," was all I said. "I've never seen any shifter who could do that. I thought it was cool."

"Didn't scare you?"

"You couldn't," I said honestly. It was true. As he focused on his return to human form, I let myself ogle him surreptitiously a little longer. Size didn't matter, he'd said. If you asked me, the extra inches on his chest mattered at least a little bit.

For some reason, the idea of measuring every inch of his skin, exploring it like he was an uncharted land, popped into my mind. One of the seams of his shirt had ripped when he shifted, and I could see exposed flesh peeking through the gap. *So. Damn. Sexy.* I shivered at the thought of stroking it.

"You okay?" He turned his head, and his short beard gleamed slightly reddish-brown in the morning sunlight. I wanted to reach out and touch one of the tiny sparks of red, see if they were as warm as they looked.

"I'm fine. I might need a cold shower after I eat something, though." I swallowed. "I mean, a shower. Just a shower. Showers at Southern were always cold, you know."

"Hmm," he replied, not looking at me, thank goodness. I knew I'd turned as red as a boiled crawdad.

I dropped back, pretending to tie my sneaker, carefully *not* noticing the way every single muscle was outlined in those sweatpants. These Northerners should really find some clothes that fit this guy. These were way too tight.

I stopped staring at Brand's butt long enough to admire the rough log stairs and granite paths that led around the sides of the enormous compound. I'd been too distracted by Vanessa to take it all in before, but the Lodge and its surroundings really were majestic. The main building was two stories tall, but sprawled across a considerable stretch of the valley. There were smaller, similar cabins—if you could call four-bedroom lodges *cabins*—spread out on both sides.

That morning, from the window of my room, I'd seen a vast training ground at the back of the main house, and more modern-looking buildings that might have been armories, gyms, stores, or even schools, for all I could tell. When I'd been running from the young males, the few shifters I'd seen in the distance had moved with purpose. Most of them had been wearing green and black fatigues, almost like they were preparing for war.

I glanced back at Brand's perfectly sculpted ass, fighting my own war against the growing urge to give in to the irresistible attraction.

In minutes, we'd reached the kitchen, where Brand ordered the staff to get me food. Then, before they could comply, he waved them aside, muttering, "I'll feed her myself," before unloading most of the fridge.

By the time he was done, the stainless-steel kitchen

prep table was practically groaning with all sorts of finger foods: pastries, small pies topped with fresh berries, mini quiches, chive-topped puffs that smelled like salmon, and a dozen other things I'd never seen before.

"Where the fuck is the real food?" Brand grumbled into the fridge.

"I think this is food," I said, popping a tiny quiche into my mouth.

"Need something more substantial. Fried chicken, or steak. Ham." He grunted, yanking open another silver refrigerator door. "Oh, venison. That'll do nicely."

One of the cooks cleared her throat. "Alpha Heir, that's the dinner."

She snapped her jaw shut when Brand whirled on her. "Did you know this young woman wasn't fed when we arrived?" When the cook only stared at him blankly, he went on. "The same woman who saved Margarette from dying."

Everyone gasped, and the kitchen staff began making a fuss, preparing a plate for me. I dug in, eating fast while Brand watched, and ignoring the whispers from the staff. Finally, when I couldn't stuff another bite in—or avoid the whispers that had become questions—he half-lifted me from the stool and gently pulled me toward the door.

"Where are we going?"

"To kill Glen," he answered matter-of-factly. "Idiot shouldn't have left you. Needs to pay."

I pulled away. "Don't bother him. He didn't know, I'm sure. And he's going through so much with his dad and mom both..."

Brand let out a sigh, then called out, "Need the butler. Norris?"

A door I hadn't even noticed opened in the wall, and a

man dressed in a far fancier version of the uniform I had on stepped out. "Alpha Heir, how may I assist?"

"This woman is a guest of the Hilliers. She was mistakenly placed in the servants' quarters. Where is her guest room?"

The man bowed, literally, to me and Brand. "We have been looking for her for hours. Mrs. Hillier has provided clothing and all the comforts in the Goldenrod Room." His eyes fell on me, moving from my ear tag to my tattered and stained maid's uniform. "Alpha Heir, you've been requested to attend Alpha Mate Hillier in the family sitting room before dinner." When Brand snarled, the butler tilted his head to one side in submission, but went on. "If you allow me, I will take our guest to her room myself. I'll be certain she comes to no further mischief."

"Mischief. Is that what they call it here?" I mumbled as Brand lifted my chin with one finger.

His voice was low and intense. "I won't leave your side."

I smirked, though his eyes had me melting just a little. "Gonna get in the shower with me, Bearman?"

His voice was rough as he replied curtly, "If you need me to."

I could tell he meant it. My ovaries practically pulsed. God, I really needed a cold shower now.

A part of me wanted to take him up on his offer, but I shook my head. "I trust Norris here to get me to my room, and Margarette asked for you. I won't leave my room until dinnertime. I'll see you there?"

Brand bowed and murmured, "I'll see you, and I'll feed you, little flower." Then he turned, purpose in his steps.

"Don't kill Glen!" I called.

"No promises," he threw over his shoulder.

I STARED into the full-length mirror that sat in one corner of the very plush, but impersonal guest room. The best part of the room—apart from the deadbolt lock on the door—was the en-suite bathroom. I'd spent a half hour in the tub, then used some of the products in the vanity to smooth my short hair into a style, rather than the now-normal ragged mop.

The clothes, though, I hadn't bothered with. They were all fancy, frilly dresses, and none of them had any place to stash my steak knife. After the initial reception I'd gotten here, I wasn't going to take one step out of this room without a weapon.

I'd found a pair of thin navy sweatpants in the bottom drawer, along with a plain sweatshirt, and decided they would have to do. I could run in this, even stash my knife in the holder the Enforcer had bought me.

I strapped it on while I thought about the day's unexpected Hunt. The young males had chased me, but they weren't like the ones at Southern. They'd seemed excited, but also confused that I'd run. I had a feeling Vanessa had told them I was interested in fucking them, and that this was some sort of foreplay thing.

But the way the other unranked girl had said she had somewhere to hide still bothered me. These males had chased unranked women before. Had those females wanted the attention?

I didn't think all of them had.

After the first hour, some older shifters had heard the young males sniffing around the base of the trees where I was hidden, and came to see what was happening. They'd forced the males hunting me to shift, explain themselves, and leave. The older males had seemed pissed at the idea of a female hiding from a pack of males, and had read the riot act to the jerks, but I still wasn't sure what the real story was.

The older ones could've been mad that the young ones had chased me, or that I had escaped them. For all I knew, all the ranked males here helped themselves to the unranked females. And maybe the women were willing.

But I hadn't been.

If those males had thought it was fine to chase down a maid, this place could be the prettiest pack house in North America, and it would still be rotten at the core. Brand's presence—and his promise—was the only reason I hadn't kept running.

I didn't want to think about how it felt to discover Northern wasn't a safe place for me, or possibly for any unranked shifters, not that I'd know who those might be. They didn't wear ear tags here, after all. Maybe they all wore servants' uniforms? My heart sank.

I should have been fine; I was used to unranked shifters like me being treated like shit. But it hurt more for some reason here, now that I'd let myself hope for something better. Fucking *hope* again. When would I learn?

A soft knock on the door kept me from dwelling on my mistake.

"Who is it?" I called out.

A young woman's voice answered, "I'm here to take you to dinner." I swung open the door. "Miss?" The maid's gaze went from my hair to my shoes, and she gulped nervously. "Did you not find the clothes?" Her eyes widened as she noted the ear tag I still wore.

"Are you... unranked?" I asked.

"Yes." She nodded, her hand moving to her neck. She didn't have a tag, but she wore a simple leather choker that must serve the same function: to mark the less worthy. Though it could have been just a piece of jewelry. Still, there were light bruises on her throat around it, like it had been used to choke her, or pull her around.

Once I tamped down my rage, I answered her. "I found some in the wardrobe, dresses mostly. They didn't suit me."

"They didn't fit? I'm so sorry; Miss Vanessa told me you wore small clothes. They're some of hers from when she was younger."

Vanessa again. I cursed quietly. "They looked like party dresses for a ten-year-old."

She cringed, for some reason. When I took a deeper breath and realized her scent had been on some of the clothes, it was my turn to be embarrassed. I hazarded a guess that she had put them here for me.

"Sorry. They're just way too fancy for someone like me. Are you going to get in trouble if I don't wear them?"

She sighed. "Probably not, but dinner here is formal. I'd try to find something else, but the meal has already started and if you're much later, I will get in trouble."

I didn't want that. "If anyone mentions the clothes, I'll take the blame. Where do unranked shifters eat?"

"So you really are unranked?" Her jaw dropped. "Why aren't you eating in the compound? Staying there?"

"Compound?" That sounded ominous. "Sounds like a prison."

"No, it's not like that. It's a block of dormitories on the other side of the training fields. They're not bad. It's just where we have to live until we test into the ranks." Something about her tone made me feel she wasn't telling the whole truth.

"Test?"

"Yes, there's one every quarter. The next one's in less than two weeks. I won't try to test until my little sister is old enough to rank up with me, though. That'll be a few years, so..." She tapped the leather choker again.

Huh. I'd have to ask about that, but she seemed skittish. Curiosity made me keep prying, though. "Why were you shocked I was eating here?"

"It's just... unranked shifters are almost never allowed in the Lodge, unless they're working. There's only twelve of us on the house staff. You met Marla, right? She said you had a room in our wing, but no assignment." I frowned. Her voice dropped below a whisper. "She was the one who told you to run."

I nodded, understanding. She started down the long hallway and motioned for me to follow. "Are the unranked ill-treated here? Starved?" I breathed the words softly, so only she would hear.

"No." Her green eyes flashed with curiosity. "Did someone say that?"

"No, but I come from Southern."

"Wow. I've heard it's a lot worse there." She stopped abruptly. "How bad is it, really?"

I'd been hunted for years, kicked, punched, beaten, starved, and almost killed. But all I said was, "Bad."

"You don't have a mate yet?" she asked, stopping at the junction of two hallways. "Most of the unmated shifters like to eat together."

"Nope. Happily unmated, thank you very much."

"Okay, then you'll be eating in the blue room, I suppose." Chewing her lip, she escorted me down the right hallway, then stopped at a door. The sounds of conversation and glasses clinking emerged from within. "Be careful in there," she whispered. "Southern won't have prepared you for this."

Before I could ask what she meant, I was escorted into a long, sumptuous room, and welcomed by a chorus of shrill laughter and raised voices.

Immediately, every eye fixed on me. Then a male voice bellowed, "Fresh meat!"

4
FRESH MEAT
FLOR

The words "fresh meat" hung in the air, and I shifted my stance, ready to run or fight.

Painted a pale turquoise shade, the room was long and narrow, taken up almost entirely by a long walnut table. There were crystal bowls with flowers floating inside, along with some pretty blown-glass centerpieces that looked kind of like seals, and fancy lace placemats for the diners.

Every seat except one was filled with a shifter, young men at one end, and women at the other. I didn't recognize any of them, except one: Vanessa.

"Our guest!" a blonde woman called out. "Finally. I'm starved."

I wanted to laugh. Not one of these shifters knew what starved was. They all glowed with health, and wore muscle and even a thin layer of fat. The scent of food in the room had my stomach growling again, even though I'd just eaten with Brand.

Before I knew what was happening, the unranked maid

had pulled out the remaining chair and I was seated at the table, wondering where the hell Brand and Glen were.

The women seated near me murmured their hellos as I placed a starched napkin on my lap and looked around. Everyone was about my age or a little older, most of them between twenty or thirty, but I felt a lot older than the way they acted and spoke. Besides me, the whole table was dressed like they were going to a fancy job interview or something, and the women were wearing so much makeup, I wasn't sure if they even had pores.

A maid set a plate filled with rich food in front of me, and I let out a sigh, noting the abundance of shining cutlery. *Eenie, meenie,* I thought as I wondered if it mattered which fork I chose.

I didn't make eye contact with anyone else as I decided not to use a fork, and began with a dry bread roll, though I could tell Vanessa was watching me closely. She'd changed into a different dress already, an emerald green one that matched her eyes, and her long dark hair was pulled into a fancy knot. She really did look like a younger version of Margarette.

"Did you hear me?" Vanessa repeated, loud enough that a few shifters near us winced.

"No." She hadn't said anything. Giving up on the roll, I grabbed a fork. I ate what I hoped was an appetizer—some sort of meat paste piled up next to the tiniest salad I'd ever seen—as quickly as possible, unsure how long I was going to be able to stand the charged atmosphere in the room.

"Right. I was just telling my friends that you're the one who hacked off Aunt Margarette's hair." She mock-frowned, and a few of the other girls at the table giggled.

One glared at me, but I had no idea why. Most of the girls, besides the glarer and Vanessa, seemed fairly decent.

A little self-absorbed, talking about the males clustered at the other end of the table, who were mostly ignoring us.

Them, I kept an eye on. I didn't think any of them had been chasing me, but I wasn't certain.

Someone had called me "fresh meat." Someone knew they'd been hunting me.

"Was it you?" Vanessa asked slowly, like I hadn't understood her.

"That's what they tell me." I stared down at the new plate the servant had placed in front of me, glad I couldn't exactly remember that gory moment. My main course was some sort of fish in pastry, swimming in a buttery sauce. My stomach churned.

She smiled with tight lips. "The story I heard was you cut it off with a butter knife, in the middle of a battle. And then you cut off the head of a Southern shifter—one of your *own*—with the same knife."

"It wasn't a butter knife." I kept my face serene, though inside I was rolling my eyes. There was no butter knife in the world that could decapitate a shifter. "It was a steak knife."

The girls around me flinched. I hoped like hell they weren't going to ask to see it.

"Why're you asking me about all this?" I stared directly into Vanessa's face, challenging her. Her eyes were narrowed, and her bright red lips pulled tight, as she dropped her gaze.

"Well, I just wondered how much of what I heard could be true." She picked at the fish on her plate. "I mean, if they were mistaken about the butter knife, they must have been mistaken about the even more... unsavory things."

"What things?"

The room had gone quiet, everyone clearly listening in.

"I heard you were unranked, and we can all see your charming earring." She giggled, like that was funny. "And yet, here you are, sitting at the table with the highest ranked unmated shifters at Northern. So, you must think you're somehow *special*. Above the rules."

"Here we go," I muttered, feeling dozens of eyes on me. I set my napkin on the table. "Does it matter?"

I fought to quiet my wolf, who was howling to put this shifter in her place. *You're not a lot of good here,* I thought to that new presence. *Unless you can shift and overcome all these wolves?*

She went quieter at that, merely snarling.

I thought so.

"I'm a guest of the pack. A visitor. Margarette invited me to stay here. She told me I'd be safe." I didn't tell them she'd adopted me into the pack, more or less. If they knew that, and knew I was unranked, it'd put me in a very tenuous position. As a new, unranked pack member, I most likely had no rights. And if anyone came after me—hunted me—I still didn't have any places carved out to hide for more than a few hours.

Not safe, my wolf whimpered. *Not safe not safe not safe.*

Suddenly, I felt utterly exposed. Where was Brand? Where the hell was Glen? Where was... No. Finnick could go fuck himself. He'd been such a rat bastard the last time I'd spoken to him, I'd be fine never seeing him again.

My mind went to Luke, shied away, then settled on the black wolf, Joaquin. *I wouldn't even mind him showing up, magic or not.*

"Well, yes, Aunt Mags makes a lot of promises," Vanessa murmured. "She told me you want to be an Enforcer. That she offered to *adopt* you." Her eyes swam with an ocean of pain for a moment, and I was shocked into answering honestly.

"She called me her foster daughter, and yeah, I am going to be an Enforcer."

Like a door being slammed shut, the pain I'd seen was closed off in an instant. "Then your rank matters rather substantially. So, tell me, *Florida*," she drawled louder now, revealing that she knew more about me than I wanted her to. Brand wouldn't have shared any of this. But Glen might have told her my name. I'd knife that asshole if it was him. "Tell us all what you told me. About that tag in your ear."

The room had gone utterly still, too silent, like the forest when a predator was on the hunt. "If you'd been at Conclave, you'd know what it means. Why weren't you there, Vanessa?"

"Oh shit," one of the guys muttered. The blonde woman sitting closest to Vanessa gave her a sympathetic look, then glared at me like I'd insulted her.

"Southern is a trash pack. I'm sure I didn't miss anything," Vanessa spat back. "But you didn't answer me. That tag means you're unranked."

I nodded calmly, but my instincts were screaming. Her eyes glittered with a dark excitement, and her scent changed to one I recognized from years of being hunted.

I had my steak knife in my hidden belt sheath, but now I stood slowly with a table knife in my hand, eyes flicking once more to the exits. I already knew there were three: two doors and one window. The door I'd come in led to the hall, but it was too far. The other door led to the kitchen, I supposed. I could smell more food and hear the noise of dishes there. The window was a last resort. It was a large picture window, and I would have to jump through it, breaking it to get away.

It might be worth the pain.

"What are you doing, Florida?" Vanessa asked, blinking innocently. "We're still eating."

The whole table was staring at me now. I sat back down, slowly. How did she know my full name?

"The other stories might be true, then." Vanessa leaned closer, like she was trying to keep the conversation between us. But from the way she glanced around, and the pitch of her voice, I wasn't fooled. "Did the males there really play a game with you called the Hunt?"

My heart raced. I gave one curt nod.

"And is it true"—she smiled, her teeth glinting in the light—"that they hunted *you*?"

I didn't nod this time. I tensed, my muscles ready to spring.

"And the prize, if they caught you, was they all got to fuck you?" I stared into her cold eyes, waiting for the attack. I could feel it coming. "So you fucked all of them?"

The blonde woman growled. "Stay away from Glen. He doesn't need the Southern pack whore sniffing around him."

At the other end of the table, one of the males stood. I wasn't sure why, whether he was going to speak, tell the girls to stop, ask for clarification.

Or ask if he could have a turn.

The movement alone, and the scent of an interested male, triggered my instinct to flee. To hide.

In my mind, the Hunt was on.

I bolted for the nearest door, but Vanessa quickly stepped in front of me, her arms wide. "You're not excused. Sit back down."

Suddenly, the steak knife was in my hand, and at her throat. "Let me go," I growled.

Her eyes went wide, her voice panicked. "Someone help me! She's gone feral. She's got a knife!"

The male shifters were there instantly, surrounding me. "Girl, put down the knife," one demanded. He was a scrawny male, about twenty, but full of himself. I sniffed, recognizing his scent. He was one of the males who had chased me.

My voice was a warning snarl. "No."

Even if they weren't planning to hunt me inside, I wouldn't survive in a strange pack with no weapons. I lunged for him, and he fell back, shocked and angry. "You *bitch!*"

Two other males reached for me, but I was already gone, leaping for the second door, yanking the tablecloth as I ran the length of the table, pulling all the plates and food onto the carpeting. That would hopefully trip a few of them.

Voices called out after me as I ran, my heart sinking.

"Get her!"

"Stop her!"

I had no idea where to go.

I prayed that whatever was through the door was better than where I'd just been. Listening to the boys taking up the howl of the Hunt behind me, I had to hope there was someone there who would help me hide, who might protect me.

Hope again, you stupid idiot? Stop. Fucking. Hoping.

As I ran, I scrambled for a plan. If I could find my way out of the house entirely, I'd run for the lake. I was a decent swimmer, and the food I'd had over the past few days had made me stronger. They'd lose my scent in the water. There had to be another shore, and I'd swim until I found it, run and run and never look back.

I plunged through another door, down a short hallway, and found a door unlocked. I burst into the room, slamming the door on the faces of the males who were chasing me.

"Flor?" Someone called my name.

I whirled, holding the knife in front of me. Large hands —*male* hands—landed on my shoulders, and I darted to one side, slicing an arm to escape.

"Let me go!" I shouted.

"Let her go, son," a voice filled with command, a feminine voice, ordered.

Margarette? I skidded to a stop.

She would protect me. I knew she was still weakened from the attack at Southern, but my wolf saw her as the one in charge. "Help me," I whimpered, running to her at the same moment the males burst through the door.

Margarette grabbed a carving knife from her table, thrusting me behind her. "Stay behind me, Flor," she yelled. I almost protested, but there was a closed door on the wall at her back. A weakness in her defenses.

I obeyed her command, feeling guilty that I'd brought the battle to her while she was still recovering. She was right, though. I could already hear howls and running feet from behind the second door.

I would protect her or die trying.

5
BATTLE IN THE DINING ROOM
FLOR

Margarette's back was so close to mine, I could feel the body heat emanating from her as we took up a fighting formation I'd never tried. I'd never had someone who would stand at my back and fight with me. Never had someone who could, since the only one who would've fought with me, Del, had also been unranked, and weapons had been illegal for us to so much as touch.

Was it possible to miss something you'd never had? To miss the experience of fighting with someone? I realized it was as I readied myself for battle now, steak knife held low in one hand.

Someone else in the room let out a deep battle cry. I knew that roar. *Brand.*

Then another joined his. *Glen.*

One more sounded. *Wait, Finnick? When did he arrive? I thought he'd stayed at Southern.* Then I had no more time to wonder.

The males chasing me tried to leap across the room, but Brand, Finnick, Glen, and another shifter—Glen's brother,

39

Patrick—were suddenly in the formation with me and Margarette, and they were armed with a hell of a lot better weapons than a steak knife. Short swords and knives sliced the air, and the snarling younger males were a pile of whimpering, bleeding idiots in a handful of seconds.

Vanessa burst through the door as the last male fell to the carpeted floor. "Aunt Mags, kill her! Glen, help your mother! Get that bitch away—she's gone feral!" Everyone still standing looked at her like she was crazy. Then she screamed, "Glen's bleeding!"

We all turned, and I gasped aloud.

She hadn't been overreacting. Glen's arm was cut almost to the bone, a deep, ragged cut across his forearm at a diagonal. With his free hand, he was struggling to hold the edges of the gash together, in an attempt to staunch the flow. The wound wasn't closing at all.

"Do you stab all your potential mates?" he joked weakly, his eyes flitting to mine. Finnick crossed the room with a white napkin and wrapped it around his arm, murmuring something I couldn't make out.

I dropped the knife, aghast. "I didn't... I didn't know who it was," I explained, as Margarette turned to me, her eyebrows flying high. "I didn't mean to..." My breath started to come fast, and dizziness threatened, but she settled one hand on my shoulder.

"Breathe slowly, Flor," she ordered. "In and out, *one*. In and out, *two*. Focus on me, nothing else. No one else."

The edges of my vision were still black, but I did as she asked. I focused on her face, breathing. Ignoring everything but her.

She had suffered at Southern, too, but I hadn't had time to really appreciate how much she'd gone through, and changed, since the battle. The cuts the Head Enforcer had given her were still scabbed up. They would scar, like silver-tipped blade wounds always did.

She had been so beautiful before, but almost too perfect, like a model. Now she looked like a heroine from some fantasy story. In the past few days, someone had cut her ragged hair into a style sort of like mine, but with asymmetric angles that mirrored the angular slices on her face. Like she was showing the scars off. Didn't she care that her face was scarred?

"Badges of honor," she told me, noting where my gaze landed. "I will tell the story of that battle to every shifter I meet. How my late sister warned me that my hair was a liability in battle, and that I almost died for my vanity. It took a teenaged warrior to get me to finally cut my hair."

Story. Margarette had heard a lot of my stories. Maybe it hadn't been Glen.

"Did you—" I paused, but I had to know. "Did you tell them?" I nodded to the pile of whimpering males, and then to Vanessa. "About the haircut, and my name. That I was unranked." I felt rage growing inside me when her face went even more pale. "Was it you who told them about the Hunt?" My voice rose, got stronger. "Did you *know* your shifters have been hunting me all day, in the woods? Here, in your own damned *house?*"

It was like I'd set off a bomb in the room.

The Alpha Heirs all began cursing. Something was happening with Brand—another partial shift, I thought—and it took Finnick and Patrick both to hold him back from the pile of wounded shifters. His snarls filled the room, and the smell of urine and fear rose from the defeated young males.

Margarette's lips trembled as she took in my words. "I

told Vanessa," she admitted, "but I only told her so she would understand, so she would help you."

That bitch.

"She set the Hunt on me," I hissed, and Margarette's eyes widened. I turned to see Vanessa wrapping a fresh cloth napkin around the soaked one on Glen's arm. It was still oozing blood, so much blood. "I should kick your ass for that, Vanessa," I told her quietly. "In fact, I plan to."

She blinked. "You want to... fight me?"

"Abso-fucking-lutely. Here and now, or in a ring." I'd love to meet this stuck-up princess in a fighting ring and let her try to laugh at me with no tongue in her damned mouth.

Brand nodded, like he agreed. The wounded males were already stirring, and I stepped as far from them as I could.

"Y-you can't fight me," Vanessa sputtered. "You're unranked."

"No, she's not." Glen shoved her away. "She's ranked higher than you. She's my—" Margarette cleared her throat, with a pointed look at me. "She's special," he finished weakly.

"Special enough to become an Enforcer?" Vanessa spat, but she was staring at Margarette.

"Vanessa, must we have this same conversation again? Glen, you'd better go see the pack doctor." Margarette sighed heavily. "You'll need to get that stitched."

"Stitches?" Vanessa's face was red, but she still sneered at me and then at Glen. "I wasn't allowed to go to the Conclave and try to find my true mate, because it was too dangerous. I guess Aunt Mags was right—Southern *was* too dangerous, if it turned you into a weak-ass wolf." Her gaze darted around the room, taking in the pile of wounded shifters, the blood splatters that decorated the carpet by

Glen, then rested once more on the cloth around his arm, which was still dripping fresh blood. "Why aren't you healing?" she demanded.

Glen didn't answer, but the males who were slowly picking themselves up off the floor and trying to leave froze. Wide-eyed, they looked at him, then over at me. The ones still on the floor began backing away on their hands and knees, eyes cast down and to the side. Like they were afraid.

They fucking should be. Finnick was still struggling to hold Brand back. And I had a feeling that with a little coaxing, Margarette might let me kill these males for their insult.

"Glen, what happened?" Vanessa's voice was fearful now.

He stayed silent, holding the napkins on his arm. But the blonde girl who'd glared at me in the blue room had slipped inside at some point, and she answered for him. "She's his true mate. She must be." Her gaze landed on me, sharp and filled with rage. "You don't deserve him."

I closed my eyes. "Not this shit again."

Margarette took charge. "Right. Why Glen is bleeding is not your concern. What *is* your concern, Vanessa, is why you would bring up the terrible abuses I told you about in confidence, so that Flor would have a friend who understood all she'd lived through."

"You expect me to be a friend to an unranked piece of fur that Glen brought home as a fu—" Vanessa couldn't finish her sentence, since she was on the floor, holding her face. Margarette had slapped her so hard, it had sounded like a gunshot.

"*Enough.* I have spoiled you, if you think you can speak to me that way—your Alpha Mate, this pack's Head Enforcer. That you can treat a guest of our pack in such a

43

manner. Vanessa, you have dishonored yourself, and our pack. I am stripping you of rank."

The room went silent. There was something I didn't understand being said.

"You've got to be joking. For *her?* I work for decades to test for Enforcer, I'm finally given the chance, and of course you're pulling the rug out. Of fucking *course*."

Margarette let out a low growl. "Get out of my sight, Vanessa. Out of this house."

"I have to move to the unranked compound?" Vanessa's jaw dropped, her eyes darting to all the others in the room, except me. "You're kicking me out of my home?"

Margarette scowled. "No. You may continue to live here as family. But you will report to the training grounds for remedial lessons with the elementary shifters on pack law and tenets tomorrow, after you clean the dining rooms."

Vanessa sputtered, "Remedial—I could teach that class! I *have* taught it!"

"That concerns me as well." Margarette's eyes clouded with grief and disappointment. "If you haven't learned the central tenet of pack law—that the pack *protects*—what have you taught the others?" She shook off her sadness when Vanessa continued to sputter and make excuses, then growled louder. "Go, now."

In seconds, all the shifters who'd been in the other dining room were gone. The blonde took Vanessa's arm and whispered something in her ear while pulling her to the door, glaring at me like she was imagining me chopped into pieces the size of stew meat.

Glen stayed, Finnick holding him still so he could bind the wound tightly. It looked like the bleeding was stopping at last. Good, maybe then they'd shut up about this true mate bullshit.

Two maids came bustling through the door, clearing away the broken dishes and spilled food, replacing it all with fresh platters and table linen, as if this sort of thing happened often. Brand stood close to me, his breathing still labored, as if he was struggling not to chase down the males.

"Where were you?" I managed to ask in a whisper. "You said you wouldn't leave me alone."

"Margarette said you were coming straight from your room, and asked me to escort her here," Brand replied quietly as he guided me to an empty space at the table. "She sent a servant to bring you to dinner; I heard her."

"She took me to the other dining room." I wasn't certain if she'd misdirected me on purpose or not. The servant had asked about my rank and mated status—but who knew what was going on in this fucked-up pack? Certainly not me.

I sniffed, and felt ill. I had blood all over my clothes. "Can I go change?" Then my stomach let out a growl. "I'm hungry, but I smell."

"Food first," Brand said, guiding me down onto a cushioned chair, then sitting beside me. "You can change after, but only if I go with you. I will never fucking leave your side from now on." That seemed a bit extreme, but I appreciated the sentiment.

"Where are your new clothes, Flor?" Margarette asked, her voice strained. "What happened in the few hours since we arrived?"

"Same old, same old, Margarette. Don't worry, I'm used to it." I patted her arm.

"Don't worry?" She was shaking with something. Pain, or exhaustion?

I peeked at her face. *Nope.*

45

Door number three: incandescent rage.

She didn't need my mess to deal with as well as her own. *Change of topic required.* "How is Alpha Hillier?"

"He's still not... The doctor says he could be healing, slowly," she said, her voice raspy. "Scars are unusual on any shifter. My mate's scars will not be as attractive as mine. But every scar on a shifter tells a story of battle, and victory."

I pressed a hand to my own chest, wanting to ask her if she was sure about that. I'd had mine since I was a baby, maybe since I was born. But I wasn't sure where mine had come from. Only that they'd been aching since I left Southern.

"Here, little badass." I flinched as Patrick moved close to my arm, serving me a large rare steak on a wide plate. Brand snarled, and Patrick returned his aggression, though he stepped backward. "Give me a break, Brand. She's hungry."

"Mine," Brand growled, and I thought he meant the steak when he pulled the plate over. But he began cutting pieces for me with his own knife and fork, and holding them up to my mouth. Feeding me? I took one, making a small sound of appreciation. Brand froze, then smiled, his teeth oddly sharp.

Okay, that was weird. He was enjoying this a little too much, and when I peeked around the room, Glen and Finnick were both staring with fascination at the next bite of steak. Or at my lips? They looked hungry for something, though Finnick's nostrils were flared. In distaste, probably. Finnick had made sure I knew exactly how much he didn't want to be around me back at Southern.

"Um, maybe I should go shower."

Brand grunted. "Eat first. You don't smell bad."

Sitting on my other side, Patrick leaned in and gave a sniff, making a face. "Don't listen to him, Flor. You do smell. But eat anyway."

"Thank you for the food." I laid a hand on his arm.

Growls erupted from all the other males in the room. I rolled my eyes when Brand moved my hand from Patrick's arm and placed it on my lap.

"As I was saying, I think my scars will be quite attractive," Margarette said, her lips twitching as she ignored whatever was going on with the guys. "I rather like the angles. They go perfectly with my haircut. I never would have tried something this modern. Thank you for giving me the idea, Flor."

"Giving you the idea? I hacked it off with a steak knife." She was bugnuts. I liked it.

"Mhmm," she murmured, turning back to her meal like it had never been interrupted. "Now, I don't want to upset you, but I would like to hear what happened with Vanessa and the others." She bared her teeth delicately. "In case I need to strip the ranks from them all."

"Who are they?" I asked, chewing the steak Brand offered me slowly. "They remind me a lot of the shifters back at Southern. They were overcome with the instinct to chase."

"Strip their ranks," Margarette instructed Patrick.

"Done," he replied.

I blinked. "No, wait!"

Margarette raised an eyebrow, tucking into her own food. "If they can't control their wolves, their instincts, they can't hold rank. That's what rank means, Flor. Strength."

Huh. I'd never heard it put that way. I wasn't altogether certain I believed it either. The maids I'd met here who were unranked had seemed as strong as most of the ranked shifters back at Southern. But I supposed I'd need to meet more of them before I could judge fairly. The young males who'd chased me definitely didn't need to have any kind of authority over other shifters, so I ended up nodding.

"Just... don't do it for me. I don't think I'm even going to be able to stay here."

"You can't leave!" Glen, Margarette, and Finnick all said at the same time.

I glanced at Brand. He mouthed one word. *Lake?*

Just seeing that made me relax. "Not yet." I turned back to Margarette. "I can leave," I said calmly. I didn't like the silence that fell in the room when I said it. "You said it yourself—I'm not a prisoner."

I stared down the woman who'd felt, for a short time, like a friend. Like safety and hope rolled into one. But her pack wasn't at all like I'd thought, like she'd led me to believe.

"Or am I?"

6

THE ALPHA'S PROTECTOR
FLOR

Margarette's beautiful eyes filled with pain, but I didn't let my own resolve falter. If she was going to change the rules now, after I'd come here, I wanted to hear it straight from her.

"Of course you're not a prisoner, Flor. You are a guest, an honored one, no matter how dishonorably my niece acted when you arrived."

She *wished* it was just her niece. From what I had heard and seen so far, unranked shifters still got the short end of the stick here. Maybe worse. Was Margarette unaware of the disparity, or did she not care? I wanted to ask her, tell her what I thought, but all I said was, "I'm not sure this is the pack for me."

"Mountain is the right place for you, little flower," Brand whispered.

The other guys heard, of course, and started arguing, until Margarette held up a hand. "Why not, sweet girl? Please, don't let today's incident sour you on all of us at Northern."

"Incidents," I told her, emphasizing the *s*.

49

"We may not deserve another chance, but I would ask you to give us one." She nodded at Patrick, and he took up the argument.

"I know the senior Enforcers have been anxiously awaiting you at the training grounds."

"Me? Why?"

Down the table, Finnick let out a sharp laugh, and Patrick joined in. "Are you kidding? The story of you saving our Alpha and Alpha Mate is all anyone's talking about. The Sergeant at Arms requisitioned an entire set of steak knives for a special training that he hopes to convince you to teach."

"I-I can't teach anyone," I sputtered. "I'm not that good."

Finnick shook his head. "She has no ego at all. None."

Patrick shushed me. "He said we all need to be trained with whatever's at hand. Our pack's too dependent on our traditional blades in this form."

I shrugged. "Tell him to throw some mop handles into the mix. You aren't always at dinner when they attack."

"But you were." Glen spoke for the first time since I'd cut him. He sounded devastated. "Today, just now, in my own home. You were attacked... twice?"

"Chased the first time. Boys being asshole boys. Not sure whether they would have touched me," I lied. Nostrils flared around the table as the metallic scent of a lie wafted through the room, and even Margarette let out a growl.

Brand snarled. "I will tear their legs off and sear the stumps. That will keep them from chasing you ever again."

To my surprise, Finnick muttered, "Sounds fun. I'll help."

I didn't want to talk about the first attack, and Brand looked like he might force the issue. So instead, I circled the table to Glen's side, gently pressing my hand onto the cloth on his arm that they'd bound the wound with. I didn't think it was still bleeding, but more pressure seemed like a good idea. "Where's the pack doctor? You need to get this looked at."

He swallowed. "It... It actually feels better with your hand on it," he murmured, pressing his fingers over mine. "Could you keep holding it?"

"Sure," I said, trying not to show how his touch affected me. I knew my face was turning red, but no one said anything about it.

Except Finnick, of fucking course. He rolled his eyes and muttered, "It feels better when you hold it, Flor. Hold it harder, *harder*—ugh." He broke off when someone, probably Brand, kicked him under the table.

"Boys, manners." Margarette took charge again. "I'm still just *stunned* that you were attacked at dinner in our own home. You have my sincerest apologies. What happened? Help me understand."

I figured Vanessa was unranked now, so it wouldn't hurt if I went ahead and told them everything. "Someone— I know now it was *you*—told Vanessa that I was unranked. She was talking shit about my pack, and me, and how trashy I am, but then she brought up the Hunt. I think it got the younger males a little worked up."

"What did she say exactly?"

"That I fucked every wolf who caught me in the Hunt." I took a shaky breath. "That was their prize. And that I was the pack whore."

Glen rose. "Mother, I'm sorry. Stripping her rank isn't enough. I'm killing her."

"I'll help," Brand muttered.

"No," I said, as calmly as I could. "It's pretty much true,

what she said." I turned back to my plate and took another bite of my steak, pretending it tasted delicious, even though my appetite had fled. "I was the prey in the Hunt for... I guess it was just over four years now. And after the first time I was caught, and my mama got me free, I did fuck every wolf who caught me." I took in their reactions, keeping my own face still.

"Damnit," Patrick breathed, dropping his gaze. "You were a *child*." Margarette's eyes glittered with fury. Brand just smiled that tiny, quiet smile. He knew.

Glen sat back down, getting it at last. "You avoided every single unmated male in your pack for over *four years?* I'd heard that, but I wasn't sure it was true."

Finnick choked on something, then rasped, "They hunted you every day?"

"Every night, more like." I shrugged, trying not to shiver as Glen's hand moved across my jawline and grazed my neck as he sat again. "From dusk to midnight. After Trevor's attack, they started enforcing the official rules of the Hunt. I think Luke was the one who convinced his dad to hold them to it."

Patrick spat out another curse. "I thought Luke was a decent shifter, at least for Southern."

Luke wasn't the worst of the shifters at Southern, but he was no saint. "It actually made things better. Before then, it was sort of a free-for-all. I was never safe. But when Mama was sentenced to death by banishment—"

"Rogues," Margarette murmured, and I nodded. "I've heard about your problems with rogues at Southern."

"Yeah. Back then, the males were hunting me all the time, and Luke convinced Alpha Callaway that the males were coming to training exhausted from hunting me through the nights." I blinked, remembering my own exhaustion, and those three nights in the tree when I'd thought I would die. When I'd almost wanted to. "Anyway, then they could only hunt me between six p.m. and midnight, and not when I was doing my pack duties in the dining hall. I got really good at washing dishes and sweeping up. It took a long, long time to finish each job, though. Nobody ever figured out Del was helping me."

Brand spoke at last. "That's when Del started teaching you to defend yourself?"

Patrick's mouth gaped. "You mean you've only been training for four years?"

"No, closer to ten." I smiled at their reactions. "He started teaching me to hunt and work on conditioning when I was really small, about five or six. Once I was old enough, he'd sneak us into an unused pack gym before breakfast and school, and we'd spar for an hour at least. And after dinner, when we hunted in the woods for squirrels and rabbits where nobody else was around, he taught me martial arts."

"Which styles?" Patrick's tone sounded casual, but the look in his eyes was pure excitement. He'd seen me fight Finnick at Southern, so he had some idea.

"Oh, you know. Muay Thai, jiu-jitsu, sword and staff forms from a couple different Korean schools. Krav Maga, a little bit of everything." I smirked. "Some street fighting."

Finnick coughed. "Dirty tricks."

I nodded at him. "I'll fight you again without dirt and kick your ass just the same," I mocked. "Oh wait, I already did."

The whole room exploded into laughter. "I deserved that," he grumbled.

I was almost proud of him. Where had that haughty shifter gone? My chest still ached when I looked at him, though. His words on my last day at Southern still rang in my mind. *I couldn't be your mate, Flor. I wouldn't ever make that mistake.*

Yeah, that chickenshit deserved to have his ass kicked a few more times. Maybe this Sergeant person would let me demonstrate my steak knife technique on Finnick's toes.

"Are you done?" Margarette asked, and I looked down at my plate, shocked to find it empty.

"Apparently, I am." My stomach felt nicely full.

"Good. Sleep well tonight. In the morning, we'll have training."

Sleep? I wasn't sure I even wanted to leave the dining room, or go anywhere alone, not in this house. Who knew if the males who'd chased me might come back? But my limbs were quivering with exhaustion. I needed to crash, and a safe place to do it.

I glanced at Brand nervously, but before I could say one word, he mumbled, "You won't be alone. I'll be right outside your door, guarding you."

Margarette started to fuss at him about needing to sleep, but let it go when he narrowed his eyes at her. "Right, let's all get to bed then. In the morning, I'll find you some clothes to fight in." She crossed the room and stared down at Glen's and my hands, like she could weld them together with her eyes. I pulled my hand back, the drying blood making the cloth sticky. "Can I take a look, Glen?"

"Sure," he answered his mother, his eyes still uncertain. He carefully pulled the napkins off. The cut was still there, bleeding sluggishly. It had healed somewhat, though. Maybe it just took a while, with a cut that deep.

I let out a sigh of relief. "See? He's healing fine. We're not true mates."

"What do you..." Margarette trailed off when Glen shook his head.

"See you in the morning, Flor," he murmured.

Brand followed me to the room and, as promised, sat outside all night. I showered, changed, and put on a set of extra-large sweats to sleep in, the only clothing I could find in the room.

I slept well, and woke up early as usual. When I heard a soft knock, I opened the door instantly. "Margarette's here with clothing," Brand mumbled, running a hand through his hair. He looked like he'd been awake all night; his long dark hair was messy and his eyes bloodshot.

"Go get some coffee, Bearman." I squeezed his hand in thanks as Margarette stepped around him and bustled inside with a bag full of clothing, followed by an unranked maid with a tray of breakfast for us. It felt peculiar to have people helping me get ready for the day, but it was better than being alone in the Lodge and running into trouble.

"I'll see you at training," he promised, though he seemed to be having a hard time leaving. "Stay with Margarette."

"I will."

IN A HALF HOUR, I was ready to go. I let out a low whistle as I stared at myself in the floor-length mirror. Margarette had found some better clothes for me than the loose sweats—all black, like the ones she'd been wearing when I first met her. The pants and shirt were a little baggy but clean, and she'd brought some sort of gel to slick my hair back. With my steak knife strapped to my waist, I thought I looked kind of badass... until she told me they were sparring clothes one of the youngest women in the pack had outgrown years before.

"I'm wearing kid's clothes?" I grumbled.

She stifled a laugh. "We won't make you new ones yet, because if the boys have their way with feeding you, you'll be bursting out of the seams in a few weeks."

"The boys?"

She shrugged, opening the door for us to go. "I'd call them men, but around you, they tend to act like boys." She laughed. "Even Brand, and he was born an old man."

I smiled as we walked toward the back of the enormous house. This hallway was brighter than the ones at the front, the walls decorated with framed blueprints of what I thought might be the buildings on the property. The main Lodge was huge, with wings that stretched out like a four-armed starfish. Then there was a clearing, with equally large rectangular buildings to one side, and more buildings that had to be the unranked dorms set farther back, almost under the trees. There were even trails marked that led into the forest, and one aerial photo that had lines drawn on it. The pack's farthest borders?

I need to memorize all of this, I thought, Del's training kicking in. This would help me if I needed to run, or if anything like the Hunt... No. I had to believe Margarette wouldn't let that sort of thing happen again.

I jogged to catch up with her. "You've known Brand a long time then?"

She grinned, her scars making the expression oddly fierce. "I don't know if they told you, but the larger packs foster out their future leaders for months at a time. Brand's mother died a while back, during an attack on their pack-

lands, so he stayed even longer with me while his dad was...
in the woods. He calls me Mom once in a while." She sighed
happily, obviously pleased by that.

"What about the others?" I asked. Had Luke ever come
here? I knew he'd gone to Eastern once; our whole pack had
been buzzing about him buying new clothing to go to New
York. I'd been bitter as hell about it, because that winter,
the food rations for the unranked had been cut even more,
supposedly to pay for those fancy clothes. I'd still been a
kid, and if Del hadn't been able to sneak me leftovers from
the ranked shifters' meals, I would have starved.

"All the Heirs had visits here," she said, but didn't
elaborate.

"Did they all call you Mom?"

She pursed her lips. "I think they all needed one, to
some extent. Finnick's parents are both alive and well, but
his mother... Well, some mothers are more hands-off in
shifter culture, especially with sons. He was always looking
for reasons to visit, even after his official foster stay was
over. I think Finnick needed an affectionate foster mother
more than most, but he was taught that wanting love was
weakness."

My heart ached a little. I was still pissed at him, but her
story made me wonder if Finnick was as much of an asshole
as he pretended to be. He seemed cold, but lonely, like his
icy distance wasn't by choice.

"Luke went to Finnick's pack once, but not for long.
Days, not months. Why was that?"

Margarette frowned in thought. "Glen mentioned that.
I always assumed there was friction between Finnick's
parents and the Southern Alpha, and that Luke was recalled
early." Then we turned a corner, and she threw open the
door to the vast yard behind the house.

I squinted into the sunlight. It was green, bright, and noisy. Shifters were moving everywhere, wearing either camo fatigues or black and gray sweats, sparring in rings that had been marked out with colored chalk on the grass. I saw groups of shifters play fighting in wolf form, and others in human form doing movements in slow motion. It looked like some sort of tai chi, but they had knives in their hands.

There was a group of older children, too, six to eight of them meditating in the sunlight, legs crossed, and eyes mostly shut. One of the smallest ones wasn't meditating very successfully, and she let out a tiny howl of victory when she spied us. "She's here! The Alpha's Protector is here!"

The whole yard went still, every head swiveling toward me.

Margarette watched the tiny shifter as she pelted across the lawn, greeting the child with an indulgent kiss on top of her hair. "You're right, the Alpha's Protector is here. And did you know she has a name like yours? She's Flor."

"Like flower," the girl said, smiling up through a gap in her front teeth. Her hair was a wild mess of brown tangles, and her face and clothes looked like she'd been berry picking—or berry fighting—all day. She hugged Margarette, but before I knew what was happening, she threw herself at me, up into my arms.

I caught her, wondering what to do with her. Children were rarer now, so holding one felt like holding the Northern pack's treasure. And I could tell from the way every shifter in the yard fixed their eyes on me, that that's exactly what I was doing.

"This is Daisy," Margarette said, placing her hand on my shoulder, showing everyone who was watching me—a little too closely—that she trusted me. "She's one of the youngest members of Northern."

"I'm seven!" she announced. "I like your hair, Flor. Yours too, Aunt Mags."

"Aunt Mags?" I asked.

"My parents are dead," Daisy said matter-of-factly, tugging at the ends of my hair. "Aunt Mags, I want to cut my hair all off. Can I?" The older male wolf who had been leading the meditation called out for her to return, and Daisy pulled free, lightly dropping to the ground. She smacked a kiss on my hand and giggled.

"What was that for?"

She wrinkled her nose up at me. "Don't you know? If you kiss the Protector, you get good luck."

"What... Why—" But she was gone. And all that was left was a yard filled with shifters.

All laughing at me.

7
THE MOST IMPORTANT WEAPON
FLOR

My cheeks burned as the laughter grew louder. Some of it was genuine, but I recognized the hard edge in it. There were at least two hundred shifters close enough for me to hear them, and more than a few were mocking me.

"If you kiss the Protector, you get good luck?" Brand was suddenly beside me, glaring around the grounds as if daring anyone to speak. He roared his next words. "If I hear *any* male repeat that, I will remove his spleen with my teeth."

The shifters nearby stifled their laughter quickly, but one or two of the males were still smiling in a suggestive way that indicated I'd need to squash that rumor, fast.

Or keep a steak knife at my waist to teach them better. I set my hand on top of it now.

"Thanks, Bearman," I called, sending him a wink. His sun-bronzed skin went a deeper hue above his short beard.

"They should show more respect." I couldn't help my grin at his fierce declaration.

But then the atmosphere shifted in the training yard. The males who had been smirking snapped to attention as an older man approached from the far corner of the yard. He was a huge shifter with camouflage-speckled pants and a faded black t-shirt that looked like it was about to start unraveling at the seams. He had to be sixty, but he stalked rather than walked. He was confident and calm, and the other shifters all bowed their heads as he passed.

"Who is that?" I whispered to Margarette, trying not to gawk. He wasn't as tall as Brand, but he was wide—all of it muscle—and dominance rolled off him like a wave. "How is he not Alpha?" I breathed, then bit my lip, hoping I hadn't just insulted her husband.

"Possibly because he never found a mate," Margarette answered softly. "He's a dedicated fighter, and an incredible teacher. Our pack is lucky to have him."

"You," the man barked out as he got closer. He had shaved, light gray hair, and strange markings all over him. They were silver scars on his exposed skin, but done in patterns, whorls and loops.

Holy crap. He'd scarred himself on purpose, like tattoos. The pain he must've gone through... But the designs were pretty cool. I wanted some.

"Sir," I answered, when it became obvious he was waiting for me to answer.

He circled me slowly. My wolf did not like having him at my back. I stifled the urge to growl, but circled with him, keeping both eyes on him at all times. He didn't carry any weapons that I could see, but it was clear he *was* a weapon. And I'd never let one this strong anywhere near my unprotected back.

"Hmph," he grunted, stopping. "Alpha Mate, leave us. You're not well enough to train."

She sputtered. "What? I can train—"

"Margarette." He shot her a glance, and she submitted, her eyes hitting the ground before she turned and strode away, agitation in every step.

Holy shit. The Alpha Mate couldn't hold this shifter's gaze?

"Eyes up, shifter," he barked, and I obeyed, meeting his gaze.

I froze. His eyes were amber, like mine. Almost the exact shade. His jawline had the same angle, and his skin the same color. Was there some chance... some way we were related?

No, it wasn't possible. As far as I knew, my mom had come from Southern. *But her parents had to have come from somewhere. He could be my great-uncle or something.*

His gaze burned into mine, and I felt sweat begin to pop out on my upper lip. But his eyes weren't threatening. Just dominant. It felt almost... safe, to be caught in his gaze. I felt connected to him somehow. I didn't want to drop my gaze, and I didn't have to. We were matched in dominance, or close to it.

Somewhere close by, a shifter let out a low whistle. Another one murmured, "Holy shit, she's held Sergeant's gaze for..."

"Two minutes, forty-five seconds and counting," the grizzled soldier interrupted, still staring into my eyes. I saw one corner of his mouth twitching, like he was trying to smile, but had forgotten. "And she's not stopping. Are you, girl?"

I kept staring, unsure if I could answer. My legs were trembling, and I felt like I might shit my pants if this kept going for much longer, but something in me would not let me look away.

"What's your rank, shifter?"

"I'm unranked, sir." Not that I'd ever had the chance to try for rank.

Shifters all around us stopped talking, and whispers broke out.

"It's true."

"She's the one."

"Unranked. But you're living in the Lodge. I see." Sergeant nodded, and for some reason, I had a feeling he understood more than I'd said aloud. More than *I* understood. "Enforcer Patrick Hillier informed me our Alpha forced your first shift to heal some severe wounds. You haven't even shifted on your own."

Embarrassed, I shook my head slightly, wondering where this was going. Were unranked wolves not allowed to learn to fight here after all? Did he think I was weak? I knew I was an underfed, unranked stranger.

Maybe he wasn't going to train me. Maybe he just wanted me to show what I could do with a steak knife and that was all.

Fuck that noise. I stared harder into his eyes, feeling the stirrings of anger, ignoring the small trickle of blood I could feel starting to roll down from my nostril.

"No quit, huh?" he breathed. "You'd keep this up until you passed out, I bet."

"Yes, sir," I said, the words respectful, but the tone the same one I used to tell assholes to fuck off. "But I been told more'n once that I'm stubborn as a mule and only half as smart, so I mightn't stop even then."

Still holding my gaze, he let out a bark of laughter. Someone choked out, "Sergeant *laughed.*"

The older shifter's eyes flicked once to my shoulder. Then, next to me, something shifted. I saw something, or someone, moving toward me, too fast. I whirled, hands up, the knife out of my belt and in my grip. Seeking the threat.

It was Brand. He tilted his head, eyes on my knife. "Please don't stab me, little flower."

Sergeant let out another bark and grabbed Brand, pounding him on the back hard enough to break ribs. "Boy, step aside. You may have fought me to a draw earlier, but I can still beat your ass."

"I know you can," Brand replied. "But I was hoping instead of me, you'd train my friend, Flor."

Sergeant grunted one word. "No."

My heart sank. "You're not going to train me? Because I'm unranked?" I backed away, not bothering to hide my sneer. "Fucking packs are all the same."

Brand's hand landed gently on my arm, flooding me with warmth. "Flor, no." He gently steered me back toward the soldier.

Sergeant's obvious confusion made his features seem less forbidding. "That is not what I meant. My apologies, shifter. I've been given the task of *testing* you so we can determine what level you'll start at in training." His lips tightened. "I only personally train the highest level of Enforcer. If I spar against shifters who aren't skilled enough, I can... Well, we've learned that's a bad idea."

I took a calming breath. "Okay. What tests do you want to do?"

"What weapons training have you had?"

"None," I announced baldly. He lifted a bushy eyebrow at the steak knife in my hand. "Unless you count silverware and cleaning supplies," I amended. "I'm pretty good with those."

"I've heard," he said. "Heard you sliced open our Alpha

Heir last night." His eyes gleamed. "Rumor is he's still not healed."

"Want me to show you what I did to him, sir?" I asked, flipping the knife expertly in my hand. Brand let out a low hiss of breath at the implied threat.

I thought, for a second, I might make the soldier laugh a third time. Instead, his mouth just did a weird twitching thing. "Call me Sergeant." He held out a hand.

"Call me Wills." I grasped his forearm, and he returned the hold, both of us staring into each other's faces again. Something in me recognized him. He felt like... pack. Like family.

"Right, Wills," he said after a long minute. "Put away your knife and let me see what you can do."

What I could do without a knife? "With what weapon, Sergeant?"

"With the most important weapon you have, shifter."

Something in his tone caught my attention. This was a test. Del had asked a lot of questions just like this, trying to trick me. Checking to make sure I knew better than to chase down the obvious prey, in case something more important —or more dangerous—was waiting in the bushes nearby.

"Well, then, you need to ask me a question, I guess," I said slowly.

He narrowed his eyes, but a glint of something that may have been respect was in his amber gaze.

I lifted an eyebrow, knowing I'd answered correctly. "A puzzle? A riddle, maybe?"

His nostrils flared slightly. "Thought you said you had no training."

"At Southern, it was against pack law and Alpha command to train an unranked shifter to fight." That was completely true, and he could hear it in my voice.

"Then who taught you the most important weapon a shifter has—"

"Is your brain? Try being unranked for a while, Sergeant. You learn pretty fast that you have to outthink the rest of your pack, just to stay alive."

"Fucking Southern," Brand muttered behind me. He sounded pissed.

But the Sergeant at Arms just looked intrigued. "Southern, hm? I've never been there. Never had an interest in visiting. I think that may have been a mistake." Those amber eyes caught mine again, and I almost flinched at the storm of emotions there. Memories, or maybe nightmares, swirled in the depths of the soldier's stern gaze for an instant, and I bit my tongue to keep from asking who he was. If he knew who I was. The only thing stopping me was the presence of so many others around us.

But then he shook off whatever thoughts had caught him, and barked out a question. "Second most effective weapon, then, shifter?"

I almost reached for my knife again, but stopped. After my mind, my second most effective weapon was... "Got it," I replied, rotating my ankles. "Where's the track?"

"The track?" He almost seemed pissed, and sniffed the air, like he was trying to scent a lie.

"You said my second most important weapon." Del had always told me that after intellect, speed was any shifter's most vital tool. Speed and endurance.

"Hmph. No training, she says," he growled to himself, but was obviously happy with my answer. "Run until you can't anymore, then do five more laps."

"Yes, Sergeant."

"Boys, take flank." I frowned, then saw that Glen and Finnick had joined us and were standing a few yards off.

"Yes, Sergeant," Glen and Brand answered.

Finnick just groaned. He was wearing the gray sweatpants like many of the other shifters, but his t-shirt looked like it had been ironed. Ironed over a set of ridiculous, sculpted abs and stretched over broad shoulders. Somehow, he made the simple workout clothes look like a magazine spread, maybe for Ireland, with his short red hair and piercing green eyes. Why did my eyes keep going back to his torso, like they had special ab-magnets stuck inside?

I forced myself to remember his words again, the ones he'd repeated. They'd hurt like knives being plunged into me. *"I am not your true mate, Florida Wills, and you are not mine."* Like I'd even hinted that it could be true. Why were the hottest guys always the worst assholes?

"C'mon, Cityboy," I teased him, trying to keep my voice flat. "I'm sure a grown-ass shifter like you can keep up with me. Even if you can't beat me in a fight."

Finnick glared, but Glen kept pace at my side as I began to run. "Not sure any shifter can keep up with you. But I think you can keep a lot of shifters *up*." He waggled his eyebrows. When I didn't respond, he pointed to his crotch with both hands. I stuck a foot out and tripped him hard. Sexual banter wasn't my thing.

Running, however? I could run all day. I ran, and remembered training with Del, and thought about the amazing food I'd eaten the day before, and that bitch Vanessa, and wondered what was for dinner tonight. Or lunch. Maybe more steak? I'd seen venison in the fridge, though. And ham. I couldn't remember the last time I'd tasted ham.

Then I let myself think about the shifter hierarchy here. I'd seen plenty of shifters with leather necklaces who were training in the yard, which reassured me this place wasn't exactly like Southern. Some of those unranked shifters had been holding real weapons, learning to fight. Some of them were really good.

I still wanted to talk to those fighters, the ones with the chokers on, and figure out how the ranking system really worked, before I trusted Margarette's assurances that Northern was better than my old pack.

My thoughts glided through my mind as effortlessly as my feet did around the three-mile track surrounding the Northern main compound. I was just starting to wonder when dinner was, when I heard Sergeant calling.

"Wills, enough!"

"Sir?" I stopped, panting. My legs were humming, still full of energy. "I haven't gotten to my limit yet."

"I can see that." He glared past me, to where Glen and Brand were grinning like idiots. Red-faced, sweaty idiots.

Finnick was nowhere to be seen. Brand answered my unspoken question. "Finn twisted an ankle about ten miles ago."

Ah. I hadn't noticed. I turned back to Sergeant.

"You went thirty-one miles, Wills," he stated. He seemed pissed. "I should have put some weights on you; I wanted to test your endurance."

"I ran a lot at Southern." *Ran for my life.*

"Not as part of training, though," he said, once again seeming to hear the words I hadn't said out loud. "I can't break protocol. It sets a bad precedent for the young bloods who think they can do better than my routine." He frowned even harder. "It'll be conditioning for at least a week for you, then basic forms and drills. You'll be with our Enforcers-in-training, but no sparring just yet." He nodded to Brand and Glen. "I want her ready for rank testing and weapons training by the next full moon."

"Yes, sir," they both shouted. Sergeant marched off, glaring at the grass like he was mad at each blade he passed.

As soon as he was out of earshot, I let out a laugh and fell to the ground. "He's terrifying!"

Glen slumped next to me. "*He's* terrifying? You're every bit as bad. You just ran me and Brand into the ground."

"She killed Finnick," Brand snickered, from where he was lying face down on the grass at my other side. "He gave up and went inside and died."

Glen groaned. "More like he gave up staring at her ass, and went inside to eat the dessert buffet."

"Dessert buffet?" I perked up, ignoring the ass comment. "That's a real thing? What's on it?"

"When I can feel my legs again, I'll show you," Glen said. "Give me a minute."

Brand started doing some stretches, and I followed suit. Glen just sat there, staring at me like I'd grown feathers or something. It made me super self-conscious. "What?" I wiped at my face, wondering if I'd slobbered on myself while I was running.

"I just realized I don't know what your favorite dessert is. Or your favorite anything. How will I know how to woo you, milady?" He fluttered his lashes and grinned.

I rolled my eyes, but couldn't help smiling back. "Wanna play Twenty Questions?" I'd overheard some of the other shifters playing that game at Southern. It seemed dumb, giving up that much information to someone who might use it against you. But I didn't think Glen or Brand would do that, and I kind of wanted to know more about him, too.

He shrugged. "Why not?"

"Okay, favorite dessert is... ice cream." I'd only had it a

couple of times, but I remembered thinking it was what I'd request for a final meal. Just a giant bowl of ice cream the size of my head. "Chocolate ice cream."

Glen nodded. "Good choice. I'm a rocky road guy, but I can deal with chocolate. Next question: favorite movie? Mine is *Fast and Furious 6*."

For some reason, Brand snorted, then muttered, "More like *Pride and Prejudice*, Glenda."

"*Princess Bride*," I shot back.

Glen's smile got wider. "Want to watch it tonight? I have—I mean, Mom has that in our collection."

"Heck yeah!" I'd watched it a bunch of times, since it was one of the only movies Del had sneaked in to play while we did dishes in the kitchen.

Glen reached over, picked up my hand and kissed it. "As you wish, Alpha Protector." His deep blue eyes caught me, and I felt the whirlpool of his attention pulling me under. I leaned forward, and so did he, like some sort of gravity field had caught both of us, drawing our lips together...

Smack! Until an acorn hit him in the middle of his forehead.

"What the hell, Brand?" He grabbed it and tossed it away.

I blushed and scooted back. Brand was glaring at Glen, and I could feel the tension rising between the two. "So, um, Brand says he likes to sculpt. What's your hobby, Glen?"

Brand snorted something that sounded like, "Semi-professional fornication."

Glen glared him to silence. "I read," he replied. "A lot."

"Oh, is that what we're calling it now, brother? So you *read* to all those women," Brand mumbled. "Keep a lot of books in your bedroom these days?"

Glen bristled visibly, but his face was flushed. He was really upset, or embarrassed. "What the hell, *brother*?"

"Ignore him." I grabbed Glen's hand again to distract myself from the upwelling of anger I felt just thinking about him with other women, then dropped it when the tornado energy started up. "What do you like to read?"

"Nonfiction," he said, staring down at my hand, or the ground, I wasn't sure. "Pack histories, human histories, biographies."

I swallowed, the bitter taste of aluminum foil in my mouth. Why was he lying?

Brand snickered. "Tell the truth, Glenda."

"Fuck off, Brand."

"Glenda?" I asked, mock-glaring at him. "Is there something you'd like to share?"

"No." Was he pouting? His lower lip was jutting out slightly. It made me want to bite it.

"He's extremely ticklish, you know," Brand whispered. "I bet you can torture the truth out of him."

"Hmm, is that so?" I reached over, running my fingers across Glen's ribs while I held him in place with a hand on his arm. He could've gotten away, but he wasn't really trying. "What do you *really* read, Glenda?"

"Stop. I'm not kidding, stop!" He lurched, letting out a very non-masculine giggle.

"Why? You gonna pee your pants?" I tickled him even more viciously, following him as he tried to squirm away. "How about now? Gonna tell me what you read?"

"No!" He flopped onto his stomach, army-crawling away.

I rolled over on top of him, straddling his back, and kept torturing him with my fingers on his sides. "What do you read, Glenda? What's your little secret?"

He let out a groan and lay still under my relentless hands. "I'll never tell."

I tickled him more ferociously. "Don't you want me to stop?"

Glen groaned again, and Brand grumbled, "Pretty sure there's not a man alive who would want you to stop, Flor."

Wait... What am I doing? I was lying on Glen's back, my whole body flattened against him, my arms and legs wrapped around his waist. The energy between us felt like a heat lamp had been turned on in between our bodies.

Shit. *Shit.*

I jumped up, horrified. I'd basically molested him. "I didn't mean to... I was just playing."

Glen lay motionless, but he muttered, "Keep playing." I lifted my shirt halfway up to cover my face, pretending to rub away the sweat, but really just trying to hide.

"Um, Flor?" Brand's voice was a squeak.

I pulled my shirt down and saw his eyes on my chest. "What?" I lifted the shirt again and checked to see if there was something there. I'd only flashed him my sports bra. Well, that and my scar.

Brand came from a pack that valued strength, and I'd always been told that scars were signs of weakness. But Margarette had changed my mind about what a scar meant. They could be more. Signs of valor. Although, I'd been born with this scar so it was probably more a sign of a botched delivery. But no one knew that.

I glared at him, daring him to mention it. "What, Brand?"

"Um, you. Um..." He'd slammed his eyes shut, like I was naked.

"Brand, I barely have boobs. I may as well be a twelve-year-old boy. I could probably walk around without any clothes on—"

"*Stop*," Glen moaned. "Stop talking, Flor, or I'm never going to be able to turn over."

"Turn over?" Finally, my brain put it together. He was hiding a hard-on. I glanced at Brand, who'd moved one of his legs to hide his own crotch. I giggled. "You boys need to get out more."

"Glen gets out plenty," Brand mumbled.

For some reason, the thought of Glen "getting out" with the females in his pack pissed me off again. *Why do I care?* "Right. Time for lunch?"

"Give me a minute," Glen muttered, rolling to face away from me. "And I haven't 'gotten out' in weeks."

"Whatever," I sneered. "Hope I haven't been cramping your style." I shot Brand a look, just to be fair. "Or yours. Y'all don't have to babysit me."

Brand ducked his head sheepishly. "I didn't mean to... I'm..." His cheeks above his dark beard were flushed, and he looked miserable. "I'm sorry."

Scowling at his friend, Glen stood and offered me his arm. I took it, being careful of the bandaged part, though it seemed like it wasn't bothering him at all. "Go to lunch with me, Flor?" I stood, wiping the grass off my pants and very carefully not looking below his waist, or Brand's as he stood. Glen let out an exaggerated sigh. "I like Regency romances, okay? My Aunt Linn loved them, and she read them out loud to me when I was little. Innocent, kissing on the hand kind of things."

It was a conversational olive branch. I took it. "Oh. That's not silly. That's nice. Maybe, um, you could lend me one." I hadn't had a new book to read in a year.

Glen brightened. "Sure. You can have any of mine."

We walked quietly until Brand spoke. "You know what we do for fun now. I sculpt and carve. Glen reads and fu— well, Glen reads. What are your hobbies, Flor?"

"Um, cooking, I guess?"

He shook his head. "That was your pack job. Do you really like cooking?"

"No," I blurted out, surprising myself. "I hate cooking." I stopped, feeling an emptiness inside. "I used to sketch a little, but I wasn't very good. It was just... stubby pencils and paper were free, right?"

"We can get you art supplies," Glen told me. "I'll tell Mom, and we'll make an order—"

"No, please!" I laughed ruefully. Margarette would probably buy an entire art store, and I didn't want to put her to any trouble. Or, to be honest, feel any more indebted to her. But I couldn't say that out loud. "Like I said, I wasn't good at it."

Brand spoke quietly. "Was there anything you wanted to do, just for fun? You don't have to be good at something to enjoy it."

I made a face. "I guess the only things I enjoyed were things I *could* do well, that helped me survive. Like fighting, or hunting. Even running."

"Please, no more running," Glen groaned. "Books. What kind of books do you like?"

I shrugged, feeling awkward. I didn't even know what kinds of books I'd pick, if I had a choice. "I'll read anything. I never had enough to decide what I liked best. Do I have to choose?"

They both said no, but it was obvious the game was over, and the flirting along with it. I was such a freak. I couldn't even answer basic questions like what my favorite class was in high school, or what I liked to read, or what was my fucking hobby—unless you counted staying alive and away from rapists as a hobby.

My chest felt tight. I didn't belong here, with normal shifters like these guys.

"You can read anything in our library, Flor," Glen said as we reached the back doors to the Lodge. "In fact, after the movie, I'll turn you loose there. You can take as many books to your room as you like."

I forced a smile and followed him to lunch. I might not belong at Northern, but I would do what Del had taught me: learn everything I could, as fast as possible.

And someday, I'd find a place I did belong. A pack that felt like I fit in. Then I'd rest.

But not yet.

8

ALPHAS AND THEIR MATES
FLOR

The next few days fell into a pattern. Breakfast was followed by three hours of running and strength conditioning. After that, I had lunch inside with the Alpha Heirs and senior Enforcers, followed by more running and the most basic fighting exercises with a group of young Enforcers-in-training. I wanted to laugh at how easy the training was, and the Heirs were all confused as to why I was going along with the rudimentary program I'd been assigned.

Brand asked me more than once if I wanted him to say something to Sergeant, but I told him not to bother. "It's just until the full moon. I can handle a little bit of easy training after last month. I want to do this. It makes me feel... normal." It was so damned true. Brand had rolled his eyes, but I guessed he'd spread the word that this was my choice. Nobody tried to force me to show my skills, anyway.

Though I would have liked to do a demonstration on Vanessa's face. She'd obviously spread rumors about me among her friends, so none of them did much more than smile or say hello. Glen assured me that would end as soon as I took my ranking test.

"I can't wait for everyone to see what you're capable of." When I asked if I could test straight into the highest rank of Enforcer, he'd grinned. "Unranked to Enforcer? That's not normally how it works. You get your rank, and then you eventually test into the Enforcers. It takes years."

"But could I? Like, has it ever been done?"

He'd admitted it hadn't, but ran off to place a bet with Patrick that I would be the first.

Margarette was more annoyed at me, grumbling that I was wasting my time, hiding my light, or some shit. When I'd mentioned that if I did become an Enforcer or a trainer here, I'd need to know what the regular process looked like, she quieted down and left me alone. I'm not sure she would have been able to keep her mouth shut if she saw me doing such basic moves, though.

It didn't matter since she spent most of her time inside the Lodge, setting up patrols to watch for groups of rogues everyone seemed concerned about, yelling at doctors, or sitting at Bradley's bedside. He was doing worse every day, and Margarette was a wreck.

While I trained, Glen and Brand stayed close at all times, though Finnick made himself scarce. I still had no idea why he was at Northern, and when I asked him outright, he dodged the question, so I let it go. Maybe what Margarette had said about him needing a mom was part of it. But he watched me constantly, not like he was suspicious of me, but like I was a puzzle he was trying to figure out.

His words on my last day at Southern haunted me, though. I was still pissed that he'd thought he needed to say all of that mean shit out loud. I'd known I was nowhere near his league, and I knew now that just changing my address hadn't made me any higher class. Why would a shifter like him even look twice at me?

But he was looking twice now, and for some reason, the thing he'd said before rejecting me—before my heart had started hurting when I even glanced his way—kept looping in my thoughts.

If you were mine, I would cover you in jewels. I would show you what a woman like you deserves, show the world your beauty.

That meant he thought I was beautiful. He'd thought that at Southern, when I was at my worst. He'd thought I deserved jewels when almost everyone else around me thought I was trash. But he'd taken it all back so fast. It made my mind spin and my heart ache every time I remembered.

There was only one explanation: Finnick was a douche. I forced myself to run harder and faster every time I thought of him, and do a hundred pushups when I even thought about touching him. It worked, mostly.

After dinner each night, I watched a movie with the Heirs, and sometimes Patrick and another Enforcer or two —though they made certain none of the shifters who'd chased me into the dining room were ever in the house. Then I read in my room until I fell asleep.

I avoided Vanessa as much as possible, given we now had rooms in the same wing. She'd been ordered not to speak to me, or confront me. But every time she saw me, she stopped and stared like my continued breathing was her problem to solve. Luckily, she went on runs into the nearest town to get supplies or something, and more or less avoided me.

Her best friend Clara took up Vanessa's bitch slack, though. She practically stalked Glen through the house, always asking for his opinion and trying to sit next to him, though I wasn't sure he noticed her. She lived in the Lodge, and called Margarette Aunt Mags as well. When I asked, Glen told me that Clara's parents had been war heroes who died alongside Vanessa's mother. I wanted to feel sorry for her, but she was mean as fuck.

Whenever the Heirs weren't near, she honest-to-goodness hissed like a cornered possum and called me a whore, or something like that. I just laughed it off; I'd been called so much worse that "whore" was a step up.

Everything felt almost normal, except for Finnick's way of watching from the corner, like a cat watching a goldfish circling in a bowl. One night in the library, I snapped.

"I don't like feeling hunted, Finnick," I spat out when the weight of his gaze pulled me away from the book I was reading. It was a good book, a Regency romance Glen had recommended, with a handsome Duke who was pining for a chambermaid, but no amount of wrist kissing could compete with Finnick's staring.

"I'm sorry," he blurted out, then strode from the room like someone had lit his tail on fire.

What the hell? He didn't want to insult me, or fight?

Come to think of it, we'd been here for well over a week, and he hadn't said anything snarky, although someone had left etiquette books inside my room after dinner for the first few nights, with pages marked at the table manners sections.

I'd thought it was Margarette, but the last time they'd been left there, I'd smelled Finnick's ginger scent on the books, so I knew it had to be him. I'd confronted him, though he'd denied it. I retaliated by using more coarse manners at every dinner.

The books had stopped arriving after a meal when I

didn't even bother with silverware, but drank my soup from the bowl and ate my salad with my fingers, staring at Finnick the whole time. Patrick and Brand had both thought it was hilarious, but for some reason, the whole drama irked Glen.

Drama was the theme when it came to Margarette's interactions with me. When she took breaks from being at her mate's bedside, she would try to manufacture reasons for Glen and me to be alone. Patrick confided in me that his mom had a true mate obsession, and always had. She'd been obsessed with finding his and Glen's true mates, ever since they were old enough to like girls.

"Her mom was the same way before she died at the end of the war," he murmured at dinner one night, when Margarette had oysters served and made what she probably thought were subtle jokes about them being aphrodisiacs. I thought they tasted like cold snot, and gave all mine to Glen.

I still felt uneasy, living in the house around all the elite of the pack. Uneasy and uneducated. I'd asked for some books, hoping to delve into the ranking structures in all the packs, and figure out where it had come from. I'd also tried to speak about it with some of the unranked shifters, but the Heirs were around most of the time, and they didn't trust them at all, or me. Not yet, anyway.

Instead of what I asked for, Margarette gave me pack law to read, and what she said was basic shifter education I'd been denied. The texts were long and sort of boring, but I learned about some of the rituals shifters were supposed to have as they went through different stages of life, like mating, births, and even death. I thought the sections on true mates were intriguing, though I would never, ever mention that to Margarette.

"Did you know that every North American Alpha has been mated when they ascended to Alpha, except Callaway?" I panted to Brand as we ran around the track. I was wearing ankle and wrist weights and carrying a backpack full of stones to build strength. "It's not a law they have to be, but there hasn't been a single other one not mated in history."

"Yes, I knew that," he replied, annoyingly *not* panting.

Damn my short, stumpy legs. "Were they all true mates?" I wondered aloud.

Brand didn't answer, not even when I nudged him, so I let it go.

After another half lap, I asked, "Did you know there's a ritual for rejecting a true mate, as long as you do it before you actually have sex?" The book hadn't said what the words were, but I was almost certain they'd be in some book in Margarette's collection. A small part of me wondered if the harsh words Finnick had uttered back at Southern were something similar.

Brand choked on something, probably a gnat flying in his mouth. I pounded on his back without stopping.

"Need a rest?" He shook his head, looking perturbed but not tired. He wasn't even sweating. Of course, if he had half his body weight in rocks in a pack like I did, he'd probably be slowing down. I eyed his massive biceps and his muscular calves. *Or not.*

He straightened up, and I realized he wasn't choking anymore. He wasn't even breathing hard, unlike me.

"Ugh, bear shifters must have amazing endurance."

He blushed and wouldn't look at me. Had I embarrassed him? I tried to think what I'd said to cause his reaction.

Endurance... Oh, yeah. I'd heard women gossiping about how important that was in sex. I scowled at Brand's red cheeks, unimpressed. "I'm not Glen, Brand. Not everything is about sex."

"Did I hear the words Glen and sex?" Glen called, running past. He turned around, jogging backward. "You called, Princess?" I licked my lips, wondering why I got so damned thirsty every time he was close. Maybe I was dehydrated.

I ignored the sensation and rolled my eyes. "Watch out, Glenda, your magic sparkles have attracted some nasty fairies. If one catches you, she gets to kiss you." I nodded at the group of unmated females who had once again—coincidentally, of course—chosen to do a few laps at the same time as Glen, wearing nothing but exercise bras and teeny-tiny shorts. I stifled a giggle at the look of panic that crossed his face.

"I'm not... not... I mean, they're not with me!" he sputtered.

"They will be, if you don't run faster," I said, and tripped him as I put on a burst of speed and ran ahead. I didn't look back when I heard the girls cooing over him and helping him up.

"Vicious," Brand muttered. I stared at the tiny twitching corner of his mouth and kept running. Eventually, we were far enough away from Glen and the gaggle of Glen-chasers that I could ask the question that had been bugging me.

"So, I need to ask you something about true mates."

Brand stumbled slightly. "You do?"

"Yep." I took a breath and focused on my stride as I ran. "I would go to Margarette, but she's made it her full-time job to hook me up with Glen. I don't know anyone else here enough to ask. You're the only one I trust to be honest."

"You t-trust me?"

How was stammering and blushing so cute on such a

huge, masculine guy? I wanted to squeeze his cheeks. My gaze dropped unconsciously to his toned ass. *All of his cheeks.*

Ugh, I was creeping on him. Maybe I'd been hanging around Glen too long. I felt a matching heat cover my face.

I tried to sound casual. "Sure, I trust you. You're the only guy I've ever known well enough to talk to, other than Del. And you haven't tried to pull that true mate line on me like Luke and Glen did. Such bullshit."

"Oh." Suddenly, Brand's eyes looked... shifty. What was that about?

Whatever. I went on. "And I sure as heck can't ask Finnick."

"Finnick?" Brand growled. "He said you're his mate?"

"Nah." I ignored the twist in my gut. "You were there. Like, he said he wasn't straight out, so I wouldn't misunderstand. Probably worried I was getting 'ideas above my station.'" I rubbed my chest, which still hurt.

"I was there," Brand grumbled. "Still has his head in his ass, if you ask me." He let out a long breath. "You should know, Finn isn't interested in any woman, as a mate. His pack... Well, I can understand why, even if he did meet a special woman, he wouldn't want to take her home to that hellhole."

"Hellhole?"

He shrugged. "Cities are all bad. But his may be the worst. A trap for any decent shifter."

I refused to think about what he meant. "Whatever. So Finnick's not mate shopping, like ever. But the whole conversation back at Southern made me twitchy. Also, he's a prick."

"True." Brand let out a huffing laugh. "Ask your question."

"Do you have to mate before you can be an Alpha? Like, you and Glen and Finnick. Is it a requirement that you find your mates before you can ascend?"

Brand slowed. "No one will ever admit to this," he said, as softly as I'd ever heard him speak. "But yes, we are expected to mate. Preferably to our true mate, if we find her. It's not written in pack law or our histories. But Alphas pass it down to their Heirs."

"Why?" I demanded. "Is it just more patriarchal bullshit?"

"Power," he answered. "It's about power, Flor." He glanced at the Lodge, as if he expected his admission to bring troops running. Or someone.

Huh. I chewed on my lower lip. "So Alpha Callaway, at Southern. He didn't have a true mate, as far as the pack knew." I avoided the truth I knew.

"No one ever understood that," Brand replied. "But we believe he had a mate, a true mate, and that was how he grew strong enough to be Alpha."

"A mate makes you stronger?"

"A true mate, yes. You felt Callaway's dominance?" I nodded, and he went on. "I think he could only have that level of power because he'd found his true mate. Luke found some proof of that, days before your fight."

"He did?" I tried to keep my face expressionless. Did Luke know my secret?

"Yes. It checked out. And that proof answered a lot of questions the rest of the Council had for years."

"The Council?"

"Finnick gave a full report on everything he found out to his father. He's the Acting Head of the North American Council while Alpha Hillier is recovering."

I didn't like thinking about Finnick's dad being in

charge. He was oily, and too smart for me to go up against. "How does being mated give someone more power?"

"It gives both mates more," Brand admitted. "My mother was what your pack would call low ranked before she met my dad. Once they mated, he ascended to Alpha, but her level of dominance rose as well. Margarette was already powerful, but once Bradley mated her... Well, he was nowhere near as dominant as my father originally, but Bradley became Head of the Council because of their shared power."

"So, if Luke doesn't find his mate, he'd be what? A weak Alpha?"

Brand stopped, a flash of pain crossing his features. "He already met his true mate, Flor. I know you don't want to believe it, but we all saw it, felt it. His wolf's power was much more potent than it should have been, given how long he'd gone without shifting. I met him ten years ago. He showed unusual dominance, even back then. His wolf has known you were his, ever since he was young. Since he was a child."

"Since he was a child?" My thoughts whirled. Luke had first shifted when he was ten or something; I'd heard Del talking about it more than once. It was some sort of shifter record. "Wait. Are you saying Luke knew I was his—I mean, he *believed* I was his true mate, from when I was a baby or something?" If he had, and he'd let me suffer... It made me want to go back to Southern, to kick Luke Callaway's ass from one side of the county to the next. "What a rat's ass!"

Brand didn't answer, but his lips had gone tight, and his eyes shifty again. I bared my teeth. "Tell me *everything,* Brand, or I'll make you wish you had."

I harassed him for a half hour as we ran, but "That's not my secret to tell," was all he would say.

Finally, Brand started back to the training camp, with me on his heels, the bag of rocks on my back taking its toll on my endurance. "Flor, don't worry about Luke. He'll be Alpha as soon as Callaway dies. After that? Well, he made his choices. Your choices are all that matter now." He gritted his teeth and ran faster, like someone or something was chasing him. "And I'll do whatever I need to, to make sure no one takes those choices from you."

"My choices?" I had no idea what he meant by that. "Brand, there's something you're not telling me."

He didn't answer, just squeezed my arm lightly— setting off that feeling of home, of grounding, of safety— then picked up the pace again.

9
A THREAT TO FLOR
GLEN

My true mate ran ahead of me with my best friend, ignoring me, as usual.

It didn't surprise me. I hadn't done a damned thing right since the moment I met her. Why would she want to be near me?

It didn't help that Mom had been more and more overtly manufacturing ways to throw us together, going so far as to try and assign seating at our casual lunches with the other Heirs and pack leadership.

Flor had not responded well. She'd bared her teeth when our butler had tried to escort her away from Brand's side. Brand had calmly torn his and her paper name cards into pieces, poured gravy over them, and eaten them with his steak while she smirked.

If it wasn't for the Regency romances that I left for her, which she read and returned to the library every day, the pages rich with her jasmine and cinnamon scent, I would have felt totally cut off from her. No one knew I took those borrowed books to my room, just to smell them.

Well, I *hoped* no one knew.

"Stop mooning over the girl," Finn muttered from beside me, where he panted slightly. I wasn't sure when he'd gotten so out of shape. He'd always been at least as fit as me, and we both knew he was a better fighter. But I had a feeling right now I could take him on one-handed and not embarrass myself.

"Stop *wheezing*, asshole," I shot back.

He punched me lightly in the side. "If you don't go faster, the hyenas will catch up."

I groaned, knowing what he meant. The unmated women had never been as keen on running laps of the training yard as when Finn and I were on the track. A group of them had been trying, and failing, to catch up with us for the past few minutes. I picked up the pace, but then almost tripped, as I heard Flor say my name.

And the word *sex*.

"Did I hear the words Glen and sex?" I left Finn behind, sprinting ahead to take in Flor's face. I jogged backward, showing off my speed. Brand might have bulk and fighting skills, but I was one of the fastest runners in either form. "You called, Princess?"

Her cheeks went an even rosier shade of pink at the nickname. Her tongue darted out, and she fired back with her usual sass, a quick eye roll thrown in, "Watch out, Glenda, your magic sparkles have attracted some nasty fairies. If one catches you, she gets to kiss you."

Fairies? What was she talking abou— *Oh shit.* I'd stopped paying attention to the gaggle of females, but Flor wiggled her eyebrows at them and giggled.

I sputtered something at her, my heart flipping that she was talking to me, paying attention to me. Maybe if I could make her laugh, she'd laugh again, and she would remember I was here. See that I was waiting for her to notice me. But before I could come up with a witty reply, she'd stuck out one small foot and tripped me.

A split second after I hit the ground, the other women were gathered around me, cooing and acting like I needed medical attention. "I'm not hurt," I protested. I tried to get up, to get back to Flor, but they kept crowding me.

Not just crowding. *Touching.* Reaching for the few parts of me that didn't show in my sweats.

I didn't want to hurt them—most of them were just googly-eyed and giggling for the chance to get the attention of the Northern Heir—but if I felt one more soft hand slip under my waistband, I didn't know what I'd do.

"How would you like it if some shifter touched you without your permission?" Finn barked at the group. "How can you treat your own Heir this way? As if he were a toy, something to be haggled over like a steak at the grocery store? You may not be decent shifters, but you could at least act like it."

As one, they gasped and backed away, apologizing, though a few muttered uncomplimentary things at Finn as well. Slightly unnerved by the vitriol in his tone, I took the hand he held out. "Thanks, Finn."

He let go of my hand as soon as I was standing. "Don't mention it," he replied, walking by my side.

But I had to. His words had been filled with more than just censure. There had been pain in his tone. As if he'd lived through something like that, maybe even worse... Could it be that? Had he been touched without permission? Or maybe someone he loved.

I felt sick. Finn had fostered here, and we'd become good friends over the years, though not quite like Brand. He'd never shared much about his own pack. But he had a younger sister, Tana, who would be around seventeen now.

I'd met her a few times, and she'd seemed sweet and shy. Could something have happened to her that had made Finn react that way to the ones groping me?

I waited a few minutes, until we were completely alone. "Finn, what you just said—"

"Don't mention it, I told you. I just can't stand to see anyone treated that way."

"They're just girls," I said, but went quiet when he shuddered. I changed the subject. "I'm surprised your family let you come to our packlands." He hadn't mentioned the dispensation he'd obviously been given. "Your dad…"

Finn let out a short bark of laughter. "When I mentioned that I'd noticed his convenient disappearance during the fight at Southern, and suggested that public questions as to where he'd gone during the fighting might be awkward, he couldn't see the back of me fast enough."

Rage filled me. "I'd assumed he was fighting somewhere else, out of sight. You mean to tell me—"

He dropped his head, obviously ashamed. "Yes. Whatever he was doing, it wasn't fighting. He didn't have a drop of blood on him, though someone had ripped at his clothing, it looked like. And judging by the bright lipstick on his collar, it may not have been him who ripped it."

"He was fucking a woman while we fought?" I took a few deep breaths. If his dad had been in the battle, my own might not still be fighting for his life. "He doesn't deserve to be the Interim Council Alpha."

"Truer words have never been spoken." Finn sighed. "I always wished I'd been born here, or even at Mountain."

"If they let Alpha Heirs change packs, you know you would've been welcome to move to Northern." The rules about us staying on our own packlands, with very rare dispensation given for Council duties, the Conclaves and Enforcer Games, and a few foster seasons before we took on the mantle of Alpha, were one of the only truly awful parts about being an Heir. We were princes of our kind, but we were confined in ways no one besides us ever thought about.

"If only. I'm still slightly shocked they let me come here without a return date specified. I'll pay for this trip, though. That's for certain," he muttered.

I didn't ask what he meant. Finn had more than a few secrets. Both he and Luke had kept a lot to themselves, apparently.

Somehow, I'd gotten the feeling Finn and Luke had been close, even though the Southern Heir had only ever gone to Eastern for a very short while. It had only been a few days before Luke had become ill and had to go back to his packlands. Finn had spent at least two of those days locked in his room with him, talking while the doctors tried to figure out what could make a young, strong shifter so sick.

A thought hit me that would have seemed ridiculous a few short days ago. Luke may have had mate sickness.

I needed to call him soon. If it had been mate sickness, it had only taken days for him to fall ill back then. It might be even worse now, with Flor older and connected to her own wolf. Though she hadn't shown any signs of shifting again. Maybe she didn't feel safe yet.

I had just opened my mouth to ask Finn what he thought, when he held up a hand, his eyes on the trees. I scented the breeze, quickly realizing what was wrong.

Someone else was here, or had been very recently. My eyes met Finn's, and I mouthed the word. *Stranger?*

He gave a curt shake of his head and tapped his nose

slightly. I took in the hint of cold water and ozone. He was right. I knew that scent.

It was the black wolf we'd met at Southern. What in the hell was he doing here? The last I'd heard, he'd opened the armory at Southern to the Mountain shifters, showing them all the weapons Alpha Callaway had been stockpiling. He'd helped us then, but if he was here now, without declaring his presence, he might not be our ally.

He could be a threat. *A threat to her.* My wolf howled to be released, to find him, and make sure he could never hurt her.

Now, Finn mouthed. He tilted his head to the left, and I knew what that meant. We would run fast, try to flank the shifter, and drive him out of the trees and back toward the training ground.

Finn and I had hunted together before, many times. But there was no time to shift, with the scent already fading. So we'd need to run in human form. When he tensed, I did the same, ready for answers. At his signal, we sprinted into the woods together, intent on eliminating any threat to Flor.

IO

A LIFE TAKEN, A PROMISE KEPT
JOAQUIN

I heard them coming long before I saw them, though they were quiet, for such young shifters, especially in their human forms. They moved gracefully on two feet, alert for any movement, their eyes on the forest floor. Of course, that was their mistake.

I spied on them from the tops of the trees, knowing I could not speak to them, not yet. Still, I wanted to learn all I could about these males who would be my little one's consorts beside me.

They seemed worthy, though the red-haired one had come close to dying, even if he never knew it, when he rejected her. From the shadows, I had watched her face pale, seen the trembling and pain his callous words of rejection had caused. If he hadn't thought better of it, if he had fully rejected her, I would have made certain he didn't live more than a few hours to regret it.

Finnick was his name. Finnick McDonnell, son of the repulsive Aidan and his reclusive mate, Elina. My teeth grew sharp as I considered Aidan. He was a coward, weak in spirit as well as body. How had he ascended to his current position? How had a shifter like that, vain and corrupt, produced a strong Heir such as this? There was something I didn't know about the wolves of the Eastern pack, but my instincts warned me to keep my little queen away from them.

Hmmm. Perhaps that was why Finnick had tried to reject her. To *protect* her. I could forgive that. Still, he had wounded her heart, and he would be held accountable. She was in pain even now.

Though some of that was the fault of the first mate, the one who lived in agony now, as he should. The unworthy one who had allowed her to be hunted and abused. Luke, the broken, weak male who had watched our little one suffer for years.

I knew more about him than he would ever dream. While he slept, I had entered the Southern Pack House and stood over his bed with a magical blade in my hand. I had been hunting her enemies: the disgraced Alpha Callaway, the Enforcer Trevor. But someone had taken them far enough from the Southern packlands that I could not find them by scent or magic.

Which meant a vehicle. But there had only been the cars and trucks that the visiting Alphas and their contingents had arrived in. Which meant the enemies of my mate had been taken to safety inside one of those. What allies could such dishonorable men have? I had suspicions, but no proof.

For her sake, I had left Luke alive, but stayed long enough to learn every secret the shadows of that Pack House had to tell. They had stored up so many. Gleaning them all had kept me from coming for my little queen sooner, though the delay would most likely work in my favor. She needed time to grow more confident, to learn what it meant to be a shifter.

Though for some reason, she had not taken her wolf form again, since the first time, when she was wounded. I worried about what that might mean.

Shaking the thought away, I concentrated on weaving the shadows under my perch in the tall pine. The two young males hunted well, their tactics proven, if predictable. If Flor accepted them—when she did—I would teach them a few of the oldest methods of hunting.

"He's not here," Finnick said, his shoulders slumping. I almost smiled. If I dropped a pinecone, it would land on his shoulder.

"But he was," the blond replied, sniffing around the base of the tree, then looking up. He leaped up on the wide trunk, climbing near enough that if it had not been for my magic shielding me, he might have caught me. His inner beast could sense me. Through our mutual connection to the little queen? Perhaps. I felt inexplicably proud that he'd come so close.

Glen Hillier, son of Bradley and Margarette. He was a bit of a fool, unaware of so much that was going on in his pack, right under his nose. I hoped for his sake that he had more integrity than his parents.

He continued quietly talking to his friend, while he scented the air. "I don't like it. We don't know anything about him. A new Alpha from the Borderlands? Which ones? Texas? New Mexico? The rogues own all of what used to be the true packlands to the west. Their incursions are what's kept any Alpha from holding onto more than a few acres of land long enough to establish a pack. My father said he hadn't heard of a new Alpha, but his power when Flor was hurt... He was definitely an Alpha; there's no denying it." He climbed back down, resting on his haunches on the pine-needle-strewn ground.

Finnick grunted as he paced around the tree, still searching for me, though Glen had stopped. "He spoke Spanish with a strange accent. If I had to guess, he's not from Mexico, or the Americas."

"Spain?" Their voices grew quieter as they walked away, back to the Lodge.

"Wherever he's from, if he hurts Flor, we'll kill him," Finnick called back over his shoulder, his narrowed eyes lifted to the trees.

Had he seen through my magical concealment? I smiled, half-hoping he had. If Flor did choose him as a consort, that particular sort of strength would give her even more protection.

A part of me liked that the Eastern Heir had paid enough attention to me to realize my accent wasn't perfect. I had only been speaking Spanish for nineteen years, since I crossed the Arctic circle and made my way from Canada, then down to Texas.

Nineteen years since I felt her wolf's spirit enter the world, and knew I had to find her.

I waited for a few more moments, until I was sure the males had gone and no one else was near, then climbed down to the forest floor. It was time to visit my little queen, and keep my promise.

I CREPT past the unranked housing, where voices were still raised. Did the leaders of Northern know how pervasive the rot was in this glittering gem of a pack? It wasn't the Alpha and his Enforcers doling out cruelty here, though they most likely suspected at least some of the abuses. In a pack of thousands, I supposed it could be difficult to keep track of a few dozen ill-doers.

But too many of the stronger unranked shifters here, along with a few of the lower-ranked Enforcers, used the petty power they had to force the others to do their bidding. And the blanket of the deep night to hide their crimes.

From what I had gleaned, listening to the women's soft voices over the past week, the system the Alpha had in place for rising in rank was a large part of the problem. Hidden corruption, as well as stagnant thinking about who deserved the chance to rise, made for an atmosphere of frustration and hopelessness, even in a pack that pretended to be forward-thinking.

Hopelessness had a stench, and I stopped, smelling it now. Along with blood, and... other fluids.

Soft words accompanied the scents. "Stay quiet and take it, bitch." I heard a slap, and a stifled, feminine cry, and knew what was happening.

It had been centuries since my heart had been touched by the plight of shifters so far beneath my notice, but now, understanding my little queen had been one like them, suffering under the injustice, I was compelled to intervene.

I didn't hesitate. His death would be a gift to her, though she would not know I had given it. I might tell her someday.

Sliding next to the rough wooden door, I sent a tendril of magic underneath the doorframe. Seconds later, the sounds of a male choking to death joined the quiet insects that hummed in the nearby woods.

A woman whispered, "Stan's gone purple. Is he... dying? Should we help him?"

Another girl's bitter laugh caught my ear. "Let him choke on his own spit. He's spit on us enough times." A clawing sound and a crash of a dish breaking split the air—this Stan's death throes.

A raspy voice, thick with tears, added, "It's not right, though, to let him die without telling someone."

"It's perfect. I wouldn't spit on Stan if he was on fire. After what he did to you? Tried to do to me?"

They argued for a moment that he couldn't be dying, until one announced, "Too late now. He's not dying. He's dead."

Gasps. "It's magic."

"No. This is the Moon Goddess, wreaking Her justice."

Of course they thought it was magic, or a miracle. Choking on spit was an impossible death for a shifter, and for a moment, I let amusement flow through me at the confusion it would sow the next day. Then I moved past again, trying not to allow myself to get lost in the heady pleasure of killing a worthless male. I needed to hurry.

I had to time my visits to her window just right.

She shone so brightly in my mind's eye that it almost felt like I could see her through the thick stone wall of the Lodge. I slid from shadow to shadow across the training ground, making no sound, and arrived at the exterior of her room. I climbed a few feet, using the wide stones, and placed my ear against the window. She was muttering in her sleep again, her dreams painful, as they often seemed to be. Her limbs moved restlessly under the quilts, her hands smoothing the fabric, then gripping it.

My own hands still burned from the small touches we'd shared. When I'd tucked her red hair behind her ear. When

I'd bound her wounds in the ring, after her fight. I longed to touch her again, with her consent.

With her eyes on mine, her lips opening to me. Her arms embracing me. Her heart softening, though there was little chance a young, bright soul like hers would want to dwell alongside the darkness for long.

It would be enough to be near her as she grew, and accept whatever affection she would give me. To be close, protecting.

Killing. She would need a shadow to kill for her.

I unlocked the window and slid it open an inch, enough to allow my voice to enter the room, but not too much of the cold night air. Then I sang an old lullaby, keeping my voice as quiet as possible. She settled instantly, a long sigh emerging from her lips.

"I will sing for you every night, my love," I whispered, then slid to the ground, just as a howl rose up from the unranked housing.

II

ANY MATE WILL DO

FLOR

I t was all I could do not to jump up and run outside when the morning of the full moon arrived. I was so worked up, my insides felt like I had a cricket jumping around in my belly. I'd never had a birthday party, though I'd read about them.

But today felt bigger than a birthday. Bigger and a little scarier.

The morning meal had been oddly tense, Patrick and the other senior Enforcers who ate with us muttering to each other about a death a few nights before in the unranked housing. A choking death, which was unusual. I'd never heard of a shifter choking to death. This one had been a low-level Enforcer himself, though from Patrick's muttered comments, not one who had deserved his position.

Vanessa and Clara had come to sit with us, staying even more quiet than usual, though Clara had glared at me throughout the meal, until Patrick asked her to leave.

At the end of the meal, Vanessa had wished me luck. Well, she'd actually said, "I'd wish you luck, but there's no way Aunt Mags would let you lose today, so you won't need it."

I'd seen Vanessa sparring over the past weeks, and I nodded. "You don't need luck either. You're a better fighter than most of the ranked shifters at Southern. You'll get your rank back. Heck, I don't know why you're not an Enforcer."

"You don't?" She let out a humorless laugh. "You're sweet, aren't you? I see why Glen likes you." She ruined it then, of course. "But don't compare me to your trash pack again, Florida."

Glen and Finnick hadn't made it to the table for the first time since we'd arrived. Brand—who was still sleeping outside my bedroom door—had walked me to the dining room door before excusing himself, making me promise to stick close to another Enforcer or Margarette until he saw me again.

Of course I was going to stick close. Margarette was escorting me to my first fight at Northern. Well, first sparring match. Supposedly, we weren't going to use weapons, not even steak knives. My blood hummed with excitement anyway. I'd been actually humming, too—some pretty song I never remembered learning, but it kept me more relaxed than I would have been otherwise.

"Finally ready to spar, Flor?" Margarette's smile was strained and her eyes a bit dull as she met me at the door of the breakfast room, dressed in her black combat gear. She'd been with Bradley almost constantly for the past two weeks, and I'd hoped she could come out today, though I hadn't expected her to. Patrick had confided that he'd taken a turn for the worse, and the doctors were out of ideas.

I returned Margarette's effort with a warm smile of my own, nodding at her outfit, which matched my newer clothing, a set made just for me that had shown up in my room the evening before. "We're twins."

"I hope you don't mind. I wanted you to look your best today, and feel comfortable."

I flexed my arm, loving how the fabric moved and felt. The areas over my breasts and abdomen were reinforced, making it look a bit like a superhero costume. There were clever Velcro closures on the sleeves and down the front of the top, which I assumed was in case I shifted, not that I was in any danger of that. I still hadn't felt even the first stirrings of my wolf wanting to come out. But tonight was the full moon; anything was possible.

I smiled at the woman who'd made this all happen for me. "They're my favorite clothes ever. Thank you."

"You're more than welcome." The pride and affection in her gaze felt motherly. Not that I'd ever had that. But it was what I'd always longed for from my own mother.

What would she have been like, if she hadn't been driven crazy by... I shook the thought away. My life at Southern had no place here. Not today, anyway.

"I knew you'd look great in black," Margarette said, tucking a stray lock of hair behind my ear. It was growing faster than usual, hanging down around my neck at an awkward length. "It's gorgeous with that red hair. Are you looking forward to showing off your skills today?"

"Heck, yes." It felt surreal. After almost twenty years of living with no rank, of being at the bottom of the pack, my rank would be decided today. I would finally know where I stood.

Well, if I passed Sergeant's skills assessment. But the guys had all assured me I had more than proved myself over the past weeks.

Of course, I hadn't made many new friends in the Lodge

—not ranked ones, in any case. Clara had made sure of that, keeping me on the outside of any circle of females I tried to approach.

At least the unranked shifters had begun to trust me a little. A few of the women had even taken to bringing me water and snacks during my training breaks.

The ranking structure was still confusing to me. I'd noticed that there were plenty of ranked females in the pack, but none of them besides Margarette were Enforcers. When I'd seen some of the unranked women fight, and even the ranked ones, it had seemed odd. A few of them had exceptional skills, and some unranked women were better fighters than the lower-level Enforcers, even if they weren't as strong. Strength seemed to be the way to become an Enforcer here. It sucked, but made sense.

The unranked women were kind and had answered some of my questions about what to expect. One had mentioned in passing that she was testing along with me tonight, and she'd seemed excited and hopeful. But mostly the unranked women came off as either weak, or incredibly shy, since none of them would meet my gaze.

I'd asked Glen and Brand about the leather chokers, but neither one of them knew what they stood for. Finally, one of the maids had shared that they weren't forced to wear them by the Alpha or Head Enforcer, unlike my tag. Apparently, it was just a way of signaling to the pack that they were satisfied with their position, and not planning to move up. She was careful to make sure I knew she'd chosen to wear the collar, and that none of the leadership had anything to do with it.

"I can take it off any time I like, Miss Flor," she'd said when I pressed her about it. "See?" She'd handed it to me right then, proving it. It was just a circle of leather with a brass clasp.

Though something about that bothered me. Why would she need to wear a leather choker so everyone knew? What if she changed her mind after a while, and wanted to spar again and move up? I'd asked her while she put the thing back on.

"I'm not a fighter, and I never will be. I want a mate who'll fight for me, and pups someday. Not to be"—she'd giggled—"a badass, like you." I hadn't been convinced. A cage was still a cage, even if the shifter had let themselves be locked inside.

I shook the thought away as Margarette cleared her throat. "Who's going to be there to watch the sparring?"

At that moment, Vanessa exited her bedroom, dressed in clothes like ours. "Aunt Mags." She dipped her head to Margarette, but didn't speak to me as she passed us.

Margarette put a hand on my arm. "She hasn't been bothering you, has she? You know I'll make her behave appropriately."

"No, thanks. I can take care of myself."

"Of course you can." She squeezed my arm gently, the touch reassuring. "But I don't want you to have to. Neither does Glen. He loves that you're so strong, you know. It's a Hillier trait to be drawn only to the very strongest."

Ugh. Time to change the subject. "Glen said your sister was an Enforcer in your pack, like you. Is that true?"

Margarette sighed. "Linn was the strongest Enforcer anyone had seen. It was a shame she was born a female; she would have made an incredible Alpha."

I told her I was sorry for her loss, but asked more questions as we walked. "Yeah, so, why can't females be Alphas?

Do the job requirements include peeing while standing or something?"

She laughed. "Linn used to complain about that, too! She had plans to go to the Mountain pack and ransack their library—they have the most extensive collection of pack histories—and find out if there was a way she could become Alpha." Margarette's eyes grew misty. "Then she met her true mate, Randolph. He was the most submissive male anyone had ever seen. When they mated... well, she didn't get weaker, but she never got stronger either." She shook her head. "What the moon was thinking, I don't know. If she'd had a stronger mate, she might have survived."

Her gaze slid to me, and I could practically hear the gears in her head turning. "You know, if you were an Alpha's mate, you'd probably be the strongest female shifter in history. You met my gaze the first time we met. You met Bradley's and didn't flinch."

I shivered, hearing the echoes of the Hunt in her words. "I was supposed to flinch?"

Margarette's eyes twinkled. "You don't even feel it, do you? The raw Alpha dominance my husband possesses can send young shifters to their knees. How you were marked as an unranked shifter is a travesty. You know, if you mated Glen, you wouldn't even have to fight—"

I cut her off. "No. I'll earn my rank in the fighting ring."

"I understand. You want it to mean something." She nodded, then tucked my hair behind my ear, exposing my ear tag. "You know, you told me you were going to get that removed when we arrived. Will you let me remove it today, after your fight?"

"I don't know," I admitted. I'd told her I was planning to

do just that when she'd asked about the tag the week before. "I think I'm keeping it."

"What?" She was horrified. "But you'll be ranked!"

"Sure. I never want to forget how wrong the ranking system was at Southern. How Callaway used it to keep a foot on all the necks he wanted to, whether or not they deserved it." I felt familiar anger rise up in me again. "You know, females there only earned rank through their mates. There was no way to be anything but trash without a male attached to you." I narrowed my eyes, thinking of what Vanessa had said. "It's a good thing you let the unranked fight their way up here. That anyone can be an Enforcer, if they prove they're strong enough. A damn good thing."

I glanced over at Margarette, who had gone slightly pale. "Why do you say that, Flor?"

I shrugged. "I'd never voluntarily stay with a pack that was like Southern."

Her lips twisted into a weirdly nervous smile. "Well, you have nothing to worry about. You'll make an incredible Enforcer, if that's what you want."

"Why aren't there any more women Enforcers here?" I asked bluntly, thinking of Vanessa.

"Not all women are fighters like us. Most of them are happy to settle down and bear pups... or try to."

"Are they, though?" I muttered, but she was already going on, explaining how ranking worked here.

I'd already learned quite a bit from the other shifters I'd trained with, though. Shifters were assigned their parents' rank when they were born, just like at Southern. Ranked shifters lived to the east of the training grounds in the buildings I'd seen in the blueprints, closer to the Lodge. The unranked lived farther away, across from the training grounds, in communal dorms called the compound that were practically in the forest.

Food allowances were the same for both sets, though ranked shifters had their pick of the best jobs, so they were able to afford more luxuries. Schooling was the same, too, and everyone got the same medical care, though mostly it was only the younger ones who needed much.

The unranked children also trained after school. When they were old enough to shift, they were given the chance to spar, and establish their own rank. All they had to do was defeat their opponent, a ranked shifter randomly assigned. If they didn't win, they could test again the next quarter as often as necessary until they won, or decided not to try again.

It all sounded so fair, but I wouldn't pass judgment until I'd seen the quarterly fights.

I tried to tune back into whatever Margarette was saying. "...and since most shifter females desire mates with higher ranks—to help themselves and any future children gain status—the males' ranks are weighted slightly higher than females."

What the fuck? Having a dick earned you extra points here, too? No one had mentioned that to me. I had to bite my lip to keep from sharing my disapproval. Margarette was so strong; surely she had to see how stupid it was to rank males over females for no more reason than a handful of flesh.

My thoughts flitted to Brand. Well, maybe two handfuls.

I had to say something. This wasn't the moment, though. "Where are the guys?" I asked as we finally headed out to the back exit.

"Brand is helping set up for the fights. Finnick and Glen

are checking on the pack boundaries today with a group of our senior Enforcers," she replied. "They didn't want to go and miss your sparring, so I've asked Sergeant to have you go last."

"Something's wrong at the pack border?"

"There was a report of a small group of rogues passing by the northernmost border of our hunting grounds. Normally, if they stay outside our borders, we don't respond with force, but we've had too much activity recently to ignore it. Their attacks have been coordinated, unlike... Well, never mind. It's only about a two-hour run, so we'll see them later this morning." She linked her arm in mine as we walked. "I wanted to chat with you about Glen anyway."

Suddenly, her arm felt like a trap. "Sure. But first, what did the new doctors say?" Medical specialists had arrived from the Eastern pack's shifter hospital two days before, since Northern didn't have their own specialists in silver poisoning.

"Nothing good. They... They don't know if he'll ever fully recover."

"I'm so sorry." My heart ached for her. "Is there anything I can do?"

"Yes, actually." Her arm tightened on mine. "I would like for you to open your mind, your heart, to the mating bond that exists between you and my son."

Ugh. This was the most direct she'd been yet, even though I'd shut her down every time she'd tried to force the issue. Margarette could teach a donkey how to be stubborn. "Open my mind? You mean, you want me to mate with Glen."

"Well, of course I do." She sighed, like I was being a

brat. "Why do you sound angry? This is an honor, Flor. He's as close to royalty as a shifter can be."

"Well, I figured out the Alpha thing," I said, trying not to let my rage seep into my tone. "That if Glen wants to ascend to Alpha, he has to have a mate."

"Yes," she said baldly, pulling me to a stop in the middle of the hall. "But it's not for selfish reasons. My husband may not recover. With the ever-present threat of Russian shifters, rogues, and now the trouble at Southern, we need an Alpha who can help plan our defense. Glen is ready; he's been trained. The Council is waiting on word that Bradley is stepping down, and they'll test Glen and promote him."

I fought back my anger, ignoring the more devastating emotion of disappointment that swirled in my gut along-side it. "Is that why you brought me here, Margarette? Why you've been so nice?"

She stepped back, her eyes widening. "Flor, no. I wanted you for Glen, of course. Mother Moon, you're every-thing I could've dreamed of for a daughter-in-law. Strong and resilient, quick, smart—"

"I haven't even finished ninth grade," I interrupted.

"No one needs to know that," she replied smoothly.

"I'm unranked."

"Not once you're Glen's mate." Her lips twisted when I released the growl that had been building. "Not after today's sparring either, Flor. Don't worry, I know you want to earn it."

I took a deep, measured breath, shocked that I'd need the techniques Del had taught me for battle here, with the woman I'd hoped was a friend. "I don't have the manners or the training to be an Alpha's mate. It's apparent to the casual observer—"

"I can help you, even stand in for you until you do

learn," she interrupted again, smiling as if I'd agreed. "You can keep training, go to school. Be an Enforcer. Once you're ready, you can step into my shoes."

I glanced at her shoes, the red combat boots she loved. They were fancy, glossy and showy. Perfect for the sort of statement an Alpha Mate needed to make. And the thought of trying to fill those shoes made me want to puke.

"I don't want to mate, Margarette, *ever*. You know this."

"But would you do it for the good of the pack? For me?" she pleaded, a hard, desperate note in her voice.

"Sounds like you had this idea from the get-go. That's why you gave me all the clothes and all that good food. Were you just working me around to sayin' yes to something I already told you I wasn't gonna do?"

She sputtered for a few seconds. "We didn't feed you and clothe you because you were Glen's mate—of course not. But if *you* aren't going to mate him…" There was something desperate in her gaze.

"Oh," I whispered, finally understanding. "He doesn't have to have a *true* mate. He just has to have a mate, any mate."

Margarette's lips went tight, but she nodded sharply. "You don't understand. Bradley… Bradley may die. When he goes, I will, too."

Suddenly, I got it. "You're true mates. You can't live without him."

"I wouldn't want to," she confessed. "*Please* understand, Flor. I want my son to have what would make him happiest, and that's you. But if you won't, if there's no hope, then happiness comes second to strengthening the pack."

I pushed down the fury building inside me, not certain if it was from her pressuring me, or the thought of Glen with some other female, mated to some woman like that bitch Clara, touching her... My gums prickled, as if sharp teeth were trying to emerge.

"That's why all those women run after him, even though they know he's not their true mate, right?"

One perfectly tweezed eyebrow flew up. "Exactly. He won't ever be as happy, or as powerful, but we don't have time for perfect right now, Flor. Our pack is in crisis. I have to steer us through." Her lips dipped into a pretty frown. "We saved you. I had hoped you would care enough about Glen and me and... and Bradley to save us now."

With that, she walked through the door to the training grounds. I followed, my head buzzing, pounding like I'd fallen face first into a beehive.

Strings. There were strings attached to her love, to her "saving" me. Of course there were. I had hoped...

Hope. There it was again, kicking me in the teeth as always.

12

A RIGGED RANK TEST
FLOR

B y the time I walked into the sunlight of the training yard, I didn't want to fight anymore. I *needed* to.

"Wills!" Sergeant yelled from across the yard. "Stretch and do bag work until your opponent is ready. You're fighting last, at the request of our Head Enforcer." He nodded across the training grounds at Margarette, who was walking away as fast as her boots could move.

The word *opponent* got my blood racing. Who would I be fighting? I didn't care, but I hoped they were strong and healed fast. I had a lot of aggression to work out.

I obeyed Sergeant's shouted command mindlessly, imagining the heavy punching bag was Margarette's perfect face, hinting that the price of acceptance at Northern was marrying her son. Then I replaced her face with Vanessa's. That was far more satisfying. I didn't stop until I heard a voice shouting and noticed the punching bag had split down one seam.

"I'll tell you this, Wills—you have more potential than I've seen in years," Sergeant said as he pulled me away from the bag. He nodded at my gloves, and I started taking them off. "I've been watching you every day since you arrived."

"You have?" I hadn't seen him around much at all, and the weird feeling that I got around him—that we were connected somehow—had made me look out for him most days. But he'd either been training with senior Enforcers at the far end of the grounds, or running patrols after rogues, from what Glen and Brand had told me.

"Yeah. You're solid. Great basic moves, stamina, flexibility. Now, the others are ready. But before your ranking match, I want to see what you can do with a weapon. Boy? You come, too." He motioned to Brand, then jogged away to speak with the other shifters who would be rank testing today.

From his concerned expression, Brand had been watching me take out my aggression on the bag. "You sure you want to test today, Flor?" he grumbled as he passed me. "There's no rush to become an Enforcer."

"Apparently, there is," I hissed, only loud enough for him to hear, I hoped. I scanned the area around us. Margarette was on the far side of the grounds talking to a red-faced, angry Patrick, so I went on. "Margarette just asked me to mate with Glen for the good of the pack."

"*What?*" His dark eyes blazed, and he went dangerously still. "She asked... No. I can't believe it."

I fought to control my breathing. He didn't mean he thought I was lying. He couldn't mean that. "She said it her damned self. She's clothed me, fed me, and I should be grateful. I should want to do her a favor now. If I'd known the food at Northern was so expensive, I would have hunted some fucking squirrels instead."

"I'll talk to her," he promised, looking toward where she had been, but she'd now left the yard completely. "She knows better. It must be her fear over Bradley's weakness—"

I couldn't help the bitter chuckle that escaped. "Yeah, that's a big part of it. I even sympathize, to a point. But one thing I've learned is there's always a reason to force an unranked female to mate against her will. And if there's not, I'm sure an Alpha's mate can find one. If I never talk to another ranked shifter again, it'll be too soon." I half-expected him to make fun of me for losing my cool. I was about to join the ranked cohort, if my fight went well, anyway.

But Brand's head dipped, and he frowned, like I'd hurt his feelings. "Not all of us are without honor, Flor."

Ah, crap. I reached for his arm, letting myself relax into the strange warmth that filled me as it always did when I felt his skin on mine. "Brand, you're the only one I trust. The only one who hasn't..." I almost said *pressured me into mating*, but it wasn't true. Glen hadn't been the one pushing that bullshit on me. That was his mom. And Finnick had done the exact opposite. Still, I didn't know how I could stay here, feeling this way. Hunted. "You're the only one who hasn't made it weird, by claiming me or trying to. If I need to get out of here, will you still help me?"

He gulped, then nodded. "Sure, Flor. I'll always help you, no strings. Lake, remember?"

Hope flared back to life, the tiniest bit. "We'll go there together someday," I murmured. "I can see your sculptures."

"Right." His voice sounded strangled now as he led me across to the central ring. Shifters were starting to filter into the inner yard around the ring to watch. There was a crowd of unranked shifters—identifiable only by the number of the females wearing collars, and the mismatched sparring clothing they wore—gathered on one side of the slightly raised, packed earth sparring ring.

A long table, draped with a black cloth, marked the other side. Patrick stood beside the table, still looking pissed, but Margarette was nowhere to be seen. *Good.*

Sergeant took up position by a group of three female shifters and one male, all of them muscled and wearing fierce expressions—except Vanessa, who looked pissed to be rubbing elbows with the others. Her black clothing, similar to mine but more form-fitted, stood out. It was so much nicer than the other unranked shifters' clothing, that I wished I'd worn my old shit from Southern to make a point.

Sergeant called out, "One of the ranked shifters assisting today is Curtis Yellen. He will be fighting Flor Wills last." He pointed to a skinny male, who swallowed hard when my name was announced. "Also, Patrick Hillier, Erik Adair, Steven Bates, and Stan—"

"Sergeant," Patrick interrupted. "Stan was the one who... choked."

The yard went quiet, though I didn't know why. For some reason, a few of the unranked females were clutching each other's hands, and I wondered if he'd been a friend. But then one of them met my eyes for an instant. She wore a collar, and she was pretty, if almost as thin as me. But I recognized the gleam in her eyes.

She was *glad* he was dead.

One of the males barked out, "He was murdered." The woman flinched.

Sergeant spat on the ground. "There wasn't a mark on him. No trace of poison, no silver dust. He was executed by the moon, as far as I can tell. And if any of the rest of you males happen to find yourselves in or near the unranked girls' rooms some night, like Stan did? If the moon doesn't wreak her vengeance on you, I will."

Ah, so he'd needed to die. I didn't know the guy, but I nodded at the female and mouthed, *Good riddance.* The corners of her lips turned up, and she nodded back.

Sergeant stared every one of the males who tried to meet his eyes into submission, then he spoke. "Patrick, can you do two rounds?"

Patrick looked down. "Yes, Sergeant." He didn't sound happy about it.

What followed was disturbing. Vanessa took the ring first, choosing to fight in human form. Her opponent was the one named Erik Adair. He was massive, not as burly as Brand, but he dwarfed Vanessa. She moved with the ease of years of practice, but so did he, and his reach and sheer strength so far exceeded hers that the match up didn't seem fair.

About five minutes into the round, it became clear that a point was being made here. Vanessa was being punished.

Her fighting was beautiful to watch, though, and the fight went on for a lot longer than anyone expected, from the crowd's reactions. Ten minutes in, Erik caught a break when a hard punch landed on Vanessa's temple, and she staggered. He bent her arm behind her back, taking her to the ground, then holding her cheek to the packed earth until she yielded.

No one seemed surprised, no one cheered, and when Vanessa returned to the sidelines, the only one who stood beside her was Clara.

"Vanessa, you'll have another chance at the next full moon to regain ranked status," Sergeant announced. "Train harder."

Vanessa didn't reply, but her jaw was trembling with suppressed rage.

Next, the other three shifters who were trying to earn their rank went up against Patrick and a massive shifter I'd only seen from a distance, Steven. When the Enforcers stood next to the unranked shifters, I wrinkled my nose.

This was who they had to beat? They were the top Enforcers here. Curtis wasn't even an Enforcer. Why was I fighting him?

Maybe this was just their bad luck. Mine usually ran that way, and I was due for a change. But after what Vanessa had said at breakfast about there being no way I could lose, this seemed suspicious.

I wanted to ask Brand, but the fights distracted me. They were sparring hand-to-hand, no weapons. Though each one of the unranked opponents were given the choice, none of them elected to take wolf form for their fights.

The females were fast, strong, and creative, but they were no match for the most senior Enforcers of the pack, though the crowd cheered them on. Patrick looked almost embarrassed when he fought the first woman, and Steven seemed just as troubled defeating his first opponent in under a minute. By the time the sole unranked male stepped into the ring to face Patrick, the whole crowd was subdued.

The women hadn't complained when they'd lost, but this guy spoke up. "You know this is bullshit. I've been trying to earn rank for five years, Enforcer." He pointed to one of the defeated females. "She's been in the ring *twelve times.* There have only been a handful of instances when the 'random selection' put an opponent any of us had any hope of beating in this ring. Only two unranked wolves have earned their rank here in a decade."

Patrick scowled. "Are you accusing me of something?"

The man swallowed hard. "No. Not you. I just want you to wake the fuck up." He went quiet, shaking his head. "Never mind. Let's just get this over with."

I stared at the back of Sergeant's head while Patrick delivered the quick defeat. They shook hands at the side of the ring when it was over, and Patrick leaned down to whisper something in the man's ear. Something that made the guy slump, even more defeated than he'd been in the ring.

"Is it rigged?" I breathed the question to Brand.

"I never would have thought so, though I haven't actually been present for one of these," he replied, just as quietly. "It's odd, now that I think of it. I was always assigned to run the borders during the ranking fights, with the other Heirs." Our eyes met. "I was asked to go with Glen and Finn today, but I refused."

I swallowed a ball of rage, and mouthed one name. A question. *Glen?*

Brand shook his head. "Glen isn't any part of it, if it is. He would have spoken out. He would have told me."

"Sergeant?" I whispered, a little louder. Brand's eyes darted away as a shadow fell between us.

"Yes, it's time," the man whose honor I'd been questioning called out.

Had he heard us? His expression was as stony as ever, but when I met his eyes, there was something there I hadn't seen before. It looked a lot like shame.

I didn't have time to wonder. "Flor, I'd like to do things a little differently with you." I wasn't sure if he was asking, so I just nodded. "I've already seen you do basic hand fighting with our Enforcers-in-training, so I'm giving you a pass on that part

of the assessment. Before you spar against young Curtis here"
—he nodded to the skinny shifter, who looked like he might
puke at any moment—"I'd like to find out if you have natural
skill with a blade. Have you ever handled a sword?"

"Never touched one," I said truthfully.

Sergeant grunted, then barked a command at an
unranked shifter who stood by the cloth-covered table. The
guy rolled the cloth away, exposing a row of swords in every
size and shape I could imagine.

Sergeant's young helper tried to hand us both short
swords, but Brand shook his head. He had a long bag with
him, and pulled out his sword belt and two swords,
perfectly sized for him.

I stifled a sigh as I hefted the one I'd been given. It
didn't feel like the right length or weight for me, but I didn't
want to complain. I'd fought with a lot worse.

"Let's see your sword technique," Sergeant instructed.
"No fighting just yet, just forms. You know some forms?" I
shrugged, then moved clumsily through some basic
patterns until Sergeant caught me glaring at the blade. "Get
her a better sword."

Brand interrupted. "I'll give her one."

He had an extra in his sword belt and kneeled to pull it
out, but Sergeant thumped him on the back of the head.
"She's not seven feet tall."

"The only smaller ones are the children's swords,
Sergeant." He gestured to the table.

"Hey!" I complained. "I can handle a big sword." I held
my hand out toward Brand. "Give me yours, and I'll show
you."

Shifters all around us started coughing, like they'd been
caught in a dust storm. Somebody muttered, "No way a

little thing like her can take his sword." Some of the teenagers giggled.

Brand's cheeks were bright red over his beard. "This whole place is full of perverts," I muttered, feeling my anger at Glen flare again. Closing my eyes, I took a few deep breaths.

Sergeant had jogged away to his cabin, but was on his way back in less than a minute with a new sword, a much smaller one. It wasn't really a child's blade, definitely not a toy. In fact, it was a work of art. Delicate silver etchings scrolled up and down both sides of the shimmering steel, blooming flowers and vines and berries. He handed it to me hilt-first, over his forearm. It seemed like a formal presentation somehow.

The sword was light and precisely balanced, a weapon for a master fighter. "I can't use this," I protested. "It's too valuable."

Sergeant cursed, but there was no anger in his voice. "Did you or did you not place yourself between our Alpha and his mate, and an attacking enemy Enforcer?"

The whole yard had gone silent again. I nodded mutely.

"Did you or did you not use a steak knife to kill that Enforcer so he could not murder my Alpha and his mate?"

I nodded again. When he put it that way, I sounded like a badass.

Slightly elongated canines peeked out over his lips, and his eyes glinted bright gold. I heard gasps all around; apparently, Sergeant didn't show his wolf side often. "And did you or did you not then decapitate that individual with that steak knife, delivering the traditional dishonorable death sentence as any shifter in leadership of the Northern pack would have been within their rights to do?" His snarl broadened. "But at the hands of an unranked teenage girl, which made it even more dishonorable?" I let out a warning growl, until he went on. "Thus earning not only my undying admiration, but also the permanent loan of my mother's sword?"

"Yes," I snapped. "And if I could do it again, I would." Wait. His *admiration*? His mother's... "Y-your mother's sword?"

For an instant, his snarl became a smile filled with a warm respect and humor, then vanished, like the flick of a moth's wing. "Yes. Keep it oiled and polished. And remember, the value of a blade exists only in the heart and hands of its wielder."

I swallowed hard. "You sound like Del... like Del used to."

"Del? Delmar Talbot?" He froze when I nodded. "You knew Del?"

13
A DEEP CUT
FLOR

The heavily scarred shifter glowered down at me, as if I'd kept a secret. I supposed I had; I hadn't stormed across the training grounds any time in the past few weeks to tell him I already knew how to fight. But I hadn't wanted the pack here to think I was trying for special treatment, that just because I'd saved Margarette didn't mean I thought I was special. I'd enjoyed the training, even if it was too easy. It had given me a chance to meet more shifters, to observe the pack's structure.

But Sergeant seemed super worked up that no one had told him about Del. It did sort of stink. If Del was this guy's friend, I would've thought someone here would've mentioned it to him, even if Sergeant gave off a *talk to me and die* vibe. These Northern shifters must not be as gossipy as the ones at Southern.

"Of course you knew him," he muttered before I could answer. "I should have recognized your style, those forms. He trained you, didn't he? For how long?"

"Since I was a little girl," I replied, feeling awkward with

so many eyes on me. "He raised me. He taught me everything he could."

Sergeant's brow furrowed. "Why the hell did you say
you had no training? You lied to me."

My jaw dropped. I was a lot of things, and a liar was one
of them, when my life depended on it. I'd been accused of
plenty I hadn't done. Being a whore, for one. But his accusation stung me deeper than it should have, coming from a
man who felt like some sort of family.

"She's had no *formal* training," Brand muttered when I
didn't answer fast enough. "Del had lost his rank."

Sergeant began to pace back and forth, almost like his
wolf was rising again. "Well, someone here lost their mind.
We've wasted weeks conditioning her, when she came
through *Del's* training? Why didn't someone say something
before?" He stopped and directed the last question at me.

I shrugged. "Beats me. Lots of the Enforcers knew about
it. Glen and his mom knew, and Patrick, too. I just figured it
was the same rules here as at Southern. Formal training
was all that counted there—not lessons after the dishes
were done."

"Right, enough talk." Sergeant shook his head, as if
severely disappointed. "I wanted to see you fight, and now
I'm not worried about who I'll match you against. If Del
trained you for years, there won't be more than a few
shifters who can safely spar against you, not when I want to
see everything you've got. Curtis, you can go." He dismissed
the young shifter and motioned to Brand. "You, get in the
ring with her. Don't hold back."

A thrill of alarm ran through me. "Um, I've never actually fought with a real—"

Sergeant cut me off. "No more talking." Brand opened

his mouth to say something, but Sergeant barked, "*Now, boy, not yesterday!*"

In under a minute, we were inside the large dirt ring, the assembled shifters crowding around to watch. They gathered in a loose circle, the ranked shifters in their uniforms standing in front of the unranked. Vanessa and the ranked girls who'd been chasing after Glen were all lined up in the front row, their expressions ranging from curiosity to disgust to grade A hatred.

A shiver ran up my spine, as I noted the excited gleam in the eyes of some of the male shifters who'd lost their rank hunting me. They wanted to watch me lose.

Screw that. I eyed Brand. He was huge, the short-sleeved black t-shirt and painted-on sweats not hiding much of what was underneath. I'd seen him training with some of the older Enforcers over the past weeks, though, and I knew he was good. I'd have to feel him out, find a weakness. He had to have one.

His muscles flexed as he took a fighting stance, his arms and legs honed, every inch of skin that showed gleaming bronze like a gladiator from the textbooks in school.

Okay, he might not have a weakness. I might have to be sneaky.

"First blood wins," Sergeant announced.

Ugh. I'd hoped we were pulling our strokes. I didn't want to bleed, even though I knew I'd heal faster now that I'd shifted. I sure didn't want to cut Brand, who I genuinely liked.

Maybe more than liked.

The small sword in my hand sang as I moved it through the air, waiting for Brand to make the first move. I'd only ever seen him fight in real battle, and that had been against multiple opponents. To be fair, I hadn't stopped to watch, since I'd been too busy taking care of Van.

Finally, Brand stepped closer, beginning the fight with a series of predictable, slow parries. I lifted one eyebrow. "Really? You know I'm pissed off; don't make it worse. Help me work out some of this aggression."

His eyes glinted, and he picked up the tempo of his attacks. Soon we were both moving quickly, dancing around the ring.

For a giant man, Brand moved like a dream, almost floated. His sword was longer than mine, but I was used to mop-sparring against Del, who hadn't been much smaller. Brand was stronger, though, and his hits were punishing. I made sure to let the blows he meted out hit my blade at an angle to deflect the power behind them, but even then, I found myself growing tired.

"This isn't the damn ballet, Brand," Sergeant yelled from the edge of the circle over the sound of our swords clashing. "Fight her, or I will, and I'll cut her deep enough that it won't heal for a week."

Brand's eyes blazed at Sergeant's threat, but he stepped closer, coming at me with a barrage of quick, sharp blows.

Shit. I had to end this, had to figure out a way to get past those freakishly long arms and into his guard. All I needed to do was slice him the tiniest bit.

Only a very small bit, a voice inside warned. *Not a deep cut.* For some reason, Glen's wound, and Luke's, flashed through my mind.

What if...

My hand holding the sword trembled.

Suddenly, I was afraid to cut him. Those feelings that flooded through me when we touched, that sense of safety and home—it wasn't like what I felt with the other guys, but it was close. Would he be hurt in the way Luke and Glen had been?

Wouldn't Brand have said something if he thought he was my mate? I'd confided in him, since he'd never acted like that mattered to him. Had he ever denied it? I parried mindlessly while I fought to remember. No, he'd never explicitly said he *wasn't* my mate. He'd never acted like it... but Brand was quiet. Thoughtful. Unassuming.

Respectful and patient. Strong and perfect.

Mother. Fucker.

That's why I was afraid. What if I was his weakness, like Luke and Glen? If I cut Brand, I could hurt him, maybe kill him. I might be one of the only shifters alive who could do that.

I *never* wanted to hurt Brand. I wanted to kiss him. No, I *needed* to. Of all the guys, Brand was the only one I would consider mating with, if I hadn't vowed never to do it. He was perfect enough to make me consider breaking that promise.

The thought shocked me, and my eyes went fuzzy, my heart racing as an image of me lying on top of Brand, naked, flashed through my mind.

A vision, almost.

I heard the gasp from the crowd before I felt the pain. A stinging burn that zapped like a bolt of white-hot fire from my shoulder down my arm.

Flor, you stupid girl. Del would be disappointed as hell. While I was caught in the vision, I'd dropped my sword. Now, an arc of blood gushed out from a deep cut that stretched across my upper arm to my shoulder, pulsing, bright.

Someone in the crowd laughed. Vanessa, probably.

I collapsed, Brand's arms around me before I hit the

ground. He was covered in my blood, too. "Hey, Bearman. Ya got me good, huh?"

The shifters around me were shouting, Sergeant yelling orders, someone screaming to find Margarette, and the much closer but softer noise of Brand... crying?

No. Sobbing, like he'd lost everything.

"No, no," he rasped, his voice cracking as he held the wound closed, his fingers instantly slippery from the blood. "Please, I didn't mean to, I wasn't trying, I knew better... What have I fucking done? *I knew*. I should have said something. Flor, I can't lose you."

Margarette's voice intruded. "She was supposed to be fighting Curtis! Whose idea was this?"

"What's the issue?" Sergeant demanded. "She's shifted before. Hold it tight, boy—it'll knit."

It wasn't knitting; I could tell from the lethargy slowly stealing over me, from Brand's face, from Margarette's screams, from the pounding pulse and flow of blood leaving my body.

Sergeant shouted, "She's a shifter! Why isn't she *healing?*"

Brand's eyes were haunted. "She's my true mate," he whispered. "Flor, I didn't mean to. I knew you didn't want me, but I would never..."

"By the moon..." Sergeant's voice was growing fuzzy, distant. "I never would have put you in the ring, with or without a weapon. Margarette, you said she was Glen's... *Shit.*" Then his face was directly in front of mine. I felt a searing pain as someone tried to hold my arm together, or tear it open, I wasn't sure. "Flor, can you shift while Brand holds you? It might help."

I shook my head the tiniest bit. "I don't know. I've never shifted on my own." I concentrated, but I had no idea what I was doing. All I could feel was pain. My wolf was silent.

"Brand, if you're her mate, you can force her to shift. You can call out her wolf."

Brand let out a strange, choked howl. "We're not... We've never... completed the bond."

Sergeant's eyes went wide, darting around. "Everyone clear out. *Now!*" He murmured to Brand, "Keep your hand directly on it. That'll help a bit."

I couldn't see everyone else leaving, but I could hear them. Heard their murmurs of shock and confusion.

Suddenly, no one was there but me, Brand, and Sergeant. *It's better this way,* I thought, my brain going slightly hazy. I didn't want too many of them around when I died. I wished for a second that Glen and Finnick were here.

At least I had Brand. "Kiss me."

He shook his head.

I tried to smile, even though his denial hurt. "Asshole. A dying girl can't even... get a kiss. Guess I am pretty gross." Bloody, thin, ugly, compared to the girls at Northern.

"You're gorgeous," Brand ground out. "You're perfect in every way."

"Then why... won't you kiss me?"

Sergeant was doing something painful to my arm, and I tried to twist free. "Hold still," he commanded. I might have been able to match his dominance the week before, but I sure as hell couldn't now. My body went utterly still, obeying on a cellular level. The blood even seemed to flow more slowly.

I glanced at the mess of red that I could see on my upper arm. He was taping it. Literally holding my wound together with... duct tape? I snorted.

"What is it?" Brand's eyes moved wildly over my face.

"It's just... so Southern," I managed to croak out. "We use duct tape for everything."

Sergeant let out a snort as well. "There. That'll hold until you can..."

I blinked, waiting. "Until what?" I managed to say.

His brow furrowed. "Until you can mate, of course."

Wait, what?

14

THE WORST WAY TO CLAIM A MATE

BRAND

My blood turned to ice as Flor's eyes closed. She'd never intended to take a mate. I knew this. I'd hoped to have years to show her that I was honorable, that she could learn to trust me and—if she chose them as well—all of her other mates. Even if the idea of her having more mates rankled.

But with one clumsy move, I'd thrown my patient plan away. Why had she dropped her sword? I hadn't been using my full speed or strength; I'd made certain of that. I hadn't even been looking for an opening.

From the moment Sergeant had announced first blood and the fight began, I'd been trying to find the right moment to give Flor her chance to win. Not to truly wound me, but to nick me. I could have hidden a small cut, bandaged it later. I was skilled enough to allow her blade past my defenses. How had that stroke landed?

It didn't matter now. That cut had ended any hope I had of her believing I was good enough for her. I'd deceived her, and she knew it. I'd been hiding who I really was to her, who she was to me, and she'd just discovered it in the most painful way.

Her eyes still closed, she whispered, "What does that mean?"

By my side, Sergeant shifted restlessly and cleared his throat. "Ah, you know... it means to secure the bond in the, ah, traditional way." When Flor frowned, he went on. "With, ah, intercourse."

I cringed at how awkward he was. I'd wanted to bond with her someday, but I'd never imagined a worse scenario than this one. It was practically a forced bond, one of the worst crimes a shifter could commit. But there was no other way, outside of her choosing death.

Her death would mean my own. And maybe the end of my brothers as well. *Ah, shit.* No matter how this ended, Glen would never forgive me.

My thoughts darted to Luke, who was still at Southern, growing weaker by the day. What would this do to the strained bond between them? She was theirs, too. But what if my claiming her severed those incomplete bonds?

"Do you want this, Brand?" Flor rasped.

"No," I replied truthfully, then realized what I'd said when she flinched. I rushed to explain. "I mean, yes, of course, I want you, Flor. I've wanted you since the first moment I smelled you."

"I smelled... like shit." Her brow furrowed even farther, and a strange, wheezing sound emerged. Was she laughing? "I was covered in... literal shit."

"I liked it," I repeated, doubling down. "No. I *loved* it."

"All of you... perverts," she whispered, then opened her eyes. "Any other way?"

I fought to keep my expression calm as I took in the

blood rhythmically seeping out of the sides of the mass of silver duct tape. "No, the wound is too deep."

The wound *I'd* made. Fur prickled along the backs of my hands as I fought to control my beast, who insisted on being let out to howl our guilt and shame. Our anger. Our love.

I forced him back down. She wasn't able to shift into her wolf form; I could barely sense her wolf within her, as if that side of her had taken the lion's share of the injury. My wolf couldn't help her. Only I could. As if he understood, my wild nature subsided slightly.

I shook my head. "Glen isn't here. Finn... No. This is it. If I mate with you, you'll heal. I can call your shift. No one else can, except your Alpha, and Bradley's still unconscious."

Her next words were as quiet as a breath, but they still carried in the ominous silence of the training ground. "The guys said you're the best hunter of them all. Well, you hunted me... caught me." Her next words to herself were even softer. "Stupid Flor. You were bein' hunted in this pack, just like at Southern, and didn't even notice."

Sergeant gasped, horrified. I flinched; I'd forgotten he was there. "Hunt? What sort of hunt is she talking about?" he demanded.

I swallowed hard, shame making it hard to speak. "Her old pack. It was how they tortured her. And no, Flor, I swear to you on my pack's honor, and on the memory of my mother. I wasn't hunting you. I would never take anything you're not willing to give. It's still your choice—I told you I'd make sure that was never taken away."

"Mating or death? Some choice." Her sigh was small, but it felt like a knife in my gut to hear it. "I'm... supposed to have sex for the first time while I'm bleeding to death?"

I didn't have it in me to blush, but I wanted to. "I don't

132

like it any more than you do. But there's no other way to save you now." I steeled myself to offer what I knew I had to. "If you don't want me afterward, I'll let you go. We can be mates in name only."

Her pale lips twisted. "If you really are my true mate, won't that be impossible? Won't you go crazy? Won't we both?"

She knew so little of our ways. That was my fault, too. I should have made certain I'd told her everything, so she could protect herself. So she knew what lay ahead. "That's only for incomplete mate bonds. Those can be very dangerous. If we mate, we'll be fine."

That wasn't quite true. A strained new mate bond was dangerous. Mates were meant to stay close to each other for the first few months at the very least, to cement the bond. At Mountain, new couples were given a private cabin and two months' worth of food, and left alone to do just that. But she was in too much pain to notice the sour note of deception in my words.

I was dimly aware of Sergeant moving away, of the training ground emptying out completely, until our hearts were the only two beating in this place.

Though her heartbeat was sluggish, and thready. We were alone.

Her breathing stuttered. "Flor, please," I begged now, my wolf panting and pacing inside our shared soul. He knew this wasn't something he could help with, or he'd have burst forth and claimed her by now. "I swear I won't take advantage. If you don't want me, I won't force you to stay with me. Please let me heal you?"

15

A PERFECT MATING

FLOR

Brand's words seemed to come from far away, though the warmth of his hands made me understand he was right there, holding me. "Please let me heal you?"

I had no choice, if I wanted to live.

At Southern, I'd experienced this. Not this situation, but the feeling. There was nowhere for me to go. No other option. I was treed, like a possum. Like I'd been once before, in the Hunt.

I'd promised my mama I would run from my true mate. I'd sworn to stay away from men who wanted to own me, who would hurt me. And Brand *had* hurt me.

But unlike all the others who'd done so before him, he hadn't meant to.

Underneath that bear-sized exterior, he was the gentlest, kindest, most thoughtful shifter I'd ever met. And he was still attempting to honor my right to choose my path forward. If he'd kept the truth from me about being my mate, he obviously hadn't done it for his own gain. Even now, he was giving me a choice.

I thought about trying to live as his mate. Living in the mountains, in the wilderness. Seeing his lake. Flickers of Finnick, Glen, and even Luke flashed in my mind. If I chose Brand, did I have to let them go permanently?

My blood raced, and I felt it begin to spill again, moving past the tape, my life ebbing.

Flor. Hold on. Stay.

A voice—though I wasn't sure it was in this world—called to me, called to my blood, slowing it further. Commanding it to stop flowing, as if such a thing were possible.

I heard the distant howl of a dark wolf, running to me, trying to reach me in time. The thud of those feet matched the race of my heart.

I wanted to live. I had to.

I took a shaky breath, my decision made. *Sorry, Mama. I have to try to heal. Have to survive, and maybe someday... live.*

Though it felt like it weighed a thousand pounds, I lifted my good hand and placed it on his bearded jaw, letting my fingers delve into the soft hair. "Yes," I answered. He shuddered, then gently, carefully, lowered his face to mine.

For so many years, I had been terrified of the day a shifter would catch me and mate me, so I wasn't sure what to do with the desire that swamped me now. His lips were on mine, kisses soft and sweet landing on my closed mouth. His tongue lapped gently at my lower lip, enticing, inviting.

I wanted more of that feeling. Heady, rich, deep like the waters of his lake. I wanted to drown in him.

I opened my lips, and the kiss became demanding, insistent, like he was the air I had needed all along, and I was taking my first breath, my first taste of passion. "More," I mumbled into his mouth, and he answered, slanting his lips against mine, exploring my mouth with his tongue, smothering me in the scent of pine. Brushing his beard over my softer skin, waking every nerve.

I was overcome with hunger. I wanted him, wanted *more*. More kissing, more of his hands on me, more lips, even teeth.

The thought of his strong teeth closing gently on my earlobe... As if I'd whispered it into his mind, he moved his mouth to my neck and I felt it, a gentle bite that sent shivers throughout my body and turned my legs to liquid.

He pulled away, and I whimpered. Was he stopping? Then I saw his face; the emotions painted there were ones I had never imagined.

Admiration. *Awe.* He looked at me with eyes filled with wonder, his heart shining in them.

"Brand?" I wasn't sure what I was asking, but he smiled and nodded once.

"I would have filled a room with flowers," he said, his large hands infinitely gentle as he used a pocketknife to cut my shirt away, exposing my chest to the air. With a small snick, then another, he cut away my sports bra. "Courted you. I would have carved you gifts, sung you love songs. Danced with you."

My throat tightened as he spoke reverently, romantically, revealing a gentle heart that astonished me. He paused in undressing me. I couldn't meet his eyes, so I stared at the top of his head, wondering what he thought of his soon-to-be mate. Knowing what I looked like, knowing how much less beautiful I was than him.

"By the moon, little flower, you're... exquisite."

"E-exquisite?" My eyes dropped to his heavy-lidded ones.

"Perfect. So fucking beautiful." He groaned as if he

couldn't stop himself, as if I were overwhelming him. He lowered his head to my chest, teasing one sensitive tip into an ever-tighter peak, nibbling, biting until I squirmed against the ground.

The wound in my shoulder didn't exist now. All that was left in the world was Brand's mouth. Then I felt his fingers, those huge, strong hands, moving toward the waistband of my pants.

"Are you sure?" I let my eyes answer him, but he stopped. "Words, Flor. I won't do this if you have any doubts."

"I want this," I whispered, closing my eyes at the cool air that rushed to kiss the skin on my bare legs. He pulled my underwear off as well, and my socks, and I lay bare under his gaze. I kept my own eyes closed, too shy to see what he might be thinking as he looked at all of me.

But then I felt the air move, and let my eyes fly wide, taking in his body as he tore—literally *tore*—his clothes into pieces. "Brand!"

His chest was covered with dark, luxurious whorls of hair, and I wanted to dig my hands into it, wanted to pull him to me. I lifted my good hand and did just that, using my nails to scrape his dark nipples as I explored that chest I'd been longing to map for days.

I wasn't planning to let my gaze drop lower—not yet—but I couldn't help it. I followed the arrow of dark hair down, down, to where his thick length pointed at me. Veins stood out along the shaft, the head exposed and purplish. I gulped, wondering if he thought that whole thing was going inside me.

"I'm big," he said, his voice an apology. He sounded embarrassed.

"Well, size doesn't matter, right?" I joked.

He let out a short laugh, and some of the tension in his eyes eased. "I'll make it good for you, Flor."

"You've had a lot of practice?" I teased, amazed that I had the energy to do such a thing. But the wound in my shoulder already felt slightly better.

"No," he murmured. "I mean, a little, a few things. But not... *that*. The girls were always... Well, I never wanted to do everything."

Unexpectedly charmed, I stroked a lock of his long hair. "It's your first time, too?"

"I wanted to wait for my mate. For you." A tiny smile crept out. "I thought it would be in a bed, with sheets and pillows, maybe."

"It's perfect here." It really was. No one was watching; Sergeant had cleared everyone out. And we were doing this under the sky, like shifters had mated in the old times.

Suddenly, all my doubts vanished. This was right. In fact, it was more than right.

"It's perfect," I repeated, gripping his firm bicep with my good hand, hoping he understood.

"*You're* perfect," he replied, shifting his weight.

I let out a small cry, as blood from my shoulder oozed past the tape with the sudden movement. A wave of dizziness assailed me, and I let go of him, needing to feel the earth beneath me. "Um, Bearman? We may have to speed things up."

"Shhh. I've got you." He dipped his head, and I closed my eyes, bracing myself for the pain of him.

But instead, I felt wetness, warmth, pressure.

I opened my eyes again, shocked. He was licking me, moving from my breasts, to my waist, to my mound. His tongue traveled in a glorious path from my opening and around, mapping every inch of me, plundering me, and ending up at the top of my slit, at the bundle of nerves that ached for his touch.

The rasp of his beard teased as he circled over and over just there. He moved fast, using firm pressure, then gentled before he stopped. I protested as he blew a stream of cool air on my heated flesh before returning to his task with intensity, and focus.

I'd never felt anything like this. I hadn't known this was possible, that pleasure could build, even though I was in pain. That someone could care this much about how I felt. Every time I reacted with a sigh or a shiver, he took note and repeated that motion, as if he were hunting my greatest pleasure.

A good hunter indeed, my wolf purred, waking up and stretching inside me.

An ache started building in my core, and I thrashed my legs. "More. Please, I need... something."

"Shhh. I'll give it to you." He put his tongue and lips back to work, then moved two slick fingers slightly down, toying with my opening. I moaned as he slowly slid one finger inside me. It was already tight, but he thrust it deliberately in and out, feeling for something, searching... and then finding it. He crooked his finger, and that place, the little bit of sensitive inner flesh he'd found, sent shocks of pleasure that bordered on pain throughout my system.

"Brand!" I shouted, and he hummed his satisfaction against my achingly sensitive flesh, his clever tongue never stopping, moving in time with his finger.

My heart felt like it would pound out of my chest, making me wonder for a moment if I could die from bliss. With the wound I had, it seemed possible, but I wasn't certain I cared at this point.

It would be the best way to die. I almost said it out loud, but then Brand added another finger, stretching me, moving at an increasing tempo, and all that came out was a garbled moan of pleasure.

It burned, and ached, and the spirals that were looping through my core began to coil tighter and tighter. Then, just as I was afraid I would actually die—from the wound in my arm, or the tension that was coiling in my center, I wasn't sure—it all exploded.

I became fire, light, and joy. The air around us filled with the mingled scents of cinnamon and pine, jasmine and woodsmoke, salt and musk. His fingers kept moving, drawing the incredible sensations out, then stopped as he withdrew. I cried out unintelligibly, reaching for him, and then he was back, his chest pressing against mine, his fingers being slowly, inexorably replaced with his smooth, hard cock.

I cried out as the thick head pressed into me, not sure whether I wanted him to stop or never stop. It hurt, stinging deep inside, and it kept going. He moved so slowly that I found myself whimpering.

"Are you okay?" he panted.

I grabbed a handful of the luxurious hair that flowed down to his shoulders, and lifted my head to one of his nipples, biting down hard. "More," I demanded, tasting his blood on my lips.

He listened, sliding deeper, stopping only when he was as far inside of me as he could go. "It feels like—"

I finished for him. "Home."

"Flor!" He started thrusting, groaning, nonsense words of praise and love falling from his lips. Something was building inside me again as he moved, coming closer.

It felt like running feet, sounded like howling.

"More," I demanded, breathing through the slight pain, the intense stretch. "Faster."

Brand picked up the tempo. We had to hurry, had to finish before those feet arrived, before anyone arrived...

Brand's length seemed to grow even thicker as he thrust and moved, becoming impossibly harder. His thrusts became almost brutal as he now chased his own pleasure, dark eyes blazing. I felt my own bliss begin to spiral upward again, tightening my core. I clenched around him, another spasm taking me over the edge, pulling me down, down into an ocean of pleasure.

"It's too much," I gasped when it felt like I might drown in sensation.

"Stop?" he demanded, his voice strained.

"No," I sobbed, and he let out a joyful laugh, thrusting even harder.

The world spun as he got close, and he set his mouth to the juncture of my neck and shoulder. He released a groan of pleasure, then bit down, his sharp teeth sinking into my flesh, marking me.

It was painful. It was *perfect*.

And then he bent, so I could easily reach his throat. I didn't hesitate. I lunged for him, marking him as well, his warm skin breaking under my small, sharp teeth.

His blood filled my mouth, and I swallowed it down as he continued to fill me, pounding into me, holding me almost too hard. I could barely breathe under his weight, but I didn't care. I didn't care about anything but this moment. I could feel the energy of his wolf, and when our eyes met, our inner beasts rejoiced.

He was mine. This steady, kind, strong, patient male. He was mine for now, and forever. My mate, my lover, my only—

Ahoooo! The howls that interrupted my inner rejoicing weren't my imagination. They were real, and angry, and very close. My gaze flew to the side, to the nearest trees.

Two wolves—one russet, the other a deep gray—emerged from under the shadowy cover of the forest, approaching silently now.

Brand's movements were slowing and relaxing, while my heart raced at the danger he didn't seem to notice. I pushed on his chest. "Brand, get up. There are two wolves." I didn't know who they were; I'd never seen them before. At least, not in fur. I couldn't smell them, since the breeze had gone still.

They could be rogues.

"Brand!"

"Hmm." He nudged my neck, scraping his teeth against the skin there. "Just m'brothers," he finally responded. "They'll watch over us."

Brothers? Did he mean shifters from the Mountain pack? Curiosity joined my concern, and I tried to pull myself away to see them, but felt the duct tape tear loose.

I blinked and reached for my damaged shoulder. Was it healed? I grabbed one end of the tape and started ripping it loose, glad I didn't have much hair on my arm to pull with it.

It had worked. The wound was healed, not even a scar remaining.

"But... I didn't shift," I said, stunned.

Brand smiled sleepily, his hand coming up to stroke my hair. "You did, a bit. Your eyes changed, and your claws." He glanced down at his sides and chest, and I saw cuts there. Claw marks.

I blushed. "By the moon, I'm so sorry. I didn't know I had—"

"I wanted more." He growled, pressing his lips to mine and plundering them with a savage kiss. "I *wanted* to feel your claws in me, in my back. I wanted you to bite me a hundred times, to mark me as yours so no one would see anything but your brand on me. Your claim." Impossibly, I felt him start to harden again inside me.

"You are mine." I touched the mark at my throat that had almost healed, leaving only a slightly raised scar in the shape of his bite. "My mate."

For the first time in my life, that idea of having a mate didn't appall me, because it was Brand. I leaned in to kiss him once more, but paused when the wolves I'd heard before howled again, a duet of pain. They'd stopped, watching us, only a few feet away.

"What?" I pulled my torso free from Brand's grip and watched as the wolves transformed into Finnick and Glen.

A naked Finnick and Glen.

Brand used his bulk to cover my bare flesh, and I made sure to keep my eyes on their faces. But their expressions were every bit as naked as their bodies.

Finnick seemed enraged for some reason, his features as cold and severe as the first day I'd met him. His words were harsh and dismissive, but that didn't surprise me. "Quick work, Wills. We were gone for what? A few hours?"

But Glen was broken. "You chose him," he said, his hands making fists and releasing them repeatedly, as if he wanted to fight but had no opponent. "You mated Brand." A tear trickled down from one beautiful blue eye, and he turned, shoulders slumped, his posture submissive.

Fuck.

16

UNDER HOPE'S KNIFE
FLOR

Brand wrapped his arms around me, and I let him shield me from the hurt in Glen's gaze and the judgment in Finnick's.

"Finn, blanket for her," Brand snapped. "Glen, clothes for me." Still facing away from us, Glen went to do as he'd asked—or ordered—though Finnick just sneered before stalking away.

Even with Brand's warmth surrounding me, I felt the chill of being naked in the open air. When I shivered, he wrapped himself even more tightly around me, blocking the cold almost entirely. How was he as big as a blanket? His chest was almost as furry as one, too. If I hadn't been perishing from embarrassment, I would have laughed.

He leaned close, rumbling in my ear, "We'll need to clean up. Would you prefer to go inside the Lodge, or to the lake?"

"The lake." The thought of facing the shifters inside the Lodge horrified me. They all knew what we'd been doing. Margarette... *Shit.* Margarette might throw me out, for all I knew. I wasn't going to be her son's mate now.

I couldn't be.

The thought of facing Sergeant or the other Enforcers was almost as bad. Heck, I couldn't even look directly at Brand. The things I'd let him do to me, that I'd *wanted* him to do.

My face went hot. "You think anyone would notice if I jumped in and kept swimming? I can't go back to the Lodge."

"Flor, it was necessary," he said gently. "You're alive. That's all that matters." His hands moved down my arms, and I ducked my head, hoping he couldn't tell how turned on I still was. "You know, if you don't want me to help you clean up, it's your choice, always."

"There wasn't much of a choice a little while ago. It was you or no one." I meant that in more ways than the obvious one. My own body had betrayed me, driving me to kiss him, touch him... But who was I kidding? I'd wanted that all along, since the moment I'd first touched him.

Even if there had been a thousand other choices, I still would have picked Brand for my first time.

My wolf, who was practically yipping with happiness at the bond between us, had wanted him, too. She didn't feel any embarrassment or shame. She only felt ready to do it again.

Simmer down, hussy. We'll get a reputation, I warned her.

She did not simmer down. How could she, when he was rubbing our bare skin with those strong, massive hands?

Brand's voice cracked when he murmured, "I don't blame you if you're disappointed. I know I'm not much."

I lifted my head so fast, my neck cracked. "What?" *Oh, Mother Moon.* I had never seen eyes so full of pain. "Aw, Brand, that's not what I meant. You're the best shifter I've ever met. It ain't... It's not that I didn't want you—I did, too much! I couldn't stop myself from wanting you, from saying yes." My cheeks burned. "Even if I wouldn't have... acted on it normally. You're pretty much irresistible."

"Ah." Now it was his turn to blush and duck his head. "That's not so bad then." He ran a huge hand over my hair, smoothing my short strands. "Maybe I'll grow on you?"

I almost cracked a joke about what parts would grow, but decided it wasn't appropriate. *Huh.* Maybe being mated was making me more mature.

Probably not, though.

"Guess we'll find out. We'll be joined at the hip from now on, right? We kind of have to be."

His face went still. "The mate bond is complete, so we can handle distance from each other. It's not ideal. But if you didn't want me around, we could just... meet up every few weeks."

"Like fuck buddies?" He blanched, and I grinned. "That's *so* not me. And definitely not you." I whispered into his ear, "You're a poet, Brand. You're a romantic. That'd never be enough for you."

His eyes shone like dark pools of melted chocolate, as he stared wistfully down at me. His hands never stopped moving, as if this might be the last time he got to touch me. As if I was precious. "I'll take what you offer, Flor. But I will never take more than you give me."

My heart felt like it was carbonated, the fizzy, dizzying bubbles of hope lifting it up inside me, as if it were trying to fly to him.

Hope. I shivered, knowing what happened every time I let myself feel that seductive emotion. I couldn't fall under hope's knife again.

"Blanket." Finnick's voice interrupted my spiraling

thoughts. He dropped a plaid wool blanket directly on our heads.

I thanked him with a few choice curse words.

Brand, on the other hand, let out a joyful laugh. "Thanks, brother. Run interference. We'll be at the lake and don't want company."

Finnick's reply was surprisingly warm. "Fine. I'll drop clothes and towels at the dock. I'm pretty sure Glen's already getting drunk." He called over his shoulder as he left, "Have fun, children."

Brand wrapped me in the blanket and carried me in front of him to the lake, while my mind spun. "Children," I finally gasped as we waded into the freezing water, the blanket tossed onto the rocks. "I didn't even think—what if I'm pregnant?"

Brand hummed, but he didn't sound even slightly concerned. I muttered a few more curses as he sluiced water over me, wiping at the drying blood and other things that crusted my skin.

"Hold still, little flower," he said, using his giant hands to cup water to rinse my hair. "My beautiful wildflower."

I grabbed his hands. "Brand, seriously. We didn't use any protection."

"You mean, like a condom?" His eyes twinkled. "Are you in heat?"

"Heat? I-I don't know." I'd heard older females talking about it back at Southern, but no one had explained any of it. "I'm not on my period, if that's what you mean."

"You never had shifter sex ed?" He sounded appalled.

I shook my head. "My guess is that was covered in high school. Dropout, remember?"

He lifted me back out of the water and cradled me

against his chest. I felt tiny, like a doll. "I could go back and slaughter them all, for not giving you all you deserved."

"I'd just as soon learn about it from you. If you know about... heats."

He set his face into serious lines, though his eyes were still shining. "I never thought I'd have to explain this until I had a son or daughter. But I can give you the facts."

"Please."

He waded to the shore and wrapped the blanket around us both, facing me toward the lake in front of him. His warm chest was pressed up against my back, and I could feel the thick length between his legs hardening slightly. I almost giggled, until he shifted his pelvis back, tweaking my earlobe. "Be still and listen."

He explained that shifter females held to normal human patterns of menstruation until their first shift, then cycled through heats instead. Since I'd shifted once at Southern, I'd experienced my last period over a month ago. I almost did a happy dance at the thought of no more periods ever. But there had to be a catch.

"What are heats like?"

"You won't bleed much, if at all. But every few months —sometimes more or less, depending—you'll feel heightened sexual desire."

"Maybe I was already in heat," I grumbled, and he laughed.

"Well, to be fair, most females say it's not that much different than usual." He paused. "The Mountain elders say it was different back when we lived closer to the land. When our packs were more... functional. If an Alpha's mate went into heat, her heat could affect the whole pack, and six months later, pups would be popping out everywhere."

"Pups?" I twisted to glare at him. "Don't even try to tell me we give birth to pups. I've seen newborns."

"No," he replied, kissing me quickly before turning me back around. "My pack just calls our children that. Not that we've had as many pups born as we once did. Though we have far more than they have here, or at Eastern."

I knew what he was talking about. "We've only had three births at Southern in the past four years. Does your pack know why our birth rates have dropped?"

"No. Some think it's pollution, others say witchcraft. But my father suspects it's something else."

"What?"

He looked up at the sky, where clouds moved across the deep blue dome. "How much of the shifter histories have you read?"

"Some," I said. "Margarette gave me a stack of books." I didn't mention that I'd mostly been reading Glen's romances over the past few days.

"Keep reading. I'm not sure there'll be much in the books here. In my pack, we have more, the whole reason for the eradication..." He rubbed at his head, as if it suddenly hurt.

Oddly, I felt an echo of pain in my own skull. *What the fuck?*

"What eradication?"

His mouth worked for a few seconds, like he was trying to speak, and the pain increased in my skull, like ants were gnawing at my brain.

He noticed me wincing. "Shit! Sorry, Flor. Strongest damned Alpha command ever given," he muttered, massaging my temples lightly.

"What Alpha command, Brand?"

He didn't answer, and I let it go, not wanting to attract

the invisible ants again. We sat in silence for a while, listening to the waves lap against the shore, the stones rolling and clicking as the water moved.

"When we go to my pack, I'm going to give you a mating gift, if that's okay," he murmured. "Traditionally, males give courtship gifts before the mating. I'd like to take a few steps back and give you some of that."

"The romance?" I teased, and he nodded. "You don't need to do that."

He nuzzled into my hair, and I could feel his lips curling. "I think you'd be surprised at what I'd do for your happiness, my wildflower. I think the whole world would be shocked to know how far I'll go for you."

It was so sweet, I turned around and stood so my face was a few inches above his. I tried not to blush, as I was still naked. His eyes traced the mating bite on my neck and the older scar over my heart, shaped like a star with five jagged arms.

I shivered under the heat of his gaze. "Bearman," I said quietly. "You're very dangerous."

"I know." He pressed a kiss to the newest scar. "But not to you. I swear, I'll never raise a weapon to you again."

"I believe that," I told him, although that wasn't what I'd meant at all. His sword might have pierced my shoulder, but his gentle, patient nature was putting my heart in much deeper danger.

17

FRAGMENTS OF A BOND

GLEN

"She betrayed you, Glennie. I know it hurts. Let me make you feel better." The perfumed woman next to me stroked my arm, either scent marking me or comforting me, I wasn't sure which. All I knew was she was wrong.

Wrong scent, wrong voice, wrong everything. I didn't want any hands on me but Flor's.

And now Flor was my best friend's mate.

That was wrong, too, even if there was nothing I could do now to make it right.

Tables of food lined one wall, with a buffet of finger food and plenty of drinks. It was a party to celebrate Flor and Brand's mate bond. Everyone was here except Mom, Dad, and... Vanessa, actually. I thought I'd seen her at the beginning of the party, talking to her friend in the corner—the friend who was now trying to stick her hand up my shirt. I batted it away, without looking at her.

I couldn't look at any woman, other than *her*. My perfect, vicious, beautiful, forbidden mate sat only a handful of yards away. So close, I could hear her breathing.

So far from being mine, she may as well be sitting on the moon.

Flor was ranked now. She was the mate to an Alpha Heir. Just not the one I'd hoped for.

She and Brand were nestled in a love seat together where they'd been all night, Flor draped across his lap. While she tried to read some dusty pack history book, Brand was picking up small pieces of fruit and cheese from a plate and feeding them bit by bit between her lips.

Her pink, delicate lips that had kissed him. It was fucking disgusting.

At least she was rolling her eyes and punching him every once in a while, at his over-the-top romantic actions. But she kept taking the fruit.

Of course she did. She'd taken more than fruit from him, and I was the worst friend in the world to be staring at her, wishing him gone, and her in my arms.

Their mating had been four days ago, and the pain was still as intense as the moment I'd seen them, seen her beautiful body under his.

I understood why he had mated her; I was even glad. After all, he'd saved her life, when I had been too far to help. But every time she touched him, every time he laughed— serious Brand, laughing like a kid!—something in me died.

At least they hadn't been sleeping together at night. For some reason, Brand had encouraged her to stay in her room, though I'd caught him sleeping outside her door, on the fucking floor, the night before.

I didn't get it. If she was mine, I'd have been with her every moment of the day, and every night, all night long. I'd keep her so exhausted, so physically fulfilled, she wouldn't be able to see anyone but me.

I'd finally asked Brand about their sleeping arrangements that morning at training. He'd answered in his usual terse way. "When she's ready."

Whatever that meant. She had obviously been ready for him before. But when I'd thrown that back at him, he'd lost his shit and beaten me down so hard, I'd had at least three fractures to heal.

I was haunted by what-ifs. If I had been in the training yard when she needed me, maybe she would have chosen me. The thought soured my gut and twisted inside me, poisoning my thoughts. I hadn't been there, and the choice had been made. I'd lost her forever.

I slammed back my whiskey and poured another crystal tumbler almost to the brim. It was harder than hell for a shifter to get drunk, but I'd made it my goal for the foreseeable future. I had lost my only other goal in life this week. Might as well make a new one.

Of course, Mom had fucked everything up for me, in more ways than one. She'd explained—or tried to—the day before.

"Glen, I'm sorry. I know you're angry." Mom tried to pry the crystal decanter of whiskey out of my hand. She was speaking softly, since we were outside Dad's sickroom.

Well, Mom called it his recovery room, but as far as I could tell, he wasn't recovering. He was getting worse. Outside of a very few, no one in the pack knew, but he was on a ventilator now. The doctor acted like he was doing everything he could, but there was no record of any shifter even needing a ventilator for this long.

His healing wasn't kicking in. The silver had gotten into his lungs and his blood, and it was taking him from us.

I was devastated about Dad. But I was every bit as gutted by the loss of my mate.

"Glen, listen to me."

"I am listening." I let Mom take the whiskey, knowing I could get more once I left, and crossed my arms over my chest, hoping to hide the tremors that had started the night before.

"I need you to move past this thing with Flor," she began.

I let loose a short, humorless laugh. "This thing? Thing? Mom, she's my true mate."

Or at least, she had been. It felt like she still was, even though I knew that was impossible. The ache inside, the longing to be with her, it hadn't lessened, even after she'd bonded with Brand.

Mom frowned, insistent. "She can't be, Glen. She would never have mated Brand if she was meant for y—"

"She was dying. She would have died. She had no choice."

"I could never have made that choice," she said, almost cautiously. "Once I met your father, I only had eyes for him. That's how I knew we were fated by the moon." She rubbed a hand over her face. She'd been crying again, and I pulled her in for a brief hug.

My voice cracked as I replied, "That's how I felt about her. How I still feel, Mom. She's all I see. She's all I'll ever want." I took a deep breath, ignoring her sharp gasp. "I shouldn't have gone with Finn. I knew she was going to spar. If I'd been there, maybe she would have chosen me. I could have saved her."

"She wouldn't have let you." Her voice was muffled by my shirt.

My blood went cold. "What?"

Mom's voice was filled with remorse. "She was so angry with me, and she was right to be. I was... I was pushing her to choose you. I told her, I insinuated, that she owed it to us."

It was all I could do not to shove her away. But she was in so much pain, and I knew adding to it would not be right. Not honorable. And, like it or not, my questionable honor might be all I had left. "What exactly do you mean, Mom?"

In short bursts, she admitted what she'd done. I'd known she'd been trying to push Flor and me together. I'd suspected it was making Flor even less likely to spend time with me. She hated being forced into anything, with good reason.

"You tried to force her hand, Mom," I said gently, though inside I was raging. Had Mom's meddling had even more severe effects? Patrick had said Flor had seemed distracted during her fight. Angry, emotional. Sloppy.

Had that anger been what made her drop her guard, when Brand injured her?

"Well, she had to choose one of you, didn't she? She left Luke to die. She looks at Finnick like he's shit on the trail. You weren't pursuing her like a shifter needs to, not that Brand was either. I thought if it was between you and him, and she knew why she needed to choose you—that we needed her..." She let go of my arms. "I fucked up."

I nodded. "We all did. Well, not Brand. He was the only one of us who didn't fuck up. He was the only one who didn't pursue her. And that's why she chose him."

"What do you mean?"

I met her confused, teary gaze. "She's been hunted for years. Every instinct she has says to stay as far away as she can from males who pursue her. I fucked up from the very start, but you..." *I wanted to lay the blame at Mom's door. Tell her that she was the reason I would never have my mate.*

But she was losing hers, and my pack needed me. I closed my eyes and took a few more deep breaths, fighting to accept what had happened. Knowing I had to accept the blame as well.

"We can all share the blame. But when it comes down to it, I'm glad she's alive, even if it means I live my life alone. Maybe someday, I'll even be happy for Brand and for her. For now?" *I picked the whiskey back up off the floor.* "I need to numb the pain."

Mom opened her mouth to say something, but the doctor chose that moment to exit the sickroom. His expression was grim.

"Is there any change?" Mom asked, straightening.

"He's losing strength," the doctor admitted. "His blood pressure is dropping; his heart is beating more erratically. I think... you need to make certain the pack is protected." The hiss and hum of the machines keeping my dad alive slithered around us like invisible snakes.

Without answering, Mom walked into the room and closed the door behind her.

I blinked. It was me the doctor was talking to.

"Alpha Heir, you need to make certain the pack is protected. When he passes, your mother..."

I finished his sentence. "She'll follow."

I pushed the woman's hands from my chest and reached for the crystal decanter again, needing whisky to wash down my dark thoughts. If my father died, my mother would, too. That's what it meant to be soulmates.

I hadn't needed Dad's doctor to say it to know the truth. I sure as hell hadn't needed him to remind me of my duty to the pack. My duty to take up the mantle of leadership... and take a mate.

But I didn't want to be Alpha. Without Flor, I didn't want to be *anything*.

I poured another three fingers of my father's favorite Macallan and drank it in one gulp. The den was growing raucous, more shifters coming to the party as the night wore on. I hated it. Hated them. Hated myself.

"Glennie..." The woman's hands were back on my arms, then my shirt, patting, buttoning—no, unbuttoning, practically stripping my shirt away.

What? I grabbed one of the hands and tried to focus my

eyes. I recognized her long blonde hair, her watery blue eyes. "Clara?"

Oh, yeah. This was the one of the women Mom had said she wanted me to "consider." Though she hadn't said it out loud. She'd left a note that morning, a list, in my room. Six names, all ranked females, all worthy of "consideration."

I didn't have the heart to tell Mom I'd already considered all the names on her list rather thoroughly a few years before. Clara had been one of the more memorable, but only because she'd followed me around for a week, whining, after we'd stopped fucking.

She obviously still hadn't given up.

I didn't hold it against her. We'd both been twenty-one and working our way through the unmated ranks, knowing we wouldn't find our true mates in our own pack—all the single shifters made sure to casually touch every other shifter of age as soon as they met, just in case—but willing to see if there was enough chemistry there for a back-up plan.

So few of us met our true mates anymore. In my mom's generation, at least a third of all shifters found theirs. But a few decades ago, that had changed. Now, it was only one in eight who found the love that the moon had meant for us. Or was it one in ten?

"Glen, come on. We were good together. Good enough," Clara murmured in my ear.

"Maybe." I finished off another tumbler of whiskey.

She wasn't wrong. The sex had been good, for a while. Until she'd started hinting that she would settle for a chosen mating, not a true one. I'd fucked around, sure. But I'd never really given up hope. How could I settle for an insipid almost-mating, when my fated love could be out there, waiting?

Only she hadn't waited.

I glared at Flor's thigh, where Brand had wrapped one of his huge hands. For a flash, I slipped into a fantasy, an impossible dream. Brand would hold her slender thighs open for me to taste her, bury my face in her.

He would play with her small tits, murmuring filthy praise in her ear as I worked her close to her peak, as I set myself at the entrance to her pussy, sliding insi—

"Is that for me, Glennie?" Clara's hand landed, a little too hard, on my erection.

I shoved it off, and she fell to the rug, crying out like I'd clawed her or something. My eyes locked with Brand's for a moment. He was frowning at me.

Flor, on the other hand, was very carefully not looking at the cluster of females who were helping Clara off the floor. Or at least, I didn't think she was. Her hair was long enough to partially cover her face now, ever since Brand had saved her. For all I knew, her eyes were on mine.

I tried to fill my gaze with all the longing, pain, and hope that swirled in my mind.

Finn was there suddenly, whispering, though that didn't matter with shifter hearing. "Stop staring like a fucking lunatic, Glen. She's Brand's now, and he's two seconds away from coming over here and gouging your eyes out. Pull yourself together."

"Come sit with us, Finnick," Clara said, sliding down next to me again, as if I hadn't just thrown her on the floor. Maybe if I gouged *her* eyes out, Flor would notice.

Finn growled. "Get off him, Clara, and go put some clothes on. You look like you're auditioning for a part in *Chicago*."

"I'm auditioning for something far more important," Clara hissed.

"The part of the pack whore?"

What? I blinked, my vision wavering. I'd never been this drunk before. It felt odd. Numb. I decided I liked it. "Who're you calling a whore, Finn?"

"Hear that, Clara? He doesn't even know you're still here. Give up."

"Glennie, I can't stay in the room with him." She rubbed her hand up and down my arm, then up and down her own body, drawing my attention.

Huh. She *was* dressed far too provocatively for a night in the Lodge, her skirt and bustier top all black leather and metal hardware.

"Where ya goin'?" I murmured as she stalked away, still snarling at Finn, who brushed dust off his dark sweater as she wandered over to a group of Enforcers who'd just come through the door.

He scoffed, "She's going to find out if a shifter can get an STD, it looks like."

Flor's voice was soft and censuring. "Finnick, that was mean."

He sniffed. "She had it coming."

My mind spinning, I stumbled to the far side of the room, where a wet bar beckoned. Once I had another full glass in my hand, I turned back to the vital task at hand: staring at Flor and wondering how I'd lost her.

"Stop moping, brother," Finn whispered again. "You're pathetic."

"Yes," I agreed. "That's probably why she mated him instead." He snorted. "No, it's *true.* Brand is the best of all of us. The best hunter, most honorable, best shifter of us all. She made a good choice."

"From what I heard, she made the choice to stay alive," Finn muttered. "If one of us—if *you* had been there, we would be celebrating very differently tonight." He paused. "Not that our dear Brand has done much celebrating with the little spitfire."

As if he heard us, Brand took that moment to lift Flor's hand to his lips and kiss it gently.

"Why was she sparring with him in the first place? Why the hell were they fighting with weapons?" I slammed my whiskey glass down. The crystal shattered, and blood seeped from a cut on my hand for an instant.

Finn made a disapproving cluck and waved for a servant to clear away the broken glass and ice. "She was following orders. I think Sergeant blames himself, but he said at the end, she just froze. Didn't block Brand's blow at all."

I grunted. "I heard she was distracted." Finn shrugged silently, distracted himself. He was watching Flor as intently as I had, his thumb rubbing his lower lip. I pulled him over to an empty sofa. "It would have killed Brand, if she'd died."

Finn lowered himself onto the sofa next to me. "Yes, literally. As it would all of—both of you. He saved her life, and yours. And Luke's."

Our eyes met. Luke was not doing well, from the reports we'd had. Of course, those reports hadn't come from shifters we trusted, but from the Council's Enforcers who'd arrived at Southern not long ago. But we had bigger problems here. I gestured for an unranked servant to bring us water; I needed to be a little more sober for this conversation.

I lowered my voice, hoping the distance from Flor would keep her from hearing. Though her hearing didn't seem to be as good as most shifters. Maybe once she'd shifted a few more times… "It doesn't make sense.

How could we both have been her true mates? And Luke?"

Finn's expression was inscrutable. "Just because something seems unbelievable, doesn't mean that it is. It's just unexpected."

"It should have faded, this feeling. I shouldn't still be drawn to her. She's his mate. But she's all I see, Finn."

"I know," he said. "I wondered..." He took a breath, shook his head, then took another breath. My eyes narrowed. Finn didn't do uncertainty.

"What?" I felt a flicker of hope. "What just occurred to you?"

"I wonder if she feels the mate bonds to all of you... a bit differently."

"Differently?"

"Less intensely. She hasn't shifted since the battle at Southern. Maybe her wolf is suppressed, somehow." He pressed a hand to his heart, and I noted his fingers were trembling slightly.

"You think she might still be able to feel for me... might feel a bond with me as well?" My head pounded almost as hard as my heart at the thought. "Maybe her wolf would?"

He shook his head. "I'm fairly certain she never felt the way we—I mean, that you and Brand did. And Luke. It's as if the bond is stifled. Buried under something, fragmented. She feels *something*; you can smell it on her. She jumps a little when either of you touches her."

"Yes," I agreed, thinking of the reactions she'd had when I was close enough to note them over the past weeks. The goosebumps on her arms when I ran close to her. The heady scent of cinnamon and jasmine when I stripped off my shirt in her presence.

Finn went on. "But she didn't seem to feel the

compelling urge to be near us—or Luke, obviously. Look at her now, though. Tell me she's not feeling the mate bond." Brand was teasing her with a grape, holding it out of reach until she snarled, then placing it between his lips for her to retrieve. She moved her lips over his, sucking at the sweet fruit—but her eyes were open, and for a split second, her heavy-lidded gaze was on me.

As I watched, her tongue darted out to lick her lower lip. I let out a near-silent growl, but she shivered, like she'd heard me across the room.

Holy shit.

Her cheeks pinkened, and her eyes darted away, but for that one second, I knew without a doubt she *knew* what I was feeling, and had responded.

Next to me, Finn shifted on the sofa. I copied his movement to discreetly camouflage my hard-on. He let out a sound that was between a sigh and a groan and murmured, "I think you should test it. See if she still feels any attraction."

My jaw dropped, and my whisper was more of a breath. "Seduce her? My best friend's mate?" Finn was rubbing his chest slowly, like his heart ached. But he also had a tent pole in his damned pants. "She's his now, Finn. What the fuck are you *thinking?*"

"His? Yes. But that doesn't necessarily mean she won't respond to you. Or others."

I could hear the lust in his voice, and I growled low. "That's not right. That's the sort of thing your parents might say about her. Seducing a newly mated female out from under her male is exactly the sort of thing they would do, from what you've said. Try not to act like your parents."

He shrugged, but I could smell the hurt on him. It was pretty low for me to bring up his parents. They'd hurt him in so many ways, not the least of which was his mother's constant attempts to mate him with shifters who could help their family fortune.

"I can't hurt him, Finn. I can't have her."

"Then don't. Just live with this." He waved at the way Flor was trailing her fingers over Brand's neck unconsciously, tugging at his beard. The scent that was rising from them was suffocating. I noticed a few of the shifters nearby drifting away, smiling.

"I have to respect her choice."

"Starting *now*, Mr. Peeping Tom?"

"Fuck you." I wanted to argue, but he wasn't wrong. I still felt the hot burn of shame when I thought about the first day I'd met her.

Shame, and desire.

"I don't know if I *could* have looked away," I groaned softly into my hands. "Could you, Finn? If you'd seen her and she'd called your name?"

He stood. "She's nothing to look at. I dare say I could have resisted." With that, he left, and I laughed harder than I had in weeks at the obvious lie.

I lifted my glass to Brand and Flor. "To the true mates!" I shouted, and all the other shifters in the room echoed my toast.

To the true mates.

Clara returned to me later, her hands on my shoulders and my hair, and I felt Flor's eyes on me again. But I didn't return her gaze. Why bother? She was forbidden, and I was alone.

And that was why, a few minutes later, I let Clara take me to my bedroom.

18

CONFESSIONS IN THE NIGHT
FLOR

I had no right to be angry. But I was. Alone, in my bed, filled with an uncomfortable anger.

And a more uncomfortable sexual frustration.

I'd mated the most honorable shifter in the universe. Brand felt so strongly that our mating—which he'd referred to today as "medically necessary," forcing me to punch him in the nuts—had been too rushed. He wouldn't push me for intimacy he said he hadn't earned. He barely kissed me.

While that sounded like one of the heroes in Glen's romances, I was horrified to realize I *wanted* Brand to push me. I dreamed of his hands on me again, his body in me. It was making me crazy.

In my darkest thoughts, I wondered if he really wanted me. Maybe the sex part hadn't been that good for him. I thought of it as earth-shattering. Life-changing. Glorious.

He'd called it *medically* fucking *necessary*. If I couldn't feel his emotions in the bond between us, I would've doubted his affections entirely. But underneath all the turbulent currents of guilt, remorse, and longing... there was something that could even have been love.

I wanted it to be that, but I wasn't sure enough to just ask him. The tie between us was so new and thin, it felt like demanding answers might fray or break it. Brand had said he didn't want to make me feel tied down, and he'd succeeded. I felt insecure and alone, like I was adrift.

But the pack around us had done a damn fine job of making sure I knew I wasn't my own person anymore. I was mated now, not a threat. Not a potential match for anyone else. The females took pains to keep Glen and Finnick away from me, and they sat Brand and me together at all times at the social events that had exploded after our mating.

Margarette's absence at what was supposed to be a mating celebration for me and Brand had made it plain that she disapproved of my choice of mate. The scores of unmated females who came to celebrate made certain to let me know they were "personally invited" by our hostess, as "special friends" of Glen's. I wasn't surprised that she was still pursuing her main goal to mate Glen off as soon as possible. Or at least, get him laid as often as possible.

I punched my pillow, refusing to think about him and that bitch Clara. *Ugh.* That female needed to be slapped into next week. All week, she'd been on Glen like white on rice, wearing more and more revealing clothing every time she showed up. It made me laugh to watch the girl who'd repeatedly hissed the word "whore" at me in the hallways prove to be such an attention whore herself. But Glen seemed to like her fine.

I turned onto my side, wondering for the thousandth time if I'd made the wrong choice. Brand was wonderful, and the bond felt... right. I felt protected for the first time in my life.

But would it last? Would he change, like my mother's

true mate had? Would those hands that had shown me pleasure begin to dole out pain?

He'd insisted I could leave. He'd even assured me that if I did, I'd keep my rank, as mate of an Alpha Heir.

The fact that I hadn't even been able to test for rank chapped my ass more than almost anything. After all the build-up, I had earned my new rank like all the other females at Southern did. By spreading my legs.

I needed to fight. Needed to prove myself.

Need to claw Clara's bitch face off, my wolf suggested. Her thoughts were clearer now that I was mated, but she still hadn't come out to play, even though the moon was full.

Shut up, you, I shot back.

She whined, still pacing inside our shared mind.

I slipped silently out of bed, pulling on shorts and a shirt, but no shoes. At the last minute, I grabbed my beautiful new sword. I was never walking anywhere unarmed again.

I padded down the hallway past Brand's door, pausing there on the thick wool rug. He'd insisted on sleeping outside my door even after we'd bonded, until I'd pointed out that the dark circles under my eyes were at least partly there because he was keeping me awake with his snoring. He'd finally caved, and agreed to sleep most of the night in his own room.

I pressed my ear to his door. It sounded like he'd invited a lumberjack to join him in bed. That might get old if we stayed together.

I passed the door to the kitchen and kept going. I had planned to get some water, but something was drawing me in this direction.

Something? I knew exactly what. *Fucking Glen.*

How could he act so drawn to me, so affected by me? I'd

almost kissed him, for crying out loud. I'd felt something for him, something deep.

Everyone had thought we were true mates, by the way his healing was delayed after I'd slashed him. But it had only been delayed, hadn't it? It hadn't remained open, like Luke's wound. But it also hadn't healed, like mine when I joined with Brand.

I found myself following Glen's scent down one hallway and another, until I was standing outside what had to be his room, sniffing the air. Was he still in there with that gorgeous blonde woman, that Clara? Was he touching her?

She was everything I wasn't, and had never wanted to be. Feminine, flirty. She wore makeup and hair products that made my nose sting. But all the eyes followed her when she moved through a room, and not because they were wondering who let the unranked trash in.

I let out a sharp breath, feeling the twist of murderous rage in my gut. My wolf rose, asserting her dominance over our shared consciousness. I was only hazily aware of what was happening in her thoughts, but I could feel the physical changes as they rolled through me.

My nails began to change into claws, my eyes seeing things more clearly.

My teeth ached, lengthened.

My hand reached for the doorknob.

The door opened before I had the chance to turn the knob, revealing a shirtless Glen, illuminated by the soft light of a lamp inside the room. His hair was a greasy mess, and he had deep, dark circles under his eyes... and lipstick on his neck.

I went still, sniffing, smelling him, his normally pleasant scent soured with whiskey and traces of *her*. She was in this room, or had been.

"Where is she?" I spat, stalking into his bedroom.

He just blinked, not answering.

"Where is she, Glen? Is she still here?" I sniffed the wide bed. I could smell she had lain there, and it filled me with rage. I tore at the sheets, shredding them with my shifted claws. "Is she hiding? I'll call my own fuckin' Hunt on her skanky ass."

"What are you doing, Flor?" Glen asked, his voice subdued. "No one else is here. Why are you?"

I stopped, panting. "I d-don't know."

He stood in front of me, his hands half-raised, as if he wanted to touch me, but was afraid. Or felt he didn't have the right to.

"Did you fuck her?" The words escaped before I could control my mouth, and I pulled the sword out of the leather sheath on my waist.

"What do you mean?" He looked concerned now. A little panicky.

I wanted to stop talking, but my wolf was in charge, apparently. "Did you have sex with Clara, that woman?"

His eyes narrowed. "What if I did? Why would that matter to you?" He stepped toward me, and I stepped back. Something about the way he paced toward me, his steps full of intention, his blue eyes deepening, darkening with each breath, frightened me.

Thrilled me.

I had been hunted for years and had resented every moment.

But now, I felt hunted in a new way. My pulse quickening, my nerves singing with anticipation. I wanted him to chase me.

What was I thinking?

"Why would you care if she took off my clothes, Flor?

Would it bother you to know that she's had my cock in her mouth? That I've been buried balls deep in her, felt her nails on my back? Would that matter one bit to you?"

I wanted to scream out, *Yes!* I wanted to fight him. I found my arm lifting with my sword in my hand, rage filling me. His eyes flickered.

"Go ahead," he said, raising his chin to expose his neck. "You might as well kill me fast. I don't want to go slow, like Luke will. I'd rather know the most terrifying, beautiful warrior I ever met had ended me. I would welcome that death."

"What the fuck, Glen?" I dropped the sword on his bed like it was a snake and stared at him. His neck was still extended, and the golden skin there shone in the dim lamplight.

Slit his throat? All I wanted to do was lick it.

Okay, maybe bite a little. But not slit it.

I shook my head. "Glen, what are you saying?"

In an instant, he was in front of me, inches away, his hands outstretched again, reaching for me like he couldn't resist. "I am saying I've fallen in love with you, Flor. You saved my mother. You tried to save my father. You saved *yourself* for years. You came out of that dishonorable fucking pack shining, like Joan of Arc. Everyone who sees you either wants you or wants to be like you. You're the most glorious shifter I've ever met. And you can never be mine. I can never touch you, have you, fuck you."

"What—wait—" *Glen's in love with me?* I tried to interrupt, but his words rushed over mine in a torrent of longing and self-condemnation.

"Not that I ever deserved that. I trusted my pack here to take care of you when I was at my father's bedside, and instead, they hunted you for sport." His voice was filled with rage. "I trusted my snake of a cousin to look after you, and she set you up to be hunted."

I cursed softly, and he echoed me, louder. "I trusted my mother to be a support, a role model and caregiver, not to take advantage of you, or make you feel as if you owed me a mate bond. I failed you again and again, and even though I know I'll never be worthy of your love, I still want it. Want *you*. I still get hard every time you pass by, still dream of biting your neck, marking you and claiming you. Still dream of giving you everything you never had, but always deserved. Love and affection, respect, fucking *reverence*.

"You're a queen among shifters, Flor. I told Clara that tonight. I told her you were my true mate, no matter if I can never claim you. That I long for you, even though I can never have you."

His eyes kept shifting between wolf and man, swirling with light and dark blue and black. The true scent of him, citrus and salt, swirled between us, and I leaned in the tiniest bit, drawing him into my lungs.

"Why not?"

His pupils dilated, black swallowing all but the thinnest rim of blue. "What are you saying, Flor?" he growled. His teeth... His teeth were too long. His canines had shifted.

"I'm saying..." I let my hand rise between us, hovering over his heart, feeling it pounding from an inch away. Heat was radiating off him, and I licked my lips, wanting to feel that heat on me. "I'm saying, why can't you touch me?" I let my hand rest on his chest. "What's stopping you?"

Glen took in a deep breath of my scent, his lips curling into a smile that was filled with pain. "Honor." He grasped both of my hands in his and held them tightly. "It's all I have now. I dishonored myself and my pack. I swore to you that I'd respect you, that I'd never take advantage of you in any way. And I would never betray my best friend, my brother." His voice broke. "Please don't make me."

"Betray..." I didn't know what I was saying. What was I *doing* here, in his room?

I didn't know, but I was sure I'd been just one more step, one more touch away from being unfaithful to my mate.

Oh, Mother Moon. I hadn't even thought about Brand at all. My stomach lurched. My wolf fled, running on silent feet to the back of my mind, tail between her legs.

"Glen," I whimpered, hating the weak sound of my voice. "I'm scared."

"Flor, what's wrong?" He gathered me in and held me, nothing sexual in his scent now, just concern.

"This isn't me," I admitted. "I mean, I've never even wanted anyone to touch me before. I sure wasn't jealous of anyone else. I don't sneak into men's bedrooms and try to convince 'em to..." My cheeks burned with shame.

"Flor, about Clara—"

"No, it's okay. None of my business."

"I did have sex with her," he admitted. I felt like I might throw up, until he continued. "Not tonight, but many years ago." He pulled me closer. "Are you disappointed?"

I managed to scoff. "I didn't think you were a virgin, Glen."

"Brand waited for you, though, didn't he?" He sighed into my hair when I nodded. "I figured. We spoke about it a long time ago, and he's not the kind to change his mind about the things that matter."

"Right," I agreed.

"I wish I'd waited for you, too. After I saw you, I knew no other woman would ever measure up."

"Glen, that's ridiculous." All his talk about me being

somehow better than other women was crazy. I backed away, waiting to see if he was joking. He had to be. "Look at me."

He did, his gaze dropping slowly to my bare legs, lingering on my hips and chest, and then settling back on my face, his eyes banked fires smoldering. "What is it you want me to see?"

"I'm skinny," I explained. "Like, prisoner-of-war skinny. No hips, no tits, none of the things males want. And I had to cut off my hair." I swallowed a stupid fucking sob. "Which, to be honest, was actually really pretty. I know your mom likes my short hair, but it was the only thing I liked about my looks, before."

"Grow it out," he said, running his hands across my short locks. "Keep it short, shave it off, dye it purple. I'll love it any way you wear it." He cleared his throat. "I mean, Brand will. Anyone who sees you thinks you're gorgeous—I promise you that. If they don't say it out loud, it's because they're afraid."

"Of me?"

Glen snorted. "Sure, princess. Also a little scared of Brand ripping their arms off."

I tried not to melt into his touch as he kept stroking my hair. "Glen, come on. I haven't met a single female at Northern who didn't look like she could moonlight as a model. I'm not... I'm not like the other shifters here."

"Good," he said fiercely. "None of them can hold a damned candle to you. And I've been with more of them than I should, so I would know."

I punched him in the gut. "Didn't need to hear about all the candles you've lit with your dick, Glen." For a second, we both smiled.

"Let's sit, Flor."

I pulled away slightly. "Sit?"

"Just sit, though I might fall asleep. I'm exhausted, princess, and maybe a little drunk. I promise I won't do anything. Not even if you ask me nicely."

He pulled me down on the bed before I could punch him again. It still smelled like Clara, and I bristled again. "You really didn't sleep with her?"

He groaned. "I couldn't even kiss her. I kept almost throwing up in her mouth when she came close."

"Too much booze."

"Hmm." He nuzzled my hair. "She smelled wrong. Like treacle and cigarettes. Yuck."

"You smell amazing." My voice was throaty and low. "Like the ocean, and oranges."

He squeezed me tighter. "You do, too. Though different, now that you're mated with Brand."

I didn't think I smelled any different. "I can't smell it."

"That's interesting," Glen mused blearily, but his eyes had gone sharp. "You can't smell his spicy pine mixed with yours? You smell like... like a Christmas party. Cinnamon, mulled spices, and a pine tree in the background."

"Does he smell like me now?" The thought sort of appealed to me.

"He smells slightly of cinnamon."

"Cinnamon bear. That's a candy, right?"

Glen laughed and stood. "Yes. Are you ready to go back to your room?"

"Yeah," I said, suddenly shy. "Thanks, Glen. For, you know, talking me down. Or my wolf, anyway. I wouldn't want to hurt Brand."

"I wouldn't either. But I'm more concerned with you." Stepping close, he let out a deep breath. "Don't misunderstand. I'm not a saint. If there was a way I could be with you, and not damage your bond with Brand, not hurt him, I would take it. I would take you for my own, in an instant."

"I think you're pretty amazing, too." I backed out of the room, waving goodbye with my fingertips, closing the door and wondering if I had been wrong about Glen from the start. Maybe it wasn't just Brand who was honorable.

I was meandering back to my room, my hand on my doorknob when I remembered I'd left my sword in his room. I turned just in time to feel something come up and over my head, a cloth that smelled strongly of something pungent and poisonous.

I struggled, drawing a breath to cry out, but that was a mistake. A fist, or a rock, hit my gut, knocking the wind out of me, and my cry emerged as a wheeze.

I tried to send a shout down the bond to Brand, but sensed he was still asleep.

Then I was falling asleep as well, and someone was binding my arms, covering my mouth, keeping me from calling out.

I sent one more desperate plea to Brand. It went unanswered.

And then all I knew was darkness.

19

QUIET SUSPICION

FINNICK

S leep eluded me. After the conversation with Glen, I
hadn't been able to concentrate on anything but
Flor. Not that *that* was anything new. Even when I'd
tried to avoid her, my mind had been fixed on her.

The part of my heart that had splintered when I rejected
her back at Southern was still aching, like a blistered
wound, seeping into my thoughts. My soul.

Even now. Even after she'd been claimed by Brand.

I'd spent weeks immersed in the Northern pack's
library, and I headed there again tonight, using my senses
to find my way in the near-total darkness. With the excep-
tion of the sections covering true mates, mate bonds, and
shifter fertility studies—Margarette's obsession—the
library here wasn't as extensive as the Eastern collection,
but the main texts dealing with Pack law and history were
well represented.

Once inside the library, I flicked on a lamp and pulled a
book from the shelf I'd located the day before. I flipped idly
through the pages, on my own personal hunt, as usual. At
first, I'd been seeking an answer to how one woman could

be a true mate to more than one male. But for the past few days, I'd been obsessed with a new question. I had to find something about mate bonds to help me understand why I wasn't free. Why I still longed for the small, boyish Flor, who was already claimed.

Not that she is boyish, I admitted to myself. When my wolf had heard her cries with Brand, when Glen and I had interrupted their mating, I'd seen her body.

She'd been naked after her first shift at Southern as well, but covered with blood. I hadn't truly registered her shape, her slight curves, her rounded, tight breasts. The gentle slope of her neck, and the stubborn tilt of her chin. Most shifter women were long, lush. She was like a fairy, some sort of pixie-shifter blend. Magical.

But when Brand was moving inside her, when she was crying out... Hell, even just the memory of her tight, feminine body made me hard. She was more than magical. She was strong and fierce, angry and intelligent, generous and good, even after all she'd suffered. When she'd fallen apart in my brother's arms, I'd seen why he'd fallen so hard for her so fast. Her soul had shone around them, transforming her, and him. She was miraculous, a goddess on earth.

I pulled out another text, appropriately titled *The Magic of Mating,* and began to read theories about how precisely the mating bond developed, and how it could be damaged. My mind kept returning to Flor, though.

Had the years of the Hunt done something to her? Suppressed the natural urge to bond emotionally and physically with one other soul? Perhaps the sheer number of males who'd preyed on her had damaged her psyche somehow.

Perhaps those males had given her that scar on her chest—the small, five-pointed, jagged star that began at her heart and ran up toward her collarbone and down to the bottom of her breast. She'd obviously been injured in some way, perhaps when she was very young.

The whispers of witchcraft bubbled up in my mind. It wasn't possible, was it? Had she been attacked by someone with magic, and come so close to death that her... soul had splintered?

Callaway had no magic; I knew that. But Brand had murmured something about the black wolf, Joaquin. He'd seen him use magic at Southern, before the great battle. Perhaps he was a witch, one of the witches from the remains of the last known coven in Florida, coming back to the scene of a magical crime. Maybe the money Callaway had paid to break the bond with his mate hadn't been enough. Maybe he'd offered up a child from his pack.

Or a baby.

My wolf went still, scenting something. A clue, a hint at what lay at the heart of all these mysteries. Luke had claimed that the witches had been employed by Callaway to break his true mate bond over twenty years ago. What if Luke had been hiding something, a secret, to protect Flor?

He'd been adamant that Flor should leave Southern. Had seemed almost panicked that she might not get away, though with Margarette's invitation, there should have been no issue at all. Flor had been unranked, after all. There was no reason to worry that an unranked female might slip away from a pack.

Unless...

The only shifters who could never leave home, not even if they won every Enforcer Game in the world... The only rank a shifter could hold that would bind them to their pack so tightly, they could never escape... "*Fuck.*"

I knew who Flor was.

I sat down before I fell, my breath coming fast, my heart racing. I wasn't *absolutely* sure. I would need Luke to verify my guess, or Flor herself, but if it was true, she was far more important and powerful than anyone suspected. And I could never, ever let my parents find out who she was.

I closed my eyes and forced all thoughts of Flor's suspected identity to the back of my mind, placing them in a mental box and shutting them away. If my parents questioned me together, if they tortured me, I needed to know she was safe.

ONCE I'D REGAINED control of my emotions, I returned to my reading, looking for more clues about mate bonds.

Flor was bonded to more than one shifter. There was no longer a question about that, only as to how it had occurred at all. But more important was to know if my brothers could be saved—Glen from a life mated to a woman he could never love, and Luke from almost certain death from mate sickness. If she could save them.

Was it possible she could truly develop a bond with more than one mate, making Glen and Luke into co-mates with Brand of some sort? It had never been done; shifters were beyond possessive. But the thought of her with Brand alone, and my brothers suffering, was what drove me to read deep into the night.

In another life, I would have been searching for myself as well. The thought of her turning from the embrace of Brand's massive arms to my more elegant ones... That thought did not repulse me at all.

My heart ached again, and I pressed a hand against my chest. That I still desired to be with Flor, to share her, shocked me to the core. My brothers had teased me over and over about being sexually repressed. I was, but by choice, and only Luke knew the reason, though Glen had his own quiet suspicions.

Quiet suspicions. For some reason, those words triggered my wolf to alert inside me, the hairs on the back of my neck standing up as a feeling of wrongness, of danger, pulsed in the air. I stopped breathing, hearing something on this side of the house. A servant?

A dragging sound. Not of a piece of furniture, but the sort of slow, uneven pull of something softer, like a heavy sack of laundry. Or a body.

As I listened, I knew it was a body.

Possibly one of the younger wolves escorting a drunken pack member back to their bedroom. But shifters were rarely drunk enough to need help, even if Glen had proved it possible earlier tonight.

I set the book down soundlessly, reaching for the light switch when I heard something else: the side door to the Lodge opening. The main exit that led to the garage.

The desk clock read 2:17 a.m. Who would be going for a vehicle at this time of night? The person dragging the "laundry" right past the library? Opening the door, I took a quick breath.

Chemicals assaulted my nose. Some sort of medicinal smell. Blood, though not a lot. Adrenaline, fear, and cloying roses. And then, underneath it all, cinnamon and jasmine and a faint hint of pine.

She was being taken.

20

A MATING GIFT

JOAQUIN

The Northern Lodge was quiet tonight, and I was vexed. The Sergeant at Arms had made an error that could have cost my fiery mate-to-be her life, and I had been hard pressed not to punish him for his idiocy. But when I went to his cabin, set apart from the other ranked Enforcers' lodging, he had been aware of my presence, though he hadn't seen me.

Something about him—a scent, or the angle of his jaw —reminded me of my perfect little female. He bore scars far more extensive than hers, of course, lines put there with magic that had me wondering how he'd survived them. Of course, if he was related to my mate, his inner strength would be a match for almost anything.

I'd kept my magic and my claws to myself. Not only because of the resemblance, but also because of his behavior. For some reason, he'd seemed concerned about the unranked shifters compound. He'd stood guard, sword in hand for hours that first night after Flor's injury, as alert as any shifter I'd ever seen. Waiting for something nefarious.

Aware that something was afoot. Each night, he returned to guard, scenting the air until dawn.

I felt it, too, and the knowledge that something, or someone, was approaching the Lodge while my Flor was tucked inside her room, sent me in ever-widening circles each night, seeking the unseen enemy.

When I finally circled close to the wing of the Lodge that housed the dying Alpha, I wondered if the enemy was death itself. Flor admired the Alpha shifter, Bradley Hillier. Personally, I had no use for him. He had inherited reprehensible traditions regarding the ranked wolves from his own father, and hadn't cared enough to change them. Though I understood in part how such things could escape a leader's notice, when far more insidious threats abounded.

But he had allowed his pack's wounds to fester, and his ranks to weaken. He himself would have stayed a weak Alpha, unworthy to lead the Council, if not for his mate, the charismatic Margarette.

I considered them both. I had a feeling he would have been dead weeks before, if she didn't tether him to this world. The silver he'd been dosed with had gone into his blood, his bones, and even his brain. I'd looked in on him once before, deep in the night. He lay in a coma, only slightly less horrifying than the agony he'd endured until they had given him the sedatives to help him sleep. I'd been able to taste the silver on the back of my tongue as it ate away at him from the inside out.

I didn't like him, but it was a horrific death. And Flor, she did like him. What to do? Put him out of his misery? It would be a kindness at this point.

I had left a courting present at Southern for my love, and hoped she would return to find it soon. But perhaps I could give her a mating gift as well, to celebrate the first of her lovers. I approved of the one she had claimed, even if I detested how the event had transpired.

The Mountain Heir was strong, taciturn, and humble. He worshiped her with his eyes, and cared for her in unobtrusive ways, not assuming he had earned the right to her bed just because he had saved her. His habit of sleeping outside her bedroom door kept her safe from the snakes inside the den. So yes, I approved of him.

Hmm. Brand had a fondness for the dying Alpha as well. *A worthy mating gift for them both.*

I would not kill the Alpha. I would save him, I decided, unlocking a window with my magic and slipping through a maid's room as I followed the stink of death and silver to the sickroom.

The Alpha's mate sat in a chair beside his sickbed, her arms draped over him, her eyes shut. She dreamed, whimpering, and her lids moved with what had to be a nightmare. The Alpha was hooked to machines that were breathing for him. Their sound and her exhaustion were the only reasons she hadn't noticed the door opening.

I noted the mate magic that flowed between them. She pulsed with hidden fire, even asleep, at his side. Funneling it into her mate.

These North American wolves were such foolish children to believe that magic could be forbidden, when we were beings made of it. I spun a filament of my own power into a pillow and slid it under her head.

She had not proved to be quite the maternal figure my little Flor had desired, though her motivations were sound. In a way, it was for the best. I had a very strong feeling the shifters of Boreal—of *Northern*, I reminded myself—would not welcome me into the pack, and if Flor had truly bonded with this woman, it would have made our eventual relationship more difficult.

I placed my hands on the sides of the Alpha's head, at his temples, and sent my energy through his body. Using my power to kill was far easier than to heal, and I'd taxed myself only days before, when Flor's blood had been spilling too quickly. Now, it was sluggish to respond. I pulled my focus away from everything but his healing, and began.

With each breath the machines forced into the Alpha's lungs, he took in a little more of my magic. When there was enough of my power inside him, I exhaled and sent a command through him, coaxing his own cells to hunt beside mine, our prey every infinitely small particle of silver in his body. We hunted them, and devoured them.

His blood began to flow more easily, his skin losing some of its gray pallor. With the silver dissipating, his own innate healing ability surged to the fore. His mind began to stir, fighting off the sedatives. He was aware of me beside him, but unable to move.

For Flor, do you understand? I whispered into his mind. *This is my gift to her. Protect her at all costs, Alpha of the Northern pack.*

The Alpha's machine was no longer breathing for him when I straightened and slipped out the door. His mate was awake by the time I reached the end of the hallway.

I stopped there, supporting myself with one hand on the wall, fighting exhaustion. The Alpha had been less than a day from his death, and I had underestimated how much it would take from me to pull him back.

I needed to rest. Perhaps with my little one? I could sneak into her room again, sing a few verses. No one would note my passing; it was the witching hour, my favorite time of any night. But the air in the hallway that led to my little one's room spoke of her absence.

And when I turned, the walls in the next hallway told a tale of her being attacked. Taken.

Silently, I cursed myself, understanding the cost of healing the Alpha. My attention had been focused on him, giving her enemies their opportunity. My mouth tasted of silver, and I spat a glob of tarry black to the carpet, then sucked in a sharp breath. There was a spot of blood on the carpet. Her blood.

I pulled on my power, and in seconds I knew who had taken her, and could guess at why. I also knew they would be dead soon—at my hand, if the moon was merciful. The only question that remained was where they had gone. Where was my Flor?

In the Lodge, voices cried out, in joy and then in fear. Feet pounded down corridors, and weapons were taken in hand as they realized they had been betrayed.

I felt neither joy nor fear. My entire being was consumed with rage as I tracked her, and her captors, over the dark landscape.

21

TRAITORS AND ENEMIES
FINNICK

"Flor!" I roared out her name, hoping she could hear me—or that my shout might rouse the rest of the Lodge. But I didn't stop to wake anyone. There was no time.

I was running down the hallway just as I heard the screech of tires on the drive. *Fuck.* Whoever had taken her had a car with a powerful engine, by the sound of it.

I didn't have keys to any of the Northern vehicles, and if I waited to get some, she would be gone. The night was windy and cold, and tracking a car would have to be done by sight since the wind would carry the exhaust for miles. So I'd have to run, which meant I'd need to move faster than I could on human feet.

I changed directions, racing for the front door, shifting as soon as I'd used my human hand to turn the knob. My clothing shredded around me, falling in tatters to the ground.

Behind me, the house was beginning to waken. A few lights shone from the compound behind the Lodge. I didn't turn, not even when my name was shouted. Instead, I howled, knowing the sound would travel. I hoped someone would follow in a vehicle.

I ran as fast as I ever had in my life, suddenly glad for all the recent patrols along the Northern pack's border that had restored some of the stamina I'd lost in my years as a virtual slave to my parents. Glad for the runs these past few weeks with Flor, which I'd complained so bitterly about, but secretly looked forward to since it meant I could run behind her and let myself look at her, take in the way she moved. Her confidence and inner strength, her inability to quit, even when she was tired.

I had to reach her. She'd been drugged, and taken, and even if I could never have her for myself...

My wolf snarled one word. *Mate.*

I shook away his rage and disgust. My wolf had been sulking and raging ever since that last day at Southern. Now, he was intent on reaching her, saving her, claiming her.

Though the cost for that would be higher than I was willing to pay. But I would remind him why we had allowed ourselves to be leashed for so long.

After we found her.

I ran for miles, catching sight of the car's brake lights as it crested a hill, then losing it again. I cut straight to where the next road would be, knowing if I ran faster than I ever had, I might catch them in the nearest town, where the roundabouts would slow them.

There was only one problem. The car was heading northwest, which meant that soon I would be beyond the Northern pack's territory lines. I couldn't howl to draw the Northern reinforcements to me, and announce to all who knew what that howl meant—that I was alone. Not unless I wanted to be attacked by rogues.

The rogues outside Southern had been a beaten-down group. Brand and Glen and I had come across them in our runs just outside the packlands. They had a white-haired female for a leader, and they were mostly starved, a ragtag band of ten or twelve. We hadn't even bothered to clean out their nest. They posed no danger, even though Callaway had acted as if they were one of his main concerns, and had claimed their presence was why he hadn't offered to host a Conclave since the war ended.

But the rogues outside Northern were a mix of disgraced wolves from more than one territory, Russian defectors from the last war, and criminals who had spurned their packs, or been driven out. Glen and I had found evidence of them over the past weeks on our patrols, but the traces had always been old, the scents stale. But still, they'd come far closer to the borders of the main compound than they should have. They'd been emboldened by something. Or someone.

An imminent rogue attack was the reason the Hilliers had been late arriving at the Conclave. Patrick and Glen had been concerned about how fast the group had been able to move to avoid being rounded up. They'd seemed more organized than usual, more skilled.

My mind spun. Was the rogue pack's presence connected to Flor's abduction? It could be a coincidence.

My father had always treated me as if I were a disappointment, but he'd taught me, nonetheless. His business acumen came from his wolf's strategic ability, and I'd inherited that. I was known as the tactician among my brothers and their Enforcers. I planned the missions, I could predict where they might fail, I planned ahead for success. Even my father had said I was adequate when it came to planning our pack Enforcers' battle exercises.

As I ran, I let my mind slip into the cold, calculating state I inhabited when planning battles. Who was the enemy here? Someone with access, one of the key cards. Someone whose scent would not alert any guards. I'd checked the hallway briefly, and there had been no unusual scents. The alarms hadn't been triggered in the Lodge, so it had to be a ranked member of the family, or a trusted servant.

My mind flew as I broke it all down, unfolding the mystery like an old paper map. How many perpetrators had been involved? The hallway was too small for more than one or two shifters dragging Flor. There was one accomplice, possibly.

What if the black wolf, the one who called himself Joaquin, and whose scent Glen and I had picked up once or twice nearby in the past days—what if he wasn't a friend to Flor, as we'd hoped? There was no record of a new Alpha in the Borderlands, and Joaquin had the skills to obscure his scent, even inside the Lodge, if he had been let in.

Of course, Brand had reported that the black wolf had some strange magic as well. Who knew what his motivations were, when it came to Flor? He'd shouted out that she was his mate, back at Southern. What if he had come to claim her?

What if he was a rogue?

Had one of the pack let him, a rogue, into the house to take Flor? It was almost impossible to believe.

What would entice a ranked Northern wolf, close enough to the inner circle of the Alpha to have free run of the Lodge, a key card to the doors, to treason? Northern shifters had plenty of money, so greed for material gain was not an issue. Greed for power was always a motivator.

But that possibility didn't resonate. What else could

have enticed someone to take Flor far from the borders of the Northern pack, to do who knows what with her?

The answer, when my wolf sent it to me as an image, was obvious.

Revenge.

Who would have a reason to hurt Flor, or to hurt the Northern pack? That sour-faced woman who was always mooning after Glen? She was too stupid, too weak to get the better of Flor in a fight.

But Vanessa wasn't. She was strong, self-centered, and spoiled. She was also understandably pissed about being forced to face Erik in a doomed ranking fight. She'd been acting strange, as well, taking more than one trip into the closest town over the past few weeks, since Flor arrived.

It was entirely possible that Vanessa had done this. I wanted to think there was no way a family member could betray their pack to outside enemies. Even my own reprehensible family was loyal, in their own sick ways.

But I remembered the day after we'd arrived. Vanessa losing her rank. Her affronted hurt and growing anger, blooming from her deep-seated sense of superiority. The way her friends had slid away, one by one, not wanting to be near their former social leader when she had nothing to offer them.

Vanessa might be planning to run away, of course. She might think she had nothing to lose.

She wouldn't be wrong. I wasn't certain if anyone else at Northern owned up to their skewed ranking system—I had a feeling Glen, with his wide-eyed, optimistic worldview, hadn't even realized what was going on. But the way they'd set up the ranking to promote only the physically stronger members of the pack, and the extremely lopsided pairings I'd heard about at the ranking fights four days ago, made one thing apparent.

If you were an unranked female at Northern? The only way you were getting ranked was by taking a mate. Even for a warrior like Flor.

Vanessa was proud, and the only one with a motive. But why would anyone have helped her betray her pack? I ran faster, my limbs aching, my thoughts racing ahead. I had to figure it out before I caught up with them.

Who was she working with?

I'd heard some Northerners grumbling that Glen was supposed to be Flor's true mate. They'd seen his slow-healing wound, they'd witnessed his possessive, protective actions, and everyone had noted the moments of intimacy between the two of them. They'd shared books and movies, spent time laughing together, sometimes at Margarette's obvious machinations to throw the two together.

These were all small things, but Vanessa may have seen Flor's bond with Brand as a betrayal.

Vanessa had at least a few allies, others she might have convinced that helping her was a way of showing loyalty to the pack. That they were getting rid of a female who had hurt their Heir. Or they might have seen Glen's obsession with Flor, and think that getting rid of her would mean less competition for the position of Alpha Mate once Bradley died.

I ran on, my wolf's strength keeping my feet moving at an incredible pace, ignoring the pain as my paws left a trail of blood across the rocks and asphalt. As I put myself in Vanessa's mind, a possible plan unfolded.

She would take Flor to a remote location to kill her before fleeing the packlands or the country entirely. My wolf howled inside at the mere thought of Flor's death.

Flor would have to be unconscious and possibly bound; Vanessa would have made certain of that, as we'd all seen Flor's exceptional fighting skills.

The traitorous bitch would act fast. As family of the Alpha, she had access to silver blades. She may have taken one. She would use it and dump Flor's body in moving water. The river was still a mile ahead. I had time.

Or did I?

The roar of the car's engine had stopped. I sped up, knowing Flor might have minutes to live, only slowing when I came to the crest of a hill. Then I crouched low, seeking my prey.

There was a vague scent of scorched rubber and exhaust not too far north of where I was. I slowed, prowling closer through mixed pines and aspens, the night wind blowing voices toward me. Voices, and scents.

I caught Vanessa, with her rose perfume. Then another one, a masculine ashy musk, and then Flor.

"You came after all," the ashy male crooned, his voice smooth.

"Of course I did. You said you had a place for me in your pack."

"But only one place. Who is this you brought with you?"

"A friend helped me get away from the Lodge. But she asked me to take out the trash on my way." Vanessa kicked at the too-still form at her feet.

"Trash, you say." The male let out a short whistle.

"What…" Vanessa went quiet as at least a dozen scents came swirling on the breeze.

As if an entire pack had dropped out of the trees.

I lifted my head slightly as they surrounded her, circling

her on silent feet. Watched as she realized she was at the center of what was unmistakably a hunt.

It was an entire, organized group of rogues, almost definitely the ones who'd been testing the borders of Northern for months now.

I heard a rustling above me. *Fuck.* I froze in place, remembering Flor back at Southern. How she'd used the trees to conceal her scent and her presence from her pack for years. The trees were exactly where they'd been hiding.

I slid against a trunk as a shifter not thirty feet ahead of me silently dropped on a thin rope from the canopy to the forest floor. He held a silver blade, and I felt queasy at the thought of shifters carrying those weapons.

In reputable packs, silver blades were only carried by the Alpha's family and used in ceremonial ways, or for executions. In my own pack, both my parents kept them on hand, but also armed their assassins and bodyguards with silver blades and even silver wire, though no one spoke of it. If these rogues had more than a few such blades, and I couldn't rescue Flor without drawing their attention, getting out of this alive would be trickier than I'd hoped.

My belly low to the ground, I followed the shifter closer to the meeting site. I recognized their uniforms and some of the decorations a few of them wore on their sleeves, tattered though they were. The Cyrillic letters on the caps two of them wore were obvious even at a distance, and their accents were too as I grew closer.

At least some of these were Russian rogues, the ones who had fled into the Canadian wilderness after failing in their attempt to take over Northern years ago. They had not been welcome to return to their own country, since their failure had brought dishonor to their pack, and fleeing with their tails between their legs meant death.

As I watched Vanessa stand with her chin up while the rogues surrounded her, my thoughts were scattered. I'd guessed she was at the heart of Flor's abduction. But seeing it was devastating in a way I hadn't expected.

Vanessa was a true traitor to her pack, and to all of the North American wolves. She hadn't colluded with one other shifter to kill a rival, or get revenge, but had made a deal with some of the very same wolves who'd killed her own mother years ago. Did she know who these shifters were?

I forced myself to focus, moving silently as I eavesdropped. By the time they had all assembled, there were fourteen shifters there, including Vanessa and Flor. I stifled a snarl as I smelled her blood in the air.

"The area is clear, sir," the shifter from the tree said.

Another one, a female, affirmed, "Clear in all directions, sir. They were not followed—not by car, in any case."

Flor was slumped on the ground in front of them, her head obscured by a black bag of some sort. I couldn't tell if she was breathing. I had to believe she was. If I let myself think otherwise, I would lose control of my wolf and attack.

I swallowed a whimper at the thought. No, I would *know* if she was gone; I would feel it. I had to stay calm, wait and watch, and gather intelligence.

Vanessa made an impatient sound, though her voice trembled. "Listen, I think there was a misunderstanding. I'll just go back. No one knows I'm gone, but they will if I hang around here much longer."

The night air filled with the metallic tinge of deceit. She knew there was no going home.

A small man stepped up, tilting his shaved head. "You are the traitor, then? You believe you can betray your own blood, and go running back to your home? Why would we want a traitor in our pack?" He had a pronounced Russian accent, and the moment he'd begun to speak, Vanessa had started looking around in a panic, searching for a way out.

Her head swung my way, though I knew she couldn't see me. Her face was a mask of horror. "What do you—wait, you're not... Are you Russians?"

A tiny part of me was glad that at least she hadn't known that.

"You may call me General," he replied. "You contacted one of my shifters weeks ago. You said you wanted a new pack, yes?" The dominance in his voice was apparent, even from a distance. "Who are you?"

Vanessa choked on her instant answer, but she was powerful enough to avoid giving her name. "I-I'm an unranked wolf. I'm no one important."

It was a stupid ploy. She was a bad liar to begin with, and her fear made it clear that she was trying to cover up who she really was.

"Unranked? Yet you had a key to the Northern Lodge?"

"I live in the Lodge. They trust me."

Some of the shifters standing around her grunted. Others laughed.

"Trusted, I see. And if we let you go back home—if this is a misunderstanding, as you said—are you certain you will still be able to return and slip in unnoticed?" The general's voice oozed insincerity. "We wouldn't want you to be punished."

"The one who helped me before will cover for me. They shouldn't even know I was gone."

The man sighed. "Such a pretty face on such an ugly wolf. What was the Moon Goddess thinking? Never mind, you'll make a decent hostage. Take her key, Mila," he said to the female rogue, who did exactly that, slapping Vanessa so hard when she tried to struggle that blood sprayed from her mouth.

The general ignored them, speaking to his other shifters. "Use the key, and place the explosives inside the Lodge if you can. In the Enforcers' barracks, if the house is too risky. Then get out. Wait until you are well away before you detonate. No one on my team dies tonight."

"E-explosives?" Vanessa mumbled. It sounded like some of her teeth had been broken with the slap. "That wasn't the deal."

The man just smiled, his silver-coated teeth glinting above and below gums that were swollen and bleeding. "Deals with traitors are worth less than nothing."

"Why are you *doing* this? Just let me go." Her gaze flickered around the group, looking for help. None was coming.

"You have our gratitude, Vanessa Parker, niece of Margarette Hillier and daughter of the late and infamous Enforcer Linn Parker. Thank you for betraying your pack. You have helped our cause immeasurably."

Vanessa whimpered, her wordless sounds reminding me of a dying rabbit, as a half-dozen rogues gathered their belongings and prepared to go. The shifters saluted the general, then raced off toward the road. A few seconds later, I heard an engine start up.

"General, do you think they'll encounter resistance? They may send Enforcers in this direction."

Suddenly, I felt the cold sting of silver cutting through my fur, into the side of my neck.

Shit.

A voice behind me growled, "They may have already sent one, General."

Of course, they'd left a guard in the trees. Father was right; I was a disappointment.

"Shift, now," the general ordered, Alpha command in his voice.

His dominance wasn't any greater than mine, but I knew I needed to obey him so he wouldn't know who I was, what I was capable of. I had to keep my secrets. Instead of changing form quickly as I usually did, I took a few extra minutes, prolonging the shift so I would seem less of a threat.

Vanessa let out a gasp as I stepped into the light. "Finnick," she cried, rushing toward me, but stopping when she saw my eyes. "You came for me?"

"You stupid *bitch,*" I cursed. Not only had she betrayed her pack, she'd just told our enemies who I was.

"Did she say Finnick?" The general crossed to me, staying out of range.

Smart. If he came the tiniest bit closer, I might be able to shift my teeth and claws quickly enough to tear his face off.

"I cannot believe my luck tonight! Finnick McDonnell, Alpha Heir of the Eastern pack. What are you doing here?"

"Do I know you?" I raked him with a glance. "I can't imagine we run in similar circles."

The man let out a high-pitched laugh. "No, indeed. But I know your excellent parents." I tasted bile. He hadn't said he'd known them in the past. He'd said he *knew* them.

Is he insinuating...

I didn't have time to wonder, as he circled me, still talking. "I have followed your career as a strategist for some time, though I must say I'm disappointed in you tonight."

I kept my gaze still. This shifter knew too much. He had called himself a general, which meant nothing. But if he was a general... There was only one true Russian general who may have escaped the war. At least, one whose body had never been found and burned, though there had been reports of his death.

"Who are you?"

The clouds above parted, and his silver teeth glinted in the approaching dawn. "The answer will cost you some information in exchange."

Trying not to look down at Flor's too-still form, I nodded, then ignored Vanessa's muffled sobs as one of the other shifters tied her up and stuffed a cloth gag in her mouth. They could cut her throat for all I cared. It would save me the trouble later.

The silver-toothed man pulled the bag off Flor's head, revealing her closed eyes, her slack features. When I saw her chest rise and fall, it was all I could not to show my relief. I made my face a mask of granite. "What do you want to know?"

"Who is this girl the traitor brought us? I have no idea who she is, and I have extensive lists of all the shifters in all the packs."

Well, that was fucking concerning. That meant he absolutely had connections inside the North American Council. *Shit.* Did he mean my parents?

He used the toe of his boot to turn Flor slightly so I could see her face more clearly. She'd been hurt; dried blood trickled from the corner of her mouth. I glanced at her eyelids. They were shut tight. Too tight, perhaps. Was she really sleeping?

I didn't think so. She seemed unconscious, but this was the girl who'd avoided the Hunt for years. She knew how to be still, stay quiet, and find the right moment to escape. I had to give her some distraction, keep their eyes off her while she worked herself free of the cord around her wrists. If she was awake.

And if she wasn't, I needed to give them some reason to keep her alive. Some reason that didn't give this criminal leverage over one of the Alpha Heir's packs. I couldn't tell them she was Brand's mate, or mine, or Luke's, or Glen's.

Not that he would believe that she could be all of ours. I barely believed it myself.

So I told another truth. "She is the only child of the deposed Southern Alpha, Calvin Callaway."

22

NOT TODAY, SATAN
FLOR

My heart almost stopped beating when I heard Finnick's voice, revealing my deepest secret to the enemy. "She is the only child of the deposed Southern Alpha, Calvin Callaway." Hearing my connection stated out loud made me want to vomit.

I had no idea how Finnick had known, no idea how anyone might. Callaway would never have told anyone, and Del had died before Finnick came to Southern.

Did all the Heirs know? Did Luke?

Fuck. I didn't have time to think about this. I had to listen and keep playing possum, which meant keeping my heart rate steady and slow, my breathing shallow. Even if I wanted to jump up and murder Finnick.

I'd come to when Vanessa had called out, but kept still, listening as other shifters had gathered around. I'd known from the rustling sounds that there were at least a half-dozen shifters around me, and my wolf had roused enough to help me sort out a few more scents. Luckily for me, I'd been able to remain silent and still and gather as much information as I could. So before Finnick stuck his nose in, I'd already been well aware that I was screwed ten ways to Sunday.

And then he'd screwed me once more. But not in the way I'd wanted in my weak moments. Not now that I knew he wasn't just a chickenshit, he was a traitor, too.

It was all I could do not to react, not to jump up and punch him in the ballsack. I was going to end his shit once and for all after this. Selling me out to a bunch of rogues? As soon as I got my hands untied, I would prioritize his punishment. Ghost pepper juice in his eyes. Poison ivy in his butt crack. I'd duct tape him to a chair and make him watch reality TV for a solid week.

I allowed my thoughts to run free but held my body utterly immobile as he spoke to the "general," letting only the tips of my fingers and my thumbs work beneath me. When the man had so obligingly rolled me over to show Finnick, meaning my tied hands were hidden behind my back at last, I'd fought a smile. Thank goodness that incompetent traitor bitch Vanessa had tied me. She'd apparently slept through not only pack law and the code of honor lessons, but also knot tying.

In seconds, my hands were freed, though I kept the ends of the rope tucked into my palms, loops still around my wrists. It was paracord, nice and strong, and would serve as a weapon when the moment came.

Weapons. It was time to make a mental list. My most important one was... My wolf cackled inside me. These stupid fucks hadn't tied my feet. I had two weapons now—the cord and my ability to run.

Then another thought occurred to me. Maybe I could shift my claws.

I asked my wolf, and for once, she answered. Slowly,

achingly, I felt my fingernails change, and my claws emerge, a centimeter at a time. There was a little blood when they came through, but I was already pretty scratched up, so I didn't think they'd smell it. And Vanessa's blood was in the air as well.

If only there was time to spill more of it.

I tuned back into the conversation, and almost choked. Finnick was spinning some crazy story about how the Southern Alpha and I were estranged—*yeah, that's the word for it*—but he would want to see me again. Be *desperate* to see me. Finnick was clever with his truths.

My old Alpha probably *would* love to see me... dead.

The story Finnick told made me sound valuable, too important to kill. Possibly ransom worthy. But he was so full of it, I wondered what his game was. Why was he making all this up? Why was he painting me to be a hidden princess, or some shit?

"Fine," the general said at last. "You have answered my question."

"Now you'll answer mine?" Finnick demanded. He was using his ultra-snooty voice, the one that made me want to belch out loud and scratch my armpits, just to annoy him.

There was a weird, metallic clicking sound from the vicinity of the general's mouth. "Amusing. No, dearest Alpha Heir. You are a tool now. I owe you no answers." He hummed. "If you prove useful to me, I may not kill you."

I wasn't certain why it made my heart warm to hear the quasi-death threat, to know that Finnick wasn't friends with these assholes. I was relieved that he wasn't a traitor. Maybe I would only put pepper juice in one of his eyes.

Finnick cursed. "Who are you, then? Besides a dishonorable pretender?"

"Pretender?" A low growl rattled the air. "You're the one

who must pretend to have power he clearly doesn't possess. Just like your father, desperate and grasping, believing you have something I could want or need."

Finnick spat something in a language I didn't know, but assumed was Russian.

The general answered calmly. "*Menya zavut Ivan. Alpha Ivan.*"

I didn't need to know what the other words meant. I knew the name.

My heart sank. Del had shared shifter gossip while we worked in the kitchens. More than once, he'd muttered about the Russian ex-Enforcer Ivan, who'd fled after the final battle against Northern. He had deserted, but rumor said he had since been forming some sort of rogue army, where they espoused everything that was the antithesis of pack law. Del had said they were out west near California, though, not up here.

And no matter how often I'd asked about the area past the Borderlands, Del had never said a word about that place. I'd assumed it was populated by rogues. But if the rogue army was in Canada, who knew what was out west? Sandworms like in that movie, *Dune*, maybe.

Finnick and the general were jabbering away, but from the tightness in Finnick's tone, he knew as well as I did that we were screwed. I cracked my eyes open to find him staring right at me, even though he was spitting more Russian words at Ivan. He began pacing, drawing the gaze of the rogues away from me. Helping me.

Fuck. There were a half-dozen of them, from what I could tell. All lean, hardened shifters. All armed with military tactical knives. I didn't want to have to fight them, and knew I couldn't, not all at once. They'd be a real bitch to outrun as well, but maybe not impossible. My bare feet were still calloused, though not nearly as much as they had been back at Southern.

When Finnick was far enough away, he rubbed a hand over his mouth, and when he dropped it to his side, he soundlessly mouthed the word *go* in my direction, not meeting my gaze. Instead, he turned his head to a dark group of trees downwind.

I widened my eyes, thinking the question, though I knew he couldn't hear: *What about you?* He shook his head a fraction as he jabbered on in Russian, his jaw tightening.

He wanted me to run away without him? I mentally rolled my eyes. *Mother Moon, save me from martyrs and idiots.* Even if I could leave him here, I was in the middle of an enemy pack. It was all about timing.

While I waited for my moment, Vanessa started yelling again. Someone knocked her out with a blow to the head that might have cracked her skull, and it took a lot not to mutter a thank you.

I slammed my eyes shut again as the group's leader spat out curt orders, and I was lifted onto a shifter's shoulder. I had to keep playing dead for a little bit, until we were moving and the group naturally drifted farther apart. I needed to buy us time, slow us down.

I felt a short, sharp tugging at the bite mark at the top of my shoulder. I shouldn't have been surprised. Brand had to be missing me by now, right? If Finnick knew I'd been taken, others would know, too. Brand would come, or even Glen, if he'd sobered up.

Why hadn't someone arrived already? I worried for a moment. Had anyone else been hurt or drugged when I was taken? Or killed?

Had *Brand* been hurt? No, I would have felt it in the bond. I focused on that connection now, and my mind hazed with a red rage.

Okay, Brand definitely knew I'd been taken. My breath stuttered, as I felt him reach back to me in the bond, all sorts of wild emotions zinging through me. I shut it down, knowing I needed to concentrate.

"Bring her up here to me," Ivan called back from twenty feet ahead. "She's awake."

Showtime.

I let my eyes fly open and did a flip, twisting free of the shifter who had me over his shoulder. On the way down, I stabbed him with my claws in the kidney as hard as I could, then twisted around and sliced his hamstring on one leg. I made a lunge for his knife, but it was out of reach.

I spun away, taking in the scene in an instant. The gloomy pre-dawn light showed me all I needed. Two shifters were about fifty feet ahead of us, and three or four were behind us, all in human form, and all dressed, so they wouldn't be shifting too quickly.

Finnick and I were in the middle of the group, of course. I couldn't find an obvious escape route. Then I heard a distant howl, filled with rage, power, and a promise.

Help was on the way.

"Mila, take the niece," Ivan ordered, sniffing the air. "We're compromised."

"What about the others, General?"

"I'll take care of them." He pulled something out of his pocket. A gun? A knife? No, a dark stick. It looked like some sort of wand.

It was fucking *magic*. I threw myself to the side just as he pointed it at me, and some sort of red light flared. It missed me, mostly. The left side of my calf went slightly numb, my leg a little slow to respond as I tried to regain my feet.

Finnick leaped after Ivan, but the wand's blast caught him in the chest, and he dropped mid-leap, like a giant hand had smashed him to the ground.

My heart skipped a beat. Was Finnick dead? Everything in me was screaming for me to run, but I couldn't leave him here. I knelt beside him, feeling a thready pulse.

"You're very good." Ivan paced over to me. "I may keep you."

I sneered, unimpressed. "I get that a lot."

I took up a fighting stance, although I had a feeling my moves wouldn't work against his magic fucking wand. Why the hell hadn't Del taught me how to combat magic?

"You can fight!" Ivan grinned, like he'd found out we shared a birthday. I tried not to react as I realized what the metallic sound had been.

His teeth. His damned teeth were silver, though they weren't doing his gums any favors. The silver smell alone would make a normal shifter feel sick. The sight of his rotting, bleeding gums around them... I shuddered.

"Oh, we have a few minutes. Let's play, little wolf." He dropped the wand into his pocket, and I backed up, not sure what this guy was doing. He seemed like a great tactician and a pretty effective leader, if a little bad-guy-monologue-y now and then. But stopping an evacuation to play with a captive?

"It's your funeral."

"Wouldn't be my first one," he murmured, swiping at me with his claws. I felt one slide over my arm before I could dart away, felt rivulets of fire as my skin parted beneath the thick, sharp points.

Holy shit, that hurt. I didn't cry out or react, just took a new stance and raised my own claws.

"Strong, little wolf. I'm impressed."

I didn't want him to like anything about me. Sticking out my tongue, I blew a raspberry to distract him.

He blinked. "What?"

I used the split second of confusion to whirl under his guard and punch the side of one knee, twisting to avoid his hands. His arms caught me, though, and before I could slip free, he was lifting me to his mouth, to those silver teeth.

Shit! He was going to tear my throat out.

I begged my wolf to come out a little more, and felt my own teeth change. I sank into the circle of his arms, wrapping my hands around his biceps, then vaulted up and through his loosened hold, squirming around to the top of his shoulders like a squirrel.

He let out a coughing laugh. "You're not a wolf. You're a little monkey."

Yeah, actual warriors never saw that one coming. They also never saw the next one. *Time to use my most effective weapon.* I vaulted off his back and ran like a rabbit on speed, ignoring the shocked yells behind me.

What this general asshole didn't know was that I'd been hunted hard for years, and I'd learned how to be very good, extremely elusive prey. How to climb, and hide, and become nearly invisible. How to obscure my scent, even traces of blood. I didn't have time to use all my years of honed skills, but I'd surprised these asshole rogues enough that I got a decent head start.

Behind me, the woods filled with howls as their instinct to chase took over. *Good.* I needed to keep them busy until backup arrived, and keep this Voldemort-wannabe shifter away from Finnick.

And keep my ass as far from these toadfuckers as possible. Silver-toothed Ivan had been clear he was going to do something nefarious with me. I shuddered, recalling what he'd said about keeping me.

Not today, Satan.

23

TWO MATES IN A TRAP
GLEN

I'd thought the worst day of my life was the one where both my parents had almost died. I'd been wrong. This was the worst, and it felt as if it might turn out to be the longest.

"Tell me exactly what happened," Mom snapped, taking a corner in her Lotus, the one Dad had given her for their twenty-fifth mating anniversary.

"Turn here," I shouted, my eyes on the tracking app on her phone. The air filled with the scent of burned rubber, and I careened into the side of the door. Mom drove like she'd learned on a Formula One racetrack, but I didn't care if she rolled the damn car as long as she got me to Flor.

Brand had woken me up from my drunken sleep, shouting that Finn was chasing Flor. I described the scene to Mom as she drove through the pre-dawn gloom of the forest.

Screams roused me from a dream of running in my wolf form alongside Flor and my brothers. We were on our way to Southern, to save Luke.

Then Brand's voice from outside had me on my feet. "They

took her!" I tumbled from my bed and was in the hallway just as he came racing past, wearing sweats and nothing else.

He yelled again, when he saw me. His breath heaved in and out of his lungs, those massive shoulders moving like he was barely suppressing his shift, his expression feral. "Glen, they took my mate. I fucking listened to her, and they took her."

"Took Flor?" I was suddenly stone-cold sober, grabbing his arm. I had to know who the enemy was. "Who would dare?"

"Traitors." He wrenched away, heading for the front door.

I sniffed the hallway, and my heart felt like a metal trap had closed around it. It reeked of chemicals and faint traces of blood. Flor's blood. The rest of the scents were jumbled together, just shifters who used this hallway often.

I ran to catch up with Brand. "Finn?"

"He woke me, calling out. He's not here; I heard his howls, moving away. He's tracking them." Brand grunted as he threw open the front door, scenting the air. "They took a car."

I felt the bands of pain around my heart loosen slightly. Finn may have acted like he wasn't as attracted to Flor as the rest of us, but I'd seen him watching her. Stalking her from the shadows.

A cry went up in the wing my father was in now, and I wondered if this night was about to get worse. But I didn't feel the dissolution of the Alpha bond, so Dad was still alive, at least. And he had Mom. Flor had no one.

Brand obviously had no time for whatever was happening there. He had shifted abruptly, leaving the torn fabric of his sweatpants on the floor.

His wolf was enraged and frantic, and I thought he might attack when I told him to wait. I thrust my phone into his enormous jaws. "Hold onto this. Finn might not be able to keep up, but you can find her through the mate bond. I'll track you this *way, and bring reinforcements. We'll get her back," I vowed. Brand snarled and raced away, the phone in his jaws.*

I almost ran into Mom on her way out of Dad's room. She was pulling on her fighting clothes, strapping her leather belt around her waist. The doctor was inside, and Dad was sitting up, more than alive. He was awake.

But there was no time to celebrate.

"Glen, what's happened? I heard Brand."

"Flor's gone. Taken."

Mom's eyes went wide, then narrowed. "What direction?"

"Brand's got my phone. We can follow the GPS," I told her as we raced toward the garage. "He's tracking her along their bond." I described the general direction he'd gone.

"He'll go straight to her, run straight into them. He'll be slaughtered," she murmured. I felt myself begin to change, needing to go to her, to Brand, to be there to protect them.

She'd said slaughtered. *"More than one? Is it rogues?" I managed to ask with a mouth full of sharp teeth. "The rogue pack?"*

Mom snarled. "Worse."

"Who?" I demanded, but Mom was barking out orders into her phone, calling Sergeant and then Patrick, putting the entire packlands on high alert as we raced for the car.

I'd been half-shifted, unable to drive and barely able to control my wolf's rage, so I hadn't argued when Mom slid into the driver's seat. It had been a solid half hour since we left the Lodge, and every mile we drove took us farther away from the packlands, deeper into rogue territory.

She hadn't answered my question when I'd asked it the first time, so I repeated it now. "Who? What could be worse than rogues working together, pulling this kind of thing off?"

"Magic. Your father's room reeked of it when I woke," Mom said quietly.

"Magic?" A shiver ran up my spine.

"Yes. I haven't smelled anything like it since the war. It filled the room. I think it kept me asleep while Flor was taken. Your father was trying to pull out his breathing tube when I woke. He's healed, almost entirely."

My heart leaped. "Dad's going to live? How?" The doctors had given up. *Mom* had all but given up.

"He is. I dreamed... I *thought* I dreamed that he was healed by the Alpha from the Borderlands. But it wasn't a dream."

Joaquin? "The black wolf? He took her?" He'd been sneaking around the borders of Northern, and we'd caught scent of him once or twice inside the packlands.

Had he been planning for this? Hunting her for weeks?

"It's the most likely explanation," Mom said. "He did claim her at Southern. He believes she's his mate."

The car went quiet, save for the engine's roar. Was it possible that Luke, Brand, and Joaquin were *all* her mates? And me as well? Could one young shifter truly have multiple mates? I shook away the thought, even though it came with an insidious thread of hope.

"The hallway smelled of blood and chemicals. It wasn't just magic, Mom. Someone turned off the alarms."

Mom's phone lit up in my hand. I accepted the call, and Mom spoke. "Sergeant?"

"Head Enforcer, we've secured the main Lodge. Everyone is safe and accounted for, except... your niece is missing."

"Vanessa?" Margarette gasped. "Taken?"

"No. A servant says she saw her dressed in black, waiting in a hallway near your son's room. Vanessa ordered the girl to return to her rooms, threatened her." Sergeant's voice dropped. "Vanessa's involved, Margarette. We believe she took the chloroform from the pack medical supplies as well."

Mom's jaw went hard. "She will be punished accordingly." She shared our location with Sergeant, who swore when he realized where we were.

His voice bristled with rage. "Working with rogues? How could she dishonor her mother like this?"

"I don't know," Mom answered at last. "But be watchful for anything suspicious. From outside the packlands, or within." Sergeant agreed and hung up.

I breathed deeply, trying to keep my wolf from emerging, and watched Brand's locator dot moving more slowly. "You think it's a conspiracy? That Vanessa, maybe others, are working with the rogues to take Flor? To weaken us somehow?"

"It would weaken us, to lose Flor," Mom said quietly. "She's your true mate, after all."

I closed my eyes, overcome by emotion. Somehow, hearing it out loud made it more real. Made it inescapably true. "She is."

Mom spoke again after a long moment. "There may be some conspiracy at work. There have been rumors about the rogue activity. They installed cameras in some of the trees on our hunting grounds."

I blinked. "That takes money. A lot of money." The type of cameras that didn't give off any hint of sound, even a tiny electronic whine, were prohibitively expensive.

"It does. And they've shown excellent strategy, with well-coordinated, small attacks."

"Testing us? Or preparing for something?"

"I don't know. It doesn't add up. I don't know that

Vanessa's clever enough to have accomplished this on her own. With your father sick until tonight, there was unrest in the pack. It seems convenient that Vanessa chose this moment to do... well, whatever she's doing."

"Betraying the pack," I supplied.

She nodded. "The rogue presence at our western border doubled while we were at the Conclave. Sergeant informed me last night that they've been seen taking to the trees, apparently. We can't get good numbers, but he believes there are a lot more than we'd first suspected. Vanessa must have known, must have been in contact with them, since she headed straight toward them."

It seemed unthinkable. Then I thought about how Vanessa had looked when Mom stripped her of her rank. How Clara had mentioned something about Flor's "betrayal" of me.

"Mom, watch Clara as well." Her jaw clenched tighter. "She was pissed about Flor mating with Brand. Said she *betrayed* me."

"She did no such thing. We betrayed that girl." Mom's voice broke. "I did."

"And we'll save her now." I laid my hand over one of hers. "But you need to know, I'm not giving up. Even if I can never be with her in the way I want, even if it means abjuring Northern and leaving the packlands, I can't be without her."

"We won't have an Heir," Mom whispered.

"Patrick is more than worthy. And if Dad is truly healed, he'll have time to prepare."

"What if she doesn't..." She went silent, unable to speak the worst possibility aloud.

I was trembling now, my nails shifting into claws at the need to be with her. To save her. "She'll make it, Mom. If she doesn't… I'm not sure any of the packs will have Heirs."

Mom sucked in a breath, like she wanted to say something else, but then changed the subject. "Flor's the best fighter I've seen in decades, since my sister. She'll survive. I have a feeling that when we find her, she'll be the last one standing."

I agreed. "Finn's with her. Brand's on his way. All she has to do is make it until help arrives." I glanced in the rearview mirror. We'd left all the others far behind.

The cell phone pinged, and I peeked at the incoming message. One of the pack's drones had picked up movement in the woods a few miles west of the Lodge. Two vehicles, and at least a half-dozen occupants. I called it in, wondering just how deep Vanessa's betrayal ran.

"Sergeant?" I shared my suspicions with him.

"We're on it," he snapped out, then hung up.

When I glanced back at the phone, we were practically on top of Brand's GPS locator dot, though it was just a little behind us. *There.* An overgrown track veered into the woods.

"Mom, he's close," I urged. "Turn back. There's a gravel trail on the right." Mom did a quick U-turn and tore down the road, fishtailing wildly as we reached the gravel.

In minutes, we spotted the phone on the ground, next to an abandoned pack car. I jumped out of the Lotus before it even stopped, scenting the air, listening for any noise. After a long, breathless moment, I heard a soft, distant whine and ran into the woods, keeping an eye on the trees.

After a minute of running, I smelled wolves. Traces of Flor, Vanessa, and at least a dozen more, and… *Oh shit.* It was Finn.

And Brand.

Both of them were injured, though I couldn't tell how severely. Finn lay on his side in human form in the shadow of a grouping of pines, and Brand as his wolf nearby. Some strange web of deep red light was wrapped around both of them. Neither one was breathing, though they were both alive. Was the magic crushing their lungs? I wasn't sure.

But it was hurting them. Bloody pinpricks oozed wherever the web touched Finn's bare skin, and Brand's fur was scorched where it met his pelt.

"Mom!" I yelled, unsure what to do. Magic had been outlawed so long ago, and no one used it. No honorable wolves did, anyway. I had no idea what to do.

Mom came running, but stopped with a short curse. "Don't touch it," she warned. "It's a trap."

Obviously. "Can you get them out?"

"Maybe. I'll need a silver blade and... Wait." She leaned down, picking up a familiar knife from the ground. Our family's crest decorated the hilt, two wolves racing around a full moon. It was Vanessa's, but had belonged to her mother. I turned away as Mom's eyes welled up. My own had to be filled with shock.

That Vanessa would use her mother's ceremonial blade to betray her own pack... I felt ill. I couldn't imagine how Mom was feeling.

Mom cleared her throat as she kneeled beside my trapped friends, then took off her wide leather belt and wrapped it around one hand. "Go. I can cut the bindings."

"You know how?" I shouldn't have been shocked; Mom had been young during the war, when the Russians and the rogues had attacked with magic, but she'd fought in more than one battle.

She nodded grimly. "I'll guard them while they recover. You need to go find Flor. Whoever did this has a lot of power and influence. You can't buy a spell like this with cash. You have to promise something to the witch."

"You really think Joaquin...?"

She didn't answer, and my gut churned with fear.

The tracks I saw were human. I'd be faster on four feet, so I shifted and ran. A few dozen yards away, the tracks changed as the shifters who had passed this way took on wolf form. I spied a small footprint that I knew. One that smelled of cinnamon.

Flor, barefoot.

Then her footprints vanished. I nosed around, using all the tracking skills I'd learned in Alpha training, and during my years fostering at Mountain. But all I could find were vague hints of her scent.

A dozen yards away, I found pieces of her clothing. That explained why her scent was so scattered—she'd stripped, maybe shifted.

Half a mile later, I came across a stretch of disturbed ground bearing some half-prints that smelled vaguely of her. At least two wolves' tracks followed her there. But then nothing.

How could she just vanish?

I thought about the Hunt, how she'd been able to hide from a whole pack of dishonorable wolves for years. She probably had more woodcraft than any other wolf I knew. She knew how to move through a forest quickly. The forests at Southern weren't anywhere near as dense as this one, but that would be to her advantage.

I noticed a tree that had new punctures and was weeping a little sap. *Right.* She'd shifted her claws and climbed up into the canopy.

I followed what I imagined would be a pathway through the forest if she'd followed the densest branches.

Some of the leaps looked impossible, but there were no tracks on the ground. It had to be the way.

Finally, I smelled water. The lake. In the far distance, I heard a loud splash. It could be a deer jumping in, or an elk.

But I had a feeling it was Flor.

The wind shifted, and I caught a hint of jasmine, followed by the dark iron tang of blood. A lot of blood. Letting out a howl, I raced faster than I had ever run to the water.

To Flor.

24

FOCUS ON NOT DYING

FLOR

I'd been called a freak plenty of times. Running for my life through the forest, my heart lifting, I knew it was true. I felt at home for the first time in weeks.

The Hunt had defined my existence for so long that I'd kind of missed it, in some awful way. At least, when I was being hunted, I knew who my friends were. I knew who I could count on. No one, except Del.

When I'd known everyone else was my enemy, I'd been careful not to trust another soul. That was why I never would've been surprised in a hallway at night back home. It was only once I'd let my guard down, once I'd thought the people around me were safe, on my side, that I was caught. Once I'd let myself get lulled by the promise—the *hope*—of safety.

I'd never make that mistake again. If I lived to make another mistake, that was.

I tried not to give despair any room in my thoughts, as I focused on moving from tree to rock and back to tree again. I might not have Del, or any real knowledge of this area, but I had claws now, so I could catch myself when I started to fall from smaller branches, dig in and climb higher than I'd ever been able to at Southern. Once I got high enough, I could look for an escape route, rest, and plan.

Water could save me. I was a decent swimmer, and could hold my breath. I'd had to do just that for almost three minutes once, when the Hunt had caught up with me at the narrow river that crossed our hunting grounds at Southern.

I was close to a lake now; I could smell it. I'd have to climb down to swim for safety—toward the Lodge, maybe.

Or maybe not. They'd expect that, all of them. Ivan and the Northern traitors, too, because I was certain there had been someone else there when Vanessa knocked me out.

No, I couldn't go back to the Lodge alone. Who knew what was waiting for me there?

I'd swim in the other direction, keep going once I hit land, toward Colorado. Maybe someday, I'd run into Brand again. When we were older, and the rest of the world had forgotten about us.

What was I thinking? He was an Alpha Heir. He would never be forgotten. But I could be; I could vanish for good. Brand had said he would be fine, that we would be fine, even if we separated.

My wolf snarled inside. She did not agree.

Nearby, a branch cracked.

Snakeshit. Del had always said I let myself lose focus too often. And that's just what I'd done.

The silver-toothed asshole Ivan stood at the base of the most recent pine I had climbed, naked, wand in hand. Where had he hidden the wand when he shifted? I sort of wanted to ask, since there were really only so many possibilities.

No, Flor. Focus on not dying.

"Excellent effort, girl. Now come down. It's time to go." He'd infused Alpha dominance into his voice, but he wasn't nearly powerful enough to force me to obey.

I peered through the pine needles for any other rogues, but he was alone. My bad luck, to be caught by the head honcho. His voice as he repeated his command carried over the wind in the trees and the shifters in the distance, who were yipping every once in a while as they hunted me. Wolves were better at tracking than humans, so it was smart to stay in that form.

They really were smart. They'd underestimated me once, but I didn't dare to hope they would do that again. The general let out a howl when I didn't obey him immediately, calling them to us.

I couldn't think of a way out of this. If I stayed in this tree like a raccoon, they'd climb up and haul me down, or just shoot me, with guns or with magic.

What would Del have said? I could almost hear his voice in my head, though I was certain he'd never said these exact words. *Other than that too-clever brain of yours, you've got three main weapons, girlie: your feet, your fists, and your foul mouth.*

Plan A was run. Plan B was fight.

Time for Plan C.

"Why do you even want me, ya ratfucker?" I yelled a lot louder than I needed to.

"There are so many reasons, girl. For one, you're the Southern Heir. Or, Heiress."

"They don't let girls be Heirs, toadface. I'm nothing."

"I know better. But you're also the true mate of the Northern Alpha Heir," he said, his voice smooth, calm. "Of course I'd want you. You're the perfect vehicle for my revenge."

"My mate is Brand," I shouted. "The Mountain Heir."

He stopped circling the tree. Clearly, I'd shocked him. "That was the truth. How? More than one mate bond?" His wide smile glinted. "Very nice to know, but your true mate must be Glen Hillier. We heard about your little knife mishap."

Wait, how did he know about that? *Fucking Vanessa.* I was gonna tit punch her the next time I got close enough. I started climbing higher, looking for an escape route. But the other trees weren't quite close enough, and I was running out of branches on this one.

"And now I'll mate you, too. Or at least, I'll fuck you, before I deliver you to my colleagues."

I was breathless for a moment. What was it with males always wanting to rape me? I didn't have time to ask, as the villain was still monologuing, but this time he was doing it with a stiffy.

"And the beautiful thing is that I'll make you ask for it. *Beg* for me. Can you imagine Glen Hillier's rage at knowing you gave yourself not only to his best friend, but also his worst enemy? It's like a Shakespearean tragedy." He paused, tilting his head. "Of course, I'd love to have Margarette under my blade as well. Maybe in Act Three."

"Ew! Keep it in your pants, Gramps," I yelled as loud as I could. "I'm pretty sure your *blade* is rusty with age." I let myself cackle, even though I didn't think it had been that funny. But Plan C was all I had left. Time for some major trash talk, and a quick peek at his naked form gave me plenty of ammunition.

"Also, I can promise I've had a lot better than your little 'magic wand.' You know, I've heard of you. Yeah, they call you Ivan the Tiny at Southern. You have a tiny rogue pack, a tiny bit of power, and a teeny-tiny Vienna sausage pe—" I ducked as he shot a bolt of magic at the branches around me.

Apparently, this rogue Alpha was a typical male after all. Teasing him about his dick clearly annoyed him.

"Yeah, they said your tiny wand didn't pack much punch. Kinda fizzling out there, huh?"

He kept shooting. "I'll tear you from this tree and show you how to submit to your betters!" I ducked and dodged the reddish globs of magical fire that arced through the air and landed on the pine needles at his feet. "You *will* respect me."

With his wand still clenched in one hand, he used the other to begin climbing.

Shit. Maybe the other trees were close enough after all.

"Respect is earned, Tiny Ivan," I called, flinging myself across the air and using my claws to catch onto the thick trunk of another pine. I wanted to celebrate setting a new shifter record for the jump, but just took a second to catch my breath before I went back to pissing off the magician. "Can a rogue pretender Alpha even *get* respect from other rogues? I mean, they know you're like the Emperor with no clothes. Although I wish you did have some clothes on, because it's super hard not to laugh right now. Maybe it's just the cold up here in Canada? For your sake, I hope so."

He shouted in Russian, dropping down and following me along the ground. As I caught a clear glimpse of it through the pine needles, I saw that he held the wand somewhat awkwardly. Like it was a borrowed weapon, not one he was completely comfortable with.

Probably why I'm still alive, I thought, scurrying around to the other side of the trunk like a squirrel as he shot another burst of red magic at me.

A blob of red, glowing whatever-the-fuck hit my left

side again. I screamed, losing my grip with that hand. I swung drunkenly, my toes finding a thin branch to hold a little of my weight as I clung to the trunk with my right-hand claws.

Pain blurring my vision, I took in the gathered wolves at the base of the pine. There were more than six down there now. I couldn't fight off that many with one arm and no other weapons, not when they had magic on their side.

I was shit out of luck. But I wasn't out of shit. Shit *talk*, that was.

I'd probably been born with a foul mouth. It would stay that way to the end, I decided, as I kicked with my one good leg at the trunk, somehow catching a pinecone in between my toes. "Stick this in your ass, you Russian warlord-wannabe!" I used my toes to fling the pinecone in his general direction. It didn't hit the general, though I'd nailed someone, judging by the yelp.

But there were no more pinecones. No more weapons at all.

Hmm. My mind darted like a crazed hummingbird from thought to thought. *Del said never to give up. That there's always a weapon, even if you can't do more than blink. That time itself could be a—*

"Aoooooooo!"

"Well, butter my butt and call me a biscuit," I whispered. I'd stalled long enough for help to arrive.

"Aooooooo!" It was closer now.

The howl was familiar, kind of. I couldn't remember where I'd heard it before. I didn't think it was Brand. Glen, maybe? Or Finnick?

I threw my head back and howled a reply, then ducked another blob of magic. The next one hit my right leg, and I found myself dangling by one hand from the tree. I tried to jam the claws of my numb hand in the bark. At least if I was immobilized while I was stuck up in the tree, they'd have to climb up to get me. It might give Brand—or whoever was howling—more time to find me. I both hoped it was Brand, and wished for him to stay far away from this magical fucker. I didn't want my Bearman hurt.

I had just decided to fling a few more insults at Ivan, when something crashed into the wolves clustered near the base of my tree. Like a wrecking ball made of darkness and teeth, it bowled through them, leaving torn flesh and howling madness behind. In a blink, it came back again, moving too fast for my eyes to track.

What was it? Shifters *couldn't* move that fast.

I couldn't move; all I could do was try to watch, and wonder. I'd thought vampires were a myth—everyone did—although Southern kids thought it was hilarious to play shifters and vampires. But this attacker was doing the sorts of things a vampire might.

Then a real wolf appeared, tearing into the crowd as well. A gray one that I knew.

Glen! I stopped myself from shouting his name; I knew better than to distract a wolf in battle. There was still a sizable group of rogues standing, and they'd circled into a defensive position, the wizard wolf in the center.

Glen feinted in and out, harrying the rogues, as the general attempted to hit him with magic fire. But the blobs coming from the wand were smaller now and not as bright. Was his magic wearing out? Running out? I hoped so.

Maybe I could distract him, make him use up his juice on me, and give Glen and the vampire-wolf thing a chance to take down a few more of the regulars.

"Hey, baldy," I called. "I wanted to ask you about your pack dentist. Is he the same guy who did your nails?

Because I think you could get a better manicure at a human strip mall."

Ivan glanced up at me like I'd lost my mind, but then I pretended to start down the tree, and he shot another ball of magical fire my way. And hit me.

Ouch. I didn't have much game left, physically or mentally at this point.

But my stupid taunt had been effective enough. Ivan had turned his attention on me, which meant he'd stopped watching Glen and what I could see now was the other wolf. It wasn't a vampire. It was a small, nondescript-looking black wolf, with glowing red eyes.

Okay, that part wasn't nondescript. The eyes were creepy as fuck.

The two of them savaged the gathered rogues as a unit, like some sort of eight-footed fighting machine. They moved together, almost as if they were connected some-how. They seemed to sense what the other wolf would do, knew when to defend the other's flank, when to drop back and allow their partner to attack.

It was beautiful to watch. But none of the rogue wolves were dying or fleeing. They kept getting back up, ready to fight. Fucking magic again? It had to be.

Ivan let another blob of light fly, and to my dismay, it hit Glen in his chest. He collapsed, just like Finnick had. Red light webbed out all over Glen's furry form, tethering him to the earth.

The black wolf was all that was left, against seven enemies. He was still, panting with his head hanging low, as if he were already defeated. I shut my eyes, unwilling to see him die, my heart aching for some reason, like I was losing some part of myself.

I didn't even know this guy. Yet, if I'd been able to move,

I would have thrown myself out of the tree and taken down at least one of the rogues, or climbed down and fought beside him. Or met my end with him.

My eyes were stinging, and I blinked to clear them. Then I realized the area was silent.

I looked down, wishing I could move my head to see around, though the view directly below was now interesting enough. It reminded me of one of those human psychological tests.

Rorschach? Yeah, I thought, trying to make sense of what I was seeing.

Ivan and the black wolf were gone, but the other rogue wolves were dead. And not slightly dead, either. They were in pieces, bits of flesh and bone, not one of them bigger than my hand.

What the actual...

There were two splintered halves of the wand below me as well, glimmering and sputtering with a few sparks of red fire on the forest floor. Was Ivan's body part of the splatters around it? There was no way to tell.

"Holy shit," I breathed, and felt something touch my neck. I lurched forward, almost falling.

Someone behind me tsked. "Careful, little one. I don't want you to fall."

25

THE BLACK WOLF'S NAME

FLOR

"Careful, little one. I don't want you to fall." The voice in my ear was a whisper, and hard to place. A foreign accent, like the general.

My heart raced, but I knew immediately it was not Ivan. This man smelled like ancient spices, rich and exotic, but slightly familiar.

"Who are you?" I couldn't see him, couldn't move my neck. He shifted slightly, and the magic holding me to the tree fell away.

It had to be the wolf with glowing eyes, shifted into his human form. I tried to turn to be sure, careful to keep my claws in the bark. I couldn't move on my own, but he helped me.

It was the shifter from the fight at Southern. The one who'd brought me the water and sang outside the storm drain. I knew his name, but my mind was buzzing as if the magic that had held me had numbed my thoughts, and I couldn't remember it. I remembered his voice, though. "It's you."

"Yes, little one," he murmured. "It is I." He ducked his head in a sort of bow.

Before I could think about it, I had returned the gesture. It felt like some sort of formal recognition. But of what? "Did you... follow me here? From Southern?"

He nodded. "May I carry you down?"

"Yes." I wrapped my arms around him, piggyback-style. Against all common sense, I trusted him, although a cold breeze came up when we touched, and I shivered all the way down the trunk. It was odd. The wind wasn't blowing now, but the sensation of a breeze moving around me, and an icy, sharp pleasure raced along all my limbs, bring every part that had been numbed back to life.

Curious, I shifted against his skin, then became aware of his length hardening as it bumped against my calves. He gave an odd grunt once we reached the bottom, mumbled a word I didn't recognize, and shifted me higher on his back. An odd, twisting need started up in my core, making me clench.

Down, hussy, I chastised my wolf, who had gone quiet except for some very questionable muffled pants. I needed to put some space between my slutty wolf nature and this far-too-powerful, naked stranger. "You can put me down."

"In a moment." He stepped us away from the gory scene; the ground near the tree was saturated with blood.

"Is Ivan dead, the wizard?"

He scoffed. "Wizard, pah. He's nothing. A tool in the hands of far greater evil. He is gone, I'm afraid. But your friend is safe. I had to choose whether to track the magic thief, or return so your friend could breathe again." He set me down at last, and gestured to a dark form, crumpled on the ground. "I can always hunt the thief another night. Anyway, I thought you'd prefer this one to live."

Glen. I raced to his body, rolling him over. "He's not waking up!"

"A healing sleep," the man explained. "Leave him a moment. I'm sending energy into him through the earth."

"Healing him?" I turned away from Glen to see if he was saying some sort of spell, and froze. *Holy shit.* The black wolf looked like some sort of old-fashioned prince, his bearing unquestioningly regal, even though he was naked. Power practically radiated from him in an invisible haze that teased my senses.

He was shorter than Finnick and Glen, but still a few inches taller than me. His muscles were chiseled and perfect, like a sculpture from Ancient Greece. My eyes dropped below his waist. I was pretty sure he'd need more than a few fig leaves to cover *that* up.

I gulped and focused on his face.

His eyes were dancing, aware I'd been checking him out. "Thank you, little one. It is nice to know you are attracted to an old man like me. You have so many young ones."

"Old?" I had no idea what he meant about me having so many young ones. My eyes moved to his dark hair. There were a few silvered strands here and there. "You can't be much older than... forty?"

He laughed, and the sound was as musical as his singing had been. "Oh, my little flame, I am much too old for you." But his eyes told me he didn't believe that or didn't care. "Come, let me heal those scratches now. Then we will wait together for the rest of your suitors."

"Suitors?"

Silent, he held out a hand and led me toward the lake. Though it meant leaving Glen to sleep there, I was glad. I didn't really want to stand around barefoot near the remains of the slaughtered rogue pack. I trusted his promise that Glen would be fine, and I could see this stranger better in the moonlight. Though he didn't feel like a stranger at all.

"So, um, you killed all those wolves?" He shot me a questioning look. "I mean, of course you did. I just, I closed my eyes so I didn't see the, um, battle. I was worried you were going to die."

He grinned, placing his hands on the bleeding gashes where the general had scratched me. They were mostly healed, but he sent a small pulse of magic into me. I tried not to react, since it didn't just go to my tiny wounds, but *everywhere*.

I squeezed my thighs together slightly, and his grin grew wider. "I am glad you were concerned. But you should not fear, those wolves were no match for someone like me."

The strange thought I'd had earlier popped back up. He definitely had that dark prince vibe. "Are you... I mean, you *are* a shifter, right? Not like, a vampire or something?"

His eyes flew wide. "What an imagination you have." He grabbed my hand and kissed it. My body broke out in shivers as that sudden cold wind feeling started back up. He frowned when an actual wind blew around us. "I cannot stay long. Others are coming soon. Not your suitors."

"I can't hear anyone." It was more of an accusation than a statement. "You sure you're not a vampire?"

"I can feel them. Can't you?" His dark eyebrows rose, as if I'd surprised him.

"No," I said. *Wait.* I felt something shiver inside. Or was it on the outside, where his hand touched me? "Maybe." I grabbed his hands again. "Don't go. I need... I need something."

As I held onto his hands, the cold wind died down and a

vibration under my feet began, making me lean into him. I grabbed hold of his arms as it grew stronger, my chest pressing up against his, that bronzed skin softer than satin, the muscles underneath hard as iron.

Without meaning to, I uttered a soft moan. His hands wrapped around me as he let out a soft word in some odd language, and everything around us started shaking in earnest. Was it an earthquake? I'd never felt one before, but I imagined it would be like this. Pinecones began falling from the trees around us, and a pleasurable rumble began deep inside my core.

"What's going on?" I gasped. He pulled his hands away, mumbling more words in that foreign tongue. Suddenly, the tremors stopped. "Was that an earthquake? Did... Did we do that?"

"Oh, little *behrserk*, when we come together, the earth will indeed move."

My cheeks flamed at that. "What did you call me? What does that mean?"

He smiled mischievously, but didn't answer. "I'll tell you someday."

My heart lurched. "Wait, what's your name?"

He brushed a strand of hair away from my face, his thumb moving along my hairline, leaving a trail of icy heat. "Your *other* mates know me as Joaquin."

Other mates? I glared. I was just wrapping my head around the idea of having one mate... even though I knew Luke and Glen were probably somehow connected to me as well. But this guy, too? "You'd better not be saying what I think you are."

He laughed. "My name is Grigor Dimitrivich, and I will see you soon. At Southern, yes?"

231

"Southern?" I was confused. "Why?" I was never going back there.

"The mate called Luke, the useless, broken one you left there?" He spat to the side, saying without words what he thought—of Luke or of Southern, I wasn't sure.

"I know Luke Callaway, but he's not my mate."

He blinked slowly. Both of us could hear the tinny ring of untruth in my words. "I can understand your hesitance. He is diminishing. You can choose to leave him to it, but I fear your kind heart would not rest easily with that decision. And your wolf may mourn."

My heart constricted. *Mourn. Diminishing.* What was Grigor talking about? "Have you seen him?"

He shrugged, walking to the shoreline. "I had some work to do at your old pack."

"Work?" He stepped into the water, wading up to his waist. What was he doing? Washing off the blood? "What kind of work? Were you helping Luke?"

"No," he said, his eyes glittering. Deep in his pupils were sparks, both red and blue, like shining stones at the bottom of a dark lake. "I left you a courting gift at Southern, little one. And a mating gift at Northern, for you and your Mountain mate. I hope you enjoy them both." He hummed a few bars of a tune that was instantly familiar.

"Wait—" I called out.

He didn't wait. Before I could ask anything else, he dove under the surface and vanished, not even leaving a ripple. I watched the lake to see where he would come up for a breath, to track him somehow... but he never reappeared.

I knew he hadn't drowned. He was too magical. And like he'd said, I could feel him. In my heart. His name felt like a secret for me alone.

Grigor. His name is Grigor Dimitrivich.

It wasn't until much later that I realized he hadn't answered my question about *what* he was. He'd used magic like a witch or wizard, but shifted into wolf form. He'd comforted me, but was a ruthless, slightly unhinged killer.

It really wasn't fair for one guy to have all the goods.

Other mates, he'd said. *Hmmmm.*

Curiosity burning through me, I sat by Glen's side as he slept and healed, waiting for our rescuers.

It didn't take long. Thirty minutes later, when the pink sunrise had covered the lake, four wolves emerged from the nearby trees. When I didn't recognize them, I jumped to my feet, ready to protect Glen with my claws if I had to—if I could get them to come out again. My wolf was exhausted, and I wasn't sure she could help us now.

But one of the wolves transformed quickly into a man. "Patrick," I gasped.

He scanned me quickly, but kneeled beside his brother, checking his pulse and breathing. The other wolves stayed in fur, padding around the lake with their hackles up and their noses busy sniffing. I knew they smelled Grigor.

"There's no one here," I said, then gasped as I remembered. "But there's going to be an attack on Northern. A bomb—they've got a key from Vanessa, and they're going to bomb the Lodge!"

"Understood. Erik, tell Mom to call Sergeant." Patrick sent two of the wolves to run back, then picked Glen up. "We need to hurry, and scoop up Brand and Finn on the way."

"Are they—"

"Unconscious, but healing. Mom's with them. Flor, can you run? Steven can shift if you need to be carried."

I was already shaking my head when Glen whispered, "Don't... touch her." Patrick raised an eyebrow. I sneered, then followed them, running as fast as I could, grateful that the callouses I'd developed at Southern hadn't entirely faded.

Brand and Finnick had already been loaded into a dark gray van. Patrick handed me some black sweats from a pile in the back of the van, then threw some on as well. The Enforcer who had loaded the guys up explained that Margarette and Erik had taken her car back to the Lodge.

"Did they stop the rogues?" I asked as I followed Patrick into the back of the van, wedging myself in between the furry wolf form of my mate, and the naked one of Finnick. They both had marks all over them, wounds from what Patrick explained was some kind of magical net.

The other Enforcer started the van, driving fast, and Patrick leaned against the side of the empty cargo bay, obviously exhausted. He still mustered a smile. "If you touch Brand, it should help him heal faster."

I didn't need to be told twice. I wrapped an arm around my mate's neck, and when the van bounced over a pothole a few minutes later, I grabbed Finnick's bare arm as well. Patrick didn't say anything about it, but his eyebrows rose as Finnick's wounds started to heal fast enough to see.

I didn't have time to think about what that might mean, since the driver took a call a few seconds later. It was Margarette.

"We've secured the Lodge, but they bombed the compound."

My heart raced. How many of the shifters I'd trained with, how many of the unranked wolves who I'd only begun to get to know, had been hurt or killed?

Patrick shouted over the seat, "Mom, is it safe for us to come back? Should I take Glen and the others to the city instead?"

Her voice was raw. "No, get them home. They'll be needed here."

We rode in silence. Brand woke just before we reached the Lodge, and tried to change, but it was obviously agonizingly painful.

"Please, don't. I can hug you just as well like this." He laid his massive head in my lap and whined as we bounced down the long drive. I couldn't see a thing as we pulled up to the Lodge, but I could smell smoke and hear shouting.

Northern's safety had been shattered.

26

BACK AT THE LODGE
FLOR

Margarette and Bradley had turned me away when I tried to help the night before, insisting I rest. So I did, and for the first time since I could remember, I slept the day away, though I was chased by nightmares. First, I was running from rogues and Alpha Callaway. Only the strains of a guitar playing a song I knew I'd never learned as a child kept them from catching me.

Then the dream changed, and I was staring down at Vanessa's dead form, an older woman who looked like her weeping at my side. Her dead mother? She grasped my arms with clawed hands, and I noted eyes just like Margarette's. The stranger didn't speak, but turned me to face another figure—a hazy, familiar one—who stood on my other side. Luke?

"What are you doing here, little fighter?" He was gaunt and gray, his dark hair grown out, his eyes dim. Blood flowed from the gut wound I'd given him, and from his ears as well. "I didn't want you to see me like this. Go back. Live."

"Luke!" I tried to scream his name, but the word came out a whimper. He reached for my face with one hand and mouthed something more, but I couldn't make out the words.

The woman turned me back to face her, taking a breath to say something, but before she spoke, I woke up, feeling a warm, bristling coat under my fingers. I was on my bed, not alone.

A raspy tongue lapped my face, removing the tears that streamed down my cheeks. "Thank you, Brand," I whispered, trying not to wake Finnick or Glen, who were both asleep in their wolf forms on the floor beside the bed. The curtains were drawn, but it felt like late afternoon.

I spent a moment quietly petting Brand, trying to shake off the sense from the dream that I needed to hurry, I needed to run... somewhere. That it was almost too late.

But there was so much to do here. Hard truths to share, mysteries to unravel. Secrets that had burrowed their way into the heart of this pack that should have been a refuge, but had turned out to be the opposite.

Warm fur moved beneath my fingers, and I resumed my petting as I worried about Brand. When we'd reached the Lodge the night before, and dragged ourselves into my bedroom. Brand still hadn't been able to change back without excruciating pain, so I'd asked him not to try.

He stood now, shaking his fur, waking the others. The next second, a knock came, and a maid called out, "Alpha Hillier requests your presence in the family sitting room."

Waking instantly, Glen and Finnick leaped to their feet as I rose and opened the door for them. Glen whined softly, rubbing his coat against me as he left. Finnick didn't even glance my way.

Asshole.

"Time for the meeting," I said to Brand. He huffed, turning his back as I changed. We were going to have a long talk about why he was fighting his attraction to me, and keeping his distance. But not yet. Not while he was still injured.

I stripped out of the too-large sweats from the night before, showered in record time, and threw on a set of black sparring clothing. At the last minute, I tucked my steak knife into my belt and grabbed my sword, glad someone had returned it to my room. I wasn't going to be taken by surprise again.

Brand and I were the last ones to arrive. Margarette's face as we entered betrayed her inner turmoil. It looked like she couldn't decide if she was pissed, ashamed, confused, worried, or overjoyed.

"Flor, it's good to see you awake," she said, rising from Alpha Hillier's side. I nodded to him, but Margarette had me in an awkward hug before I could greet anyone. "We're beside ourselves. Northern was meant to be your refuge."

The Alpha agreed, promising to make amends for what happened. I wasn't sure how, but Patrick had told me his dad had experienced a full and miraculous recovery, around the time I had been abducted. I'd been skeptical, but it looked like the truth. The Alpha looked better than ever, except for the dark circles under his eyes and the pain reflected in them. Everyone in the room looked like they might fall over from exhaustion, except for him.

Was it possible that his recovery was Grigor's doing? *A mating gift at Northern, for you and your Mountain mate...* The more I thought about it, the more I knew it was likely.

I pulled away from Margarette, mumbling some vague words to them both about water under the bridge. I wasn't sticking around long enough to find out if Northern could pull their collective heads out of their communal ass. I knew they had more snakes in this den.

A fancy den it was, too. The room was probably twenty feet square, with dark wood paneling and oversized furniture that made it feel smaller. Right now, there were seven grown shifters gathered inside: the Alpha and Margarette, Patrick, Glen, Finnick, me, and Brand. Everyone else had changed clothing, and my enormous mate was the only one still in his wolf form.

Finnick had shifted at some point after leaving my room, and had put on dress pants and a cable-knit sweater, but it must have taken every last ounce of his strength to do so. His pale skin was almost translucent.

I looked around like I was trying to find a seat, but I was taking in the windows and doors, all the exits, and any possible weapons. There were almost too many, since someone had hung a whole assortment of swords and daggers on one wall.

I wandered to a long table under the sword wall that had a selection of food on it, taking enough of the carved meat on a plate for Brand and a selection of sandwiches for me, then settling on a sofa, where Finnick and Glen moved to make room. Brand settled at my feet, making a furry barrier between the sofa and the rest of the room.

"Flor, please let me express our remorse as a pack, and my own as the one who brought you here," Margarette murmured as she sat back beside Alpha Hillier, who wrapped his arm around her as she launched into a longer apology.

Brand and I ate while she talked, and our first helpings of food were gone long before she finished. Apparently, escaping magical chains and certain death and then sleeping for a whole day built up an appetite.

Glen, Finnick, and Brand all waited patiently for me to finish my meal, not leaving my side until I was done. Then Glen cleared my plate, while Finnick got me a drink. It made me feel weird to be waited on, but good weird, even if I was still worried about their slow healing.

"...the honor of our pack has been besmirched, and we will not rest until..."

Huh. This sounded a lot like Glenda after he'd creeped on me at the stream in Southern. I leaned down and whispered in Brand's ear, "I see where Glen gets his drama llama tendencies." He gave a wolfy huff that sounded like a chuckle.

Alpha Hillier frowned slightly, and I wondered if he'd heard me.

Brand pressed against my legs. I could feel his need to be closer to me. Now that his hunger for food was sated, the emotional hunger in our bond came close to overwhelming me. Shame, rage, guilt, desire, and something that felt like grief kept seeping through. Until we spoke, I wouldn't know exactly what was going on, but it wasn't good.

My own moods were a bit turbulent, too. My head ached, and Margarette's protracted guilt and shame-filled apologies were making it worse.

"...never once imagined she was a viper in our den, and I know you may not ever forgive us..."

What the hell was I supposed to say to that? I wasn't sure that they deserved forgiveness. I half-wished I'd jumped out the window when the maid had knocked on my bedroom door. I didn't need apologies. I needed action.

I tuned Margarette out, sipping on the lemonade Finnick had brought me, and wondering if the rogues were really taken care of, like the Alpha had assured us when we returned.

Since the Lodge was well protected, and the Enforcer barracks were too close to the well-guarded main house, the assholes had decided to blow up the unranked compound as a consolation prize before they abandoned their attack. No one had been killed, though more than a few of the unranked shifters had been injured enough to need medical care.

Conveniently, Northern had a doctor on hand whose patient no longer needed him, and others who knew enough first aid to help the unshifted younger ones.

By the time I finished my drink, Alpha Hillier had started talking again, answering a question I hadn't even heard Glen ask. "Yes, the injured unranked shifters have been moved into the servants' quarters of the Lodge, and the uninjured ones have been moved to tents in the training yard."

Was he kidding? I felt rage well up in me and almost cussed out the Alpha, but Del's voice rang in my head. *Pick your battles, girlie, and make sure you're willing to die on whatever hill you decide is worth claiming.*

Did I want to fight this fight? Was this hill worth dying on?

I lifted a hand to my ear, feeling the tag that hung there, and knew the answer wasn't yes.

It was *hell yes.*

I was about to leave this pack, and not look back. But before I went, I had to make sure a few things changed. Not for me, but for the unranked at Northern.

"Excuse the shit out of me, but why aren't the unranked shifters being given rooms in the Enforcer barracks?" I muttered, interrupting Margarette's renewed rant about betrayal and traitors. My simple question brought every conversation in the room to a halt. "Or in the Lodge? There are extra bedrooms here." Vanessa's was probably fancy as fuck.

The whole room stayed silent for a moment, like I'd said something they'd never thought of. To my surprise, the Alpha answered me first. "We can't let anyone into the Lodge right now who we don't trust implicitly. The unranked, well... some of them may have been a part of the attack."

I fought to keep from rolling my eyes. "No offense, but that shit's so fresh, you could cook an egg in it."

More awkward silence ensued, though Brand sent a wave of agreement through our bond, and Glen nodded slightly.

For some reason, Patrick was the only one who spoke. "Damn straight."

Finnick coughed, but I thought he was covering a smile.

The Alpha gave one of those *I'm not mad, I'm disappointed* sighs. "I'm not sure what you know about our ranking system here, Flor—"

Oh, buddy, mansplain to me about ranking bullshit. It was a good thing I was on my way out. I had a lot to say. "Ya know, maybe Vanessa wouldn't have made the choices she did, Alpha, and sold y'all out to the enemy, if your shit wasn't as rigged as an eighteen-wheeler haulin' two trailers."

The room went completely still, like a photograph. Or a grenade, before it exploded.

Glen's curse cut through the silence. "Rigged? What is she talking about? Dad?"

The Alpha stayed quiet.

Glen's blue eyes went stony as he met his father's gaze, then looked to his mother and brother. "It's not true, is it?"

"Abso... lutely... is." Patrick was fighting to get the words out, the tendons on his neck stretched taut.

"Aw, you see? That's some bullshit right there," I murmured.

I was sick of it all. Leaving everything I knew at Southern to come to a paradise that was every bit as shitty, being treated like crap by the Northern ranked shifters, then abducted. All of it. So the tiny bit of tact I sometimes had was nowhere to be found.

I gave a low, mocking whistle. "That's some serious Alpha command. Won't even let your own sons talk about how fucked up this pack is. I shouldn't be shocked, but... I am, a little."

Glen stood up, facing his father. "Alpha command? What's she talking about? Mom?"

Margarette had gone still in the Alpha's arms. "Bradley. You have to tell him."

The air crackled with unspoken emotion, and my heart broke for Glen.

He turned to me, a question in his agonized gaze. I shrugged. "You weren't here to see the ranking tests. The part where I almost died wasn't the worst of it. It was how the unranked shifters were set up to fail. All of them. And they knew it. Vanessa knew it."

At the sound of her name, Brand snarled, snapping at the air, then glared at the Alpha.

Alpha Hillier looked around the room, taking in the universally horrified and confused expressions. He rubbed his forehead with one hand before he spoke. "It's not my command, or wasn't originally. It's a... policy that's been in place since my father was Alpha, when the war started."

"The war that ended just before I was born?" I asked, wanting clarification. I hadn't had much schooling, but Del had told stories about a big shifter war before I was born. "Against the Russian shifters and... some rogues or somethin'."

He nodded. "The North American Council declared that all able-bodied ranked shifters would need to fight if and when the Russians came close to pack borders. Of course, our pack was the only one that bore the brunt of the attacks, since they invaded our land." When Brand curled his lip and let out a nearly silent growl, he amended, "Our pack, and yours, Brand. Mountain was always our most reliable ally."

"What *policy?*" Glen demanded. I wondered for a moment how he couldn't know about something so fundamental in his own pack.

Then I thought about Glen, how important his honor was to him. If he'd known about the rigged ranking, it would have destroyed his own belief in his pack. In its honor. No father would want to snuff out that faith.

I knew I was right when guilt shone from the Alpha's face as he explained, and watched the last of the innocence sputter and die in his Heir's eyes. I could almost feel Glen's pain as his dad spoke. It had to hurt to discover his role model was every bit as flawed as the rest of us.

No, role models. Because Margarette had known as well. I tried not to let my own pain show. There would be time for me to cry about that betrayal later.

Alpha Hillier went on. "Our losses were severe. Dad told me we were likely to lose the entire pack, if we couldn't get more help from the others. Even our youngest shifters were trained in combat, our girls. They were so proud to be ranked, even if they weren't skilled enough to be Enforcers, until the Council's decision meant they were on the front lines of the battle against wolves that used magic. Dark magic that killed almost every one of ours it touched."

His hand tightened around Margarette's. "To get the Southern and Eastern packs to commit their own ranked shifters, as well as to keep our own younger shifters and women from being slaughtered, we had to come up with a way to be certain our ranked members didn't include the generation we would need. My father had to be sure they didn't move up."

"So, what? You just... cheat?" I was about fucking done. I leaned down to Brand and whispered, "That lake is sounding good right about now." His massive head swiveled to me, and I could see he was ready to do it. To take me, right now, out of here and to his pack.

His ears twitched forward, and the bond inside me shivered with the unspoken question. I was tempted to jump up and run out of the room, run on two feet all the way to Mountain if I needed to.

All the Northern pack had done was show me that there was no such thing as a safe place, no real system of honor. "Maybe they aren't as rotten as Southern, but that remains to be seen," I leaned down and whispered into Brand's fur.

Or thought I'd whispered.

"As rotten as Southern?" Glen repeated.

I cringed at the roomful of horrified faces. "I probably shouldn't have said that." *Even if it is true.*

Glen turned back to his father. "Who knew about this, besides you and Mom? Patrick?"

Patrick's glare at his father, as well as his jaw that was working like he had an entire mouthful of taffy, gave the answer.

Clearly shaken, Alpha Hillier walked to his son and put

a hand on one shoulder. "You may speak of the ranking." A rush of Alpha power rippled in the air around the two males, then retreated.

"Sergeant knew," Patrick spat out, once he could speak. "He was the one who ran the tests. He was the one who set up the fights."

27
WHAT KIND OF PACK?
FLOR

S ergeant had been the one behind the rigged ranking system at Northern? I couldn't believe it.

And it wasn't true. At least, not entirely.

"He was the one who followed orders," Alpha Hillier corrected sternly. "Sergeant came to Northern near the end of the war, and is the only reason we didn't lose more of our members. Why we kept the packlands intact. He enforced the ranking scheme."

Scheme. I tasted bile.

When Glen let out a soft curse, the Alpha hurried to add, "He had no choice at the time. My father was still leading the pack then, and he placed the Alpha command on him, too. He could not have disobeyed."

"There are ways around Alpha commands," I said, thinking of Sergeant's strength, and the ways I'd subverted some of the commands at Southern. "If he had wanted to—"

"Don't blame him for my mistake. I should have rescinded the command, changed the policy. It was always intended to be a temporary measure. It's just... I understood why my father did it."

"Oh, this should be good," I muttered. Brand lowered his ears.

The Alpha ignored us both. "When the war broke out, I wasn't Alpha. I was young, but I had two friends, younger than me. One was Darwick. He wasn't physically strong, but he was the heart of our cohort, and made us all laugh. He and his little sister Sera had both tested for rank a month before the Council's decision was made." He paused, taking a drink of water, but no one else in the room even moved.

Brand was still gazing at me, and I tried to push a little reassurance down the bond. I wasn't sure if it worked, but he didn't herd me out of the room. I wanted to hear this story. I *needed* to. What had gone so wrong in this pack?

"They were some of our first casualties. After they died, my father explained to me and the senior Enforcers why we needed the more fixed ranking structure to keep our vulnerable members safe. Then after the war, the Council's law was rescinded. But by then so many had died, and our birth rates had dropped so rapidly, it seemed prudent to continue what we'd started as an emergency measure. We were protecting the pack. You have to understand."

I wasn't sure I was the one he was talking to. His pleading gaze was fixed on his Heir.

I glanced over at Margarette. Her shoulders were hunched. "I was just as much to blame," she whispered. "Maybe more so. I just wanted to protect the young ones. The girls." Her red-rimmed eyes found my face, and I shook my head. I was so disappointed, so angry, I almost couldn't keep from shouting.

"I don't understand. You told me Northern was a place

where women could be Enforcers. You were so proud of your sister."

"She died, Flor. She died, and I couldn't protect her. When I learned about the ranking... process, I didn't change it, because it was the only way we could *protect* the ones who might have died like she did. Our Enforcers live dangerous lives."

"Vanessa," I murmured. "She was ranked. The women in this pack who hold rank—they didn't fight for it, did they? They train alongside the men, but the ones who have rank were born with it, right? None of your unranked women were ever going to move up." It was all I could do not to spit on the floor. "At least at Southern, they didn't lie to the girls about it. We all knew we'd have to fuck some ranked asshole if we wanted to eat."

Margarette opened her mouth to protest, but she was cut off by a loud snarl. I glanced at Glen, who had fur bristling on his neck, and looked seconds from tearing out his own mother's throat. I stood and moved to his side, placing a hand on his arm. His deep blue eyes, lit from within by his wolf side, met mine. I squeezed his arm, letting the magnetic spiraling sensation that always came from touching him move between us for a moment before letting go.

Alpha Hillier addressed me now. "Flor, it was for the good of our young."

"If I had a nickel for every time I've seen someone perpetrate a crime on someone else 'for their own good,' I'd have enough money to buy a ticket to Hawaii," I said, not even trying to keep the disappointment from my tone. "Why do you think having less power in a pack as large as this would be safe for anyone—especially a female?"

I met his gaze and did not look down, though a slight

headache started at the base of my neck after a few seconds. "I'm not certain you've had a chance to hear about this, but the day I arrived here, Vanessa set your young males on me. They hunted me—a stranger, an unranked female—through the woods around the Lodge. And I'm certain it wasn't the first time they'd done something like that."

I walked back over to the sofa, laying a hand on Brand's neck to stop him from growling. "You took away the most vulnerable pack members' power and gave them lies about ever moving up. The ones who figured it out put on leather collars to show they were your dogs. To gain a little bit of protection, by making sure everyone knew they weren't going to try for more. Not that their dog collars granted them much."

At the word *dogs*, everyone had flinched. I just tapped my ear tag, to drive home the point.

Alpha Hillier went pale, but didn't look away, so I went on, not dropping my stare. "And the ones who stayed in the housing you gave them? You think living even farther from the Lodge did anything but make their screams harder for anyone who gave a shit to hear? Did you know an Enforcer 'choked' to death not even a week ago? Choked while he was inside the unranked compound, helping himself to the young women there."

He let out a shocked breath. "How did this happen?"

Patrick broke in and gave a quick recitation of the facts. To my shock, it was the Alpha who eventually dropped his eyes.

Inside, my wolf snarled. *That should not have happened. An Alpha cannot show such weakness. This one should not be leading.* My gaze moved to Margarette. *She would be a better Alpha.*

250

I forced the thoughts aside. My wolf was a stone-cold bitch. But not wrong.

Everyone was looking at me again, and I decided to really let my inner fury out. "Good job protecting your females, Alpha. What kind of Alpha wouldn't know what was happening to his own most vulnerable members?" I swept the room with my gaze. "What kind of pack?"

"Not mine," Glen whispered. "This is no longer my pack."

No longer his pack? I sat down slowly, moving like I would if I'd been handed a cottonmouth. Beside me, Finnick stopped breathing. Brand lifted his head, assessing Glen.

Alpha Hillier lost his balance, sitting back down abruptly. "You can't—" he began, but Glen's scathing look cut him off.

"We'll talk about it later, Dad. We need to go over what happened yesterday. How Flor was taken, and who was really behind it. Obviously, the unranked shifters here weren't the problem. It was our own damned *family* working with the rogues. Flor was right. We're as bad as Southern."

Ugh. I wished I hadn't said that now; it wasn't really true.

"We have a bigger problem," Finnick broke in, surprising me with a gentle hand on my shoulder. "There was an accomplice. Someone else inside the Lodge."

"It was that wizard," Margarette declared. "He was in the Lodge."

Grigor? Oh hell no. "He saved me. He's not the bad guy here."

"We'll look into every possible suspect. Patrick and Glen?" Alpha Hillier seemed to shake off the emotions that had filled the room only seconds before, an invisible mantle of Alpha power forcing our silence and attention. "We have things that must be discussed, and quickly. Finnick? I phoned your father this morning to tell him I'd recovered. He's recalled you to Eastern, effective immediately. I'll have a car ready for you in an hour."

"My phone," Finnick murmured, his hand dropping. I missed the sensation immediately, but tried not to let it show.

Patrick crossed the room and handed a phone to him. "We found it with your clothing, where you shifted."

"Thanks," Finnick muttered, then cursed as he glanced down at his messages. His expression grew darker as he read, and his green eyes were haunted when he finally met my gaze. "I have to go. I have no choice."

I frowned at the ache in my chest. No choice? What was going on at Eastern?

"It's probably for the best," Alpha Hillier muttered. "I know I'd want my Heir well away from a pack as exposed as ours is now. Your father just wants to keep you safe."

Finnick's jaw hardened. "As you say."

My wolf was growling and snapping inside as Glen moved over to Finnick's side, grasping his shoulder with a hand in support. "You'll be all right," he whispered. "We'll get you back as soon as we can." I *really* didn't want to know what Eastern was like, I decided.

The Alpha sighed deeply. "Before you go, Finnick, I'd like for you to tell your version of last night's events, please. Don't leave anything out. Every detail could be vital." There was more than a hint of Alpha command in Bradley's voice now, and I could tell Finnick felt it from how he stiffened at the order.

"I was up in the library researching mate bonds," he began. His mouth closed, as if he were trying to omit some detail, and the next words exploded out of him on a breath. "I haven't been able to control my feelings for Flor, even after she and Brand claimed one another, so I was looking for a way to understand, to see if there was any way I could —*damnit*, Bradley!" He shot to his feet.

I blinked. Finnick covered his red face with one hand. Brand whuffed once, the wolf equivalent of shock. Or laughter, maybe?

Patrick whispered, "Fuck." Margarette's reddened eyes narrowed. For some reason, Glen winked at me. I just sneered back.

The Alpha cleared his throat. "Ah, sorry. I mean, don't omit any *pertinent* detail, please."

His eyes on the carpet, Finnick described what had happened. How he had scented my blood in the hallway, and chemicals.

"Not Vanessa, though? No other shifters?"

"That hallway sees enough traffic that the scents were layered," he explained, and Alpha Hillier waved a hand.

"Understood. Go on."

"When I reached the area where Vanessa stopped the car, she was meeting with a group of rogues. At least a dozen, but possibly more were still in the trees. Some spoke Russian, some did not. The leader was Alpha Ivan."

"Who is that guy anyway?" I wondered aloud.

Margarette's answer was instant, and agonized. "He was the shifter who killed my sister Linn."

Patrick shook his head. "I can't believe Vanessa betrayed our pack to her own mother's murderer."

Finnick was already shaking his head, too. "She'd

253

planned to run away, but it was clear she didn't know about Ivan. I'm not sure she understood the Russians were a part of the group. But I don't think Flor's abduction was a part of her original plan. She said she was taking out the trash for another member of our pack."

"Fucking Clara," I muttered. Every head turned to me, but I waved at Finnick. "Continue."

He was still listing the details of who had been gathered around the Russian meeting site, when his voice changed. It sounded strained, like he was trying not to say something. "He asked... I needed a reason for them to keep her alive... *Fuck.*" His face turned toward me.

Snakeshit! He was about to tell this whole group about my father.

He slapped a hand over his own mouth to stop the words, but the Alpha's gaze narrowed. "What are you hiding, Finnick? I may not be your pack's Alpha, but I am the Alpha of the North American Council, or I will be when I retake my seat. *Speak.*"

Finnick's hand flew away from his face, and he drew a breath, his green eyes landing on me with apology. "They were planning to kill Flor, thinking she was unimportant. But I knew that wasn't the case. So I told them that she was —" He clenched his teeth.

"Brand's mate?" the Alpha urged.

"No. Not that. I didn't want him to know she was all of ours—" His jaw twitched, and a tiny trickle of blood began to roll down from his nostril as he fought the Alpha's command. "So I told him Flor's father—"

All I wanted to do was shut him up, but I didn't have anything to stuff in his mouth. So I leaped up before he could finish spilling my secret. He was too tall for me to reach, so I climbed up his long frame, wrapped my legs around his waist, grabbed his shoulders, and pressed one hand over his mouth.

But he kept talking, audibly. "Her father was ac—"

Shit. I grabbed his head in both hands and smashed my mouth over his, humming loudly as I did so, so the syllables were drowned out. No one could hear them, since he was speaking them into my mouth.

Dang, I was smart.

Wait. No. I was an idiot. What was I *doing?*

I stopped humming, and realized Finnick was... growling? His growl was every bit as addictive as his touch, and as warm, sending waves of sounds through my lips, down my throat. His arms landed around my waist a half-second later, his growl cut off, and suddenly he was kissing me. It was a kiss like I'd never imagined I would receive.

His lips moved on mine like a poem, like a petal smoothing lightly across the sensitive skin there. Like I was precious, and fragile, and perfect.

I was his secret treasure. His sparkling stars and shimmering moon, kept hidden deep within his heart. Kept safe.

Finnick's lips were softer than I'd imagined, and his mouth tasted slightly of ginger and mint. I felt one of his hands thread through my short hair, and heard a muffled groan from somewhere else in the room as he devoured my mouth. My eyes were closed, and yet a strange brightness began to grow behind my lids. A sun was coming up inside my mind, an unexpected dawn.

It felt like I was waking up to a new world, a new possibility. My heart, which had ached for so long, which had burned and stung when he'd told me I would never be his mate, became a flower opening under a soft pink sky. The kiss kept us connected, as we opened together.

To one another.

And then my wolf woke up as well, stronger than I'd ever felt her before. *Claim,* she insisted.

I opened my eyes and saw Finnick's green gaze fixed on me. But it wasn't him—it was his wolf, the green a darker shade, with golden flecks that glowed with power.

Claim, my wolf repeated in my mind. It began as a whisper, then grew to a steady drumbeat, a command. *Claim claim claim.*

She took control of my lips, and I breathed the word into Finnick's mouth as he kissed me. "Claim."

The instant that Finnick's head bobbed up and down, nodding at my wolf's muffled request, I was thrust to the back of my own mind. My gums itched and burned as my teeth lengthened, and my nails did the same. Before another second had passed, I had somehow taken Finnick's tongue into my mouth and bit down, hard.

Warm, rich blood filled my mouth, and the kiss became something else. Something more.

"Flor," Finnick growled, pulling back. His lips were smeared with blood, but the look in his eyes was by far the most savage thing about him. "What have you done?"

Mine, my wolf purred into his mind, along with a new connection. *Claim, mate.*

His green eyes glowed even brighter for a second, before his bloodied lips turned up in a glorious, sharp-toothed smile. It wasn't Finnick who answered. It was his wolf. "Mine," he snarled, and lunged so that his mouth was on the side of my neck, just below my right ear.

I heard someone shouting, a woman cursing. A barked command to stop that rolled over me, and Finnick as well.

"Mine," he repeated, then bit down on my neck, claiming me.

The bond shimmered into place, brightening everything inside me. That is, until my wolf hopped out of the driver's seat, and left me to explain whatever the fuck had just happened.

As if I had any idea.

28

ONE MORE SNAKE TO SKIN
FLOR

For at least a minute, Finnick and I stared into each other's eyes. I should have looked away. Then I might not have seen the too-human regret that replaced his wolf's fierce pride at our connection. Of course, I could still feel it in our bond.

How the hell had we bonded? This was the same guy who'd sworn more than once that I was not his true mate, that he didn't want me. But I could feel his desire in the connection. And his remorse.

"That was a mistake. I shouldn't have done that," he whispered, and each word was a knife that found its target in my heart. "I'm so sorry, Flor."

"No. I bit you first. I'm the one who should apologize," I managed to answer, although it wasn't altogether true. The connection between us felt strong, and right. It was his reaction to it that felt like a donkey kick to my soul.

"How is this possible?" Margarette demanded, breaking the agony of the moment. "Is this because of the magic?"

The magic? Ah, yeah. Finnick had been trapped in the stuff. At least, I thought that's what she meant.

Finnick rolled his eyes, his regular sneer covering his face even before he turned to her. I hated that expression. "Flor's appeal is magical, I'll admit. But you know Flor's bonds are unusual, and even if I would never have chosen —*damnit*, Brand!"

My wolfy mate had at some point risen and taken a huge bite of Finnick's ass. Finnick dropped me, and I fell onto Brand. My arms and legs wrapped around him, as the scent of Finnick's bloody butt cheek filled the air, and he alternated between cursing Brand and explaining what a mistake he'd made to our hosts.

As if I needed to hear him tell everyone how unworthy I was.

I buried my face in soft, deep fur. "Lake, Brand. I need the lake."

Brand shook himself and began his change right there, in the middle of the room. It was slower than it had been before, but within a minute, he was a man again. A naked, hairy man, who held out his arms to me. "Little flower, let's leave this place. Let's go home."

"I don't have a home," I murmured as I jumped up into his arms. Unlike Finnick, I knew Brand would not put me down, or cast me aside, or let me go. He moved us so his back was to the room, his bulk sheltering me. "I didn't mean to. I don't know why I did that, Brand," I tried to explain, but he covered my lips with his, silencing my apology.

"Your wolf knows. She's doing what she is compelled to do." His deep brown eyes went hard as he directed a glare at someone over his shoulder. "As we all must do." He ran his thick fingers over my hair, smoothing it, ignoring everyone around us. "And you will have a home in my pack. They will love you. We never have to leave."

He hesitated. "No one really ever does. We keep to ourselves."

I sighed, then let go of him, his reassurances subduing the urge I'd had to flee. There were things I needed to do here first. Injustices to correct... and at least one more snake in the Lodge. Vanessa had not been alone the night before.

I wriggled for Brand to put me down, and he did so reluctantly. "Before we go, where's that bitch, Clara?"

"Dead when I find her," Brand promised.

Glen nodded, picking up his phone and texting. "I've sent Enforcers to round her up." Then he put it down and faced Brand. "Alpha Heir Becker, I would very much appreciate a ride to the border of your packlands."

Brand nodded. "Of course. You'll have to ask my dad for permission to enter Mountain."

"If he'll accept a rogue into your pack, I think I'd like to join." The pain in Glen's reply had my heart aching.

Brand grabbed his arm and pressed his forehead to Glen's, with a whispered, "Brother."

I looked away, my eyes stinging. Alpha Hillier and Margarette were discussing something with Finnick—I made out a few words about a Council meeting, and a possible resolution of war—but it hurt too much to even look at him. My newest mate, though I wasn't at all fucking sure how that had happened.

"Don't you have to knock boots to claim a mate?" I muttered aloud.

Brand stifled a chuckle with a fist. "Normally, yes, my flower. But you are a miracle. The Moon Goddess allows you to break Her rules."

"I wish the Moon Goddess would get me another sandwich. I'm still starved," I grumbled.

Patrick stepped up to us, handing Brand a soft blanket

from the sofa. "Brand, go get dressed—you're making the rest of us males feel inadequate. Flor? I'll take you to the kitchen. Then we'll go talk to Clara together."

I smirked. I wasn't planning to talk. I wanted revenge, but the idea of going to the kitchen intrigued me, and for more than sandwiches. I kissed the back of Brand's hand. "Go find clothes and meet us there? Don't kill her without me."

He grumbled, unhappy to leave my side, but when I explained I'd have to gouge out the eyes of any woman who saw him naked, he smiled and jogged away. I'd set my sword down when I came in, and I picked it back up, tucking it into the sheath on my belt, my steak knife on the other side.

"Thank you, Flor," Patrick said in a low voice after we left the room.

"Don't thank me. You're the one taking me to get a sandwich."

He let out an exasperated breath. "No, thank you for shining a light on the festering wounds in my pack. I've been fighting to make someone see that just because someone isn't ranked, that doesn't necessarily mean they lack power, or skills." He waved at me, as if my existence proved his point. "Rank shouldn't just be based on physical prowess, either. There are more important things. Integrity, talent, compassion..."

His voice got louder as we walked, but the kitchen door opened in front of us, and a dark-haired girl stepping out with a platter of sausage rolls had him stopping, his hand on my arm, like I might need protecting. "What are you doing here?"

I recognized her; it was the girl from the ranking fight, the one who'd been happy that Stan had choked. She nodded to me. "I'm not regular Lodge help, but they needed hands. I was bringing food to the family sitting room, wherever that is."

Her hazel eyes flashed as she took in Patrick's hand on my arm. If looks could kill, I'd be bleeding from a mortal wound already. A slightly charred scent filled the air, like burning paper.

Huh. I took a small step away from him. The girl—she couldn't have been more than eighteen, probably not old enough to have shifted—relaxed.

"Hey, Patrick, why don't you help her? Those rolls look heavy."

He practically jumped to take the rolls from the girl. Their hands brushed, and the hallway filled with electricity. The girl stopped breathing for a moment. Patrick's breath, on the other hand, came too fast. Their scents grew thick, their eyes fixed on each other.

Holy shit. I had a feeling Patrick had just found his true mate.

"Kristin." Patrick breathed the name like a prayer. "Your name is Kristin, right?"

She just narrowed her eyes and yanked her hand away. Her fingers flew instead to the band of leather around her neck. "Does my name matter? I'm nobody." Patrick stared at the collar now, like he wanted to tear it off. It was the same way Brand looked at my ear tag.

"Patrick, why don't you help Kristin find the sitting room?" I suggested, fighting a laugh when she shook her head slightly at me. "I'll get some hot food in the kitchen."

He didn't even blink. Maybe he couldn't. "Uh, are you sure?"

"Yep," I answered, already halfway through the swinging door.

The kitchen staff should have been used to seeing me in there—I'd made a habit of hanging out there, getting to know the house staff as well as the cook, since the kitchen felt like a second home to me after my job at Southern. But when I walked in, all their jaws dropped.

The maid I knew best, Marla, rushed over and engulfed me in a too-tight hug. "By the moon, I'm glad to see you. If anything happened to you, I would have burned this Lodge to the ground." A few of the others shushed her, but she shook her head. "It's true! This pack is fucked, and it's because nobody stops those ranked assholes from getting everything they want."

I glanced around. I'd never been in the kitchen alone, and I realized this was the place the unranked gathered and spoke freely. And they were finally welcoming me into their group. All it took was getting abducted.

"I think a lot of the fuckery may change now," I said as I climbed up on a stool. "I may have told the Alpha how the cow ate the cabbage. There's at least one Alpha command that's getting rolled back. Rank testing won't be a fairytale anymore."

They all stared, like I'd just announced Santa Claus was coming. "According to who?" Marla managed to ask.

"Ah, that would be Patrick and Glen. But your Alpha will probably find himself with no Heirs left, if he doesn't listen to them about it."

At some point, the head cook had placed a huge bowl of beef stew in front of me, tutting about how she'd just started fattening me up, and I'd gone and lost precious weight. The other staff hung about, eavesdropping.

Marla handed me a basket of rolls to go with my quart of stew. "Seriously, Flor. I would have never forgiven myself or them if you hadn't come back safe. When I saw those bitches in the hallway last night, I knew they were up to something." I ate while she recounted everything that had happened since that moment.

I slid off my stool, now ready to find Clara and tear out her throat, but the door to the servants' hallways opened behind me, and the kitchen began to fill. In seconds, the room was packed with unranked shifters, some of them sporting still-healing wounds from the explosion, but all of them wearing identical expressions.

I knew the emotion. It was hope.

29

THE MATE SHE DESERVES
FINNICK

"You don't deserve her, Finn." Brand paced across the floor of my bedroom, judgment pouring off him in invisible waves and audible growls, as I packed hurriedly.

"And you think you do?" I shot back, trying not to let my inner panic show when the phone in my hand lit up with another message. I read it, cursed, and threw it down on the bed. It bounced and would have fallen to the floor, but Brand caught it.

I packed faster. There was no time left.

My father had sent an almost constant stream of angry texts since I arrived at Northern, but I'd been able to put him off, telling him I was keeping an eye on the Alpha's condition, and gathering information on Northern's defenses.

Someone had told him about Flor's mating with Brand, though, and his messages had gotten more terse since then. I'd ignored them until Bradley had handed me my phone.

At some point that day, while we slept, Mother had

texted me a request to call my sister, Tana. A veiled threat, of course.

Mother never sent a message that wasn't a demand, a threat, or both.

I hadn't seen it at the time; I'd been wrapped in dark magic and sleeping off the aftereffects. But now I knew that recovery time had borne evil fruit. While I slept, Tana had sent a flurry of desperate messages begging me to call her, until they stopped suddenly.

When I'd tried to reply earlier, none of the messages had been read. When I called, it went directly to voicemail.

The last message had come from a number I knew well. It belonged to Niall, the current Eastern pack torturer, though his official title was Second Enforcer. But the text itself was from Tana, and she'd included a code that only the two of us shared.

I miss you so much, my stomach hurts. Mom and Dad miss you too, I've never seen them this upset. I know I asked you to bring me a souvenir. But I don't need more necklaces and bracelets, just my brother home before my mating ceremony to Niall. Surprise!

"Finn, what is *this?*" Brand demanded. "Your sister is mating that sadistic fuck?"

I spun to see him staring at my phone, reading the texts. "Not if I get there in time," I muttered, slamming my suitcase shut.

"She can't want to mate him," Brand said, horror in his dark eyes. He'd met Niall. Anyone who had knew that the man shouldn't be allowed around any women, especially not young ones. "She's not even old enough to be mated. What's your father *thinking?*"

"You know an Alpha can change—even break—whatever rules he desires," I said, fighting not to scream. "He's thinking he'll get me home faster. Tana won't be able to stop the mating. Only I will."

"They're forcing the mating?" The air in the room grew heavy with Brand's horror and rage. "Are you certain?"

"She put it in the message, in code. Necklace and bracelets, those mean shackles. Her stomach hurts means she's been tortured. By our parents, and probably Niall as well."

"We have to tell Bradley. You have to tell him."

"He has no power right now, and his own pack has been bombed. Him leaving now would open Northern up to another attack. Until Bradley reports to the Council and they acknowledge his healing, my father is the final authority, the ruling shifter of the Council. There's no one to stop them, not until I get back and bargain for her. *Again.*" I tried not to show my distaste for what that bargain would cost me.

Didn't know if I could even pay the price my parents would exact this time.

"What will they ask of you in return for stopping the mating?" Brand asked quietly, getting to the heart of my fears with one question.

"The same thing they always have," I said, trying to keep my expression bland, but failing. My hand trembled as memories threatened to send me to my knees. "If I'm lucky, they won't ask for more."

"You're leaving without talking to Flor. What do I tell her?"

I had no idea. "I never would have done that, Brand. I'm not good for her." *Not good enough, either.* "I'm still not sure how our bond formed."

"The moon gave you no choice," he said gently. "Maybe it had to be this way. If you had left her before the bond, you both would have suffered horribly." He sighed. "I'm not sure being apart won't hurt you now, Finn. Or her."

I shrugged, deeply concerned about her, but knowing I had no choice but to go home. For Tana. "Luke and Flor didn't even exchange mating bites, and he's still alive."

"Barely. He's bedridden, according to the latest reports. As bad off as Bradley was."

We both stayed silent, pondering the miraculous nature of Bradley's healing. By the time we'd returned, there hadn't been any hint of the black wolf inside the Lodge, though Margarette had insisted he had been inside. And Flor had shouted at Margarette that he'd saved her in the woods. That he was on our side.

We'd agreed earlier to let it go; there was no use in chasing down a shadow, though Margarette had sent Sergeant, along with some of Northern's most senior Enforcers, to do just that.

I lifted a brow. "You know you have to tell her about Luke's condition."

"I'm not sure she's ready to go back. She asked me to take her to my lake."

A wave of longing swept through me. What would I have given for a safe place like Brand's lake? A secret haven that I could take our mate to. I'd dreamed of showing her the delights a city had to offer, the culture and arts. But that could never happen.

"She's Luke's mate as well. If he dies, she might..." His growl stopped my words. "You're strong. She'll need you. You and Glen, if you'll allow him to go with you."

"Glen can come with us. She'll need him, too."

I nodded. "Good. Whether or not he abjures his pack, he'll need to stay close to her." I let out a long breath, strangely comforted by knowing she would have two of us.

Us. The men I thought of as brothers, when I had no one else who truly cared for me, to save Tana. Even if I'd had to hide much of the shame of my pack from them. Their pity would have broken me. I knew I might not see them again for a long while.

Or her. And even if I found a way out for Tana and me, Flor wouldn't want me, not after what I knew lay ahead.

What I would have to do to survive my pack.

I cleared my throat, swallowing the grief that gathered there. "When you take her to Mountain, use the library. Try and find something to explain what's happened. How one woman can be true mates with all four Alpha Heirs..."

Our gazes clashed, and silent words moved between us. How could this work? Would our packs even believe it was true? One of the most foundational beliefs of all shifters was that we had one true mate alive in the world.

How could that be wrong?

Brand crossed to me and clasped my forearms. "I'm taking her to Mountain to meet my pack. But we'll have to return to Southern straightaway. Then we'll head to your pack, Finn."

"*No!*" The word came out as a shout. "You can never bring her there. If they get their claws into her... Brand, you have no idea what they'll do."

"You're right; I don't know. You've kept your pack's dealings secret even from your closest friends. If we knew all that happened there, we'd know how to help you. Let me understand. Tell me what's happening there."

Shame filled me. Of all the Heirs, Brand was the one I'd distanced myself from most. His pack had a reputation for being truthful and fair. Perhaps violent and brutish, but honest. The opposite of Eastern.

I picked up my case and headed for the door. "I can't,

Brand." I held his gaze, letting him see how much I wished I could.

"An Alpha command?" He breathed the question.

If only that was all that kept me silent.

I inhaled deeply, fighting panic and despair. "Tell Flor I'm... I'm not sorry." Brand's lip curled up, exposing his fangs, until I finished. "Tell her I'm not sorry she claimed me. I'm only sorry I can't be the mate she deserves."

30

LISTENING IN

BRAND

I went to find Flor, following the link between us that pointed me to her like an invisible compass needle. Instead, I found something curious: Margarette, eavesdropping outside the kitchen door.

When I approached, she cringed, but held a finger to her lips. I frowned, but her face was pleading. So we both listened to the raised voices coming from the room.

A female shifter whose voice I could not place was speaking. "Of course we couldn't tell the Alpha Mate about the assaults. We all know she and the Alpha are keeping us in our places. Why the hell would we go to her for help?"

Margarette covered her mouth with a hand, but didn't make a sound.

"You're lucky as hell you can get out of here, Flor. Unranked shifters don't get to go to the Conclaves, so we won't ever get the chance to escape."

"What about to find your true mates?" Flor asked. "She's big into that. Doesn't she want you to meet them?"

"Sure, and when the Conclaves are hosted here, we have

a chance. My cousin got out that way eight years back. She met an Enforcer from Mountain at our last hosted Conclave. But no one else has in... a long time."

Another voice chimed in. "Being a female here, especially an unranked one, is a silver chain around our necks. Vanessa was a traitorous bitch, but I know why she snapped."

Margarette was holding her breath now, frozen in shock and horror. I held just as still, feeling torn. I shouldn't eavesdrop on Flor, but Margarette needed to hear what her unranked shifters were saying. We all did.

"Why?" Flor's voice inside the kitchen was gentler than I'd ever heard.

"Vanessa was ordered to stay home from the Conclave at Southern. She was pissed as hell. Her true mate isn't at Northern, and she was convinced she'd find him there."

Flor snorted. "If she has one, he probably is at Southern. Almost any of those assholes would be a perfect match for her."

"Well, I think she met a rogue on one of her trips into town for *supplies*. She took a hell of a lot of trips into town while the Alpha and his mate were away."

Someone else laughed. "Yeah, she spent the pack's money and time getting her nails done, and buying shit for herself and her friends."

"That wasn't all she did. I work in the laundry. She came home smelling like an unknown shifter, more than once. I heard her tell Clara about him when I was serving dinner." A long pause. "Clara was helping Vanessa."

"No shit. Where's Clara now?"

"Not anywhere we've seen. Probably in some ranked asshole's bed. Where we'll probably all end up if we want a bed."

"No, you're not going to have to sleep—"

"Flor, *look around*. They have us in tents now, even the young girls. No locks, no doors, no one to stop them taking advantage of the ones who can't protect themselves. The males in our pack aren't all bad, but there are enough of them that are. And now, we'll be even easier prey."

"You're not prey; you've all had training. Do you need weapons?"

"By Alpha command, we're not allowed to handle them outside of the training grounds. We might *injure* ourselves." There was the unmistakable sound of someone spitting.

Flor's laughter was surprisingly sweet. "Are all Alphas such boneheaded fools? All right, have any of you heard about Southern? The unranked there, especially the women, weren't allowed to be trained at all, with any weapons. But there's always a workaround, ladies. Always."

When the rest of the voices suddenly joined hers in a boisterous explosion of humor and a clatter of silverware, Margarette's eyes widened. "I'm going in," I murmured, and she stepped back.

I'd almost pushed the door open, when I heard a woman say quietly, "I caught a ranked bastard sneaking into the women's shower block early this morning when Daisy was in there with two of the younger girls. Thank you, Flor. This will help."

My lip curled instinctively, my wolf enraged at the idea of the children of this pack, of any pack, in danger.

"Did he touch her? I'll fucking *kill* him," Flor swore.

"No. She yelled for help, and Sergeant came running."

"Can we trust Sergeant?"

Flor's question was met with a long, heavy silence,

followed by what sounded like over a dozen women leaving through the servants' hallways.

Fuck.

31

A PLEA FOR HELP

FLOR

My gut felt like I'd eaten stones rather than sandwiches. It was apparent that even if Sergeant had felt like family to me, like I should be able to trust him, rely on him, none of these women felt the same.

When I really looked at his actions since I'd arrived, he hadn't done anything to earn my trust. He'd set up my ranking fight with a weak shifter, then switched him out when he thought I'd lied about my training. He'd insisted on me using a steel weapon against Brand, a much more experienced, far larger shifter, as my first opponent.

And what was worse, he'd overseen the rigged ranking tests for years. Alpha Hillier hadn't breathed a word about Sergeant disagreeing with the old system. And Sergeant was ridiculously strong. He could have found a way around the Alpha command, if he'd wanted to.

My wolf wanted to trust him, I realized. But my human side knew better.

The silence in the kitchen grew thick and ominous, and I slid off my stool, heading for the door to the main Lodge hallway as most of the others slipped out through the servants' passages.

I'd felt Brand outside that door for a few minutes, and wondered why he hadn't come in, but I'd assumed he was just being polite, not wanting to interrupt the conversation.

But when I opened the door and found Margarette standing behind him, I realized why.

"There'd better be a good explanation, Bearman," I snapped, not even looking at Margarette. I had nothing to say to her. Well, the only things I had to say were words with four letters.

I was the polite one, keeping them inside.

Brand pulled me into a hug. "I'm sorry, my flower, but I thought she needed to hear what was being said. They would never have the courage to say it to her face, and she needs to understand how deep the rot goes."

"All the way to the heart, if they don't trust Sergeant." I stepped away, waiting for Margarette to speak.

But she didn't. Couldn't, it looked like. Her face was expressionless.

"What's wrong?" I asked, feeling foolish. There was so much wrong here at Northern.

Her lips went tight before she forced out the words. "I need your help." I nodded for her to continue. "Will you please come with me to the unranked housing?"

"Why?" I felt something pinch in my chest, and rubbed at it. Brand moved closer, placing a hand on my shoulder, and the sensation eased.

"I need to interview the unranked members of the pack privately. But I've just realized... they won't talk to me."

"Why should they? You betrayed them."

She flinched, but went on. "They trust you. If you stand at my side, maybe they'll listen."

"Thanks, but I'm leaving here as soon as I can. After I'm gone, whoever they tell you about will definitely strike back. I won't be a part of that."

"There will be no retribution."

I almost couldn't believe what I was about to say. At Southern, I would've been executed for questioning someone of her status. But I was on my way out of this pack, and with Brand at my side, I didn't think I had anything to lose by speaking the truth.

"Margarette, respectfully, pull your head out of your ass. Unless you change the ranking system immediately, unless you punish the abusers now, and get the unranked shifters somewhere safe, they'll never trust you or me. They shouldn't. It'll be far worse if they do, and they know it."

"There will be no retribution, because the perpetrators will all be dead," she said, her voice going steely. "And we'll change anything we need to, immediately. If you'll stay and help me, even for a few more days..." When she saw me start to shake my head, she added, "It would give you and your mates time to recover, and us a chance to make sure there aren't more bombs hidden on the roads out of our packlands."

I sighed at Brand, seeing the dream of the lake slipping farther away. One corner of his mouth curled up, and he murmured, "It's your choice."

There was no choice, though. My mates did need rest, and I wanted to watch Margarette turn her pack around, and make sure she didn't mess it up. I'd stay a few days, for Daisy, and all the unranked shifters who'd been abused here. I nodded.

Margarette spoke quickly. "First, we'll need to move the unranked into the Lodge, and the Enforcers to the tents. Then, maybe you can convince some of the women to tell us which males we can trust, and who needs to be executed. After that, I'll need to meet with whichever unranked shifters are the... well, I guess, the leaders in that group. If they *have* leaders."

I tried not to roll my eyes and failed. "You've artificially kept strong shifters from having rank, but that doesn't mean their wolves don't already know who's the strongest."

Brand hummed. "The strongest unranked may be the very ones who were the most abused. The males whose wolves could sense their superiority may have taken out their insecurity on them." He ran a hand over my cheek. "Rank or not, there is no denying the Moon Goddess's gift of power."

I wondered for a moment if my wolf—whenever she decided she would let me shift fully—would be a match for Brand's wolf. What if she was weak? I'd been starved for so long, and I hadn't been able to shift fully since I was at Southern. I wanted to be worthy of his wolf.

Margarette interrupted my musings. "Can you think of anything I've missed?"

"When they meet with you, you and the Alpha need to listen to what they say. And beg their forgiveness." I set one hand on the hilt of my steak knife, the other on the pommel of my sword, and bared my teeth. "I gave them some rudimentary weapons, but you need to give all the unranked *real* ones, immediately."

Margarette blinked. "What rudimentary weapons?"

I patted my steak knife. "The one good thing you did here was train them to defend themselves. You think I listened to them talk about not being able to protect the children, and didn't immediately liberate every kitchen knife you had, to send to those tents?"

Brand smiled savagely. "That's my sharp-petalled flower."

She was not as impressed. "What if they attack the ranked members?"

I hummed. "You know, you're right. We may not even need to convince them to tell us who's been hurting them. If we give them enough steel, my guess is they'll take care of it themselves." She started to shake her head, and I whispered, "What if some young, unranked girl is hurt because you gave her predators access, but kept weapons out of the hands of the only ones who'd protect her?"

"I'll find swords for them." She nodded stiffly, leading the way to the back of the Lodge.

At the door, my chest started burning again, like I had indigestion, and I rubbed it. Brand noticed immediately. "What's wrong?"

"I don't know. It feels like the muscles around my heart are being... pulled? Stretched too far. It hurts."

He growled. "Finn."

"What about him?"

"He left, right before I came to find you. He asked me to say goodbye for him."

"Asshole," I gasped, the vague pain now making sense. I'd formed that bullshit bond with him, and he'd taken off immediately. Not that I blamed him. "I guess he was horrified to be bonded to me. If we really are."

"You're bonded," Brand said, pressing a hand to his own chest. "I can sense it. Your scent has changed slightly as well. Cinnamon, jasmine, a little of my pine, and now a hint of ginger."

"Ew. I smell like Cityboy?" I sniffed my arm.

His dark eyes sparkled with humor as he brushed a piece of hair back from my eyes. "As to how he feels about being your mate? I think you'd be surprised at the depth of his emotions. Of course, I think he might be surprised as well."

I wanted to ask what he meant, but Margarette had opened the door for us. I walked out into the dim evening light of the training yard... which looked like a battlefield.

The Northern training yard was a kicked-over anthill of activity. The Enforcers' barracks had guards stationed all around the perimeter, and shifted wolves weaved in and out of the darkening tree line, monitoring any movement there. Patrick and Glen stood in the center of the yard in front of a table with a portable lantern on it, snapping out orders to the shifters around them.

We walked toward them slowly, taking it in. Dusk was falling, laying shadows over the whole scene, making it look like something out of a horror film. The unranked dorms were only half-standing, one third of the main building crumbled into rubble.

I gasped. "Nobody died?"

"Not yet, but two of the unranked males lost limbs," Margarette replied. "They'll be given a choice."

Memories of Del in the kitchens at Southern flooded through me. Me, rubbing the stump of his leg with oils to soothe him after a long day on an ill-fitting prosthetic. Him in his wolf form, teaching me to fight in my human one against a foe with teeth and claws.

"Where are they? Maybe I can speak to them."

"Of course. But if they choose to greet the moon, rather than—"

I cut her off. "Rather than live a life with no hope? No possibility of ever moving up in rank, of earning respect? Then you're a bigger failure as a pack than I thought." I could probably have stated that a little more tactfully, but

I'd never pretended to be classy. Why start now? I ignored her red face. "Brand, take me to see them?"

He nodded and escorted me to a tent that smelled of blood and despair. Outside the tent, I placed my hand on his arm, pausing him. His dark eyebrows rose. "Yes, little flower?"

I swallowed hard. "We need to talk. Not now, but sometime."

He smiled gently. "About us, or... them?" I could feel his emotions through our bond, a steady thrum of acceptance and strength, and found myself smiling back.

"All of it? How you're feeling about..." I placed a hand over the mark Finnick had given me, feeling a gentle, sweet ache start up there.

"I feel like I'm the luckiest shifter in the world. To walk beside you, no matter how many others the moon calls to you as mates."

My throat felt thick as I tried to answer, and found I could only duck my head in a nod. I didn't deserve this man. But I could try to change that.

Brand pulled back the canvas flap, and I stepped in, noting a half-dozen cots with residents, two of them set farther away from the others. I strode across the space, ignoring the protests from the doctor who was polishing a long, sharp blade by a steel table. Margarette went over to him, speaking softly.

I leaned down to the first unranked shifter, shocked when I recognized him. It was the male who'd fought Patrick for rank and lost, the one Patrick had whispered to at the end of the fight.

Brand hung back, not making a sound, even when I laid a hand on the unranked shifter's shoulder. "Please leave me alone," he rasped. He had tear tracks down his face, and as I let my gaze sweep over him, I realized he was missing his lower left leg below the knee, just like Del. "I don't want anyone to see me like this."

"What's your name?" I asked gently.

He didn't answer, but the other shifter, who was missing one arm, did. "He's Christophe. I'm Ralen. You're the unranked girl from Southern who was set up to die by Sergeant."

Brand growled, silencing the man.

"Set up to die?" I asked, and Ralen's lips went tight.

Brand stepped up beside me and demanded, "Do you know that for sure?"

Ralen stayed quiet, but Christophe groaned an answer. "No. It makes sense, though."

Honestly, it did, though the thought made me sick. I was glad Sergeant was away; he was one of the only fighters I didn't think I had any chance of besting.

"I'm dying anyway, Ralen. So are you. Maybe they'll make it quicker if we tell the truth."

I met Brand's gaze. Margarette hadn't announced her presence, but was listening quietly at the door. At some point, she'd escorted the doctor outside, which I appreciated. Listening to a knife being sharpened for their executions was the last thing these two needed to hear.

"We do want the truth, and you don't have to die," I said quietly. "Neither one of y'all needs to choose that. Things are changing. We're gonna ask the women who's been preying on them, and—" They both let out weak sighs, or laughs, it was hard to tell.

Ralen muttered, "They won't say a word. They know better."

Christophe added, "When they tried to complain before,

the abuse was worse for *months*. They learned not to speak up. I did complain to some of the Enforcers—the wrong ones, apparently. I was sent out to the woods for long shifts, next to the same assholes who hurt our females. They beat the shit out of me. But I kept trying to get ranked, so I could change something from within." He coughed weakly. "The women know better than to say anything. It only makes it worse."

Damnit. I should have predicted that.

Brand growled. "How many shifters here knew?"

"Plenty of the unranked. Not that many Enforcers, more of the regular ranked males. But those ranked assholes are smart. They never left evidence that couldn't be explained away."

Of fucking course not.

Ralen sighed. "But we have nothing to lose. We'll tell you everything before we meet the moon."

"You'll tell me the names of any Enforcers or ranked shifters who've harmed the unranked?"

When he murmured his assent, I waited, but his mouth twitched. "You'll need something to write on, ma'am. It's not just a couple of names."

Brand cursed aloud, but Margarette stayed quiet and out of sight, thank goodness. She'd already listened to the unranked women in the kitchen, but I realized she needed to eavesdrop a little more. These two wouldn't speak freely with any of their own pack leadership.

My mate pressed a kiss to my forehead, then walked away to get paper and a pen. I sat with the two men and told them stories about Del until he returned.

When they realized he'd been the one to teach me everything I knew—literally everything, since no one else in my pack would so much as spit on me if I was on fire—

their faces changed. I hoped they were understanding why I was telling them.

When Brand came back in, he brought bottles of water as well, setting them at the side of each man as they listed off over two dozen names. Then they went back and gave an account of their crimes, and approximate dates. I felt sick when I heard all of them. More than one of the unranked women had essentially placed herself in the sights of the worst abusers to draw attention away from the more vulnerable.

That's where we would find the leaders among the women, I knew. The ones who had already been leading, keeping the others safe. They were the natural choices.

Hours later, when the injured men finished spilling the pack's darkest secrets, it was past midnight. I was shocked to silence when Christophe said, "Flor? Can you get a chair for our Head Enforcer? It can't be comfortable squatting in the corner like that."

I hadn't even noticed her coming back in. I lifted my chin at Christophe while Margarette got herself a camp chair and approached. I liked this guy. He'd reminded me more and more of Del as the night wore on, and not only because he was missing a leg. He had a quiet strength. Christophe would make a good leader, if he decided to keep on breathing.

"You knew she was here?"

He lifted an eyebrow. "I'm not missing my nose, ma'am. I can still smell."

I blinked, impressed. Margarette's scent was so buried under layers of other, less pleasant smells, I hadn't even noticed it. "You're a shit-hot tracker, I bet."

He nodded, his cheeks going pink. "Not a patch on you, from what I heard. You escaped a hunting pack for years.

They told the stories in the unranked housing, about using spices to hide your scent, and how you rigged the trees. How you hunted to feed your pack's children. I only wish I had your woodcraft."

My cheeks went every bit as pink from the praise, and a surge of amusement poured through the bond from Brand. Margarette let out a soft laugh.

I took in her scarred face, so different from when I'd met her a handful of weeks ago at Southern. She'd seemed so perfect then, so strong. Now she looked bereft, like she'd lost something precious.

She'd also lost the arrogant pride she'd always worn like a shield. Humble looked good on her.

While Christophe and I talked, Margarette had been listening quietly. Now, she took a deep breath and spoke. "Shifter Christophe Warner and Shifter Ralen Thomas, may I address you formally?" They nodded. She knelt low between their cots and spoke with her head bowed. "You've both done a brave, selfless thing tonight, giving our pack the truth we need to go forward with justice, to regain the honor that we haven't had in so long. Now I would ask you to accept something from me and my mate."

They both made confused sounds of agreement.

My eyes flew to the tent flap, where Patrick and Glen were holding it open for their father. How long had they been outside? I wasn't sure, but I could tell they knew exactly what had been happening inside. Patrick came and took the list from Brand, then exited while reading it, his face grim.

Alpha Hillier walked to his wife's side and knelt next to her, his head lower than the injured shifters' faces. They stared wide-eyed at me, and I gave them a half smile. I had no idea what was going on, either. But Glen's small nod made me understand it wasn't bad.

It was both strange and strangely gratifying to see the two highest-ranked members of this pack kneeling before two of the least powerful, and a knot formed in my throat as Alpha Hillier took over from his mate.

"I've changed the ranking system in Northern, effective immediately. Rank will no longer be determined in the fighting ring. A shifter's worth cannot be measured by the strength of his or her body alone. From now on, we will consider all aspects of a wolf's power—their spirit, mind, body, and honor—before choosing who will earn their rank."

"That's good. That's... better than I could have hoped." Christophe let out a shuddering sob. "My life may not have had meaning, but my death will, if it means the unranked here have a chance."

"Your death?" Alpha Hillier asked.

"I'm going to meet the moon," he replied, his voice shaking.

Margarette stood. "We can't afford to lose any more Enforcers, Christophe Warner. I ask you to reconsider your choice."

"More—what do you *mean?*" His voice cracked on the last word.

"That is what I am asking you to accept. You and Ralen are Northern's newest Enforcers," Margarette said gently.

The Alpha nodded. "And more than that. You will be Senior Enforcers, bringing vital experience and knowledge of the hidden injustices that have been taking place under our noses...." His eyes met mine for a second. "Both the ones we ourselves did not knowingly commit, and the ones we allowed to take place."

I let it sink in that the head of the Northern pack had just admitted his wrongdoing to the least powerful member of the pack. My old Alpha would have died first. Would have let his entire pack die first.

When Del lost his leg, he'd been stripped of his rank and forced to do menial work. He'd been placed at the bottom of the hierarchy. Alpha Hillier had just done the opposite.

I smiled gently at the Northern Alpha. It was a start. A good start.

He went on. "Both of you more than deserve the rank, privileges, and income that comes along with the positions. Although, the Enforcers have been moved to the tents, so the lodging won't be what you might expect."

"I'm... I'm ranked?" Ralen sobbed, trying to cover his face with his remaining arm. "I can't believe it. I can't..." His words broke off, and Margarette gathered him into her arms, murmuring words of love and comfort, and promises of a pack that was ready to take care of him in his need.

Surprisingly, they didn't sound like lies.

Stunned, Christophe shook his head, leaning up on his elbows to glare at the stump of his leg under the sheet. "Enforcers need to fight. What can I do?"

I scowled at him, but only so I didn't dissolve into the puddle of emotion that was making me weak. "You can train the young unranked fighters. I saw you in the ring. You're good. You'd make an excellent teacher, like Del was for me." He looked doubtful until I said plainly, "The rogues that tried to take me, that blew up the barracks, they'll be back. Do you want the young shifters here to be ready to defend your pack? Who else will teach them?" I leaned close. "Patrick's working his way down the list right now, rounding up the bastards. There will be a lot of holes to fill."

His wolf rose in his gaze as I confronted him, and I saw a spark of hope and defiance there. He was going to be just fine.

Outside the tent, a fight was breaking out—possibly Patrick cleaning house—and the Alpha stood. "I need to take care of this. Glen? Can you stay here?"

Pulling a sword out of the sheath by his side, Glen nodded. "Of course."

But when we heard the enraged screams of women and girls outside, and the roars of anger from males that turned to howls, only the injured ones stayed—though I slipped my steak knife into Christophe's hand before I let the tent flap shut behind me.

32

ON ONE CONDITION
GLEN

The training yard outside the tent was filled with what looked like the entire pack, thousands of shifters congregating around the fighting ring where my father waited, his Alpha energy pulsing from him as he stood beside my brother. The night was lit up by torches and lanterns, shadows dancing in the nearby woods.

Shadows lay over my own thoughts as I wondered again how I'd been so fooled. I'd believed my pack was honorable. I'd been blind to the horrors our weakest members had experienced, ignorant because of my own privilege, the distance my position had provided.

I could hardly look at my father now without recoiling. I needed to leave Northern as soon as I could, and find a new home.

Flor is our home, my wolf murmured.

It was true. My wolf was ready to shift and run, as long as we were running alongside our mate.

Patrick stood next to my father in the ring, his sword drawn and stance aggressive, the list of abusive shifters and their crimes crumpled in his other hand. He was panting, stiff with anger, as he threw the balled-up paper at Erik, one of the Enforcers I genuinely liked.

Erik was facing Patrick down, his own sword in one hand. By the moon, I hoped his name was not on that list.

"Stand down, Enforcer," Dad ordered him.

Erik obeyed immediately, sheathing his sword. "Alpha, Patrick says you've stripped over two dozen shifters—some of them Enforcers—of their rank, effective immediately. That they've been accused of crimes, and I'm to round them up for judgment."

"I suggest you follow my son's instructions," Dad replied, picking up the list and reading it, his concerned gaze moving to Patrick.

My brother's face kept shifting, teeth lengthening and fur sprouting along his jawline. He was as close to losing control of his wolf as I'd ever seen him. What had he read? What had he discovered?

My mother slipped out of the tent behind us, and Dad gestured to her, his expression growing grimmer as he read the list. "Margarette, we'll need the silver blade."

She nodded, then returned to the house, the crowd parting smoothly for her. The ceremonial blade hadn't been used since the war, as far as I knew. It was stored in Dad's private office, and I'd only seen it once, back when he was teaching me what it meant to be an Alpha, or the Heir to one.

That sometimes protecting the pack meant cutting out the rot.

"Who made these accusations?" Erik demanded. "Those Enforcers are some of our most valuable fighters, and the rogues—"

Dad's eyes narrowed. "Erik, are you challenging me?'

290

"What? No, Alpha!" His shock was genuine. "But we can't afford to lose ranked wolves, not now." He wasn't wrong, but those wolves had to be culled.

Patrick shouted, his muscles rippling strangely, "We can't afford to have them in this pack. I will tear them out, all of them!" He dropped to all fours, breathing heavily.

A dark-haired shifter I vaguely recognized, a young woman with a leather collar who normally worked in the unranked housing with the children, crept closer to him and murmured something.

"What is her name?" I muttered, mostly to myself.

"Kristin Star." Flor's whisper was just loud enough for me to hear. "Patrick's... Well, Patrick has a thing for her." She was leaving something out, but I let it go.

Whatever the girl was saying to my brother wasn't helping. Patrick still fought the change, snarling at the others around them when they milled closer.

"Everyone down," Dad called. When only a few shifters obeyed, he repeated himself, a huge upwelling of Alpha power in his voice. The only people left standing were me, Brand, and Flor.

The crowd, now seated or kneeling, began to protest. I could see better now, and realized there were unranked women in a group on one side, circled around a group of our youngest. All of them were armed with what looked like butcher's knives, rolling pins, and steak knives.

Dad spoke again, every ounce of his dominance coming down on the gathered shifters. "*Silence.*"

Behind me, Flor whispered something to Brand, and I almost smiled. But Patrick's situation was worrying me. I walked over and laid a hand on his shoulder, helping him to his feet. "What's wrong?"

"They hurt her," he rasped. "One of them..."

My blood went cold as I realized what he meant. "Who is she?"

His eyes, glinting a bright blue, fell on the young woman who'd spoken to him. She had somehow managed to crawl back to the other unranked women and was crouched at the edge of the circle, a knife in each hand, her teeth bared at the ranked shifters around her.

"Kristin Star. My mate-to-be," Patrick managed to whisper, then let out a quiet howl of agony. I felt my own teeth sharpen, and tightened my grip on him.

"They must all die," Dad announced, his voice filled with power. My wolf let out a silent snarl of agreement, as we watched Dad read the list silently, his expression growing tighter with every second. "Every single one."

Dad handed the list to me, and I took it, skimming the contents quickly and feeling sicker with each name. Each crime.

I'd been so blind. I bowed my head to my brother's mate-to-be, deep sorrow filling me, and even deeper shame. "We will kill them all," I promised.

"Leave some for me," Flor whispered, moving to my side. "Or at least one." She slipped her hand in mine, and I swallowed hard at how perfect it felt. How necessary her support was right now, even if I didn't deserve it.

I would someday. I would earn a place at her side.

I squeezed her hand. "Which one do you want?"

"I'll take the traitorous bitch in the back," she said, pointing at a familiar woman who was being held by two Enforcers. Clara, her hair a tangled mess around her muddy, blood-streaked face, wearing the same cocktail dress she'd had on when she and Vanessa betrayed our pack. I'd never wanted to kill a woman before, but this one had my wolf foaming at the mouth.

Dad spoke again, louder, and we all fell silent. "Northern, I learned today that my pack has evil at its very core, and I take full responsibility for harboring it, giving it a place to flourish. In my misguided efforts to protect our weaker wolves, and our women, I allowed great harm to come to them.

"I allowed shifters who had no honor to stand with their feet on the necks of the very ones they swore to protect. While all along, they were torturing them in private, in the dark, like the cowards they are. But no more. Tonight, I am cutting the rot out, with teeth and claws. Each one of the accused will be given one chance to speak truthfully, under my power, to the accusations made against them.

"If they admit the crime, they will die by silver, a quick death. If they attempt to deceive or run, they will fall to the claws and knives of the pack they betrayed." He gestured to the unranked women. "Come forward." They shuffled closer as a group, their knives still drawn. Even the smallest of them had some sort of weapon in their hands.

My heart fell when I recognized the little girl who stood in the very heart of the group: Daisy. The women were protecting her, as if even our children were at risk.

I wanted to howl, to rage like Patrick. Instead, I held still. The air was filled with a grim expectation.

"Child," Dad murmured. "You don't need that knife. I promise I'll keep you safe."

Daisy shook her head, shocking everyone around her. A shifter child standing up to an Alpha was unheard of.

"You may speak," Dad said quietly.

Daisy answered clearly, "I do need it, Alpha. The Alpha's Protector said we could have them. This way, the mean ones can't hurt us anymore."

"The mean ones?" Dad asked, his voice breaking.

"The 'Forcers that hurt my friends."

The energy in the clearing was so tense, it was almost painful to breathe. Dad closed his eyes for a second, and I noticed that he was having trouble controlling his own shift now. "Patrick, Erik? I need you to help bring the named Enforcers and shifters into the training ring. You know who you can trust? Have them bring all the chains they can find."

Patrick glanced toward Kristin, then nodded, his movements stiff as he moved away, like it hurt him to go. I knew the feeling.

Dad went on. "Brand Becker, the Northern pack would like to formally request your assistance. Can you please stand with my Heir and guard these unranked shifters while I bring the accused to face the charges?"

"I'm not your Heir, Dad," I murmured, perhaps not quietly enough. A few of the nearby shifters began to whisper, and their eyes drilled into me.

Dad's jaw worked, and he swallowed. "With my son, then," he corrected.

"Of course," Brand replied.

Dad tore his gaze away. "Flor? Will you also guard our pack's most vulnerable while I…"

"While you clean house? Of course." Flor pulled her hand out of mine, and I tried not to whine. "On one condition."

Dad blinked at her, then me. I just shrugged.

Her smile, when it came, wasn't sweet. It was a baring of her own sharp teeth, and her wolf filled her voice with a growl that resonated in my soul. "You'll let me have Clara to punish."

I knew what Dad's answer would be before he gave it.

Flor couldn't dole out justice on our behalf. She wasn't a member of Northern anymore.

Officially, she'd never been a full member, since she'd never had her rank assigned in our pack. She'd become Brand's mate and gone from Northern pack member-to-be, to de facto Mountain pack member the instant his teeth had sunk home.

Though, come to think of it, she and Finn had a bond as well. Was she half-Mountain, half-Eastern now? My stomach churned. What I wouldn't give to have my own mark next to theirs. To have her small teeth in my neck.

To know she found me worthy.

"You're a Mountain shifter now, Flor," Dad said, almost gently. "This has to be Northern justice." He stood beside Patrick and Erik as they tapped a number of the Enforcers nearby to help them. By the time they began moving through the milling crowd, the Alpha had about three dozen burly Enforcers—trusted ones, all of them friends of mine—helping with the task.

To my surprise, Dad went with them, his Alpha power still forcing the closest shifters to their knees as he moved through the crowd of what had to be close to the entire pack, at least eighteen hundred wolves.

I'd been relieved as hell to see none of my closest pack members were on the list of criminals. But I'd been sickened at who *was* on it, and what they'd done. None of our unranked wolves had been able to hide like Flor had, and the abuses ranged from theft of their blankets and possessions, to physical and sexual assault.

A lot of shifters were about to die, and needed to.

"I didn't want Northern justice," Flor muttered grumpily. "I wanted Southern revenge. Give me a half hour with Clara, some duct tape, a jar of honey, and a fire ant mound, and I'll be your guard bitch for however long you need."

Brand let out a low chuckle, while I kneeled beside Daisy. Her small face tipped up to mine fearlessly, reminding me even more of Flor. This little shifter, the orphaned child of two unranked wolves, was the future of the pack. We had to keep her safe, even if it meant culling a hundred ranked abusers.

I tapped the end of her nose with one finger. "I think there may be things you should not see happening here soon, little wolf. Maybe you could go into the tent and help Ralen and Christophe, the two men who were hurt? There's a platter full of cookies and brownies that needs to be finished—" I stopped speaking as Daisy ran to the tent.

"That's a good place for her," Flor noted. "One entrance, easily guarded." She stepped back a few paces to be closer to the tent, resting a hand on her sword hilt. Brand and I followed her, as if an invisible magnetic force pulled us close.

Maybe one did.

"The other unranked women might also like to go into the tent as well," Brand began, but Kristin stood and spat on the dirt of the training ring.

"Are you joking? Miss the chance to see the nightmares end? Fuck that. I'll stay awake for days, paint myself in their blood."

I was impressed again at her strength, and repulsed at the lie the leather choker on her neck told the world. She couldn't hold Brand's gaze, but had been able to stand while most of the other shifters were still on their knees.

"I like her," Flor told Brand. "I wish you could come to Mountain with us, Kristin. Get you the hell out of here."

"Maybe you can ask," Kristin replied, but her gaze flitted to where Patrick had gone.

"You'll find your place here. You're my brother's—"

The young woman's eyes went dull. "I'm his nothing. He won't want me."

My heart broke. I'd seen what was written on the list, the assaults that had begun about a year before, when she was barely eighteen, and lasted until only days ago, when her attacker choked to death on his own spit.

Flor stepped closer, pulling the girl's chin up with a gentle hand so their faces were only inches away. "You're not nothing, Kristin. You're a badass, and you're about to be an Enforcer, if I guess right. If you stay here, you'll be one of the shifters who'll change this pack. You can make it what they promised. A refuge."

Kristin nodded, tears shining in her hazel eyes.

"But if any shifter—even an Alpha Heir—doesn't see how fucking valuable you are, even with that leather around your neck? Even without anyone telling you that you're worthy? Cut off his nuts and feed them to him one at a time." Flor dropped her hand to the steak knife that Kristin held, and adjusted the young woman's grip. "Hold it like this, so you don't accidentally slice your thumb when you're nut-cutting, okay?"

Kristin's tiny smile was all the answer she gave, but it was enough.

"You'll be all right," Flor said gently. "And if you ever doubt yourself, know that I think you're a fucking inspiration."

With every word, my brother's future mate stood a little straighter, her gaze a bit clearer. I'd seen how the unranked shifters had watched Flor from a distance, like she was some beacon of hope. She was. She practically vibrated with a fierce determination to get Kristin to feel proud of herself, not ashamed.

Flor was a wonder. She reminded me of the strongest shifters I'd ever seen, and the most compassionate. Bloodthirsty when the situation called for it, gentle when she could be. She was everything a man could dream of and want, far more than one could deserve.

Then she turned her head, her red hair falling around her face, her eyes flashing amber fire, and I spoke before thinking.

"I love you."

Flor's eyes went wide, her lips forming a small O of surprise. My heart skipped a beat when I realized I'd just declared my love for Flor, for my best friend's mate, right in front of him and the entire pack.

Everyone left in the training ring froze. Flor's jasmine and cinnamon scent blossomed in the night air, rising along with the fire in my cheeks. I'd slipped once before back at Southern, and told her it was just an expression. But the words had been fighting to spill out ever since.

I wasn't ashamed. I did love her.

Fuck it.

I took a deep, steadying breath and repeated it, so she would know this wasn't a mistake. So they would all know. "I love you, Flor. I'll never love any other woman. You're my true mate, and I love you completely."

Brand's hand crashed down on my back, his fingers gripping the back of my neck just shy of painful. "Not the moment, brother. Not the fucking time."

I winced, but didn't look away from Flor, until she bit her lower lip. "All the stress has gotten to him. He's cracked. There's no other explanation," she murmured, maybe to herself.

Kristin snorted. "I mean, there's one explanation..." She muttered two words that might have been, "Magical koozie."

Wait... Coochie?

Flor sneered at her, but didn't snap out a sassy answer. Instead, she shrugged. "Must not be too magical." She glanced at Brand, a whole private conversation in that one moment.

Maybe not that private. I had a feeling I knew what she was hinting at.

He hadn't been inside her bedroom, not once, since they'd mated. I may have been glad about it before, but now I saw that it had made Flor doubt herself. That would not fucking do.

"Idiot," I grumbled as Brand let go of me. "It's always time to tell the woman you love exactly how you feel."

"Glen, Brand doesn't—" Flor started, but stopped mid-word when Brand gathered her up in his arms, growling.

"Words," he muttered. "Love's not words." He nuzzled his beard into her neck. "Love is actions. Acts of service. Sacrifice." He whispered almost too quietly to hear, "Love is showing you how perfect you are, making sure you know you're the queen of my life. I made a mistake, not showing you. But I do, Flor. I do."

Flor was blushing redder than me now, her gaze flickering to me while her arms wrapped around Brand's massive torso. He kissed her, and I watched, a mixture of jealousy and satisfaction filling me as Brand worshiped her lips.

I would kiss her like that someday, if she let me. I would do whatever it took to earn that privilege.

"Save it for the lake, Bearman," Flor whispered after a

moment, pulling away quickly when shouts in the distance attracted our attention.

"*Get back here!*" Dad's voice carried over the crowd's noise, and I realized some of the accused had made a break for the woods.

Erik and Dad must have followed, since Patrick and some of the other trusted Enforcers returned. They began forcing a group of the accused shifters into a ragged line inside the ring, each of them held immobile by my dad's command and by chains.

Patrick shouted for attention, answering the shocked demands from some of the gathered shifters to explain why their friends were in chains. "They're here to receive justice for what they've done to our most vulnerable," Patrick growled. "To answer for the crimes they've committed in our own pack."

"Who accuses us?" one of the chained men demanded.

"Our newest Enforcers, shifters who almost lost their lives in the bombing. Who showed bravery when they gave testimony of your rapes, theft, and abuse." He gestured to the tent, and I heard muttering about Ralen and Christophe. Patrick nodded to me, his attention on the prisoners, until Dad called for him to help with another group. "Watch them," Patrick told me.

I nodded back, my focus on the fifteen or so burly shifters in chains, until another shifter was dragged forward and dropped with the others by two of our senior Enforcers.

She wasn't chained, but she lay still for a long moment on the packed earth, until she peered up at me through her tangled hair with tear-filled eyes.

Clara.

33

A SOUTHERN WITCH

FLOR

When the woman who had helped Vanessa abduct me, who had given me over to the enemies of her pack, crumpled onto the ground only a few feet away, a hot wave of rage rushed through me.

But I knew it wasn't because of the things she'd done to hurt me, even if everyone else would think so. It was because of the way she fixed those helpless, pale blue eyes on Glen, and pleaded with him to save her.

She was a mess, but a hot one. With one of her boobs practically popping out of a rip in her dress, her disheveled state only made her look more like a damsel in distress. As she struggled to throw all the blame Vanessa's way, claiming she was talked into helping her, I could tell that plenty of the ranked shifters around us were already giving her the benefit of the doubt. A few of them cried out in protest.

Not the unranked ones, though. Every shifter who wore a collar was holding their knife a little tighter as she spoke, her sweet voice carrying and drawing the other ranked shifters closer to hear.

"Glen, you have to understand, I never meant to hurt you or the pack," she gasped. "I was only trying to protect you."

"You knocked out my true mate and gave her to my cousin to get rid of. There wasn't anything you could do to hurt me more effectively. When you hurt her, you hurt me," Glen spat out.

"She's not your true mate, though," Clara sobbed. "She should have been, but she claimed the Mountain shifter. We all saw it; we all know she's the real traitor."

I fought to control my expression. The crowd was listening to her, and we could all hear the ring of truth in her words. Even if it wasn't true, she believed it.

She thought I'd rejected Glen. She believed, at least on some level, that getting rid of me would keep him and her pack safe.

Glen's expression didn't change, even as she kept going, professing her allegiance to the pack, her good intentions in rescuing him from me, on and on. "Glen, please, you can't think I would try to hurt you. You're our Heir. You're the only man I've ever loved!"

"Clara," Glen replied gently. Too gently. "You didn't love me, and I certainly never loved you. You only wanted a position at my side, eventually, as Alpha Mate." He gestured to me. "But my place is at her side, wherever she goes. She may be Brand's mate, but she's mine as well, and I'll do anything to stand at her side. Even if it means leaving this pack."

It was a romantic thought, but the pack members near us cried out, shifting restlessly. From the darkening mood, word had already gotten around that he planned to leave.

And when Clara shouted, "She's cast some kind of spell on you, Glen—can't you see? No wolf can have more than one mate," more than one or two voiced their agreement.

Brand was completely still by my side and didn't speak, but I could feel an odd frisson of worry in our bond. I glanced down and noted he didn't have a weapon. Then I realized he was shifting partially, long claws extending from the tips of his fingers.

Oddly, I relaxed. My Bearman *was* a weapon.

"She's got magic," someone called out. "She's a Southern witch!" The crowd milled closer, and the circle of unranked females shifted farther back, closer to the tent.

I set one hand on the hilt of my sword, ready to fight. Brand moved closer, while I scanned the crowd for Patrick and Alpha Hillier. They needed to get here *fast*.

But they hadn't returned, and the first bunch of assholes chained in the ring were adding their own voices to the angry outbursts. "She's the one who's trying to gut our pack, take our Heir, and cut the heart out of our fighters!"

"That's why I did it," Clara sobbed. "I only wanted to keep us all safe!"

We didn't have nearly enough blades if Clara convinced even just the ones around us that I was the bad guy here. "Someone cut her tongue out," I muttered.

"With pleasure." To my shock, it was Kristin who answered. She darted forward, and in an instant, Clara's hair was clutched in one hand, a kitchen knife at the bitch's throat, and Kristin was looking up at Glen. "May I, sir?"

Glen opened his mouth to answer, but before he could speak, a group of ranked shifters rushed forward to pull Kristin away. I wasn't sure if they were friends of Clara, or just shifters enraged to see an unranked woman attacking one of their own. It didn't matter. The knife fell to the ground, and she and Clara were lost under a wave of angry shifters, some shifting into wolf form, snarling.

"Brand, help her!" I shouted, and he listened, though Glen was already fighting to get to her. They weren't attacking him, but they weren't helping him get to Kristin, either.

He didn't reach her before she was hurt. She let out a high-pitched shriek, and I heard a distant answering roar in the crowd. *Patrick*, I thought.

But then there was no time to think. The chained Enforcers were using the distraction to overpower their guards, and Brand's attention had shifted to the ones headed toward us. The fight was on two fronts now.

Crap.

Clara took the opportunity when I was standing alone for a split second to grab the fallen knife and lunge for me. I rolled to one side, then leaned away, avoiding each jab and thrust of her blade. My own sword was in the way as I dodged her desperate stabs. Her face was a mask of rage. She had to know she'd signed her death warrant by attacking me. She clearly didn't care.

I almost respected that she'd chosen to die fighting, but I couldn't feel such a thing for someone who'd betrayed her own pack. She was fast, but not as fast as me. Her training at Northern had been civilized, with sparring matches and rules.

My training had been far harsher. I'd battled every day of my life, and Del had made sure I knew there was only one rule in battle. Survive.

"Fight me, you little whore," Clara spat as I weaved under her next thrust. Her movements were increasingly sloppy, and my cheeks ached with what I was sure was a feral smile. My only distraction was Brand's fury echoing down the bond, but I closed it off, letting myself enjoy this moment. "Fight me!"

"Nah." I pulled my sword free with one hand, rolling not away, but closer to her in one smooth movement. I was done playing. "This ain't a fight."

"What?" She blinked, then looked down, to where my sword was piercing her torso. "How—"

"This ain't a fight, you insignificant bitch. It's just my turn to take out the trash." I turned the blade and drew it upward, the sharp blade cutting through her, all the way to her heart. A small bubble of blood and spit emerged from her lips, and her eyes went blank as she died, but I didn't have time to consider what I'd done, or what the consequences might be.

To my left, I heard males roaring curses, and feminine screams. A battle had broken out, and the unranked women were in the very heart of it. The night filled with the sounds and smells of fighting. Clashing knives and swords, screams of rage and fright, growling and howling as the world devolved into blood, soil, sweat, and fear.

Too many of the ranked wolves had no idea who to defend or attack. One thing was clear: the chained shifters had chosen to go down fighting, and they were all expertly trained.

What was shocking many of the pack into a confused state was that the fiercest fighters, who were granting the criminals their wish to die in battle, wore leather collars and shoddy clothing, and fought with kitchen implements.

I watched a scrawny girl who couldn't have been more than twelve whack an Enforcer on the back of his legs with a rolling pin hard enough to make him fall, where he was immediately covered with a swarm of knife-brandishing women.

One of the kitchen maids I recognized was wielding a paring knife with terrifying accuracy, piercing everything from arteries to eyeballs faster than my eyes could track.

The rich scent of blood carried on the breeze. These women breathed it in like a welcome perfume.

Glen was still fighting the pack members who'd rallied to Clara's insanity, and I found myself facing a ragged wall of armed shifters who seemed keen on killing the "Southern witch." There were at least ten overgrown males bearing down on me, only my sword keeping them all from attacking at once.

My sword and, in the next instant, my mate.

Suddenly, Brand stood in front of me, his claws dripping with blood, his face half-shifted into a muzzle. "Get in the tent!" He threw the command over one shoulder, then roared to confront the now-hesitant males.

I almost protested—I wasn't running from this fight, and I sure as hell wasn't going to leave Brand to battle alone —when I saw two of the chained shifters slip past the flap.

Fuck. Daisy was in there, with the wounded men.

Her small voice carried. "Help! Alpha Protec—" The word was cut off.

My sword in hand, I sprinted for the tent, but ended up fighting a shifted wolf and almost tripping over a corpse. Sounds of a confrontation inside the medical tent had me running faster. I reached the canvas flap and batted it open with my sword, intent on saving Daisy. But I was too late.

She already had a savior.

Christophe was no longer in his bed. He stood on his remaining leg, with Daisy behind his back, an Enforcer on his knees in front of them both. I wasn't sure why the

Enforcer was kneeling, until he made a gasping sound and fell over.

My steak knife was jutting out of the side of his neck, his carotid artery neatly severed.

I didn't have time to congratulate Christophe on his technique, though. Ralen was facing the other Enforcer, and he didn't have any weapons. I knew I could use my sword to end this quickly, but the look of despair on Ralen's face when I'd first met him flashed in my mind. This pack had taken so much from him. Most importantly, his pride.

Daisy was safe enough now, but Ralen? He needed to find a reason to live. And to do that, he'd need a sword.

Good thing I had one. I let out a short whistle and yelled, "Ralen, catch!" I tossed my sword to him, and he caught it in his one hand, an expression of disbelief painting his features.

I snatched up my steak knife—giving it a final twist before pulling it out, just in case the dead guy wasn't completely dead—then watched as Ralen and the remaining Enforcer circled the hospital cot slowly.

Daisy and Christophe joined me. The Enforcer, his hands still bound by a short length of chain, started to shift into wolf form. I hoped Ralen wouldn't let him finish the shift, since he might slip free of the chains. I stepped to one side, to block the entrance in case he tried to run. Daisy followed me on silent feet, her focus intense.

"That's one of the bad ones," Daisy whispered. "He takes our food. He took my blanket last winter, when it was so cold."

Christophe snarled at that, hobbling over to stand in front of us, but the softly spoken words had an even more significant impact on Ralen. He'd seemed worried before, but his face was now wreathed with savage determination.

"You don't deserve to be called an Enforcer." Ralen threw himself low at the shifting male. He'd gone down on one knee to lunge, and the half-shifted wolf gripped Ralen's shoulder in his jaws, biting down.

But Ralen had dropped beneath the wolf, using my sword to open up an enormous gash in his belly. The wolf howled in anguish as his guts spilled out onto the floor.

Ralen pushed the dying beast away and swung the sword high, bringing it down in the perfect spot to sever the ragged, furry neck halfway through.

34

THE HEART OF THE PACK

FLOR

The sounds of fighting outside the tent went on, but inside, it was quiet, except for our breathing. Stunned, Ralen stared across the room at us, then back at the sword that was stuck in place, halfway through the Enforcer's neck.

"Good job, Enforcer," I congratulated him. "Finish it, though."

"Finish?" He panted the word.

Daisy let out a tiny howl of joy and answered for me. "You got to cut the whole head off, 'Forcer Ralen. That's what the Alpha Protector did, right?" She slipped her small hand in mine, and I smiled down at her.

"That's right. It's the traditional sentence for someone really awful. Someone who hurts their pack."

"Where did you learn that?" Ralen grimaced, but leaned over and used his knee to hold the body down, and his good arm to saw off the head.

Shrugging, I shooed Daisy away from the severed head. "Common knowledge." I didn't need to admit that I hadn't really known that until Sergeant had told me.

Sergeant. Suddenly, knowing where he was seemed vital.

I helped Christophe to a seat, listening to the fighting outside grind to a halt as a pulse of Alpha power surged through the very air. I shivered as it moved over me, then cursed as I noticed Daisy and Ralen were on the ground, bowing under the invisible weight.

Thank goodness I'd already gotten Christophe to a chair. All three of them stared at me like I'd sprouted wings or something.

"What you'll need, until Margarette can order a decent prosthetic, is a crutch," I muttered, looking around the tent for something that might work.

At that moment, Brand appeared in the tent, covered in blood, his chest heaving, Glen right behind. It sounded like the battle outside had ended. From the amount of blood coating my mates—*mate, Flor. Only one is an actual mate, remember?*—I suspected the two had slaughtered every one of the accused, and maybe a few extras who'd looked at me funny.

I hoped they'd taken care of the ones who wanted to burn the Southern witch.

"Are you all right?" Glen demanded, at my side in three huge steps. He cupped my face in his hands and stroked my hair back, assessing me. Then he leaned forward and pressed a gentle kiss to my lips.

"Ooooh," Daisy hummed, delighted. Brand just snorted, slapping the back of Glen's head as he passed.

Glen's hands moved to my shoulders. "You weren't hurt?"

I curled a lip. "By your asshole pack, who think reenacting the Salem witch trials would be a good time? Nah."

Not a second later, Margarette flew through the

opening of the tent and skidded to a stop, a strange sword in hand that smelled strongly of silver. She pulled Daisy to her feet and gently checked her for wounds, then turned to face me once she knew the girl was okay.

"Flor, my pack is once again indebted," she said. "Thanks for killing these two." Margarette looked like she'd been in a fight herself, with blood spatters across her arms and clothing.

"I didn't do any of this. Your best Enforcers did." I nodded at Ralen and Christophe, who practically glowed with pride as Margarette reached a hand out to each man. I wasn't certain how she did it, but her touch seemed to free each of the lower ranked shifters from the Alpha's power that was still bearing down on us all.

I made a note to ask Brand about that later. I'd never seen any other Alpha Mates before, and didn't know what kind of power they might have. Although, I supposed the only other one left alive that I might meet would be Finnick's mom.

"Well done, Enforcers," Margarette praised. "All of you, please come outside with me. The Alpha has commanded the pack to bear witness to his judgment."

"I'm not going out there unarmed," I protested. Ralen wiped my sword clean on his pant leg and handed it back to me. "Perfect. Now Christophe needs a crutch—ah, thanks, Ralen." The one-handed shifter had draped an arm around Christophe's waist and was helping his friend hop to the doorway.

Margarette led Daisy out by the hand ahead of them. Brand, Glen, and I followed close behind. I had no idea what to expect, but what I saw shocked me to the core.

The Alpha stood in the center of the ring once again, but in his wolf form. I had never seen him shifted, and was impressed by his beast. His gray fur gleamed with blood. The blood of the shifters that lay all around him.

From what I could tell, he'd torn the throats out of all the first group of Enforcers. Well, the ones the unranked women hadn't taken care of. Another group of ranked males and females kneeled trembling in a line, Patrick and his men standing over them.

The unranked women stood clustered loosely around the Alpha, bloodied knives in their hands, eyes gleaming with rage and pride, like some kind of honor guard. The rest of the pack had gone completely silent, staring with bewilderment and fear at the group.

Margarette walked with Daisy, who didn't look at all upset by all the blood. In fact, she gave a vicious kick to one dead male as she went past his corpse, before stopping at the Alpha's side. The torchlight threw eerie shadows over the macabre scene.

Even the wind in the trees went silent as Margarette spoke. "Our pack has lost its way. Lost its honor." Moonlight reflected in her eyes as she glanced at me, then back at her mate. "Everything changes now."

Would it, though? I felt eyes on me, some of them friendly, many of them not. Brand and Glen stepped closer, forming a rank against the judgment. I set one hand on my sword and the other on my knife, and kept my chin up.

Maybe not everything would change, or at least, not all at once. Prejudice and fear were hard to cut out, even with a thousand swords and steak knives. But change had begun.

SOME OF THE changes Margarette warned about happened fast. She read out the crimes of the accused to the silent crowd, then used the silver blade to dispatch the remaining few criminals, her mate beside her.

No one complained after she announced their crimes. A few of them cried. One or two vomited.

Then Margarette called the unranked females to stand with her and made an announcement that did raise a few eyebrows. "Our most vulnerable members have been wronged for too long. We meant to protect them, but instead, left them vulnerable. They are the Heart of the Pack."

The way she said those words made them seem like a title, and a feeling that reminded me of the magic Grigor had used rushed over my skin.

Huh. I knew Alpha Mates shared in their mate's dominance, and that the Alphas could grow stronger if they mated a powerful female. But could they also use the Alpha power and command? I packed the thought away and focused on Margarette's speech.

"...so the Heart of the Pack is kept protected. From now on, these women and all the unranked shifters and children will live inside the Lodge. They will be guarded at all times, and the adults and teens armed as well. They are to be treated with the same respect that you give me, or the Head Enforcers. Raising a hand against one of them is the same as raising it against your Alpha himself."

I glanced to the side and saw Glen smiling sadly at his mom, while Patrick stared with anguish at Kristin.

"There will be a complete restructuring of the pack hierarchy, and every member of Northern is commanded to report here tomorrow at midday. No one may leave the pack grounds. Once the Heart of the Pack is safely inside, every ranked wolf will help us burn the bodies of these criminals and clean up this mess. No questions. Get to work."

The next few hours were a buzz of activity. I helped Margarette get the unranked women into their new quarters. Ralen and Christophe chose Enforcers to help guard the Lodge, ostensibly in case the Russian rogues attacked. But I could tell they were worried about violence from within the pack as well.

Margarette called me into the family room again after the Heart was settled, asking me to listen to the changes she was planning to make at Northern. As she laid out the new pack structure for me to approve, I found tears stinging my eyes.

She and Alpha Hillier weren't just changing a few things. They were remaking the entire structure of the pack. I almost couldn't believe what she had planned, but she'd written it all out.

"Flor. Do you think it's enough?" She held out the pad of paper with a trembling hand. She was exhausted and grieving.

I took a seat and scanned the paper, swallowing hard. "Rank will be decided by a group of the most vulnerable."

She nodded. "As of today at noon, no one in the pack besides the Alpha's family, and Christophe and Ralen, will have any rank at all. The Heart of the Pack will hear the remaining Enforcers' and Alpha Hillier's suggestions for who should be elevated. Those women's wisdom and experience will help us make certain no one who should not have authority is given back that power to abuse."

"And you'll let shifters leave if they want? Travel to other packs to find their mates, maybe even move?"

"Yes. Bradley spoke to Brand, and he assured us that

Mountain pack at least will allow our wolves to visit outside of the Conclaves. He can't promise they'll be welcomed into the pack permanently, but given more time there... Well, who knows? If they decided to come back home, they'll be allowed to do that as well."

"Like dual citizenship," I murmured. "Maybe Glen won't have to abjure Northern after all."

Margarette sighed heavily. "The children of Alphas, especially the Heirs, are not allowed to leave their pack-lands outside of foster stays or official duties, by order of the North American Council. Bradley already called Acting Council Alpha McDonnell and asked if Glen could have a temporary foster stay at Mountain. He declined the request."

"That fucker." I held my face still at the bombs she'd just dropped. One of them, I'd known. But that Alphas' chil-dren—not just the Heirs—couldn't leave their own packs?

Margarette grimaced. "You should meet his mate. She's a thousand times worse. So when Glen leaves home, he can only do so as a rogue. That means he can be hunted and killed with impunity, and should not be welcomed in any of the North American packs, unless the Council changes that law."

"He won't be allowed to enter the Mountain packlands?"

Margarette shrugged. "There is some leeway given. Brand's father can choose to incarcerate him, and send a request to the Council for directions."

"Not a good option."

"Not ideal, no. Glen could enter the packlands in secret and not declare himself, staying if Samuel chooses to look the other way." She allowed herself a small smile. "Brand's father detests the Council's meddling, and Finnick's father even more. Samuel is the ultimate authority in Mountain, and he has a soft spot for you, Flor. If you ask him to let Glen stay, to let you stay, I'm sure he'll allow it."

To let me stay. I took a drink, wondering if she knew, or suspected.

"I thought it was just Alpha Heirs that couldn't leave their own lands, except for Conclaves and foster stays," I said after a moment. "So Patrick and Glen both are tied here?"

"Yes. That law was decided long ago by the Council, to keep strong wolves from setting off on their own to carve out their own packs, or take over neighboring lands."

I nodded, like I wasn't panicking.

I could never, *ever* let anyone find out who my biological father was.

I let out a breath, trying to keep my heart rate steady. "We need Finnick's dad to step down."

She nodded once. "Bradley will have to go to the city, prove that he is capable of retaking the seat as Council Head, and call an official hearing with all the packs' leaders in attendance, to change the law."

"Will he be able to do all that?"

"He should. He's well now, and well respected."

"When's he going?"

Margarette slumped onto the armchair beside my seat. "It'll take a month, at least. We have to rebuild our pack from within, repair our defenses, and schedule a meeting all the Council can attend. And Flor, we don't know what to tell them about Glen's reason for leaving to follow you. Everyone knows you're Brand's mate. The idea that you have more than one mate—"

"They're all going to want to burn the Southern witch, aren't they?" I ground my teeth. "It would be one thing if I actually had magic. Hell, I can't even shift into my wolf form."

"You've tried?"

"Every damned day."

"Then that's another concern," Margarette pointed out. "There could be some connection between your problems shifting and your... unusual mating situation. We're hoping that the library at Mountain will reveal some answers as to what perverted the bond." She swallowed when I stood to leave. "Changed it, I mean. Flor. My own collection of books has almost everything our kind knows about mate bonds. Yet there's nothing in any of these books that even hints at why this happened. How it could have happened."

She crossed the room and poured a glass of water, staring out the window. "A lot of our collected knowledge was lost in the war, of course. Libraries burned, whole packs—" She started choking and took a quick sip of water. "You should research your lineage, Flor. You might find some answers." Her gaze was assessing. "Do you know who your father was?"

Margarette knew I was hiding something, and I had a feeling she at least suspected who my father was. But if I told her outright, if she knew it definitively, I was afraid she would have to tell the Council who I was.

And that I would have to return to Southern. I would, someday. My wolf was restless, insisting that we needed to go back to Luke soon. I wasn't ready to return yet, or to share all my secrets, and while I could do a lot of things, I couldn't lie straight to Margarette's face. "I need to go." I jumped up and headed for the door, forcing myself to move slowly, trying not to make it obvious that I was running away.

She exhaled heavily, but let me duck the question. "Go where, Flor?"

"I haven't slept in days, it feels like. I need to rest."

She stood and followed me to the door. "I heard you gave your bedroom to Kristin Star." Her lips pursed as she said the name.

"Yeah. She deserved it. Nice sturdy lock on that door. I'm going to sleep outside."

"Outside?"

I shrugged. "We've moved the ranked males out of the Lodge, and Brand's wolf was throwing a tantrum when he thought he'd have to sleep far away."

"Where is he now?"

Just outside the door, Brand cleared his throat.

Margarette echoed my grin. "I see. Go to the western edge of the lake. There's an old cabin there, a few hundred feet from the water's edge. I spent more than one night out there with Bradley, long ago. I'll ask someone to make sure you're not disturbed. We'll find you another bedroom for tomorrow night."

I shook my head. "I'm sorry, Margarette. I need to go to Mountain, as soon as possible, and then back to—"

"To Southern, yes." She gripped my arm. "I'm glad. You're needed there as well."

"Yeah, I have to check on..." I didn't let myself say his name, but I rubbed my chest where the pain was sharpest.

"I'll miss you. Our pack needs energy and discernment like yours."

I met her gaze, hoping she would listen and really hear what I was saying. For all that she knew she needed to change, Margarette had some deep-seated prejudices to fight.

"I think you already have a woman with the same qualities. A natural leader, no matter what's around her neck." I flicked my ear tag, then waited until she nodded. "Kristin's lived through hell, like I did. You'd do well to listen to her advice."

"I will." She stepped close and extended her arms for a hug. "Someday, if you come back to Northern, I hope you'll see a better pack. That we learned how to be the pack, the refuge, you deserved." I let her arms enfold me, and it was like I was back at Southern again, with this woman giving me the love I'd never known from my own mother.

Only now, I knew that Margarette was almost as flawed as my own mother had been. Still, she was trying to redeem herself. For all I knew, someday I'd fuck up royally and be the one asking for forgiveness.

So I let myself sink into her as she whispered, "I hope you'll love my son enough for his family and pack. He'll need you, Flor. Please... give him a chance."

"I will," I promised as she escorted me through the doorway where Brand waited for me.

"Take good care of her. The rogues may come back," Margarette cautioned.

"I will. Thank you for the supplies." He held up a picnic basket and two pillows.

"Good. I'll set a guard to be sure no one interrupts your rest," she said, then arched a brow at Brand. "I'm glad you're finally honoring the moon with your mate. Shifter pups don't make themselves, you know."

We both blushed, but Brand muttered, "I do know that, ma'am," before we fled the Lodge, laughing as we ran.

35

HER CHOICE
BRAND

I marveled at my little mate's resilience. It seemed like only hours ago that she'd been abducted. Only minutes since she'd stared down a crowd of angry wolves, intent on casting her out.

In the past few days, she'd been taken, had dark magic used on her, returned, claimed another mate, forced the most powerful Alpha on the continent to apologize, assisted him and his mate in restructuring the pack from the bottom up, and now she was laughing.

No. *Giggling.*

I couldn't help the smile that spread over my own face at the sound. Everyone knew my mate was deadly. But not many knew that she was cute as a pup, with a giggle that sounded just like one.

"Can you believe that?" Flor called as she ran in front of me toward the western lakeshore. "'Shifter pups don't make themselves.' The look on your face!"

Pups. The thought made my wolf's ears perk up.

Not yet, I warned him.

I didn't know what to say to Flor. The idea of her growing round with my pups flooded me with a wave of longing so intense, my knees went weak. But we were in no place to even think about such things. So I gave a mock growl and chased after her, the picnic basket thumping against my leg.

When we reached the cabin, Flor explored the inside while I found a flat place on the lakeside and laid out the picnic. The kitchen staff obviously adored Flor; they'd packed enough food for a week, and all of it was exquisitely prepared.

Flor plopped down on the checkered cloth and began pulling off the lids off the small glass dishes. "What did they make? Ooooh, fancy meat stuff?" She stuck her finger into the pâté and licked it clean, moaning in appreciation. I shifted on the cloth, remembering the only other time I'd heard that sound from her lips.

She'd opened four or five dishes and sampled them all before she stopped, blinking up at me. "You're not hungry?"

I took a deep breath, then let it out. "Not for food, little flower. But I would very much like to feed you." She dropped her gaze, and the breeze blew a soft wave of her jasmine and cinnamon scent to me.

"What would you like to feed me, Bearman?" she teased, her voice a husky rasp. Her fingers toyed with the button at the top of her shirt. "I might be hungry for more than food."

"Food first. You'll need your energy," I teased back. I gathered her up and placed her on my lap, using a spoon to lift bites of quiche, beef stew, and a half-dozen other foods to her mouth.

"That's enough," she insisted when I opened a jar of honeyed custard. She took the spoon. "My turn." She turned to face me so that her legs straddled mine, carefully spooning up a bite of the sweet pudding and holding it up to my lips. I shook my head, and she rubbed the custard on my closed mouth, giggling. I leaned in and kissed her until there was not a drop of pudding left.

"Oh, I like this way of eating dessert," she said breathlessly. For a while, that was all we did—share bites of pudding and long, drugging kisses, while the bees and insects droned around us, and the frogs called out from the water's edge.

Eventually, I pulled away, stroking her hair. "What else would you like? I know you need rest."

"I don't want to rest. I want to get to know you," she said, her voice wobbling slightly. "Can I... Can I explore? Can I touch you?"

My only answer was a heartfelt groan, which made her laugh again.

Oh, Mother Moon, let me be the reason she laughs for the rest of our lives, I prayed, as Flor took the lead, kissing me more deeply. *Let me give her pleasure and joy and no pain. Whatever the cost, I accept it. Just give me the skills and knowledge to keep her happy, and safe.*

Eventually, the kisses became caresses, our clothing serving as pillows as she took her time exploring my body.

"My flower," I rasped, as her small fingers moved gently over my bare stomach and down to my groin, cupping my balls and then feathering up and down my length so lightly, it made me ache. "Love, I'm not sure I can take much more."

"I'm not good at this," she murmured, leaning back.

I gently moved her back over me, and shook my head.

322

"You're too good. Let me touch you before I embarrass myself."

"Okay." She lay back on the cloth. As I touched her with my hands and lips, the wind picked up around us, lifting the soft cries that she made over the lake. I held her core to my mouth and lapped at her, luxuriating in her pleasure as if it were my own.

Raindrops began to fall around us, and the wind grew stronger, raising goosebumps on her limbs. "I don't want to stop," Flor panted. "I want you."

I hesitated, not wanting her to grow chilled, when a soft cough drew my attention.

In an instant, I was covering her body, growling at the threat.

"Sorry, brother, it's me. Mom, uh... Shit. She probably engineered this." Glen stood downwind, carrying a thick stack of blankets, his face averted. "She asked me to guard from the woods, but said you needed bedding."

My wolf settled immediately, and I considered Glen for a long moment. I'd known him for years, respected him more than any of my friends. I called him brother and meant it.

If I had to choose one other person in the world to care for my little flower alongside me, one other mate to share a bond, it would be him. But it was her choice, always.

I glanced down at Flor, who was chewing at her lower lip. She stood, the rain dampening her flushed skin. To his credit, Glen didn't even try to steal a peek at her naked form. Her eyes caught mine, an unspoken question in them. I sent reassurance down the bond between us, and acceptance.

Flor's soft smile was shy but hopeful as she ran to Glen's side through the worsening rain, and grabbed a blanket from the top of the stack, wrapping it around herself. "You're going to stand out in a storm while Brand and I are safe and warm inside? I'm not sure you're smart enough to be my mate, Glen Hillier."

Laughing once more, she ran ahead of us both into the cabin.

We were only a breath behind.

36

FRAGMENTS OF BLISS

FLOR

T*ime to conjure my inner sex kitten,* I thought as the door behind me shut, both males inside the cabin with me.

For a long moment, they held still, watching me, waiting for me to decide what happened next. I held even more still, except for my nipples. Those little hussies were growing rock hard in anticipation.

I almost couldn't believe this was me. Only a few months before, I'd scrubbed my skin raw whenever a male touched me, even inadvertently. I would have bet cash dollars that I'd never desire a man, let alone two.

And two at one time? Even if Glen just made popcorn and watched the show, this was way more perverted than anything I'd ever fantasized might happen. My wolf snorted and assured me there was a lot more where this fantasy came from.

I shushed her, took a breath, then let it out as I turned to face the men. Brand was smiling quietly, as he turned to slide the bolt in the door, while Glen crossed the room to light the fire in front of the implausibly large bearskin rug.

Once he'd stoked the fire, I turned away from him and toward my mate, who was leaning against the wall. "Well, Brand, are you going to make me wait forever to—how did Margarette put it? *Honor the moon?*" I let the blanket fall to the floor, standing there naked. Hoping I looked confident.

With no wind or rain, and the small fire, it was warm enough to be naked in the small cabin, but my flesh prickled as two sets of hot eyes raked my body. I turned to take in the cabin—and give both of them the whole view— pretending I wasn't flushed with anticipation and close to flinging myself at one of them. Or both.

The cabin was one room, with a half-open door that led to a small bathroom, where I could see a clawfoot tub. There was a bed against one wall of the main cabin, and a small kitchen, but the soft rug in front of the fireplace called to me. I prowled over to it, sliding down to sit on the plush fur with a low hum. "So soft."

I wasn't certain where the sexpot I was acting like had come from, and I could tell the males inside the cozy cabin were as shocked as I was.

"I'm not soft," Brand teased. "And pretty sure Glen's never been harder."

"Ah, Flor..." Glen was practically breaking into a sweat as he tried to find words. "Did you mean... Should I go—I can *leave*. I didn't expect—" He stuttered to a stop.

When I forced myself to face the truth, I knew he was my mate, that somehow they all were. I wasn't sure how it could be, or if I even wanted them all. But they were mine.

"Definitely not the brightest of my suitors," I sighed, not letting myself think of Finnick or Luke.

Or Grigor.

I turned my head to Brand. "Would you like Glen to stand guard outside, Bearman?"

Brand's eyes hardened slightly. "That would serve him right, wouldn't it? After he watched you at the creek, without your permission. He shouldn't be allowed to see you, or touch you."

Glen sputtered out a curse, then sank to his knees on the very edge of the wide rug. "Whatever you want, princess. But please let me stay."

I felt Brand's acceptance in our bond before I gave a short nod.

"Thank you," Glen whispered, though I was already distracted. Brand was stalking toward me, his swollen length slapping against one thigh. I swallowed hard. If I hadn't already fit that thing inside me, I wouldn't have believed it was possible.

He stopped in front of me, lifting his hands to touch me gently, then dropping to his knees to trace my cheekbones and jawline, the curve of my neck to my shoulders, and down to my breasts. He outlined the silvered scar over my heart with his thumb, feeling the slight change in the skin there, starting from the center point and moving out along each of the five jagged lines, slowly. Intentionally.

"I don't know how I got it," I admitted. "I've had it forever."

He held out one bare arm, showing the slight silver scars that remained on his body where he'd been bound with the magical net. They had the same odd shimmer that my scar had, though his were very light compared to mine.

"A question for tomorrow," he said, then gently lowered me to the floor until my back was on the rug. He kissed me gently, thoroughly, his hands moving over my hair.

Glen's voice was soft, almost reverent as he watched Brand begin to make love to me. "She's so beautiful, isn't she, brother? So responsive. Look at how she shivers when you stroke her nipples. Have you tasted them yet?"

Brand growled in response, taking one of the taut buds between his lips. I arched my back as sparks of pleasure shot to my center. His teeth scraped across the other tight peak, and I cried out, my core going damp.

"Oh, she likes that."

Brand grumbled, "She'd like them both, wouldn't you, little flower? Both of these nipples being played with at the same—" I was already nodding my head, my cheeks flaming. Brand grunted something that must have been an assent, because Glen quickly moved over, resting on his side on one elbow, and wrapped his fingers around the other breast. Then they lowered their heads at the same moment, swirling their tongues around the sensitive flesh.

I had to bite my lip to keep from screaming. How could this feel so forbidden, and so perfectly right?

Brand used his tongue more delicately, and was far more careful with his teeth, while Glen devoured my other nipple until it ached. My breasts were small, but apparently, that hadn't made them any less sensitive. The combination of pleasure tipped with a hint of pain made me tremble from head to toe.

Could a woman have an orgasm from just this? The almost painful swirling feeling in my abdomen had me wondering that out loud.

"She's close," Glen murmured.

"I want to feel you come on my cock, little flower," Brand growled. Glen moved away as Brand rose above me, balancing his massive torso over mine on his burly, muscular arms. He reached down, coating the head of his cock in the wetness that slicked my inner thighs, and pressed forward an inch, then two, his hand guiding it slowly inside me.

I hissed as the pressure grew too intense. His cock was so thick that even though we'd had sex before, my body wasn't really prepared. Brand flinched, cursing softly, then began to withdraw.

Damnit. If he pulled out now, I wasn't sure I could keep from throwing a fit. I'd been waiting for this ever since he'd claimed me in the training ring.

"Wait," Glen and I said at the same time. Glen's eyes met mine, and he lifted an eyebrow. "Flor, can I help you? Can I touch you while Brand works his way into you?"

My wolf howled a *yes*, and Brand's concerned expression shifted instantly to one of dark amusement, but he waited for me to answer out loud. "Please."

Glen was still fully dressed, which somehow made what he did feel even more illicit. He stuck two fingers in his mouth, then moved them to the top of my mound, circling my clit with firm, even movements. His eyes never strayed from my face as the sensations began to build, and I knew he was paying attention to everything I liked. How fast or slow, how much pressure, or how little.

And he talked while he touched me. "You're so slick, princess, so hot and perfect. I could do this all day, all night. Touch you and make you come, worship this body the way I was born to. Brand, can you feel her getting even wetter? I bet she's pulsing around your cock already. Push into her, a little more; she's opening for you."

Brand's cock almost felt like it expanded as he pressed into me, and I groaned, but with pure bliss. The stretch was just on this side of painful, my mind blurring all the sensations—Brand inside me, thrusting gently, slowly, while

Glen tortured my body with too-gentle caresses and kisses until I came, writhing and begging.

"Fuck me harder, Brand, *please!*"

When Brand slid his entire length inside me and began a rhythm, Glen moved away. But the feeling of his gaze on us as Brand moved inside me, the longing that was so thick I could taste it, was what had me coming again a moment later. The cabin filled with my cries, and the scent of our lovemaking. Brand hadn't reached his climax yet, but he was moving slowly, gentling me down from the peak.

"So beautiful," Glen whispered.

"*Mine,*" Brand's wolf replied, his tone filled with dominance. Glen's lip curled slightly.

I interrupted the beginnings of their posturing. "Wrong. You're mine."

"I am?" Glen asked, his voice raw. I didn't know what to say, so I let my inner sex kitten answer for me.

"You have to be too warm in those clothes. Take them off."

Brand pressed a kiss to the corner of my mouth, then moved to nibble my neck, distracting me, but from the corner of my eye, I saw Glen moving slowly, sliding his clothing off.

Breaking the kiss, I turned my head and watched as he uncovered his muscular body. The dim light sifting through the windows illuminated him just enough to see the definition on his chest and lower, and then—

"Wow." I licked my lips, my throat suddenly dry.

Glen had the most perfect dick. It wasn't as big as Brand's, but it was just... pretty. Smooth and curved, and for some reason, it made my mouth water.

I wanted to lick it, taste it, more than *anything*. "Come closer."

Brand pulled out of me, and for a moment, I wondered if I'd hurt his feelings. But his eyes were pools of molten fire as he lifted me up and turned me so that my knees were on the rug, positioning me so I was facing Glen. "Look at my perfect queen, brother," he growled, wrapping one arm around my front, gripping one of my small breasts with a massive hand.

I wrapped my arms around his, widening my stance, though he had to lift me off the rug somewhat to make this position work. He was so much bigger than me, he had to spread his own legs wide to fit us together. He set the tip of his cock at my entrance again, teasing me. Teasing Glen.

"So small, but made to fit with me."

"With us," Glen whispered.

Brand merely growled in response. At last, he lowered me down slowly, as if he was showing off his control, his strength. His claim.

Glen's jaw had dropped as he watched Brand take me from behind, but it opened even wider when Brand said roughly, "My queen said to come closer. Don't make her wait. Kiss her, hold her, while I fill her full of my cock."

"With pleasure, brother." Glen crawled to kneel in front of me, then waited there, touching only my face, tracing his fingertips over my flushed cheeks. "I don't deserve you," he whispered.

I gasped as Brand moved suddenly upward. "None of us do, brother. None of us do. Now kiss our mate while I honor her."

I gasped as I felt his total acceptance of Glen in our bond. Acceptance, and what had to be love.

Did I love him?

The answer was immediate. Of course I did. His fierce

protectiveness, his gentleness and devotion made it impossible to do anything else.

He'd waited for me to be ready for him. He would have waited forever, I knew.

He was my rock, my mountain of a mate, the solid foundation I could build the rest of my life on. I never wanted to be apart from him.

"I love you, Brand," I murmured, though I was staring into Glen's face.

His blue eyes gleamed with understanding and joy. We didn't share a mate bond, but I could see in his eyes everything he felt. He was almost glowing with a deep joy for his brother, and me.

We don't have a mate bond with him... yet, my wolf purred.

Yet, I agreed.

As Brand lowered me to the rug, then kneeled over me, Glen backed up slightly. I was on all fours, so he could only trace the lines of my face. Glen smiled with wonder, cupping my face like I was some kind of treasure.

Brand let out a fierce growl and pressed his teeth close to my mating mark. I couldn't see his face, but I could feel his response. I'd never experienced anything like the upwelling of gratitude, and what might have been peace, that emanated from him. "Don't deserve it," he murmured at last. "But I'll spend my life trying to."

"I love you," I repeated, wondering at the emotions that shone in Glen's deep blue eyes. I was telling another male I loved him, but Glen's response was only joy.

Well, perhaps a little jealousy, too. But there was no mistaking the happiness he felt for Brand and me.

Huh. Maybe this could work after all. Maybe Glen would turn out to be a perfect mate as well. Was it possible that the Moon Goddess had known what She was doing when She gave me more mates than any one woman could handle?

My thoughts scattered as Brand surged into me, and I pushed back into his strong embrace, as Glen watched me dissolve into a thousand splintered fragments of bliss.

37
BETTER THAN OYSTERS
GLEN

W hen Flor had teased Brand about "honoring the moon," I'd laughed along with her. But what I was witnessing—what I was taking part in—was as close to a prayer as anything I'd experienced. I felt the presence of something almost divine as I watched Brand worship her with his body. Felt as if the Moon Goddess Herself was present as I touched the woman who somehow, though I did not deserve it, allowed me to drop to my knees and worship alongside my brother.

I knew I hadn't earned this moment. Nonetheless, I drank in her cries of pleasure as she moved under Brand's massive form, her own miraculous body somehow allowing him to thrust fully inside.

Flor was still thin, but her breasts had grown more lush with the regular meals since she'd escaped Southern. Her red hair was longer, almost sweeping her shoulders, and glowed like a dark net filled with rubies in the dim cabin light.

What would she look like, swollen with a child? A pup growing inside that concave belly, her breasts heavy and full... I shook the thought away, though my wolf howled as if he was on the hunt, chasing a moonlit shadow, years away in the woods.

She blinked up at me, a pink flush covering her cheeks as I stared. Her eyes were where the greatest change had occurred. She'd always had a fierce look, but now it was tempered with a touch of gentleness. "Glen. I need you."

At first, I didn't respond, until Brand slowed his thrusts, rising so that he was holding her hips, balanced on his knees. She lifted herself onto her hands and turned to face him. "I love you," she repeated.

He lifted a dark eyebrow. "But you need him, too, little flower."

She nodded, then turned to me. "Kiss me."

She didn't need to ask twice. I slid across the thick bearskin rug and cupped her cheeks in my hands. Her lips parted under mine, and I moved with her as Brand continued to fuck her gently from behind.

When she groaned out her pleasure, I smiled into the kiss. I'd never once imagined that the first time I kissed my mate, my friend would be sliding inside her. Never thought she'd proclaim her love for another man, while I felt nothing but delight.

Jealousy-flavored delight, sure. Someday, those words would be mine.

Someday, I would earn her love. Someday, I would do something heroic, something that would prove to her that I'd earned my place at her side, in her bed. She would welcome my claim then, and wear my mating bite.

I had no more than finished the thought, when she shook her head, as if she'd read my thoughts and disagreed. She kissed me harder, deeper, her teeth nipping my lower lip, until she broke away.

"I need more," she gasped.

Brand's dark eyes met mine as he held her up again, her back pressed to his torso, her body once more on display. "You want him in your mouth, my mate? Want to taste him?"

I felt the unusual sensation of a blush work its way over my cheeks. I'd done many things in my past, experimented with other shifters. But this was by far the most intimate, the most important moment of my life so far.

A hint of mischief darkened her gaze. "I don't know how."

"I think he'd like you to learn on him," Brand said, nuzzling her shoulder, his teeth moving over the mark of his claiming bite. I stared at her neck on the other side, at Finn's mark, then at her small breast.

That was where I would mark her, if she let me. On the soft swell that made my mouth water.

Or maybe on her thigh, where Brand's right hand dropped now, his fingers moving past the damp curls to her pussy and circling her clit. It was an impressive feat, holding her up with his left arm, and driving her closer to another climax with the other.

But when he stopped and spread her lips wide, tilting her so I could see his length where it stretched her small opening, I realized my own task—not tearing her away from him and pushing into that perfect pussy myself—might be the harder job. His cock was thick, but she was wet enough to take him, and his quick fingers kept her on the edge.

Brand chuckled darkly. "Brother? Don't keep our little flower waiting. I'll go slow."

"Do you want this, Flor?" I asked, moving closer, until

her mouth was only inches from my swollen cock. "Only if you're sure."

"So sure." With that, Flor pulled away from Brand's loose grip, landing on her hands and snarling up at me. "If I'm bad at this, you'd better not say a damned thing."

"Just don't bite it off, and it will be the best moment of my entire life," I replied breathlessly, making her smile. I ignored Brand's rolling eyes and moved even closer, so Flor could reach me with her hand.

"So pretty," she murmured, as she played with me for a moment, cupping my balls and gripping me. I fought not to come instantly; her touch was like fire in my veins, more sensual than anything I'd ever felt before. And the sensations kept rising, forcing me to leash my own impulses, since my wolf wasn't any help at all.

After she slipped the end of my cock into her mouth and gave a first experimental suck, then moaned around my length and started experimenting with more vigorous actions, he was howling with delight. *Shit.* My teeth were lengthening as well.

Brand glared down at me. "Not yet."

"No," I agreed, though my wolf rebelled inside.

A thought flickered through my mind. Finn hadn't earned the right either, and he'd marked her. Maybe —

"Ah!" I cried out as Flor reached under my balls and stroked my perineum with a spit-dampened finger, giving me a hard suck at the same time. I hadn't expected that, and it triggered my climax.

She held her mouth over my cock as I came, her own orgasm forcing her away at last. I watched as Brand pulled out and spilled over her back, rubbing his seed into her skin as she lay on the rug.

"Not bad," she muttered, licking her lips. "Not perfect, but not bad."

"Dream Girl?" I gasped, unsure what she meant. My performance? Hers?

Before I could start to panic, she went on. "Not the best thing I've ever eaten. But definitely not the worst."

Brand's shoulders shook, and I felt my jaw drop open again.

Flor sighed, closed her eyes, and curled up on the rug between the two of us. "Better than oysters. Not as nice as salted caramel." Before I could take a breath to argue with her, she was asleep.

38

AFTER THE FACT
FLOR

I could not stop blushing.

I couldn't believe what I'd done with Brand on the lakeshore to begin with.

But after that? I slapped my hands over my cheeks as we walked up from the cabin to the Lodge, me slightly in front of the men, glad that the gray weather was keeping the rest of the pack inside.

Of course, face after face appeared in the windows of the Lodge as we drew closer, noses smushed against the glass, eyes wide. Most of them were friendly faces, at least, since it was only the unranked living inside. Still, I blushed even harder.

I'd heard of the walk of shame in magazines. That had to be what this was, even if there was a healthy amount of smug satisfaction coming from my wolf, who hadn't stopped purring since the night before. She kept sending images of the previous night's activities into our shared mind, with hints at even more debauched activities, and I kept ignoring her suggestions.

I was going to need to wait at least a decade before I let

myself even think about what I'd done with Brand... and Glen.

"Pick up the pace, little flower, or we'll still be here for the noon meeting," Brand teased. We'd decided we didn't want to stay until the all-pack event. Brand was itching to get home, and I wasn't eager to face the screaming hordes again, just in case they decided to burn me at the stake, or threw me into the lake in a sack to see if I floated or sank.

Glen had seemed sad but resolute before the cabin. Now, he was ecstatic. I could feel his eyes on my back.

"Stop staring at me, Glenda," I snapped without looking behind me. Brand chuckled. He was amused at my conflicted emotions, but tried to hide it. "You too, Bearman. Look at the trees or something."

Patrick stepped out of the massive Lodge front door, jogging down the steps. He stopped, sniffed the air, and fought to hide his smile. "Brand, Flor, good morning. Big brother, how did the guard duty go?" His eyebrows wiggled up and down, and I gave him a sharp elbow to the gut as I passed by.

"Say one word, and I'll cut off your head," I promised. I buried my face in Brand's chest, breathing in his pine scent for a moment.

Patrick laughed and kept teasing Glen behind my back, but after a moment, I felt a gentle touch on my shoulder. "Flor, the mood in the pack is volatile. I'm not sure..."

I knew what he meant. "We're not staying for the meeting, Patrick. I think getting a fresh start would be good for all of us."

Patrick pulled me in for a firm hug, ignoring the others' growls of displeasure. "Little sister, I can never tell you how grateful I am that you fought your way into our lives. I wish more of our shifters understood who you are."

I pushed him away. "Who I am? Don't get carried away, Patty. I'm just the Southern pack reject. No manners, no class, no breeding."

Patrick shook his head slowly, lowering his voice. "You're one of the strongest shifters alive, by mate"—he nodded to Brand—"and by birth. You know Southern will want you back, don't you, Flor? Luke will need you, but no pack gives up its Alpha's blood."

I froze. "You don't know what you're talking about."

He nodded, tightlipped. "Of course not. In fact, we never spoke of this. And my father never said that Northern will keep that secret from all the others on the Council, as a sign of our appreciation. No one knows anything about you... other than that you're far too handy with a steak knife."

I set one hand on the handle of my blade, and the other on my sword. I wore them both at all times now.

Patrick pulled Glen away to chat quietly, and I glanced up at Brand. He'd heard it all, but hadn't even blinked. "You knew?" He nodded once. "How?"

"Luke gave Glen a note back at Southern, a piece of evidence against Alpha Callaway that was damning. Twenty years ago, he paid a significant sum to a coven of witches to sever a mate bond. When we asked about your father, Luke ducked the question."

"Luke knew?" I swallowed hard, waiting.

Brand's reply came slowly. "He did. I guessed from what he didn't say, and once I claimed you... I knew."

I didn't ask what he meant. It wasn't the time.

"Flor, Luke also knew the pack law that doesn't allow Alphas' Heirs—or children—to leave their packlands. He sacrificed himself to get you free. To give you the chance to see the world, and find a new home." Brand's eyes gleamed with emotion. "I will honor his sacrifice by giving you my home, if you'll have it."

My heart lurched. "His sacrifice... Is Luke going to die?"

He waited a long moment, then said gently, "I will never lie to you, my love."

And then he fell silent.

IT WAS close to noon by the time we had our bags packed, and Margarette walked us down the drive to where a car waited, with Alpha Hillier standing there. The morning sky was cloudless, though my own emotions were stormy enough to be felt. Brand kept smoothing his hand over my arm, like he could calm me with his touch.

Okay, he could, but not even his comforting warmth could keep me from worrying. My heart had started racing, like there was something terrible happening, and I had no idea what it was.

No, that was a lie. I knew it had something to do with Luke. I needed to get in touch with him somehow. But the thought of going back to Southern felt far too much like a leap from the frying pan into the fire.

I hadn't survived this long by taking those sorts of idiot chances.

When we reached the waiting car, I realized Alpha Hillier had a storm brewing in his eyes as well. As soon as we were close enough, he shared why.

"I want you to be careful on your journey. Sergeant has gone rogue."

39
A HIDDEN ALPHA
GRIGOR

The voices of the Northern hunters filtered through the pine branches to my ears, carried by a helpful breeze. "Sergeant, we need to get back. A call came on the sat phone from Erik. The Alpha's called a mandatory meeting for the entire pack at noon today. Something big is happening."

Sergeant was in wolf form, but began his shift to answer. It was done as quickly as any I'd ever seen, except my own.

His power bothered me. Who was this man? Where was he from? He had no family in the Northern pack, and I had overheard more than one of the older shifters mention Sergeant coming to them after the war.

He wasn't Russian, like the ones he hunted now. He was filled with real hatred for those rogues; I could smell it on him, sense the rage their attack on his adopted home had kindled. If he had come from one of the other packs, there should have been some added familiarity with my little one's other suitors.

Perhaps he had acted more familiar with her Mountain mate. Could he have defected from that pack? But Mountain was the most insular of all the packs on this continent, keeping to the old ways more closely than any others. It was their greatest strength. I knew they would welcome my mate with open arms, but wondered how they would feel about my presence on their lands.

It would be a challenge to keep from being spotted as I followed her to a new home.

I peered down at the group of six Northern males who were meant to be seeking out the rogues. They had only found one—the body of the traitor, the niece who had betrayed my mate. One of them carried her now over his shoulder, her naked body showing signs of mistreatment.

They'd assumed she had been killed by the rogues and dumped in their haste. But I had been the one to take her life from a distance, with a wave of my diminishing magic. Traitor or not, no woman deserved what the rogues had only just begun to do to her. Death had been a mercy.

Though I had no reason to be merciful. Perhaps my kindhearted little mate was rubbing off on me.

The pre-dawn sky cast just enough light for me to see how my hands trembled as I fought to hold onto the trunk of the vast pine I'd climbed. I'd expended far too much magic over the past several days.

Healing the Alpha had taken more energy than I'd hoped. That and defeating the Russians had left me depleted, though I knew I still had to follow the general and his remaining followers to be certain they were no threat to my little mate.

"Something big?" Sergeant demanded. "What is it?"

"Erik said the pack is being restructured." All the shifters looked uneasy at that.

"Go on," Sergeant prodded.

"He said... they figured out the ranking tests weren't... precisely fair." None of them seemed surprised at that, but when he added, "And that the Southern girl is working with the Alpha Mate to change the way rank is assigned," all of them began to bristle.

Unseen, I smiled. Of course my little miracle of a mate would be in the center of the much-needed revolution. She would be a catalyst in more ways than one.

"Right, you all go back now. I'll be along. Don't worry about me," Sergeant said curtly, taking the bag with the satellite phone and provisions from the man who had spoken.

Defying a command by someone as highly ranked as Sergeant was a grave offense. Most of the others stared, but when one finally raised his voice to argue with their leader, he found himself on the ground, in a chokehold.

"Never question me. Now, all of you, back to the Lodge. Return Vanessa's body to her family, Enforcer," Sergeant commanded. The power in his voice left no room for disobedience, or doubt.

This man should have been an Alpha. Perhaps he was one, in hiding. He was worth investigating.

Or killing. I could just kill him, and go back to my little *behrserk*'s side. Sing to her before the night had fled entirely. If I had a little more magic, I would have done just that. Or if he hadn't shared so many of the same features. So much of the same pride in their bearing.

Sergeant called out as the hunters ran on human legs in the direction of the Lodge, "I'll keep going north for a bit. Tell the Alpha I'll try to make it back to the meeting."

They were too far to hear the lie in his words, and not one of them looked back to see him face south. If he'd spoken even a little more quietly, I wouldn't have heard what he said before he sprinted away in the opposite direction of his home.

"She's alive. She has to be alive."

40
A TEMPORARY REFUGE
FLOR

"Sergeant went rogue?"

Alpha Hillier nodded as I repeated his words. Brand and Glen had both stiffened beside me, as shocked as I was. I wanted to say it didn't make sense, but my gut churned as I realized it could be true. He had been a party to the bullshit ranking scheme. He'd been the one to set me and Brand against each other with blades.

Ralen had said that Sergeant had set me up to die, as if it were a fact. Maybe it had been.

Shit.

Alpha Hillier went on. "His hunters returned for the meeting moments ago. They'd been trailing the group that set the bombs here to the east, and turned back when they got the call. He claimed he was going on alone to find them. I called him when he didn't return."

"He didn't answer?"

"He did." The Alpha's brow furrowed even more deeply. "He answered, but told me straight out he was defecting. He said he had a previous allegiance and could no longer serve Northern."

"A previous allegiance?" Brand murmured. "To whom?"

"That is a question for the Council," Margarette said. "But not for you three, and not for now. We have a pack-wide meeting to run."

Brand opened the trunk of the car while Glen and his dad shook hands, then hugged—slapping each other's backs hard enough to break a few ribs, it looked like. When I heard Alpha Hillier murmur, "I'm so proud of you. Never forget that, son. Someday I hope to make you half as proud of me," I had to swallow the lump in my throat.

Brand and Margarette hugged, and she whispered something in his ear that made him grin and blush over his dark beard, before he closed the trunk and went to open my door, waiting patiently.

Then it was my turn.

Margarette sniffled, her eyes glossy with unshed tears. "Are you sure you won't stay, Flor?"

"You know I can't. I have a lake to see at Mountain... and then, I need to go back to Southern."

She smiled and hugged me again, then pulled back and cupped my cheeks in her warm hands. My eyes burned as she kissed my forehead, whispering, "Come back to us whenever you can, my dearest daughter-to-be. These pack-lands will always be open to you and your mates, no matter what pack law says. Even if it means going to war with the Council, we are your allies. Your family. If you ever need us, send word."

Alpha Hillier stepped up to her side as she let me go, and finished for her. "Send word, and we will answer in force."

The car was now quiet, Glen in the back and Brand driving, the atmosphere somber and tense. I reached a hand over one shoulder, and Glen took it and squeezed, his grip too tight. I understood. He was leaving his comfortable home for an uncertain future.

I wasn't sure I would have had the courage he did. When I'd left Southern, I'd been glad to go. The only difficult part had been walking away from Luke. But Glen was beloved at Northern. And now, he would be rejected by every pack, if the Council wouldn't change their law.

It could mean a lifetime of living on the run. Of having no rank, no homeland. No pack.

Did I have a pack? I had thought I'd left Southern in the rearview, that I could start a new life. But if the rest of the packs found out who I was, they might force me to go back and stay.

I might have to do that anyway. I had loved Luke from my first memories, even if he had only been a childhood crush. I couldn't let him die.

I thought of Alpha Callaway, and wondered where he'd gone. He wasn't dead. Cockroaches like him were almost impossible to kill. He'd be back as soon as the lights were off, so he could scuttle around, spoiling everything he touched until he had enough power to take over again.

There wasn't a single shifter alive who deserved to die more than him. At Northern, I'd learned about pack laws and traditions, and realized just how many laws he'd bent or broken. What was worse, he'd figured out a way to break the most stringent one of all: not to use magic. I rubbed my chest, feeling the lines of the scar there. I had a feeling he'd used it on me, somehow.

Grigor's face flitted through my mind, and as I stared out the window, I thought for a moment I saw him there, a black wolf with glowing eyes, running alongside the car, just under the canopy of the forest.

"Is that—" Glen muttered, then fell silent. His

breathing was ragged, and I leaned over and gave Brand a peck on the cheek, then unbuckled and crawled over the seat.

"Flor?" Glen asked.

I didn't speak, only curled up on his lap and let him hold me, let his wolf feel mine near, until we both fell asleep as Brand drove us to his pack.

To another place that I knew, deep down, would only be a temporary refuge from the storm that was coming.

EPILOGUE
WHO IS FLOR WILLS? ~ LUKE

My thoughts were knives, slicing into my brain if I tried to focus on where I was, who I was. Who was near me.

I drew in a shallow breath, aware that I hadn't taken one in a while. My heart beat sluggishly, long moments between the weak thuds.

The scents that I drew into my lungs were acrid and vile. Herbal smoke and rancid meat. Death and decay.

Evil so strong, I tasted it in my mouth. It burned its way into my center, prying at the only thing I had left.

The only good thing.

The world I lived in now was made of pain, of loss. She had been gone for so long, the memory of her scent was all I had.

Cinnamon and jasmine.

Passion and innocence.

Fire and flowers.

I clung to the memory of her perfume in the darkness, sought it with my fevered mind. There were voices all around making demands, but none of them were hers, so I did not listen, did not answer.

Still, the harsh hands on my skin never stopped prodding, cutting, tearing.

And the voices never stopped asking their questions. "Who is Flor Wills? What did she do to you? Why are you sick?"

"Is she your mate? Is she a shifter? Is she a witch?"

"Have you seen the black wolf? Do you know who he is? Who is he to Flor Wills?"

"Who killed the Enforcers?"

"Do you know how to find him, to find her?"

The voices pretended they were friends, they were doctors, they were pack. But I knew they were hunting her. Hunting my heart.

And I would never help them catch her.

But then a new voice began asking questions, a voice with edges sharp as silver nails, jagged as shattered glass, that forced answers from my lips. An Alpha, whose power easily overcame my reluctance and my silence, tearing past the remaining defenses I had built in my mind.

An Alpha I had never met, with a feminine, snakelike command.

"Who is Flor Wills? Tell me now."

She is my heart.

"What did she do to you? Why are you dying? Answer."

Nothing. Everything. Stole.

"Stole what?"

My heart.

"Is she your mate?"

She is... my heart.

A long silence stretched out, and my limbs grew cold, heavy. The darkness grew thicker, like a suffocating blanket. Then, an icy needle plunged into me, and my heart began to beat again. The pain increased.

"Is she a witch? Does she have magic?"

I heard laughter then. My own laughter, weak and strained. *Yes.*

I let myself remember her fiery eyes, her snarl, her determination. Her fight. Her soft, sweet lips on mine. That single kiss had been so full of magic, it had kept me alive for weeks. Months? I'd lost track of time.

"Does she have magic? Tell me now."

Yes, she has magic.

The voice hissed with pleasure, and I knew I'd said too much.

"Good. She'll come for you." The words cut into me, tainting my blood, wrapping me in dark, poisoned fire, moving through my veins, freezing me in place. "And then she will be ours."

I fought to rise, to wake, to warn her. But I was tied down with tendrils of dark magic, wrapped in a shroud of agony.

I had betrayed her again. My Flor, my fighter. Even in death, I was unworthy of her love. The pain swamped me, drowned me, tore out my soul.

Finally, I did the only thing I could to protect her, my heart. I used the last of my energy, summoned my wolf, and gave him his freedom to run into the darkness, away from the pain.

And let my own heart stop.

Acknowledgments

Before I knew about knots, before I even realized angels needed glitter, I was in love with wolf shifters.

I wrote the first chapters of Pack Reject over five years ago, and then hid them on my hard drive. It took a special reader, Bekka Parker, to convince me to put this story out in the world. Bek, you are the sassy Southern cheerleader every writer needs. You are terrifying and terrific, and I adore you.

Tami, Courtney, Kristin, Lorna, Maria, and Deb, I can't begin to tell you how much your constant encouragement and friendship mean.

Iris, you make me want to run to the page every morning. Thank you for calling out the typos, and spinning scenarios on Vella!

Thank you to all the readers who share my books and share their love for Flor's story! I know that cliffhanger was a tough one. Are you dying to know what happens next? Follow me on my socials or join my newsletter to keep up with the very latest on when the next book will be out.

Also by Merri Bright

The Billionaire's Betasitter Series (MF Omegaverse)

Knotty New Year

Sunshine's Grump

Grumpy's Holiday Sweater

Valentine's Heart

Rainbow's Storm

The Splintered Bond (Paranormal Shifters)

Pack Reject

Pack Refuge

Pack Ruin

Pack Rage

An Ancient Bond, A Pack Reject Story

About the Author

Merri Bright spends her days dreaming up naughty angels, misunderstood demons, sexy shifters, growly Alpha males, and frequently refuses to limit her heroines to just one love interest.

Please join Merri's Mischief Makers on Facebook where you'll discover random giveaways, sneak peeks of new novels, book recommendations, and silly/sexy/funny stuff. You can also email her at merri@merribright.com, or follow/subscribe to reamstories.com/merribright for stories in progress.